THE DISCOVERY

When Ford and Rafe had built the cabin, they had found need of a place they could hide things they didn't want stolen, or didn't want to leave in plain view of their guests—high school girls, mostly. It took him a while to find it, a huge old gumbo limbo tree halfway down the back side of the mound with a hole near the base of the trunk. Ford got down on his knees, fished around inside, and touched something metallic. He retrieved a small fireproof box.

He snapped the latches and flipped open the lid. Inside was a blue spiral-bound address book, two hundred-dollar bills, a large empty plastic sack, and something in a cloth bag. Ford pulled the drawstrings and dumped the contents out of the bag.

He sat, staring. There were several pieces of intricately carved jade, tiny parrots and pre-Columbian god figures with bleak, drilled eyes. There were also two bright-green gemstones among the jade. The stones were large, each about the size of a robin's egg, roughly cut, multifaceted, pulsing with light in the dusty sun rays that filtered through the tree canopy.

Emeralds . . .

"Randy Wayne White is a fine storyteller!"

—Peter Matthiessen

RANDY WAYNE WHITE

SANIBEL FLATS

St. Martin's Paperbacks

This is a work of fiction. All of the characters, organizations, and events portrayed in this novel are either products of the author's imagination or are used fictitiously.

SANIBEL FLATS

Copyright © 1990 by Randy Wayne White.

All rights reserved.

For information address St. Martin's Press, 175 Fifth Avenue, New York, NY 10010.

ISBN: 978-1-250-12722-8

Our books may be purchased in bulk for promotional, educational, or business use. Please contact your local bookseller or the Macmillan Corporate and Premium Sales Department at 1-800-221-7945, ext. 5442, or by e-mail at MacmillanSpecialMarkets@macmillan.com.

Printed in the United States of America

St. Martin's Press hardcover edition published 1990
St. Martin's Paperbacks edition / April 1991

St. Martin's Paperbacks are published by St. Martin's Press, 175 Fifth Avenue, New York, NY 10010.

10 9 8 7 6 5 4 3 2 1

For three friends:
Dan Rogan, Lee Wayne, and Allan W. Eckert

AUTHOR'S NOTE

The details of Pedro de Alvarado's conquest of the Maya are historically accurate, as are accounts of the modern-day butchery by *Sendero Luminoso*, the Shining Path. The Kache and Tlaxclen are fictional peoples and should not be confused with the Quiches and Tzutuhils of fact. In all other respects this novel is a work of fiction. Names, characters, places, and incidents are either the product of the author's imagination or used fictitiously, and any resemblance to actual persons, living or dead, events, or locales is entirely coincidental. The exception is Florida, which still exists.

*Whether or not we find what we are seeking
Is idle, biologically speaking.*
—EDNA ST. VINCENT MILLAY

PROLOGUE

Ciudad de Masagua, Central America

Ford crawled to the mouth of the tunnel that connected the convent to the park outside the Presidential Palace. It was after midnight and he was wearing no pants, but he'd had time to grab his shoes—Nike Air Soles—and now he put them on. Water dripped from the ceiling, down his nose, and the cramped walls scraped at his shoulders. The convent had been built in the late 1500s; the passageway in the 1600s, during the time of the Inquisition, when the nuns of Cloister La Concepción sometimes broke their vows of solitude to save heretics condemned by the courts to die by fire.

Heretics, Ford decided, were smaller in those days.

A stone disc covered the entrance, and he pushed the stone away, looking through the bushes into the shadows of the park. Beyond the traffic of Avenida Las Americas, the windows of the Presidential Palace formed a citreous checkerboard above lighted statues and fountains. Police were everywhere, running down sidewalks, surrounding the convent. Many wore the white holster tassels of the elite guard. How in hell was he going to get past them?

He lifted himself out of the hole, replaced the stone cover, and stepped out of the bushes to find an old man staring at him. The man was dressed in the traditional clothing of a Maya *shiman*, embroidered shirt and baggy, mauve-striped pants—not unusual for the Indios who came down from the mountains to trade, for they practiced their own religion. The man had lighted rows of candles in front of a large stone artifact. There was a censer in his hand made from a bean can, and from it came the incense smell of burning copal leaves. Frightened at seeing Ford crawl out of the ground, the old man jumped back, chanting in some guttural language, Tlaxclen Mayan, probably . . . pleading, judging from his vocal inflections, or asking some question. When Ford did not respond, the old man said in Spanish: "Can this be? You do not understand . . . you really do not understand the old tongue?" He looked bewildered and a little disappointed, too.

The elite guard was moving in on the convent; Ford could see the silhouettes of policemen moving through the trees of the park. Standing naked, but speaking formally in Spanish, he said to the old man, "*Señor*, you have perhaps confused me with another. I am only an American, a *turista*. To prove it, allow me to buy your pants. As a souvenir."

The old man was staring at the stone artifact, a gray Mayan stela, staring at the candles flickering in the late wind, not listening, saying "How can it be that Quetzalcoatl does not understand the language of his people? I have been kneeling here, praying that he would come to save us—instead, he wants to negotiate for my clothing. Do the gods never tire of their shitty tricks?" He turned to Ford, considering him intently now, adding "Perhaps I am wrong; perhaps you are not Quetzalcoatl. Yes, that is it! I can see that you have been cut . . ."

Ford looked where the old man was looking, hoping he wouldn't see blood.

". . . cut in the way of the Hebrews. And you are wearing glasses. And you did not come from the sky as the sun god surely would. No, you cannot be Quetzalcoatl. But your hair is blond and you came at the moment of my prayer. And on this night, near the end of the Calendar Round and the beginning of the Year of Seven Moons—"

Ford interrupted. "I really do like those pants. They would make a very fine present. A nice souvenir. I will give you twenty—no, thirty. Thirty quetzals for your pants!"

The old man stood, wobbling, troubled. He was very drunk, Ford realized. "You came from the earth—" He looked at the bushes in sudden realization. "No . . . that is the place of the old tunnel; the tunnel that connects the palace to the convent and the convent to the park. My people still speak of it, though the knowledge has been lost to others. You did not come from the earth, you came from the convent. Yes, I understand this thing now. A naked man in the convent! A bad omen!"

The police were beginning to search the outside fringe of the park, the beams of their flashlights probing among the trees. Ford ducked as a funnel of light swept past him. "*Señor*, I will give you fifty quetzals for your pants. Have I mentioned that I am in a hurry?"

Fifty quetzals were worth about thirty-five dollars, and, though it caught the old man's attention, he was skeptical. "And where do you carry this great fortune? Behind your ears?"

Ford's hands went involuntarily to where his pockets should have been. "I can come back tonight and bring you the money."

The old man still looked skeptical.

"Or meet you in the morning. That would be better. Mercado Central, at the place where the women weave the mats and sack coffee beans. Fifty-five quetzals, I swear on my honor."

"I should take the word of a man who defiles nuns?" The man was already taking off his pants, resigned.

"I was not with a nun. What do you take me for?"

"Oh, do not tell me; do not lie. I am an old man who knows the way of people. I myself once lay with a missionary woman, an *evangélica*. Such a strange woman, but very lively in bed. Her eyelashes, she kept in a box on the table, and she made odd noises in her passion. This woman told me I had been born a second time, yet that year a certain insect came and ate my corn. Yes, most of the problems in my life have been caused by this creature which lives between my legs, so you need not lie to one such as me."

Ford accepted the pants, saying "Now your knife. I must use your knife. Hurry, please."

The old man handed over his bone-handled knife, but

reluctantly. "Do not misunderstand. I wish to keep this creature. We have had many adventures, and he refuses to grow old. Where is there a man who secretly does not covet such problems?"

"You take me for a murderer, too?"

"You do not have the look, it is true. You have the strange face of one who can be trusted, which makes me all the more suspicious. Who can tell in such a year!"

As Ford cut the legs off the pants, the old man rambled on, explaining, saying this was the end of the Calendar Round, the fifty-two-year cycle, a time of great change in the Mayan calendar. It would bring many omens, many changes—some tragic, perhaps. Long ago in such a year, on a single night, the old man said, madness swept through Guatemala and Masagua. People ran into the streets screaming without reason; old women died of fright. Men bashed their heads against walls, and thousands of people had gone insane at exactly the same time but in different parts of the land. On the very next day, earthquakes destroyed the cities.

"It is because we have lost the old ceremony," the man said. "I was praying to the blond one, Quetzalcoatl, to return and show us the way. But on the summer solstice, for that is the proper time." He took up a liter bottle of *aguardiente*, drank, drank again, wiping his mouth with the back of his hand. "Is it possible that I am imagining this? Perhaps this is such a night; perhaps I have gone insane."

The pants were now shorts. Ford put them on and began to run in place, trying to get a sweat going in the cool mountain night. "You have just sold your *pantalones* for a price twenty times what they are worth. You are not the crazy one."

He left the old man sitting in baggy underwear among the candles and ran out of the park at an easy pace. When the police noticed him, he gave a bland wave and peered at his watch: a runner intent on his training. At every intersection, he checked his watch. He ran right past the Presidential Palace and the elite guard, confirming that, even in Central America, joggers had joined beggars and stray dogs as innocuous creatures of the streets. From a balcony on the third floor of the palace, a woman with waist-length black hair watched him, but turned away when Ford caught her eye. He kept running and did not look back; jogged straight to the American Embassy. Everything he owned was there, in crates, ready to be shipped to the United States. That would be his home, now that he had resigned.

The next morning, Ford paid the old man at Mercado Central, then returned to the embassy to find a box delivered by courier. The box contained twenty thick blocks of U.S. $100 bills and the pants he had left in the palace the night before. There was also a short note. He was not surprised to find the pants; the money and the note were unexpected. The note was signed *P.B.* for Pilar Santana Fuentes Balserio, the young wife of Don Jorge Balserio, and it said that she would not be joining him as planned.

Ford rode in the cargo hold of a DC-3 to Miami that afternoon, sitting on the deck, his back braced against crates that held his books and specimens and microscopes; the things he still cared about. By morning he would be in Virgina for a week of debriefing. After that, his life as a bureaucrat was done. He could forget about Masagua and try to forget about Pilar. He'd get a place on the water and do the work he'd always wanted to do. A simple life, that's what he wanted. Just a place to do his work and no more women. Not for a while. Not after the president's wife . . .

He brought a Chevrolet pickup truck in D.C.; an old one with a pear-shaped cab, short bed, and new blue-black paint. He left with $1,500 cash in his money belt, receipts for three large separate bank deposits, and everything else he owned in back of the pickup beneath a tarp. He headed for the coast, then drove south, eating when he wanted and stopping at tide pools and estuaries to collect marine specimens. He slept outside when the weather was good; he ran each morning at sunrise. On the Outer Banks of North Carolina and in south Georgia, he found places that would be good to live, but he kept on going, crossing to the Florida Panhandle, stopping at several small towns to inquire about real estate, but ending up in Southwest Florida, as he somehow had known he would. He had grown up on this coast, yet there was no nostalgia involved in his decision—or so he told himself—for he was no less alone upon his return than he was when he had left eighteen years earlier. He wanted to buy a place, but learned of a house built on pilings right in the water—an old fish house inherited by some federal bureaucracy—that might be available on long-term lease to a marine biologist with the proper credentials or the right connections. The fish house was joined to Sanibel Island by a tide-bleached boardwalk, and there was a marina next door that sold fuel, block ice, and beer in quart bottles.

It was not a difficult decision to make.

He took possession of the stilt house in late August, sleeping on the floor while he concentrated on building the lab and office he wanted, stopping only to cook over the propane stove or talk with the marina's fishing guides or to go out collecting. Sometimes, late at night, or out on his new flats boat alone, he would think of Pilar . . . the memory electrodes keyed by an unexpected sound or fragrance, and into his mind would come gauzy images, as if etched by acid: the clean lines of her legs and hips . . . the way her head tilted in thought . . . the way she softened when surprised by his arrival, as if her aloofness was a guard to all but him. These stray remembrances were not unpleasant but he didn't allow them to linger, for they were meaningless now and uninvited. This, Ford realized finally, was the way it must feel to have once been in love.

All marinas are more than a sum total of docks and property, bait wells, ships' stores, and receipts. They are communities; ephemeral colonies with personalities as varied as the individuals who form them. Gradually Ford was accepted into the marina community—Dinkin's Bay Marina, it was called—and, as months passed, he became more than just a member of that small society, he became one of its pillars. If a fisherman had a question about species identification, Ford and his library were available. If a guide had to limp back in after dark with an empty fish box and a broken water pump, there was beer and consoling conversation to be had at Ford's stilt house. In a relatively short time, Ford became the trusted dispenser of first aid, wisdom, reluctant medical diagnoses, and unwilling advice on everything from love to law to broken timing chains—all by saying little but listening much. His rapid climb to position in the community surprised no one more than Ford. He had always been a private person, a man who attracted people and valued his friends yet went his own way. But just as the marina's society had adjusted to him, Ford adjusted to his new role, his new life, doing his work each day and sometimes far into the night, accepting callers with the offer of cold beer and letting down his guard, slowly, slowly, for it was not easy after ten years of being necessarily suspicious and living a life of professional deceit.

And just when it seemed he had finally adapted, Rafe Hollins called.

ONE

Sanibel Island, Florida
May

Ford saw the vultures from a half mile off; noticed them wheeling over the island like leaves in a summer thermal, dozens of black shapes spiraling, and he thought, *What in the hell has Rafe gotten himself into?*

He stood at the wheel of his skiff, traveling toward an island he hadn't tried to find since high school to meet a friend he'd seen only twice in the last eighteen years. He tapped the throttle and the skiff seemed to gather buoyancy as it gained speed, rising slightly as the bottom came up, a blur of sea grass and bronze sand at forty miles an hour. Ford leaned with the wheel and the skiff banked. There was the tidal rift—a green ribbon of water that crossed the shallows—and he dropped the skiff in, following the deeper water as if on a mountain road. After a quarter mile the rift thinned into a delta of old propeller scars. He touched the power trim and the outboard lifted with the whine of landing gear as he heeled the skiff, running for a time on its starboard chine. Ahead, fish and small stingrays panicked as if trapped beneath a slick of raw Plexiglas. Behind, nubs of turtle grass boiled in a marl cloud.

Then the shoal: a sandbank that encircled the island like an atoll. Ford held tight as the skiff jumped the bank then settled itself on the other side. He looked immediately for the opening in the trees, found it, and turned hard into the shadows of the island, backing quickly on the throttle as the bottom fell away in shafts of amber light and mangrove trees interlocked to form a cavern over the tidal creek that was hardly wider than the eighteen-foot Permit flats skiff that now rolled on its own wake beneath him.

Ford nudged the nose of the skiff onto a shell beach and killed the engine, then sat for a moment listening to the wash of waves, pleased that he had remembered the tricky cuts even though he hadn't made the run for all those years, thinking *Maybe the intimacies of water and women are the only two things a man never really forgets.* . . .

He thought of Pilar momentarily, but then the vultures brought his attention vectoring. He watched them circle overhead.

The surge of pleasure faded.

Where was Rafe?

Rafe Hollins had called the previous morning; called three times before he finally caught Ford at the marina. Out of all the gin joints in all the world, Hollins had said, trying too hard to keep his tone loose and easy, saying he'd been fine, staying busy, and how'd Ford like living on Sanibel Island again, the old stomping grounds, huh? Boy, they'd had some times, and, yeah, the reason Ford hadn't been able to get in touch was he'd been out of the country and the telephone company disconnected his phone 'cause he moved around so much since the divorce there just wasn't any reason to pay the bill. "I was living on Sandy Key, but now I'm mostly out of town," Hollins had said. "Traveling's the only kind of life insurance I got, Doc. When I'm travelin', there's no chance of me killing my ex-wife and spending the rest of my life in Raiford. The kind of policy State Farm doesn't offer."

The years had turned Hollins's voice gravelly, muted the Florida piney-woods twang, added something else Ford didn't recognize at first, an edge of desperation. In high school, they had been best friends: Rafe a left-handed passer and pitcher who threw bullets; Ford a mediocre linebacker and better catcher, the two of them cruising buddies. He had seen Hollins only twice after graduation: once while still in graduate school (he'd returned to Florida for a marine science workshop), then again three years ago in Central America, a coincidental meeting in San José, Costa Rica, that had shocked them both and should have turned into an all-night beer and talk session, but didn't. Hollins had been oddly distant, in a hurry, had to catch a plane. He never said why; Ford was in no position to ask. Hollins said he was looking for work outside the country. Ford gave him a few names, and that was that.

There had been no hint of desperation in Rafe's voice then. But it was evident on the phone that morning. Ford had stood at the marina desk looking out at the glittering elliptic of bay, listening while Hollins worked his way into whatever it was that was bothering him, talking about his wife like some cocktail lounge comedian. "She used my charge cards like Monopoly money. The mailman had to think she was having an affair with a guy named J.C. Penney. J.C. was probably the one guy she didn't hump. That woman handled more tally-whackers than an army urologist. And I was so busy traveling around, trying to earn enough to keep her happy, I never found out till later. Silly me."

There was the sound of traffic from Hollins's end, the wind-wake of passing trucks: Hollins was calling from a phone booth. Ford had already decided it was because he needed money, and he tried to gentle him along, saying "If there's anything I can help you with, Rafe . . ."

There was a pause, and Hollins said, "Good ol' Doc. Christ, we used to get ourselves into some shit, huh? Goddamn high school and all that stuff seems about a million miles away." The careful thread of control was beginning to unravel, his voice wistful. "Remember after that game in Key West, we marched up to Customs House in our uniforms, and you had everyone stand at attention and salute while we stole the flag? I thought we'd go to jail for that one for sure, but naw, no way, not with you. Told the cops all about flag etiquette, and there shoulda been a spotlight on the damn thing at night, and they ended up apologizing to us for interfering. God, I never met anyone could think on their feet like you, Doc. I used to tell the other chopper pilots in Nam that I had a friend back home could think his way outta any kind of shit, had balls that clanked when he walked."

Ford said, "So this call's about old times, Rafe? If it is, let's meet someplace and get a beer."

"Well, it's more than that."

"I know." Still looking at the bay, Ford's eyes had come to rest on the little house built on stilts thirty yards from shore—his stilt house now. It was a pretty little house with very thick walls (before modern refrigeration, it had been used to store ice and fish), painted gray, with water all around it and a rust-streaked tin roof. Ford said, "If you need money, I've got some."

Hollins, uneasy now, said, "I never could bullshit you, Doc. So, okay, I'm in a jam, but it's not money not really. It's something else."

"Then let's hear about something else."

"I need someone I can trust. You believe all the years I lived here, I come up with exactly one name: yours. Plus, you speak Spanish good—"

"*Spanish?* Ah, Jesus, Rafe—"

"You lived long enough in Central America, that's what you told me that time—"

"This can't be legal—"

"Guatemala, you said, and Costa Rica, too. Come on, Doc, everything's legal down there but peeking up the Pope's skirts and certain kinds of murder. But it's nothing like you think. See, I got involved with some guys, real hard cases, and they owed me a lot of money; money I earned, but they wouldn't pay up. So I took something of theirs to make sure I'd get paid. Like collateral, only without their permission. Now they've taken something of mine, and I have to get it back."

Ford said, "I knew it wasn't legal."

Hollins's tone changed, taking an edge. "I didn't think it'd bother you so much. After that time I ran into you in Costa Rica, I called the American Embassy in San José, trying to get your address. They said you weren't registered. Said you'd never registered. So then I called the embassy in Guatemala City. They said they'd never heard of you either. Alien residents have to register with their embassies, Doc—that's not the kind of thing a guy like you'd overlook . . . unless there was some reason you didn't want them to know you were around. So then I talked to some of the Americans I met. Funny, in those kind of places Americans always know about each other. But I only found one who knew of you—and she said you had a real good reason for not being on the books."

Ford said nothing for a moment. He picked up a pen and began to doodle on a tide chart, drawing tiny sharks and starfish. He said finally: "Okay, I'll listen, Rafe. No guarantees, but first I want you to tell me one thing. I want the truth, too. This problem of yours, does it have anything to do with running drugs? If it does—and I'm not kidding—you can count me out right now. I mean it." Jethro Nicholes, one of the marina's fishing guides, was sitting behind the desk reading *Field & Stream*. When Ford said "drugs," Nicholes looked up, mildly interested.

From the other end of the phone came a snort of laughter, derisive, self-directed. "It's not drugs. Shit, nothing that simple."

"Then what?"

Hollins said, "I'd rather tell you about it in person."

"I'd do anything for you but go to jail, Rafe. Tell me now."

"Okay, okay. I guess I owe you that. Let's see . . . it started with the divorce. My ex-wife got me over a barrel, man. She went into court wearing braids, looking like some kind of virgin homecoming queen. This young judge took one look at her and the horns started to grow. Sweat on his upper lip and everything, like he wanted to grab her by the hair and drag her off in his Porsche. You never saw her, Doc, but that's what she does to guys; God knows, she did it to me. I mean, she *smells* like she wants it.

"The son-of-a-bitchin' judge gave her everything: froze my assets, even got the bonds I'd been assembling to convert into a trust for my little boy. Then he provisoed my visitation rights on an alimony payment about the size of Great Britain's debt. If I didn't pay, they wouldn't let me see my son."

Ford had already heard most of this from old acquaintances. He said, "And that's when you began to press these other guys for the money they owed you."

"No, not right off. I still had ways of making money, money on the sly the court couldn't touch, but these guys owed me, damn it; owed me a bunch, and I wanted it. If they paid me, I wouldn't have to worry about alimony and all that shit for a long, long time. But I didn't start pressing till I'd taken something from them to sort of use as a bargaining tool; like I said: collateral. I knew I had to give them a good reason before they'd pay me 'cause they are first-rate dangerous; real bad cattle. After I got the collateral, that's when I began to press. I had to have the money, understand? That's why I pushed so hard. But then . . . then the money didn't matter so much anymore, but I still had the collateral. Hell, I didn't know it was that important to them. I kept it like a sort of insurance."

"Why'd the guys owe you the money?"

"I was flying for them."

"Not drugs."

"No. No way."

"And what did you steal?"

"A couple of things. It's complicated."

"I've got an orderly mind. Try me."

"I'll tell you—just not right now, okay? Not on the phone. See, it's not the money. I don't give a damn about their money anymore. That's not why I need your help. It's my little boy." Hollins's voice thickened, the emotion evident, and he paused to clear his throat. "Not being able to see my son was the real killer, Doc; the final straw. He's a really great little boy. Jake, that's his name. Throws lefty and hits from both sides, and he just turned eight. After the divorce, I stayed in touch with the old neighbor lady across the street to kind of see how things were going. She's a nosy old lady and doesn't miss much. Helen—that's my ex-wife—she was sleeping with a different guy about every night, this old lady said. Different car in the drive almost every morning. Said Helen would lay out by the pool in her bikini all day, then go off at night. So I figured she was staying wired most of the time—vodka, dope, coke; she liked it all. And her with an eight-year-old boy at home.

"I called this old lady about two weeks ago, and she was real upset. Said that morning Helen had walked some guy outside to kiss him good-bye, and Jake came wandering out, still in his pajamas. Said she could hear Helen yelling at Jake to go back inside, and Jake started crying so this guy gives my boy a slap and bloodies up his nose. The son of a bitch hit my son, Doc! The old lady called the police, but the guy turns out to be the judge who railroaded me. They're not going to touch a judge, of course, plus I've never been what you'd call A-one popular with all them Yankees on Sandy Key. That did it, Doc. I mean, I went fucking nuts when I heard that.

"I got a plane back to the States that night and waited until Helen left the house. Poor little Jake was there all alone, and he was so damn happy to see me. I didn't exactly know what I was going to do till I got there. Then I knew. There wasn't any doubt once I saw him."

Ford said, "You took him." He had heard that already, too.

Hollins said, "You're goddamn right I took him." Still angry, but desperate, too. "Jake helped pack his own suitcase, that's how anxious he was. I knew of a secluded spot on the Pacific coast of Costa Rica where no one would bother us and I could rent a place that had enough pasture to make a decent airstrip. Flying's my business and I'd done some work down there off and on over the last three years. But you already know that— hell, you're the one that give me the names and got me started. A buddy flew us cargo commercial to Mexico, then another pilot friend flew us down the rest of the way because I knew we couldn't get into Costa Rica without our names ending up on a computer someplace. There's a nice little village out there on the Pacific coast, and there's a school and nice kids, and I figured Jake and I could just live there, say screw the rest of the world. You can't blame me for that, Doc."

Ford said, "I don't blame you, Rafe. But it's called kidnapping, which is federal. And taking him out of the country is going to make them want to lock you up and melt the key."

"You think I give a shit about that? I grew up with a drunk for a mother. I wasn't going to let it happen to Jake. But Christ—" This last came out in a rush of pure despair. "—I never thought those Central American bastards would take Jake to get back at me. Hell, it never entered my mind the stuff I had was that important."

"They took your son? Who?"

"Masaguans. The Indios. You ever deal with those people? Now they've got my little boy."

Ford exhaled, a noise of disgust. "And you think you're going to work out a trade with them?"

Hollins said, "I've got to," his voice charged, near panic. "And it's got to be soon. They've already had him four days, and it's driving me crazy thinking what they might be doing to him. See, I can't go to the feds. What am I gonna tell 'em: I kidnapped my son, then someone kidnapped him from me? They'd throw me in the pen— which I wouldn't mind if it got Jake back safe. But the feds don't have any pull with those Indios. Up there in those mountains, the way the Indios stick together, they'd never find the men, let alone find Jake. It's got to be me, Doc. I'll give 'em their damn junk back. I'll do anything just so long as they give me Jake. But I need someone to help. If I tried it alone, they could cut my throat, take their stuff, and still keep my boy. See? I need a hole card. I need you."

Ford said, "Jesus, Rafe. Of all places—"

"Come on, Doc, come on. This is serious. I need help, man."

"That's the one place I can't go back to."

"What, they got a warrant out?"

"No, it just wouldn't be smart for me to go back. Not now."

"You're saying you won't help. I'm trying to get my son back, and that's what you're telling me?"

In the abrupt silence, Ford thought Hollins was about to hang up. He said quickly, "Okay, okay. Where do you want to meet?"

"You mean it?"

"But you're going to have to tell me everything. Understand? I'll help, but I need to know everything. Then maybe I can find a better way. We can figure something out."

Hollins said, "Christ, this has all gotten so crazy I can't even think anymore. It's like I'm losing my mind, the way everything's just gone all to hell at once."

"Sometimes it can seem like that."

"You got some time tomorrow?"

"I've got time today."

"Naw, tomorrow. Meet me on Tequesta Bank."

"The island? Couldn't we just meet at a restaurant or something?"

"I got people looking for me, remember?"

"Okay."

"Say . . . late afternoon, about six? I've got an appointment with some a my old buddies from Sandy Key; got to make a little money to finance this thing. Meet me at six, and I'll tell you about it. Everything."

"Tequesta Bank. Up on the mounds."

"Right. Just like old times. I've been kinda camping out there, keeping a low profile."

"The FBI's already after you?"

"Someone's after me, but it's not the FBI I'm worried about."

"Then who?"

Hollins said, "Doc, I've got more enemies than a Dallas whore with herpes. So it's hard to say."

Ford stepped out of the skiff, dropped the anchor in the bushes. He could see a boat hidden in the mangroves down the creek. The wedge of bow suggested a small trihull, a piece of junk Rafe Hollins would never have owned by choice.

The path leading into the island was overgrown, no wider than a rabbit trail. It twisted through mangroves and up a steep shell hill. Jungle crowded in beside him, above him, and there was the smell of heat and vegetation like wood ash and warm lime peelings, an odor that was pure Florida. For just a moment, the smell of the island brought it all back; made it seem as if he had never been away, back when he and Rafe were teenagers and had adopted the island as a sort of second home. Rafe's mother was a drunk, his father a commercial fisherman. Ford had lived with his uncle, an ex–triple-A pitcher who picked up the bottle the day his contract was dropped. Rafe and he had pretty much come and gone as they pleased.

They chose Tequesta Bank because of the Indian mounds and because it was uninhabited and no one was likely to bother them. They'd built a cabin on the highest mound and they had had beer parties and brought girls and sometimes just sat looking at the stars, the two of them, talking on the high mound by a campfire which flickered in a wind that blew straight out of Cuba.

Ford ducked under a spider the size of his fist. He stopped and watched the spider longer than he normally would, impatient with the charge of nostalgia, wanting it to fade. He noted that the spider was rebuilding its web, the upper half first, and that it was a golden-silk spider, a female that had recently made a kill. Probably some kind of butterfly judging from the orange dust clinging to the hair on her legs. What was butterfly dust called? Prismatic-something . . . prismatic scales, right. He stood looking at the spider; stood in the silence of his own heartbeat, his own breathing, the whine of cicadas; stood wondering why Rafe had yet to yell some greeting; realized that something really might be wrong. Eighteen years ago it could have been the prelude to a practical joke: a surprise party with a keg of beer and half the football team stashed in the bushes. But not now. Not after the urgency in Hollins's voice. Rafe was here and he was alone and he had yet to make the first sound.

Why?

Down the mound, the path disappeared into shadows.

Ford leaned and picked up a chunk of old conch shell, discarded it, then picked up a broken limb about the size of a baseball bat. Carrying the club, he moved quietly through the brush and up the highest mound, his heart pounding.

When he got to the top, he stopped again. To the west was the bay. He could see the domino shapes of condominiums on the barrier island that fronted the Gulf of Mexico three miles away: Sandy Key, the island where Rafe said he had lived. Back in high school, Sandy Key had been an undeveloped spit of land just beyond the county line, a good place for parties because it was outside the jurisdiction of the local sheriff's department. Now there was a causeway and the steady *thunk-a-thunk* of heavy construction. To the east was the grove of avocado and gumbo limbo trees where they had built the cabin. Ford stepped into the shadows of the grove, surprised to see the rotted walls of the cabin still standing and at how small it seemed; surprised that someone had thrown fresh palmetto limbs over the top . . . and then he saw what he knew must be Rafe Hollins and nothing could have surprised him more than that.

The Rafe Hollins Ford remembered best was still eighteen, long, lean, with a Kirk Douglas chin on a hell-raiser's face and hands that could palm a basketball. This Rafe Hollins was not a man but a thing, a bloated creature with a huge gray head and a shrunken distended body turning slowly in the late-afternoon shadows, his arms slack, his eyes dull slits, hanging from the limb of an avocado tree with a rope around his neck.

Ford stood motionless for a time taking it all in but

still not making any sense of it, thinking *Come on, Rafe, come on, say something because this is one poor excuse for a joke. . . .*

The vultures not in the air were perched, looking heavy as bowling balls in the sagging trees. A black vulture with a cowl like an Egyptian priest dropped down onto Rafe's shoulder, and the rope creaked as the bird's head rotated to feed.

"Hey . . . get away!"

The vulture lifted away unconcerned as Ford ran toward it. Two more birds landed on the ground behind him, their gray heads as high as Rafe's knees. Ford whirled and threw the club just to scare them. Threw it above them, but one of the vultures tried to fly at precisely the wrong time and the club caught it across the chest. The bird spun to the ground with a guttural scream that set off the other vultures and they all flushed from the trees at once, making a noise in the leaves that sounded like rain but, Ford realized, was excrement.

He covered his head for a moment, then didn't even bother because it was useless to try. The injured bird continued to thrash, making it impossible to think about anything else, so he chased the vulture down, penned it with his foot, fought the beak and the six-foot wingspan, and snapped its neck, trying to make it quick and painless. Then he stared at the fresh gouge on his hand, thinking *I survive two revolutions and a hemorrhoid operation so I can come back to Florida and die of infection from a vulture bite. Boy.*

He slung the bird back into the bushes, wiped his hands on his pants, looked up. Rafe Hollins turned in the breeze to face him then turned away again, his expression like something Ford had once seen in Amazonia, Peru, a shrunken head with its lips sewn shut, that same look of humiliation, of total submission. He stared at the corpse, which had once been his best friend, wondering why he felt no grief, none, only a sense of loss like seeing something useful wasted, nothing more. Only a few weeks ago an artist friend of his, Jessica McClure, had said, *You've got a cold, cold eye, Ford—* her talking in that analytical, dreamy way, half prophet, half Ph. D. *The way you study all the data trying to make it fit because you won't abide anything that can't be weighed or measured. Trouble is, some things don't fit, never will fit, but you still go plunking along collecting pieces, weighing the evidence, trying to neaten up a world that seems way too emotional and untidy. . . .*

Half of which was probably pure invention, but the part about the cold eye Ford now wondered about. All through high school he and Rafe had been family, done everything together. They'd had one of those closer-than-brother relationships in which they were continually plotting against each other, trying to gain advantage, laughing like hell at making life into such a game. Rafe, it seemed to Ford, usually got the better of it; not that it mattered because they were like Hope and Crosby on the road, best friends trying to catch each other out. But now the lean handsome one, Rafe, had taken a really big fall, and Ford didn't feel anything inside even close to tears, just that sense of waste.

Maybe his eyes had grown cold; maybe he'd always been cold. Or maybe four years in West Africa, a year in South America, and five years in Central America had leached away most of the emotional niceties. But Ford didn't believe that, not really. After all, before yesterday, he and Rafe hadn't exchanged a word or a letter in more than eighteen years, aside from those two brief talks, so it was almost as if a stranger had gone and gotten himself killed.

Or killed himself. . . .

Suicide?

It was the first time suicide had crossed Ford's mind. At first he had just thought dead, Rafe's dead, then he thought murder, as if maybe the Indios had gotten to him. But now the thought of suicide flashed. He didn't like the idea; couldn't reconcile it with the Rafe he had talked with the previous morning, but here it was. Ford took a few steps closer, his hands at his sides like someone in an art gallery. He began to study the body with clinical interest.

First things first: Could he be positive it was Rafe?

Not much was left of the face or ears; the eyes were gone. But what was there seemed to match—the heavy jaw, the high cheeks and broad forehead beneath a plucked mange-patch of black hair. The clothes seemed about right, too. The corpse wore khaki slacks, not the cheap kind but expensive ones with cargo pockets, and a black knit shirt with a tiny tarpon over the breast. Rafe had always liked nice clothes. There was a bulge in the rear pants pocket, and Ford removed a leather billfold. Inside was an out-of-date Visa card, a photo of a seventeen-year-old Rafe Hollins in full football gear throwing a jump pass, a photo of an older Rafe Hollins holding a tiny, wide-eyed infant, and four dollars in cash. That was all. Ford used the tail of his shirt, first to wipe the billfold clean, then as a glove as he placed the billfold back into the rear pocket.

Ford stood thinking for a moment, considering the scene before him. Was it murder, or was it suicide?

On the corpse's left foot was a pale leather boat shoe, no sock. His right foot was bare, the matching shoe on the ground four feet in front of him and to the left—his feet weren't tied and he had done some kicking. A man intent on hanging himself wouldn't tie his own legs, and that was a vote for suicide. His hands weren't tied either, hanging limp beside the distended belly, and that made it look even more like suicide. Rafe had been six two, two twenty-five, maybe; a big man. There was no way he could have been forced into a noose and up onto the chunk of log that lay nearby if his hands were free, unless he was already unconscious. But if he was unconscious, could he have kicked a shoe off? Ford didn't know. Besides, the shoe might have been placed—weren't some murderers supposed to be clever?

Ford stood on his toes and studied the face more closely. The vultures had made it impossible to tell if his friend had been beaten. Ford touched the bloated right hand for a moment, turned it and looked for rope burns on the underside of the wrist. There were none. On the left wrist was a Seiko dive watch, the lens shattered and green hands stopped at 2:18. A.M. or P.M.? Probably P.M. the previous day, judging from the condition of the body. Only a few hours after Ford spoke with him on the phone.

The heat and the vultures had had plenty of time to do their work.

Ford lifted the watch bracelet and studied the pale wrist skin beneath, then moved around to the back of the body and considered the noose. The knot attached to the tree limb was one of those overtied messes that formed a kind of loop so the running end could pass over the limb and through. The noose was formed by the same kind of bad slipknot, and it had cut into the corpse's neck, judging from the dried blood. These weren't Rafe's kind of knots, no way. He'd spent too many days on the water, working boats. The bad knots were a strong vote for murder; to Ford, in fact, they seemed conclusive. Rafe had made it clear he believed someone was after him.

Ford walked quickly away, took a breath. He looked back for a moment, used his shirt to clean his glasses, then began a slow search of the area. He didn't know what he was looking for—footprints maybe—but the ground was like mulch and didn't hold any. He poked his head into the cabin and waited for his eyes to adjust. The cabin was a mess, as if it had been ransacked. There were canned goods scattered, some clothes in a heap, a half bottle of Southern Comfort right in the doorway, six cans of Copenhagen snuff torn out of a cellophane tube, a snapshot of a little brown-haired boy with the words *Jake Age 5* written on the back. Ford almost picked up the photograph, then caught himself. He wrapped his right hand in a towel and held the photograph to the light. The child had Rafe's cleft chin, the same high cheeks, and dark, dark eyes: a bright, innocent face, open to the world. He considered putting the photograph back as he had found it, but stuck it in his pocket instead. Still using the towel, he opened the Southern Comfort and poured a quarter of the bottle over the vulture bite, letting the alcohol sting.

Outside, he stared at the dark doorway for a time, then remembered one more place he might look. When he and Rafe built the cabin, they had found need of a place they could hide things they didn't want stolen, or didn't want to leave in plain view of their guests—high school girls, mostly. It took him a while to find it, a huge old gumbo limbo tree halfway down the back side of the mound with a hole near the base of the trunk. Ford got down on his knees, fished around inside, and pulled out a package of something—a cellophane mess, black with eighteen years of humidity, TROJAN CONDOMS barely legible on the cover. Ford threw the package into the bushes, then reached in again. This time he touched something geometric, metallic, and retrieved a small fireproof box. He snapped the latches and flipped open the lid. Inside was a blue spiral-bound address book, two one-hundred-dollar bills, a large empty plastic sack, and something in a cloth bag. Ford pulled the drawstrings and dumped the contents out of the bag. He sat, staring. There were several pieces of intricately carved jade, tiny parrots and pre-Columbian god figures with bleak, drilled eyes. There were also two bright-green gemstones among the jade. The stones were large, each about the size of a robin's egg, roughly cut, multifaceted, pulsing with light in the dusty sun rays that filtered through the tree canopy.

Emeralds.

As he returned the stones and the notebook to the box, the plastic sack caught his attention. It wasn't completely empty. Gathered in one corner were small beige flakes of something; something that looked like dried leaves. Ford dipped his finger in, aware of a familiar smell; a smell similiar to that of old leather. He stood quietly for a time, thinking, then put everything back into the metal box, latched it, and carried it slowly back up the mound.

The wind had turned the body so that it now faced the cabin. The vultures were back at work, and it was when Ford averted his eyes that he noticed the note for the first time: a piece of paper tacked to the avocado tree, hanging there like some kind of public notice. Ford stood looking at the note without touching it. Finally he took a few steps closer, reading: *It is nobodys fault. I just can't take it no more. Rafe Hollins*

Ford rocked back and forth on his heels, back and forth, staring. Finally he ripped the note away, carried it out into the sunlight, and read it again. Then he folded it carefully and put it in his pocket.

Damn.

He stood on the high mound looking at the bay. The bay glittered in a grid of harsh afternoon light. It would be dark within two hours, and it was a forty-five-minute boat trip back to Sanibel Island. Ford stood thinking hard, hating his own indecision, then turned suddenly.

In the boat he found old three-strand nylon rope. He carried the rope back up the mound and used it to tie the bloated hands and legs. Finally he forced the shoe back onto the corpse's swollen foot.

TWO

The last thing Ford did was jot down the registration numbers of the trihull boat tied to the mangroves. He also made a fast trip around the perimeter of the island, kicking grass and mud the whole way, making sure there wasn't a second boat still hidden somewhere.

There was not.

On the trip back, he stopped at a bayside restaurant that had a phone booth and started to dial the sheriff's department in Fort Myers, but then remembered that Sandy Key and Tequesta Bank were in Everglades County, just across the line. He got the number of the local sheriff's department from the front of the book. He told the woman who answered: "A man named Rafe Hollins has been murdered. You can find his body on Tequesta Bank," and immediately hung up. At a 7-Eleven he bought a quart of beer—Coors in a bottle—then got in his boat and headed straight out into the Gulf, needing air. The sun grew huge at dusk, pale as a Japanese moon, and Sanibel Island materialized on the horizon as a thin black line on the gray flexure of sea.

It was nearly dark by the time he got to Lighthouse Point, and he ran beneath the causeway and turned south into Dinkin's Bay. At the mouth of the bay was a strand of beach where there were coconut palms and secluded piling homes. Jessica McClure lived alone in the last house, an old clapboard place with a tin roof that was built on a point among the gumbo limbo and casuarina pines. In his first weeks on Sanibel, he'd had occasional glimpses of Jessica standing at her easel on the dock: a striking figure in faded jeans and T-shirt, a tall, lithe woman with a private, introspective expression but a friendly wave. They finally met one morning when Ford was wading the sandbar across the channel from her house, digging beak-throwers more than a foot long with chitinous beaks and pairs of wicked-looking black teeth. Jessica had watched from the dock for a time, then climbed into her little wooden skiff and puttered over. She had waved again as she got out of the boat, strode to his side, and peered into one of the collecting buckets.

"Hum . . ." She had looked up at him, her expression quizzical, interested. "They're sea snakes, right?"

Ford told the woman they were clam worms, as he got his first close look at her: pale, pale-green eyes, long auburn hair that was copper streaked in the fresh sun-light; her face like something out of a 1940s movie, Carole Lombard maybe, high oval cheeks, full mouth set in an expression of slight bemusement, good skin and no makeup at all. She was probably in her late twenties but carried herself as if older; reserved but sure of herself; a woman who lived alone and liked it. She was almost as tall as Ford: the gawky, awkward teenager come of age whose beauty, in developing late, had probably spared her the self-consciousness common in beautiful women who had lived too long with the knowledge that they were always, always under inspection.

Looking into the bucket again, Jessica had said, "Clam worms, huh? I like the color, that iridescent green. They're really kind of pretty."

In the collecting bucket, the clam worms were writhing, their beaks protruding and retracting mechanically. Ford told her that beak-throwers had to be dug carefully, not just because they were delicate, but because they could bite, and not many people would agree with her that the worms were pretty.

Jessica had said, "I guess most people wouldn't," which could have come off sounding self-congratulatory but didn't because she said it so objectively, a simple observation which pleased Ford. She was smiling, more at ease but still aware she was standing knee-deep in water with a stranger. "I'm Jessi McClure, the woman who's been waving at you."

"I know. You're the artist."

"And you're M. D. Ford, the guy who fixed up the old stilt house. But I don't know what the initials stand for, just that everyone calls you Doc." She was still smiling, but not giving it too much. "I asked about you the last time I was at the marina. So which is it?"

"Which is what?" Ford had picked up the bucket and was moving down the sandbar again.

"Do they call you Doc because of the initials, or

because you have a lab and look at things under a microscope? Or maybe it's those wire-rimmed glasses."

"I had the initials before I had the microscope. Back in high school, though, it was because my first name is Marion."

"Marion's a nice name."

"Easy to spell, too."

They had spent the rest of the day together and then had dinner: Ford sitting across from her at a table at Gran Ma Dot's, feeling the sensual impact of her face, her body, but not quite sure he wanted to pursue the attraction. For one thing, he thought the quick pass might offend her. He had already found out she preferred classical music to cult rock, ocean swimming to aerobics, so maybe she was an anachronism when it came to curbservice sex, as well. For another, Pilar, the last woman he'd been involved with, had almost gotten him killed; worse, he'd been in love with her—a first for Ford. What he'd most enjoyed about the past year was living without the complications of romance; of doing whatever he damn well pleased without having to yield to the exigencies of emotion or the plans of some woman.

No involvements, he decided, not with her—at least until the rules had been established, the parameters set.

He saw her nearly every day after that; at first on the pretext of teaching her something about marine biology, then just because it was fun. Some evenings he would boat to her house on the point, or maybe jog the back way, come up quietly and surprise her. Other nights he would look out and see her porch light go on, a sure sign that she was leaving. A few minutes later he would hear her skiff's motor, and soon she would holler up from the darkness, "Hey, Ford—how about some company?" It was a couple of weeks before he finally kissed her; touched his lips softly to hers, then harder, feeling her mouth respond, feeling her body go soft and slack as her back arched slightly. But she had pulled away then, pressing his hand to her cheek, looking up with those eyes. "*Whew* . . . I was beginning to wonder if you were ever going to do that."

Ford had said, "I guess it just hadn't crossed my mind before," smiling with Jessica because it was such an obvious lie.

"Well, it's been on my mind. So maybe it's time we talked about it, huh? Do you know that I've told you things I've never told anyone? It's true."

"I'm flattered."

"Not so quick. Do you also realize that I've told you very little about my past? And you—you, you big lug, have told me even less about yours. In some ways we're complete intimates; in other ways, complete strangers. Don't you think it's about time we sort of dropped the shields a little; dispense with some of the cowshit?"

Grinning, Ford had said, "Sure," enjoying the way she phrased things: *You big lug . . . dispense with the cowshit*; but he was also aware, from the way her eyes bore in on him, that she was hoping for a more heartfelt response.

After a time she had said, "You've become important to me, Ford. I wake up in the morning anxious to get done with my work, wanting to hear the sound of your boat because, once you're here, it's like I can let my breath go and relax. I've had lovers before, Doc . . ." letting that hang in the air until she saw that he wasn't going to respond, then continuing, "but I guess I've never really had a male friend before; a man who was an intimate. Maybe that's why I'm having a hard time with this. But you know what I'm getting at; we're close enough that you know what I'm trying to say. I can see it in those damn chilly eyes of yours. Help me out here, buster!"

Ford had laughed with her, but said nothing because he had absolutely no idea what she was trying to say.

"I like you, Doc. I like you a lot."

Ford waited, feeling increasingly uncomfortable. *Christ, she's not going to start talking about marriage already, is she?*

Jessica had pressed on. "It frightens me a little. I keep wondering what happens to intimate friends when they become lovers. What happens to them, Doc?"

Ford, who hadn't been with a woman since the day before he left Masagua, said, "Well, we could stick with it for a while—" He meant they could try being lovers, but Jessica had interrupted.

"Then you're willing?"

"Ah . . . sure; more than willing." He had shaved until his skin burned and showered, just in case. "On a friendly sort of basis, I mean."

"I knew you could tell what was on my mind! You dog, letting me go on and on like that. It could be kind of like an experiment, Doc."

"An experiment, sure. That's one way of looking at it."

She had hugged him quickly, then stepped back. "I'm

so damn weak! I was ready to jump into bed with you that first night. And just now, when you kissed me, my knees got all watery, like some schoolgirl. But I think you're right, Ford. Why not just be friends, a man and a woman, and see where it takes us? How many people have ever had that opportunity? You know . . . I'd rather have you as a friend. And it's a great feeling knowing I can say that and you're not going to go away with a damaged ego, worrying about your sexuality or whether I find you attractive or not."

Finally realizing what he had just agreed to, and wincing at the force of her enthusiasm, Ford had said, "I'd be silly to worry about that," and immediately began to wonder about both.

In the weeks that followed, though, Ford regretted the misunderstanding less and less. Abstinence was frustrating, but it had its good points, too. There were no obligations, no hurt feelings, no bruised egos. Jessica told him things she probably never could have confided to a lover, and Ford began to take a distant, almost clinical interest in the emotional differences of men and women.

A couple of times, he actually came close to confiding in her.

Ford slowed his boat enough to look into Jessica's house. Lights were on and he could see the silhouette of wind chimes above the door transom and the outline of a cat in the window.

He idled toward the dock, turned into the current, and tied off. The metal box he had found on Tequesta Bank was beneath the console, and he considered carrying it in with him, but did not. Jessica switched on the porch light and stepped out just as he was about to knock. She was wearing a white strapless dress and her hair was combed long over one shoulder. She looked very pretty, and Ford realized he had never seen her in a dress before.

"Ford? That's you, isn't it?" She stepped out into the light, and Ford could see that her face looked different; decided it was because she was wearing makeup. She said, "I've been trying to get in touch with you all afternoon, kiddo. Where've you been? I called the marina twice and then boated over to your place. When are they going to put a phone in that house of yours—" She stopped suddenly and touched his elbow. "Hey, what's wrong? You don't look right. Your eyes look funny. You been drinking?"

"Drinking? Sure I've been drinking. But just a quart."

"You just look upset or something."

Ford said, "I got no work done; I was bitten by a bird. Mostly, I just need someone to talk to. Someone with a clear mind and an objective viewpoint."

"A *bird?*"

Ford held his hand up for inspection. "A vulture. That was after a couple of dozen of them dropped their load all over my shirt. Smell it? So maybe I can get cleaned up and we can go get something to eat. Or maybe you just got back?"

From the dirt road came the sound of a car traveling fast, and Jessica glanced at her watch. "Ah, damn it, Ford . . . that's why I was trying to find you. There's a party tonight on Captiva. A lot of New York exhibitors are going to be there, a lot of rich collectors. I've known about it for a month, and I wasn't going to go, but then Benny flew in unexpectedly. I wanted to ask you to take me, but I couldn't find you, so now—" She looked at the drive as a car turned in, still going way too fast. Dust was like smoke in the big car's headlights. "—so now I'm going with Benny. I told you about him, remember?"

"No . . . I don't think so."

"Benny from the gallery. *Benny.*"

"Oh . . . right. Benny. That one." It was the name of a man she had said owned the gallery in Manhattan that handled her work; the man who had also once been her lover, or so Jessica had implied. Ford said, "Well, that ought to be fun, you two together again."

She took his arm. "Don't be so damn big about it, Ford. Come on, at least meet him."

Benny swung open the door of the rental car and came toward them, walking fast. He was as tall as Ford, leaner, black curly hair styled close to the head, tight jeans, bright floral shirt open to the sternum showing glittering chains among the mat of chest hair, the cosmopolitan look with body by Nautilus.

"Jess! My God, it's great to see you!" Big hug and a kiss, arm thrown around her shoulder, taking no notice of Ford. "You look marvelous, just marvelous. Island life agrees with you. I've been telling everyone in the city you're in your Gauguin period, off in the sticks creating brilliant stuff."

"No, no, nothing like Gauguin, but I do have a couple of new things. . . ." Jessica was smiling, too, happy to

be talking about her work, but perhaps not as happy to
see him as her forced expression made it appear, and a
little uneasy as she made the introductions. Benny became even more magnanimous, catching Ford's hand
just right, squeezing too hard, saying "To hear Jess talk
on the phone, she doesn't have a friend in the world on
this little island. I'm damn glad you locals are around
to keep an eye on her," putting Ford right in his place
with a big grin.

Ford said, "Well, us locals think the world of little
Jess," giving the dryness an edge, but Benny was done
with it, already leading Jessica to the car, saying "What
is that *smell?*" and Jessica, glancing back, gave Ford a
searching Are-you-going-to-be-all-right? kind of look.

When Ford didn't respond, Jessica said to Benny,
"Oh, those damn vultures. You get used to it after a
while."

Ford touched the throttle and the skiff jumped on a
line through Dinkin's Bay toward a pocket of lights in the
encircling darkness: the marina. He ran straight across
the flats, not slowing until he came abreast of the double
markers beyond the marina basin. His own house was
a dim shape three hundred yards to the east: two small
cottages under a single tin roof on a wooden platform,
all built on stilts and connected to the shore by ninety
feet of old dock.

It was Friday night, clean-up and cocktail time. Fishing guides hosed their skiffs after working the late tide
and live-aboards were beginning to circulate among
neighboring houseboats, drinks in hand, smiles fixed,

everybody smelling of shampoo and looking for a party. Someone had put speakers out on the dock so that Jimmy Buffett seemed to be erupting from the water singing, saying that, on the day that John Wayne died, he'd been on the Continental Divide.

Two tarpon hung from the support over the cleaning table, one about eighty pounds, the other well over a hundred. With ropes passed through their gills they looked like giant aluminum herring, weird, misshapen, and Ford pictured the corpse. He stepped onto the dock thinking he could use a few beers, just as in the song, wondering where he had been on that day, the day that John Wayne died.

"Hey, Doc . . . come here, I ga-ga-ga-got to show you something." A man in khaki shorts and a long-billed cap was waving for him, Jethro Nicholes, muscular, dark-haired, one of the fishing guides. Nicholes was an easy laugher, good-looking, just a little younger than Ford. His stutter had burred the ego points, made him seem boyish, gave him an air of vulnerability not normally associated with men who opened Coke bottles with their teeth. Jeth made Ford wish more people stuttered.

Ford said, "Looks like you had a pretty good day out there, Jeth." His own voice sounded strange to him, oddly carefree. "You bring in both for mounts?"

Nicholes was still motioning, wanting Ford to come the rest of the way down the dock, shaking his head as he said, "Naw, Ted Cole's boat got that one there; the littler tarpon. My people got this one. Hundred twenty-six pounds by the ma-ma-market scale. Older woman on my boat caught him, blond-haired woman." He was grinning. "God, what legs, Doc. Had me keep my arms around her waist part of the time. 'Fraid the ta-ta-ta-tarpon was going to pull her in. Had to concentrate like hell to keep my mind on the fish and offa what I could see when she leaned forward 'cause she had on one of those kind of blouses and didn't wear nothing under-neath. I'm telling you, Doc, you wouldn't expect a woman her age to look like that. Lord, you'd need safety glasses, that's how those things stood up. And smell good? God da-da-da-*damn* she smelled good."

"Smell's important."

"Smell, huh? Like in biological stuff?"

"Yeah. Did MacKinley say anything about the phone guy coming? They were supposed to have my damn phone in a month ago."

"Why would MacKinley tell me? If I want to see you, I can just holler out the door." He stared at Ford for a moment. "You mad about something? You don't look right."

"I've been drinking."

"Oh. Good. Hey, look at this. See here what I saved for you?" Ford had followed the guide to his charter skiff, a blue Suncoast with *Jacks or Better* in white script on the stern. He watched as Nicholes opened the forward fish box and pulled something out. "Nice little b-b-b-bull shark, huh? Hit a pilchard of all things. You still want 'em, don't you, Doc? For your fish-selling business, I mean."

Nicholes was talking about the marine specimen busi-ness Ford had started, Sanibel Biological Supply.

Ford took the shark by the tail and swung it over onto

the dock, saying "Sure, I'll take the shark; I'll take all you can bring me." It was a male bull shark, about twenty pounds, and he could see that Jeth had clubbed it to kill it.

Nicholes said, "Tell you the truth, I thought you were kinda crazy, starting a business like that. I mean, what kind of a person would want to buy old sharks and stuff?"

Ford was standing by the tarpon, wondering how he could ask Jeth not to club the sharks without hurting his feelings. He said, "Mostly it's organizations—colleges and research firms. I got my first big order last week. Minneapolis Public Schools ordered twenty-eight sharks all dissected and injected. They ordered some sea urchin embryology slides, too, but I can't get those until this winter when the urchins are gravid. I can fill the shark order, though. See, the good thing about an order like that"—Ford kept his tone airy—"I can dissect the sharks, color-code the circulatory systems, send them off, and still keep the brains. I'm hoping I get some orders for isolated brain mounts. That way every shark I get does double duty. I won't have to kill so many that way."

Nicholes suddenly looked worried. "Jeez, Doc, I didn't know you sold their brains. I clubbed the pa-pa-piss outta that little bastard. I didn't even know they had brains."

"You clubbed him? Oh yeah, yeah, I can see now. You open them up after that and their nervous system looks like somebody glopped dark paint all over. Blood clots. I don't sell the bull sharks anyway; they're for my own work. But maybe next time—"

"No more clubbing, Doc, honest to God. What happens, I bring them sma-ma-ma-mall sharks aboard and they get to thrashing around and the people just go wild, thinking *Jaws*, like they're gonna get their toes bit off. I swear to Christ it's like the white Amos and Andy Show."

"Maybe if you just stick them right on the ice."

"Right, yeah, that's what I'll do. Stick them right on the ice. Hell, no p-p-p-problem. Hey, you see MacKinley, remind him he's got a package UPS delivered for you."

Ford had been squatting by the tarpon, picking off the dollar-sized scales, inspecting the rings as Nicholes began to ready the fish for the taxidermist. Now he stood. He was expecting a shipment of Riker mounts and two dozen Wheaton specimen jars. "You want me to bring you a bottle of beer back, Jeth?"

"Sure, yeah, if they got any left. That party's shaping up pretty good down there on the Chris Craft. They've been making ba-ba-beer runs 'bout every half hour. There's a convention of women doctors staying over at Casa Ybel. You know, the business-suit kind that don't wear no bras, like maybe they used to be rich hippies before their daddies paid their medical school. Things ought to get pretty lively tonight."

Ford said, "Oh?"

"Yeah. Women doctors ain't exactly bashful when they get a few drinks down them, and they're a thousand miles from the country club. I'm going to put on a shirt with those flaps on the shoulders and introduce myself as Captain Nicholes. You want to stick around? Bring your painter friend who lives out on the point?"

Ford shook his head. "I want to open up this shark before he gets stiff. Besides, Jessi has a date tonight."

"Oh, so that's why you're pissed off. I know just how you feel; especially a woman like that who lives off by herself and owns cats. Woman has one cat, she's just a pet owner. Woman has three or four cats, though, that's different. That's the type woman lives alone 'cause she wants to. I fell for a woman like that once. They shouldn't call it love, they should give it another name, like a disease, maybe."

Ford was already walking toward the marina office as Nicholes added, "I'd rather have a ga-ga-ga-goiter than have to go through that shit again."

MacKinley said, "They'll have your telephone in tomorrow." He was standing behind the counter counting money, enjoying it. MacKinley was a New Zealander who had sailed around, bummed around, before embracing free enterprise on Sanibel Island.

Ford said, "I heard that two weeks ago." Then, replying to MacKinley's stare: "I know, I'm grumpy. Jeth already told me."

"The phone guy said it took so long because they've been so busy they've been working overtime, plus they wanted to run the cable underwater, but it got too complicated with the permits and stuff. So the office finally said he could run the cable along your dock. They don't like to do that."

"Can I get four dollars in change for the pay phone? And two quarts of beer."

MacKinley said, "You can use this phone if you want."

"It's long distance."

"You can pay me when I get the bill."

"The pay phone's okay, Mack."

"Oh, private, huh? You got a package and some mail."

Ford said, "I'll be back in a few minutes."

He dialed the number from memory. It was a Washington, D.C., area code, but the number would ring at a compound outside Williamsburg, Virginia. Because it was after normal business hours, a woman answered, saying "Federal Transportation Pool, answering service." Ford, who knew he was not speaking to the Federal Transportation Pool or an answering service, said, "Extension W-H two oh-one." The woman said, "Who's calling, please?" A year ago he would have replied with his cryptonym— something which had always made him feel silly. Now he gave his real name. The woman said, "I'm afraid the extension is busy. Can they return your call?"

He gave her the number and stood in the neon haze of the booth watching moths, slapping mosquitoes, waiting. He was about to walk across the shell drive into the shadows of the mangroves to urinate, when the phone finally rang. A man said, "I have a message to call a Mr. Ford."

Ford said, "I need to get in touch with Harry Bernstein, Central American Division, Branch One. I don't know what his cryptonym is anymore."

"Branch what? I don't know what you're talking about. Did you want the Federal Transportation Pool?"

"I'm on Sanibel Island, Florida. I'll be at this number between nine and eleven in the morning. If he misses me, telephone information should have my home number under new listings as of tomorrow. I hope."

The man said, "I think you must have the wrong number."

Ford said, "Thanks. Tell Bernstein it's very important."

Ford was still in the marina office when Jeth Nicholes returned from his upstairs apartment, nautical in khaki shirt with epaulets. It looked as if he had maybe washed here and there and combed his hair, too. "I'm wearing cologne," he told them.

MacKinley said, "You might as well stay for the party now, Doc. Seems like the guests are arriving."

Looking past MacKinley, who was behind the counter, Ford saw a group of women in expensive leisure clothes. Creased slacks and pastel blouses; vacation women with tawny, tended hair, drinks in hand, careful expressions of professional control on their faces.

"I like women da-da-da-doctors," said Nicholes to no one in particular, all three men staring out the window. "They always look like they grew up taking vitamins and ba-ba-brushing their teeth."

"Right," said Ford, "I know what you mean."

Nicholes said, "Another hour or so the dancing'll start. Then about midnight the dirty doctor stories and maybe a little cryin' 'cause they've been through so much together. That kind of stuff. Then they're gonna want to swim in the bay, sure as hell. No clothes. That's when the real fun will start. You really ought to stay, Doc; find you a nice smart one."

Ford said, "I've got to take a shower."

"Now you're talking," said MacKinley. "Might change that shirt of yours, too."

Ford headed toward the door, then stopped. "Hey, Jeth. How many people do you figure know the way into Tequesta Bank?"

"Why, you want to ga-ga-go?"

"No. I was just wondering, that's all."

Nicholes looked at the ceiling, thinking. "All that shallow water, and there's only the one little cut takes you in, and that's not marked. Not many, I'd guess. Hardly any at all, if you don't count the commercial guys. Unless they were in a real small boat and didn't mind tearing up their prop. Anybody could make it that way."

Ford said, "Thanks. I'll see you guys later."

When he had left, Nicholes said, "I like Da-Da-Doc. He's an easy guy to get to know."

MacKinley said, "Been nice having him around."

Nicholes said, "Smart, too. But in a booky kind of way. The kind of guy who puts his hand in the fan 'cause he's concentrating so hard on the manual."

After a time MacKinley said, "Doesn't say too much, though. You ever notice? Just asks questions and listens. Ends up, he knows all about you but you don't know anything about him."

"What's wrong with that? Ma-ma-ma-most people, it's the other way around."

"Nothing wrong with it. Just an observation."

Nicholes said, "Besides, what's there to know? He likes to wade around the flats, collect stuff, and bring it back for his microscope. Doc's idea of a home entertainment center is a six-pack of beer and a dead fish. A guy like him, you trust right away."

MacKinley was nodding. "I was just saying he's different, that's all."

THREE

Ford went through Rafe Hollins's address book while he fired the little gas stove and made dinner. He dumped a can of black beans into a pot, flipped pages as he chopped onion, garlic, squeezed in lime juice, added cumin, and put coffee on to boil.

He recognized seven names in the book, three of them from Central America. Only one of the names surprised him. Most of the entries were in ink, but his own name and the marina's phone number were written in pencil—an entry Rafe had probably made within the last few days. Ford leafed through the book searching for other penciled entries, and found two, both inserted above numbers written in ink. Ford reasoned that the inked numbers had been changed, and Rafe had penciled in the new numbers after calling information. Each of the numbers had a Sandy Key prefix, but he recognized neither of the names.

He could hear Rafe saying "I got to meet some of my

buddies from Sandy Key. Make a little money to finance this thing . . ."

Ford wiped his hands on his pants and went out the door across the roofed walkway and unlocked the room that he had converted into a lab. Against the far wall was a stainless-steel dissecting table angled slightly to drain. Above it on a shelf were rows of jars containing chemicals and preserved specimens: the comb jellies and nudibranches, the sponges and brittle stars, the octopi, anemones, and unborn sharks he had collected since returning to Florida. He switched on the draftsman's lamp and in a very neat, very tiny script, he noted five of the names, addresses, and telephone numbers on a yellow legal pad. Beneath the names he wrote *Wendy Stafford?* then opened the metal box he had found on the island.

He removed one of the jade amulets from the box, a small parrot's head with wings folded close to the chest, and studied it under the light. It looked authentic, but he wanted to be sure. He crossed the room and placed the artifact on the dark stage of his Wolfe zoom binoculared microscope. He raised and rotated the binocular tube, dialed to the lowest power, and took off his glasses, focusing carefully on the parrot's drilled left eye. Through the illuminated lens, the jade—jadeite, really—was a brilliant field of translucent green, magnified seven times. Ford wanted to be certain of how the eyes had been drilled. The indigenous peoples of Central America had used wooden augers, string, and the cutting power of sand to fashion their amulets. Ford was looking for the trace spirals of a modern metal drill. Street shysters were selling mass-produced jadeite junk all over Central America, but this little parrot wasn't junk; he found no spirals. It was a little green god, cool to the touch, a dense little weight on the palm. Probably eight hundred years old or more, and Mayan, though it could have been Chorotega, Corobici, Brunca, or possibly even Inca—there had been trade between most of the Meso-American tribes. Ford didn't know enough about it to be sure.

He gave the other amulets a quick inspection, then took the plastic bag from Rafe's metal box and used a tweezers to extract a thin beige flake of residue. He dampened it, mounted it on a slide, touched the reflected light switch, upped scope power to 25x, and took a look: rough congealed particles; some kind of membrane. He chose another beige flake, the largest in the sack, and positioned it beneath the scope. This sample was blotched with a long dark stain. As Ford increased power and illumination, the hairline stain became a sweeping reddish-brown stroke that bled and faded into the beige membrane.

Ford opened the plastic sack once more and inhaled the faint odor of old leather—but now from another direction he caught a stronger odor.

Damn it!

Ford ran across the walkway into the room he thought of as his living area, and yanked the pot of burned beans off the propane stove.

Now he'd have to start supper all over again.

Through the window above the stove he could see the marina. Dock lights shimmered, strips of gold on liquid darkness, funneling out across the bay. Most of the boats were lighted, too, sitting in rows looking bright and Christmasy, vibrating with muted laughter, wild sentence fragments rising above the night sounds.

Ford listened to the party for a time as he made fresh beans, trying to pick out words, match voices with the silhouettes he could see on the docks. Then the hilarity began to underline his own sense of solitude; made him feel like an eavesdropper, so he decided to make a little noise of his own. He slid a cassette into the Maxima waterproof stereo system, The Beach Boys' *Pet Sounds*, cranked it loud, poured coffee in a mug, went out onto the porch and down the wooden steps to his fish tank while the beans simmered.

To make the tank, he'd taken a thousand-gallon wooden cistern built like a whiskey barrel, cut it in two, mounted it on the widest part of the dock, added a sub-sand filter and a hundred-gallon upper reservoir to improve water clarity. He'd spent a week checking pH, getting the raw water and overflow pumps just right, then began to slowly introduce some of the local flora and fauna: turtle grass, tunicates, sea hydroids, then a few common vertebrates, killifish, small snappers, immature groupers, then plenty of shrimp he had seined up so the fish wouldn't eat each other. Finally he'd caught three reef squid knowing that squid, because they were delicate, were good indicators of an aquarium's integrity.

The squid all died within three days.

Ford started over. He made structural adjustments. Got rid of the killifish—they attacked everything that came near them. Rechecked the tank's pH, fine-tuned the intake flow, and tried again, this time with two squid. Now he turned on the light above the tank—a bare bulb beneath a green metal shade—and watched fish scurry, saw the glowing ruby eyes of shrimp, finally found the two squid side by side, their wine-colored spots throbbing with, what seemed to Ford, outrage.

"You guys still alive?"

The squid held themselves suspended above the bottom, their keen eyes apparently fixed peripherally on Ford.

"Don't die on me. I've had enough of that for one day."

With the light on them, the squids' chromatophores were beginning to function, changing color from brown to pale yellow, matching the shade of the sand beneath them while their posterior fins fluttered, holding them in place.

Ford said, "Here it is, Friday night, and I'm talking to cephalopods. And everyone I know's at a party."

He switched out the light, went back up to the cabin, replaced The Beach Boys with shortwave, Radio Havana. He recognized the announcer's voice. She spoke a fluid, sensual Spanish that did not mesh with the way he remembered her: a nicotine-stained hulk he'd met at some long-ago embassy party. His mind slipped easily into Spanish, thinking in Spanish. He was jolted out of it, though, when the Hulk put on the New York Philharmonic doing Aaron Copeland's *Danzon Cubano*. Listening, Ford put snapper on to fry and ate alone looking out the window. The bay, calm in the June night, was a black mirror and the sky a basin of stars.

After the dishes were done, he found a local AM station on the shortwave. The news guy didn't say anything about the body of Hollins being found. Maybe the woman at Everglades County Sheriff's Department thought he was kidding, a crank. No way of telling. But the idea of Rafe still out there, still hanging in the darkness, was oddly unsettling, and Ford decided to do some work to put it out of his mind.

Tomlinson came clattering out of the darkness in the tiny painter skiff he kept tethered behind the Morgan sailboat, the boat that had been his home since his arrival in Dinkin's Bay two months earlier—and probably years before that.

He tied up at the dock beside Ford's skiff and flat-bottomed trawl boat, stepped out waving with one hand, pulling his shoulder-length hair back into a ponytail with the other, calling "Hey, Doc, hey, man, what's happening?" Then he climbed onto the stairs, into the light, saying "Sittin' out there all alone, listening to that party going on—" Tomlinson, tall and bony, blond with a black beard, shrugged. "Really got to be kind of a bummer, you know? Thought I'd stop by."

Looking at Tomlinson was like stepping into the past and seeing a child of the Sixties with that look in the eyes, still hearing music, an old hand at psychedelic visions, a man about Ford's age who had weathered badly but had visited God often enough not to care. Tomlinson had taken to stopping by the stilt house off and on in the evenings, sometimes bringing a book to read while Ford worked; other times talking away, and Ford didn't mind. He liked Tomlinson and was glad for the company.

Ford had just removed Jeth Nicholes's shark from the ice. It lay on the outside cleaning table beneath the light of the twin overhead bulbs, its three-foot body in rigid curvature. Ford said, "How's it going, Tomlinson?"

Tomlinson said, "Are you kidding? How's it going? You've got to be kidding." He made a face, showing he was not as serious as he sounded, saying "You been listening to the music they're playing over at the marina? How could you miss it, loud as hell, man. Damn people at that party are deaf or something. Going to ruin their damn inner ears playing it that loud. There's been research done on that stuff."

Ford said, "I've got some beer up in the refrigerator, you want to go get it?"

"What?"

Grinning, Ford spoke louder. "I said I've got some beer."

Tomlinson said, "Oh," reaching his hand out, touching the shark with one finger. "My God, they're playing Twisted Sister. They're playing Van Halen. They're playing *Prince,* man. Rot their damn brains, listening to junk like that. These kids today, huh?" Tomlinson shuddered. "What kind of beer?"

"I didn't even look in the sack."

"A cold beer'd be nice right now."

"Make sure you get the refrigerator closed tight. The door's got a bad seal."

Tomlinson stopped at the top of the stairs and looked down into the shark pen. The floodlight made the water the color of strong tea, and, beneath the surface, three black torpedo shapes cruised slowly into the light, following the perimeter of the pen. Tomlinson said, "Why they always swim that way, man, that direction? Every time I come here, those three big sharks are always swimming the same way, the same speed. It's weird, like they're police dogs or something."

Ford looked up from the cleaning table briefly. "I don't know why. Sharks in captivity almost always swim clockwise. In Florida, anyway. Not in Africa, though. It was different in Africa. They swam counterclockwise. Someone somewhere probably knows why, but I don't."

"You think if I fell in there, all three of them would nail me? Eat me up?"

Ford said, "If you fell in, the noise would probably scare them so bad they'd bust through the wire, so don't, okay? It's hard enough just getting them to eat fish."

Tomlinson returned with two bottles as Ford took up the scalpel and made a long cut, opening the small bull shark's belly. He penned back the skin as the huge gray liver slid out, spilling over the edge of the cleaning table as if trying to escape. He pushed the liver away and found the larger of the fish's two stomachs and snipped it open with scissors, front to back. Inside was a litter of catfish spines and bits of shell and crab carapace. Tomlinson said, "He was hungry, huh?"

"Could be. This is its cardiac stomach, the one they can expel through their mouths, inside out, if they want to get rid of something they can't digest."

"Then why's it still have all that gravelly junk in it? They can't digest that kind of stuff, can they?"

"Some of it probably. But I'm not sure."

Tomlinson finished his beer quickly and now opened Ford's bottle. "You want this?"

"No. Go ahead."

"Sharks are your thing, huh? You told me that's what you've been studying, what your work's all about."

"Now it is. For a long time my main interest was bio-luminescence. Phosphorescence. You know how sea water sparkles?"

"Yeah, man. Boat leaves a bright trail at night. I love it. Like green fire."

"Only it's cold light caused by tiny organisms that light up when they're disturbed. I got interested in a little crustacean called an ostracod. It gives off a pale-blue light; very pretty. Put a bunch of ostracods in a tube of water, shake it, and they give off enough light to read by. The Japanese used to collect them and dry them. During the war, Japanese officers would take a little ostracod powder in their palm, moisten it, and read dispatches in dark-out situations."

"Dormitory chemistry," said Tomlinson. "I used to be good at that."

The skin around Ford's eyes crinkled when he smiled. "From ostracods I went into the single-celled bioluminescent organisms, things called armored flagellates. That was my main interest for a while. Then I went to fish. Tarpon. The tarpon is one of the most popular gamefish in the world, yet hardly anything is known about its life history."

"But now it's sharks."

"Temporarily, anyway. Just bull sharks. I don't know

that much about them yet. No one does, really. I got interested when I was in Africa. Second to Australia, there used to be more shark attacks off the coast of Durban, South Africa, than any other spot in the world. The Durban businesspeople have spent a lot of money enclosing the public beaches with nets. The shark responsible for most of the attacks is the Zambezi shark. It's called that because it goes up the Zambezi River into fresh water." Ford tapped the fish he was working on. "This is the Zambezi shark. Our bull shark. The same species. Then I was in Central America. In Lake Nicaragua and in a Masaguan lake they call *Ojo de Dios,* God's Eye, there's a freshwater shark that is extremely aggressive. Attacks on people are so common that the natives won't even bathe in the lakes. The Maya considered the shark a deity; some still do. Used it in their glyphs, their carvings. They still refer to the sharks as *El Dictamen,* The Judgment. You'll see an occasional boat on the lake, but that's it. Natives consider swimming out of the question."

"And those are bull sharks, too? All the same fish, right?" Tomlinson was combing his fingers through his hair, getting into it.

"Right. So I'm interested in the bull shark for a couple of reasons. Why is it more prone to enter and live in fresh water? Why's it so aggressive off South Africa and in Central America, but not here? It's one of our most common sharks, but this area has had only four recorded shark attacks in the last hundred years, none fatal. Those attacks may have involved bull sharks, no one knows.

Even so, with all the people who swim here, the chance of shark attack is statistically insignificant. Why?"

Tomlinson said wasn't that always the stumper, why? "But what a great way to make a living, man. Catching stuff and selling it. This is what you've always done?"

Ford said, "No. Just now." Still using the scissors, he clipped away the fish's spleen, then sections of the pinkish-white pancreas and the long rectal gland at the posterior end of the intestine. He was going slower now, using a probe to reveal the shark's urogenital system, pushing apart the cloacal opening with his fingers, then using the probe again to see if the abdominal pores were closed. They were not. He said, "I got my degree when I was still in the navy. When I got out, I couldn't get a job in marine biology, so I went to work for a company that could send me to the places I wanted to go. I worked for them and did my research on the side."

"Like some kind of international corporation?"

"International, right."

"World conglomerates, man. You don't have to tell me. They recruited us heavy back at Harvard. Once I got in the wrong line and almost ended up working for IBM. LSD and IBM—that's a business trip for you. I was messed *up*. Thank God I couldn't remember my Social Security number, or I'd probably be in New York right now. Paris maybe, wearing a tie."

Ford looked up from the shark. "Harvard? You went there?" It was the first he'd heard of that.

"For seven years, man. Seven long years. And I don't mind saying, toward the end, morale was at an all-time low. You go for a doctorate at the university, you better expect to take a written test or two."

"A Ph.D.?"

"Eastern religions. My master's was in world history, but I figured what the fuck, why not shoot for enlightenment? Sometimes you got to go for broke."

Ford said, "I'm going to segment this shark's brain, then weigh the parts. How about a couple more beers?"

"I've got a number all rolled and ready . . . in my pocket here someplace if you're interested." Tomlinson was patting his pockets, searching.

"A number?" Ford knew what it meant, but it didn't register right away.

"A joint . . . someplace."

Ford said, "I thought you said you don't do that stuff anymore."

Tomlinson was smiling, suddenly sheepish. "Can't find the damn thing anyway. Maybe I did quit." He was still patting his pockets. "Yeah, I guess that's what happened. I musta quit. How about another beer?"

"Good idea."

Ford used a fillet knife to remove the skin from the shark's head, then a scalpel to scrape away the cartilage that protected the brain. There were blood clots from the clubbing Jeth had given it. Ford washed the clots away and found the cerebellum, neat as a walnut above the optic lobes. Tomlinson watched while Ford segmented and weighed the brain, and then they sat out on the dock for another hour, talking, listening to the music and the noise of the party at the marina. Ford established that Tomlinson did, indeed, know a lot about world history;

probably even enough to have majored in it at Harvard. When Ford went to bed at 1 A.M., he looked toward the mouth of the bay to see if Jessica's porch light was still on. It was . . . and it was still on when he awoke at three, made a trip to the head, then lay awake thinking. . . .

FOUR

Ford had found an old number for Harry Bernstein; so he got the operator, clunked in a pocketful of quarters, and listened to a distant, distant recording in Spanish: line disconnected, *muchas gracias*. He hadn't much hope for it anyway. So he waited around the pay phone, hoping Bernstein would call him. As he waited, Ford took out the photograph of Rafe's son. *Jake Age 5*. What was it in the faces of children, he wondered, that created the impression of innocence and keyed in some adults—himself, to name one—the urge to shield them from all harm? It was more than bone structure and the absence of facial lines. It had to be more than an experiential judgment, too, for children sometimes demonstrated the capacity for great cruelty. Perhaps the source of the emotion was some deep coding in the DNA, evolved during speciation to protect the young from marauding adults; a built-in check for the preservation of species. It would be a good one to bounce off Tomlinson some night. Whatever it was, the boy's photograph communicated that innocence: the slight, shy smile and the wide brown eyes staring out as if waiting for something; eyes that trusted and expected only good things.

Ford wondered what the expression on the boy's face would be if photographed now, this moment; wondered if young Jake still had access to that expression of trust, of pure expectation. What would it be like to be an eight-year-old boy in a strange country, unable to understand the language, stolen from his father by strangers? The child was getting the adult course in terror, and the sense of urgency Ford felt wasn't alleviated by the fact that Bernstein didn't call.

At noon, he ordered a fried conch sandwich from the marina deli and went in to talk to MacKinley. MacKinley was sitting behind the cash register reading a magazine called *This Is New Zealand*.

"Have I gotten any phone calls, Mack?"

"Had one this morning, but they didn't leave a message."

"A man?"

"Nope. A woman. Might have been that artist friend of yours out on the point."

"Oh." Ford nodded toward the magazine MacKinley was reading. "You getting homesick, Mack?"

"Homesick? Don't think of the islands as home anymore. Left when I was sixteen, and haven't been back." Speaking with a New Zealand accent, MacKinley added, "Still have a fondness for the place, though.

Like to look at the pictures—but that's as close as I care to get. All those sheep, you know. And the women aren't as pretty. Unless you go to Australia. The women in Australia are something." He put down the magazine. "You missed quite a party last night, Doc."

"It sounded fun."

"I met a lady urologist. Good dancer, as I remember."

"Hmm . . ."

"Two of the women turned out to be speech specialists. About midnight, they got into an argument about the best way to treat Jeth's stutter. Somehow the three of them ended up in Jeth's skiff, out there in the bay all alone. He made it back just in time to take his morning tarpon charter."

"Was he still stuttering?"

"Between yawns. The lady doctors were happy. Getting on quite well together. Jeth looked a bit drawn, though. Rather pale, I should say, like he'd had a tough football match."

"Maybe Jeth should send them a bill."

"Exactly what I told him."

Ford had found the Fort Myers newspaper and began to leaf through it.

MacKinley asked, "Did your telephone man show up?"

"Yeah. He's out there working on the cable right now."

"For the first two months you said you didn't want a phone. Said you didn't need it. Now you can't wait to get it in."

"Sometimes I'm just plain fickle," said Ford. "Other

times I'm just plain wrong." He turned to the inside page, local section and saw that Rafe Hollins had made the late regional edition:

The body of a Sandy Key man was found yesterday evening on a deserted island by Everglades County Sheriff's deputies. The body of Rafferty Hollins, 36, was discovered on Tequesta Bank, a remote island in Curlew Bay three miles from Sandy Key, after an anonymous caller contacted police. According to a department spokeswoman, Hollins was found with a rope around his neck, hanging from a tree. The death is being treated as a probable suicide pending an autopsy.

Everglades District Court issued a warrant for Hollins's arrest recently on kidnapping charges following the disappearance of his 8-year-old son who was in the custody of Hollins's estranged wife, Helen Burke Hollins. According to the Atlanta office of the Federal Bureau of Investigation, the case was under investigation by a federal magistrate, but no warrant had been issued. There is no information yet available on the whereabouts of the child.

A former Sanibel Island resident, Hollins was a star high school athlete. According to newspaper files, he was drafted by the Kansas City Royals in the 16th round following graduation. Hollins played one year at the Royals' Sarasota baseball school before enlisting in the Marines. He was awarded the Silver Star for valor.

"What?" Ford realized that MacKinley was talking to him.

MacKinley was standing at the counter, looking at the paper. "I asked if you knew that man. The one who did himself in on Tequesta Bank. You were just asking Jeth about Tequesta Bank yesterday, weren't you?"

"I knew him. I knew Rafe pretty well." Ford was thinking *Suicide?* How in the hell did they come up with that?

MacKinley said, "Seems a damn shame. Child involved and all. Did he seem the type?"

"To kill himself, you mean? No. Absolutely not. Rafe wasn't the type."

"You seem very sure."

"I am sure."

"Then maybe the newspaper has it wrong. It happens, you know."

"They were quoting the Everglades County Sheriff's Department. An indirect quote."

MacKinley shrugged and went back to his chair. "Can't pay much attention to those Sandy Key officials now, can we?"

"Oh?"

"Well, that's what people around here say. Sandy Key is one of those Florida phenomenons, you know. Instant city. About fifteen years ago, just before I arrived, a financial group bought the whole island. And it's a very large island. First thing they did was get rid of the old fishing shacks. Second thing they did was start spraying for mosquitoes. The damn bugs are the only thing that kept that area from building up a long time ago. The

environmentalists were all in an uproar, said they were
spraying way too much. But the developers barged
on, kept spraying, and platted their own city: churches
here, shops there, apartment complexes in one section,
residential houses in another. All concrete block, thank
you very much, no wooden structures allowed. Within six
years, it was the largest city in Everglades County. They
petitioned to become the county seat, pulled a few
financial strings, and got it. Now all the public services
there are a closed shop. Law enforcement, medical examiner, all appointed offices—the development group
controls them all. Sealife Development, that's the name
of the group. When elections come around, they let
their citizenry know the proper way to vote. They don't
always have good people in important positions, but they
always have *their* people."

"Voters stand for that?"

"Places like Sandy Key attract a certain kind of
buyer. They like rules. Everything nice and neat and
sterile." MacKinley pronounced it *stair-ile*. "And they
are very loyal in return. Their bumper stickers say 'We
Live On Sandy Key and Love It.' That type. Maybe your
friend didn't fit in. Maybe they don't care enough to
check everything out properly. But if they made a mistake, you'll never hear about it."

"The sheriff of Everglades County doesn't admit his
department makes mistakes?"

"The sheriff is Mario DeArmand, a New Jersey
builder who's a big stockholder in Sealife Development
Corporation. He was appointed by the board. The city
manager is . . . I forget his name. But he's from New

York, one of Sealife's major investors, and he was appointed, too. The district attorney is from Long Island, and he's also chairman of the board. The whole city is run like that. Like a bunch of big kids acting out their childhood fantasies, wearing uniforms and playing with sirens. Everyone stays in line, or the corporation gets rid of them. Sandy Key is a bright, sunny, cheerful place with almost no crime. If you don't believe me, just read the Sandy Key *Sentinel*, the corporate-owned newspaper. Suicide is a nasty business, but murder is so much nastier. The corporation might lose a condo sale or two if word got out there was a murderer on the loose."

Ford said, "Maybe someone needs to do some poking around down there if the medical examiner agrees with the sheriff's department. Stir things up a little," but he was thinking about that name: Mario DeArmand. It was one of the names Ford had found in Rafe's address book.

"You, for instance?" MacKinley was smiling. "Forgive me, Doc, but you really aren't the type. I'm sure you're very good in your field, bookish and studious and exacting and all, but weaving one's way into the heart of a corrupt government is an entirely different job of work. People like DeArmand are little tyrants, and tyrants have the unhappy habit of turning nasty when their competence is questioned. That sort of thing calls for someone shifty and devious; bit of a liar, too, I'm afraid. I really can't see you in that role, Doc. As Jeth says, you're a nice, quiet man; a person who can be trusted. I think you should leave the muckraking to those more suited for it."

Ford was smiling, too. "Maybe I'll just write a letter to the newspaper, tell them what I think."

"There you are. That's an idea. But there's a possibility in all this I think you should consider first."

"What's that?"

"That your friend really did commit suicide."

Jeth was just docking with his morning charter as Ford stepped outside, still listening for the pay phone. Nicholes looked grim as he tied the lines; the four big men sitting in his skiff looked grimmer. MacKinley poked his head out, saying "Those guys are pissed off about something. Look at them. I knew they'd be trouble before they even got in the boat. I told Jeth that."

Ford walked out onto the dock, hands in the pockets of his khaki fishing shorts, interested. Jeth was saying "You can ga-ga-ga-get out now," stuttering worse than usual, upset.

"Hear that boys? The ca-captain says we're allowed to leave. Always have to do what the ca-captain tells you, even if he's the screw-up that let our tarpon get away." Talking as if he were joking around, this wide-bodied man with a sunburned face twice the size of his hands jumped out, dark hair gray at the temples, early forties, pack of cigarettes in the pocket of the bathrobe he wore over a bikini bathing suit and a huge belly. Probably a little drunk, too, from the way he teetered. "Ca-ca-captain? I owe these men of mine an apology. See, they're the top salesmen in my company, and they worked their asses off to win this Florida trip. I wanted to give them a taste of big-game fishing, but it seems I chose the wrong man for the job. Fellas, I'm sorry. But it's a good lesson. I didn't do enough checking around, and I admit it. Proves even the boss makes an occasional mistake. Did the same thing off the Yucatan, hired this rookie to take me after blue marlin, and I swore I'd never let it happen again. I've fished enough around the world to know within a minute whether a guide knows his ass from a bunker, but I was wrong this time, and I'm sorry. You deserved better." Making a speech right there on the dock, people in boats listening, Jeth Nicholes turning red as he cleaned up, pretending not to hear.

"It's okay, Mr. Willis. We had a good time anyway." The three subordinates were sticking by the boss-man, jockeying for position in the executive pecking order, backing him all the way.

The big man, Willis, said, "Just one of those ba-ba-bum decisions," laughing because he was mature enough to take the good with the bad.

"That's enough! God da-da-damn it." Nicholes slammed down the line he had been coiling and jumped out of the boat, facing the four men. "I ma-ma-missed the ga-ga-gaff on one tarpon. I a-a-a . . .'mit it. Said I'm sorry, and I ca-ca-can't do no more than that," his stutter so bad he could hardly talk.

Willis took a step toward him, now the cool-headed negotiator. "But you *can* do more than that, Captain. In my business, we give the client what he wants. We work our butts off to make sure our clients are happy. That's how we built our reputation; ask anyone in Ohio. When a client isn't happy, we give him his money back. That's exactly what you're going to do for us. Give us our money back."

Nicholes's jaw was working, but no words were coming out. He finally croaked, "Okay . . . just ga-get . . . leave."

"You sure you want to do that, Jeth?" Ford had moved up the dock, hands still in pockets, smiling good-naturedly. "These guys paid you to take them tarpon fishing, right? Well, you took them. You don't owe them a thing."

Willis turned a cold eye on Ford. "I don't see how this is any of your concern, friend."

Looking past the big man, Ford asked Nicholes, "How many tarpon did they have on?"

Nicholes started to say something, then held up five fingers.

Willis said, "Friend, I personally think you ought to get the hell out of here before you get yourself into trouble." He reached into his robe, took a cigarette in his lips, and lit it.

Ford said, "You had five tarpon on, which means you and your party lost four. Right? And I think I overheard someone say Jeth missed a gaff? Well, everyone makes mistakes. You guys made four of them. Jeth made one. But it sounds to me like you had a pretty good day anyway. I don't know any fishing guide anywhere who tries harder than Jeth to keep his people happy, and that's the truth. So why don't you just drop it?"

Willis looked at his three salesmen, made an open-handed gesture; lecture time again. "This is why it's

good to get away from the office occasionally, gentlemen. Reminds us what happens when a man drops out.
Loses that competitive drive. You end up a boat bum
like the ca-ca-captain. Or one of the beach bums like
my friend here who has nothing better to do than hang
around a marina, poking his nose into places where it
doesn't belong." He looked at Ford. "See, I know your
type, friend. Can't make it in the real world, the business world, so you come down here and mix with people
who have made something of themselves, act like a real
person. Frankly, I don't have time for people like you.
So now you can get the hell out of my way, buster."

Ford was still smiling, blocking the dock, but beginning to sweat a little, hoping he could find some way
around having to actually fight the guy, thinking *I haven't
punched anyone since Coronado*, but also thinking
this pompous bastard had it coming. He said, "You're
trying too hard, Willis."

The man looked at him. "I'm *what*?"

"I said you're trying way too hard. See, you've got
those three junior executive types at your heels, judging you every step of the way, and you can't let them see
you back down now, can you? They'll smell blood,
maybe get ideas about taking your job. What are you, the
president of some small company? No, you flinched. A
vice president then—"

"More than you'll ever be, friend."

"But you'll probably never get to be president. Only
the really good ones make it in the executive world, and
the good ones would never mock a guy who stutters.

They have too much style—something you don't have, Willis. You know it, so you try too hard. You talk too loud, and you bully people when you can—like Jeth there. Jeth takes a swing at a customer, and he's liable to lose his license. You're not smart, but you're shrewd enough to know when you're on safe ground."

"I don't have to stand here and listen to this garbage—"

Ford moved to block his path once more. "But I'm not done, Willis. And you're going to stand right there and find out what it's like to have some stranger browbeat you in public. I tried to be nice; you had your chance. Now you're going to listen. Let's see . . . you drink too much and you smoke your two packs a day, and the blood pressure is way too high, but you've got to keep pressing, have to run hard to stay ahead of the parade, because these guys and probably a bunch of others are just waiting for you to drop. Now you're not sure what to do because I'm standing smack in your way. Some stranger who doesn't fit into your pecking order. And you may have to actually fight it out, and right now you're thinking you have twenty pounds on me, but you'll have to make that first punch count because you're lugging a lot of fat and you don't have much wind, and you could end up looking very, very foolish. So I'll give you an honorable way out, Willis." Ford stepped back, creating enough room on the dock for him to pass. "I admit it. I'm afraid you might connect with that first punch. So go climb into your rental car, drive to your nice motel, sit around the pool with a fresh drink, and joke about what you would have done to me if I'd said one more word." Ford looked at Nicholes. "You're not going to give them their money back, are you Jeth?"

"Na-na-no way, Doc. He just had me so mad I ca-couldn't think right."

Willis was saying "He's a coward. There, that's putting it pretty plainly. Said so himself." His face was grayish, and the three junior executives were looking here and there, avoiding his eyes. "Nothing but a fucking nobody coward. I wouldn't waste my energy on a nobody like him."

Hearing something, Ford cocked his head: The pay phone was ringing. Maybe it was Bernstein; Bernstein finally calling from Central America. Miss this call and he'd have to go through the whole process again, maybe have to wait another day. He turned to trot toward the phone and, as he did, the creaking of the dock and a guttural grunt gave him just enough warning. He pivoted sharply, feeling the wind-wake of Willis's right fist sail past his face. Willis's follow-through left him teetering sideways on the dock, and Ford hit him in the stomach, hard, kicked him behind the right knee, and caught the big man as he fell, wrapping his left arm under Willis's right elbow and arm, clamping his hand around Willis's throat, putting just enough pressure on the carotid artery and the elbow to pin him immobile on the dock.

The phone was still ringing.

Ford glanced at the junior executives, all three of them shifting nervously, not quite sure what to do; Jeth Nicholes standing behind them, ready. Ford said, "Willis, you just had a spell of very bad judgment," talking as he put enough pressure on the man's elbow to make the joint creak; watching Willis's eyes pinch, the flesh on his cheeks flush then mottle. "If you're smart, you won't try it again . . . *friend*." He released him abruptly, turned to run, but Willis got his foot out, tripped him, and Ford dove headlong onto the dock, almost into the water. Looking up, he could see MacKinley running toward them, a baseball bat in his hand.

"Mack! Get the phone!"

"What?"

"The phone!"

"I already called the police."

"Not that phone!"

A crushing weight hit him from behind, and Willis was on him, punching wildly. Ford rolled away, heard the big man's shoe smash into the planking by his face, wrestled his way to his feet suddenly not able to see so well. Where in the hell were his glasses?

Willis was coming at him, a big blurry shape pawing like some kind of boxer. Behind him, Nicholes was systematically wrestling the junior executives into the bay.

"Not now, Willis. I don't have time right now."

"Ha! That's what I thought . . . coward, trying to talk his way out."

Ford saw a big shadow coming at him, Willis's right fist. He batted the fist into a harmless trajectory and kicked him in the side of the leg, missing the knee. Willis stumbled forward, grabbed Ford by the shoulders, scratching at his face and eyes with his fingernails. Ford smacked him in the throat with his open palm, then whirled 360 degrees, his elbow out like an ax. Willis walked right into it, taking the elbow flush on the nose, blood spurting as he backpedaled into a piling and tumbled into the water.

"Jeth, make sure that asshole doesn't drown!" Ford was already running.

"Hell, Da-Da-Doc, looks like he's dead already. . . ."

Ford sprinted past MacKinley toward the pay phone, forced his way through the crowd that had gathered, skidded around the corner of the office, and lifted the receiver just as the caller hung up. He rummaged through his pockets to find a quarter, remembered he didn't need one, and dialed zero.

A woman's voice said, "Good afternoon, operator."

"Operator, I'm at a pay phone. Someone just tried to call here from Central America, probably Masagua. I need the number they called from. It's important."

"I'm sorry, sir, but I have no way of getting that information."

"Yes you do. You're in an office, right? One of the operators there had to work the call. Ask around. She can call the operator in Central America; the number had to come up on her equipment—"

"I'm very sorry, sir, we don't provide that service."

"You can try, though—"

"I'm sorry, sir."

Ford slammed the phone down, patting the pockets of his shirt absently, looking for his glasses. Then remembered he'd lost them back on the dock. The adrenaline was still pumping through him; his ribs hurt, and he could feel the raw burn of the scratches on his face.

His stomach was grumbling; maybe he was going to throw up. He walked back to the basin where the junior executives, all soaking, had just fished Willis out of the water. His bathrobe was open, showing the big hairy belly, and his face was bleeding, split from nose to left eye. MacKinley moved to Ford's side and said quietly, "He's already talking lawsuit. I think he means it, too."

From the near distance came the sound of sirens.

Ford stepped over and kicked Willis on the sole of his sandal. "I hear you're thinking about pressing charges, fat man."

Willis looked up groggily, pressing a towel against the flaps of split skin. He slid back slightly when he saw Ford. "You just wait . . . just wait till my lawyers get through with you. You and this crummy marina and that idiot fishing guide—he's guided his last trip. You have no idea who you're dealing with, buster. No fucking clue."

Nicholes was glaring at him. "Don't worry about it, Doc. He started it. We all saw. They can't ta-ta-ta-touch my license for this."

Ford said, "You go right ahead, fat man. Stir up a lot of trouble. If you do, I may just have to call your wife. Your number won't be hard to get. The marina has the name of your motel, and the motel will have your address back in Ohio."

"My wife . . . ?" He struggled to his feet. "Now just what in the hell does my wife have to do with—"

"Remember the waitress you made a fool of yourself over the other night? Or was it last night? Well, she's a friend of mine, Willis. If your wife doesn't believe me,

I'll have my friend tell her. What was it you said to that waitress again?"

"You son of a bitch—"

"Let's go, Mr. Willis." One of the junior execs had him by the arm, trying to steer him away. "I think we ought to go before the cops get here. And you're going to need some stitches."

Willis jerked his arm away. "He's bluffing. Can't you see that? He doesn't know the waitress."

"Then how did he find out? Come on, Mr. Willis. I think everyone here agrees we should go."

"Bullshit! You think I'm going to let this creep suckerpunch me and get away with it! I'm staying right here—"

The junior executive took him by the arm again, but much harder. "Willis, for once in your life, just shut that big mouth of yours and do what you're told. I'm not going to stand around and let you embarrass us more than you already have."

One of the other men took the other arm. "He's right, Mr. Willis. I'm getting a little sick of it myself. Let's go."

They half walked, half pushed Willis to the parking lot. The police pulled in just as they started their car.

Watching, MacKinley said, "I think it's time for Mr. Willis to think about a career move. Those men are never going to look at him the same again. And word spreads fast in a corporation."

"Damn, Da-da-doc, damn. Nicholes was back in his skiff, moving things that didn't need to be moved, burning nervous energy. "We lucked out. That bastard woulda had us in court all year, and I ca-can't afford no lawyer. It's a good thing you know that waitress."

Ford was rubbing his ribs. "I don't know the waitress."

"What? You're ka-ka-kiddin'?"

MacKinley studied Ford for a moment; reappraisal time. "I'm surprised you'd take a risk like that"—he looked at Nicholes—"being the nice, quiet soul you are."

Ford said, "With a guy like Willis, there was bound to be an offended waitress somewhere on the island. It wasn't much of a risk."

"And honest, too. Not the least bit sneaky or shifty."

Ford said, "If you guys don't mind, maybe you could help me find my glasses?"

Ford was lying on his bed in the stilt house. He wanted a beer, but his ribs hurt too badly to get up, and there was a fly buzzing around and he didn't want to deal with that either. His elbow hurt and his knees ached from the fall he had taken. His hands were fine, though. He'd learned a long time ago never to hit anyone with his hands unless he absolutely had to. Ford looked at his fingers without moving his head, wiggling them. Yep, they were fine.

The door of the next room banged shut and a man pressed his face against the screen. "All done, Dr. Ford"

"That's good."

"Nice black phone, just like you asked for. Desk model. I put it on your desk."

"Ah, the desk."

"Sure you don't want a call-on-hold model? Or maybe

redial? Push a button, redials last number you called. Now the cable's in, I can do anything you want. We got all kinds of models. Maybe match the decor."

Still not moving his head, Ford considered the ceiling and the walls. They had gray phones? There was no decor to match. "No, thanks. Black's just fine."

"Dr. Ford, you don't mind some advice. Well, I saw you lay it on that guy with the big mouth. Best thing to do after something like that is make sure you keep moving, get some kind of exercise, maybe do some work. You don't, you're not gonna be able to get outta bed tomorrow."

Ford shifted his eyes enough to see the man standing at the screen. "You really think so?"

"Absolutely. I saw the spill you took. Made me hurt from where I was standing. But I'll tell you, that guy didn't have much experience to take a swing at you. Those wire-kinda glasses you wear and those baggy clothes might fool some people, but me, I take a look at a man's shoulders and his wrists. Guy your size, the asshole was just plain nuts."

Ford was wondering how the telephone man would react if he asked him to get him a beer.

"Anything else I can do for you, Dr. Ford?"

"Ah . . . no, nope, not a thing. I'm going to get up and do some work here pretty quick. Maybe go for a run."

"Best thing in the world for you. Well, enjoy. Your phone works fine. Have a nice day."

Ford closed his eyes. "That's nice."

FIVE

Bernstein called at dusk, just as Ford finished dissecting ten of the twenty-eight small sharks he needed to fill the order from Minneapolis Public Schools. He'd taken the phone man's advice and gone to work. Why not? Phone men met knowledgeable people every day, and probably gleaned all sorts of useful information while buckled onto those poles, listening in on private conversations. He'd forced himself out of bed, did some pull-ups, dove off the dock and swam for twenty minutes, out to the first spoil island and back. Halfway in, he felt something brush past; something big and mobile, in the water right there beside him. Ford stopped, his heart pounding, but then this huge creature ascended, exhaling foul breath, looking him right in the eye. It was a manatee, about half the size of a Volkswagen, and Ford began to laugh, spitting water.

"If you're looking for romance, you're blinder than I am."

The sea cow submerged, rubbed past again, then came up behind him whoofing warm air.

Ford swam the rest of the way with the manatee following, goosing him along. He got out, changed clothes, began to ready the dye and dissecting instruments, and the manatee was still there, hanging around the stilt house, stirring the water with its huge fluke tail. He'd had manatee come up to his boat and rub themselves before, but never anything like this—of course, he hadn't swum with many sea cows.

He watched the animal for a while; watched it finally swim away, then took the ten sharks from the cooler. Small blacktip sharks, one to three pounds, their bodies cobalt colored, as if sculpted in metal. He worked carefully with scissors, scalpel, and dissecting pins, laying open the bodies and exposing the circulatory systems. He used red dye for the arteries, injecting the latex slowly into the dorsal aortas to begin, watching the efferent branchial arteries take definition like the branches of red rivers. He used blue latex for the veins and yellow for the hepatic portal system, enjoying the precision of the work; everything nice and neat, clear to the eye and the mind. He packaged the sharks in formalin and laminated barrier bags for shipping, and was just cleaning up when the phone rang. It was Bernstein, 1,800 miles away, but a clear connection, only a slight echo

"Buck! I'm glad you called. I appreciate it; I really mean that."

Harry Bernstein said, "The message I got said it was important so, sure, what you expect?" Dour, suspicious, Bernstein was a tall, effete Texan who spoke Spanish with a drawl so southern that he sounded like Slim Pickens in a badly dubbed movie, so everyone called him Buck. He spoke English, though, without accent, or in dialect when he was angry. With a black mother and a Peruvian father, Bernstein had been pulled in all kinds of directions, social, ethnic, and sexual. He had taken Ford's post in Masagua; hadn't liked it then, and there was no reason to think things had changed. Ford knew he must tread lightly.

"I heard you're doing a great job down there—"

"You haven't heard shit, man. You're calling 'cause you want something. What you want?"

"Come on now, Buck. You've got no reason to be mad at me—"

"Reason to be mad at you? Man, I got no *time* to be mad at you. You been reading what's going on down here? Bombs going off, taking hostages, shootin' people in the streets. Even your buddy Rivera is losing control, his goddamn guerrillas up there in the mountains splitting into all kinds a' factions."

"My buddy? Juan Rivera was never my buddy."

"Helped him start a baseball team for Christ's sake. And you the one got them uniforms, balls, bats—"

"Buck, Buck, what's more American than baseball?"

"Rivera's a damn *communist*, man. But you out there taking the hit-and-run signal from him, tellin' him when to squeeze bunt and double steal. Aiding and abetting the fucking enemy, you ask me. Playin' pepper with guerrillas . . ."

Ford said that's what they needed to talk about, the guerillas, and he was about to tell him about little Jake

Hollins, but Bernstein, still angry, cut in. "And you aren't going to say a word about President Balserio, are you? Man's gone off his rocker, walking around in robes talking about stars and moons and shit. Whatever it was got stolen from the Presidential Palace got him crazy. Happened on your watch, but you think me and my people can find out what it was—"

"Everything I know is in the files, Buck. You're taking this stuff way too seriously."

"Seriously my brown ass! Mayan artifacts got stolen; that's all you wrote down. Mayan artifacts. That's all it was, why he so worried? Why things so crazy up at the palace? You know his wife's retreated to the convent? Hasn't seen anyone for ten months—"

"Convent? Which convent? I need to get in touch with her—"

"That's just what you *don't* need to do, man. Balserio won't give me the time of day, but he still sends aides around every now and again to inquire 'bout you. Where's good old Ford? Ev'body liked Ford. His Excellency like to see that man again. They smiling but got firing squad in their eyes, and you wonder why I think you know more than you're telling? A fucking looney bin is just about exactly what this place is. But not a soul in the world blames you . . . Shit."

Ford said, "Look, Buck, listen for just a second, will you? Take a deep breath, okay?"

"I don't need no deep breath. Just tell me what you want."

"What I want is just a little of your time. Okay? The son of a friend of mine was kidnapped. By some group in Masagua. Indios. Smugglers probably, maybe guerrillas, I don't know. I just found out yesterday."

"They just kidnap him yesterday?"

"No, five, maybe six days ago. I'm not sure about that either."

"Why'nt you ask your friend for more details, do this thing proper, Ford? Go through the right channels for once—"

"My friend's dead. The proper chain of dialogue is to contact the FBI here, and they contact Balserio's law enforcement people. What good will that do? Most of Balserio's people are on the smuggler's payrolls, and they couldn't find the guerrilla camps even if they wanted to—which they don't."

"But the FBI would contact the CIA people down here on the sly. They'd find the boy. You listen to me, go through channels, let the CIA take care of it. Leave me alone."

"If your son had been kidnapped, would you want the CIA trying to help? They'd send in a squad of marines, automatic weapons, and air support."

"I don't have no son."

"Come on, Buck, you've got to help me on this. The boy's only eight years old."

Bernstein said he didn't have to do anything; the kid was no concern of his; he didn't like kids anyway.

Ford said, "I didn't ask you to help, Buck. I said you've got to help." He let that settle, listening to beeps and echos, the silence of long-distance telephone.

"Are you trying to blackmail me?" Speaking slowly, the black dialect disappeared. "You're out of your mind if you think you've got something on me. I have a clean file, man. I know that for a fact—"

"Buck, I would have never used this. Never in a thousand years. But we're talking about the life of a little boy here, the son of a friend of mine . . ."

"You son of a . . . you had me followed, didn't you?"

"I didn't say that."

"Those first two weeks I was down here, I kept thinking someone was following me, but I thought, shit, they got no reason. I was on *vacation*, man, my own private time—"

"This is important to me, Buck. I never wanted to use it, and I'll never use it again."

Bernstein said, "Well, you try using this, you sneaky motherfucker," and slammed the phone down.

Ford returned to cleaning the dissecting table, thinking maybe he had misread Bernstein, not given him high enough marks, but then the phone rang almost immediately, and Ford knew he'd read him just right.

"Ford? Buck. Ah . . . sorry about getting mad like that. I mean, you just really pissed me off. Let's admit it, that was a pretty shitty thing, having me followed."

Ford was looking through the window of his lab: The sun was a great gaseous orb of fire; the bay, molten. At the marina, the dock lights were just coming on: pale, pale rays on a lake of bronze. He said, "I do admit it, Buck, and I'm sorry. That was pretty crummy, trying to leverage you like that. I should have known you're not the type to tolerate it."

"Well, yeah, I guess that's my rep, not being an easy guy to push."

"I was stupid to even try."

Bernstein said, "But I was thinking about that kid. You know, out there in the jungle with those Indios, probably seeing blood sacrifices, watching them go crazy on psychedelic mushrooms and . . . well, Christ, the kid's probably scared shitless."

Ford was still looking out the window. At the marina, Jeth Nicholes and the other guides were washing their boats, another charter done. Across the bay, Tomlinson was meditating on the bow of his sailboat, sitting naked, blond hair hanging down. Naked? Yeah, no doubt about it, naked. Holding a stick of incense, too. Ford said, "The boy has to be scared, Buck. Like I said, he's only eight."

"Look, for someone that young, and the kid of a friend of yours . . . he's dead you say? Your friend."

"As of yesterday. Murdered."

"The Indios that took the kid?"

"I thought it was a possibility. But not now. He was murdered by someone around here. In Florida."

"For the son of a friend of yours, I guess I could help. I don't know what got into me. This mess down here just has me mean or something. What do you want me to do?"

Ford had Rafe's address book by the phone. "You have something to write with? I want you to check out three names for me. Ready? The names are Julio Zacul, Raul Arevalo, and Wendy Stafford. Find out where they are, what they're doing, if they know anything about the boy. I know the last two personally, but Zacul only by reputation."

"I know Zacul by reputation, too, man." Bernstein pronounced the name Zack-COOL, giving emphasis to the Mayan guttural, like a growl. "He's one of them that split away from Rivera; got his own band of guerrillas. Zacul got the boy, he's probably already dead. How the hell am I supposed to get in touch with him?"

"You can talk to people who know Zacul; people who've worked for him. Come on, Buck, there's nobody around better than you at that sort of thing." Ford wondered for a moment if that might be a little strong, too obvious, then decided not to bother qualifying it. Bernstein wouldn't recognize flattery. "Another angle is, whoever has the boy is smuggling something out of the country or into the country. My friend was flying for them."

"All the guerrillas smuggle stuff into the country and out of the country. They send out dope or refined coke, and bring in raw coca leaves from Peru. Or guns."

"It may have been arms, but my friend told me it wasn't drugs."

"Maybe he was lying."

"Maybe. Write this down, too: My friend's name was Rafe Hollins. He could have used an alias down there, I don't know. The boy's name is Jake Hollins. Brown hair, brown eyes, cleft chin."

"Looking for a brown-eyed, brown-haired boy in Masagua. That's just great. Aren't too many of those around." The sarcasm returning as the submissive Bernstein began to fade; an asshole to the end. "And what do I do if I find him? You going to come down and get him out?"

"I had to sign papers saying I wouldn't return to Masagua for two years, you know that. Company rules. Besides, you say Balserio's men are after me. That I don't understand at all. They have no reason." Ford listened carefully, gauging Bernstein's tone.

"Ah, shit, I don't know. Maybe I said that 'cause I was mad at you; overreacting. They just keep asking, that's all. Maybe they think you can help them find whatever it was that was stolen." A little too airy; Balserio wanted him, all right. Then: "But why you need a visa, man? Just fly into Guatemala, sneak across the border. Get in touch with me. No one has to know you're here. Not even our own people."

Ford thought, *Right, so you can have me arrested, put me in some Masaguan prison for twenty years.* He said, "That's a good idea, Buck. Maybe the best idea. We can talk about it. But first you need to locate the boy."

"And what about that other matter—my first two weeks here? Man, that really was some shitty thing to do, I hope you know."

"What I'm going to do right now is type up a memo on my old stationery, in triplicate. I'll postdate it, make it a week before you arrived, and say I received word Rivera's people were considering plans to intercept you, give you a powerful narcotic, then photograph you in various compromising positions, all staged, all without your knowledge or cooperation—"

"Photos? You got fucking photos, too! You one sneaky . . . careful dude, man."

"I'll keep the pink sheet for my files, send you the blue and the white. You should put the white copy in an

envelope, address it to D.C., then shove it down behind
the desk or a crack or something, make sure it stays
there—"

"Behind the desk?"

"If the matter ever comes up, the people in Washington are going to want to know where their copy went.
Things get rough, you can have them help you look for
it. They'll find it right behind the desk, a piece of lost
mail."

"Yeah—sneaky, sneaky. But what about the prints
and the negatives? I want those, too."

"I'll send the memo tomorrow, and everything else I
have as soon as I get it together. Things are kind of
messy around my place."

"How long?"

Ford said, "About as long as it takes you to get that
information I need."

He hung up wondering what Bernstein had done during his first two weeks in Masagua that had him so
worried.

More improper channels: Ford got the home number of
Sally Field, not the actress; the one who worked for the
Operations Data Board of National Security Affairs.
Sally was thirtyish, lush in a deceptive, secretarial sort
of way, a dedicated government employee who had only
one passion outside of her work: the bedroom. The bedroom was to her what golf or skiing were to her
co-workers. She liked men, all kinds of men, but she was
selective and discreet. She told Ford she'd kept a record of every man she had ever been with—in code, of

course, because her men often held public office. In the diary, each man was graded in a variety of categories (Ford hadn't asked what categories) so she could look back and have fun remembering when she was old and single. "Because I'm always going to be single," she had told him. "No husband could put up with my hobby." When Ford met her, there were forty-three entries in her book. By the time she confided in him, he was already number forty-four. He had always avoided promiscuous women and probably would have avoided Sally had he known in advance. But the woman was a devotee, and Ford admired dedication wherever he happened to find it.

Sally answered—sounding sleepy, he thought. But no, she wasn't busy; he wasn't interrupting. She hoped he was calling because he was either in D.C. or on his way. "You are one of my favorites, Doc. One of my very, very favorites. I hope you know that."

Ford knew that. He also knew that each of the other forty-three were favorites, too. "I'm in Florida, Sally; calling to ask a favor. A professional favor."

Her tone changed, from sleepy to slightly severe. "Oh, Doc, I hope you don't. I never mix business with pleasure. Never, ever. I'm very serious about my job, you know."

"I know that. I wouldn't ask under any other circumstances. But this is important." Ford told her about Hollins and the missing boy, adding "All I need you to do, Sally, is run a computer check on a few names for me. I need some background information, that's all. Anything you can come up with."

"That's all you need?" She was relaxed again; relieved. "I can do that on my coffee break; make it as thorough as I can, and that's as thorough as you can get. How many names?"

Ford gave her the spellings of the names and what little other information he had.

She said, "Okay, okay," her voice changing; her dictation voice. "Last name T-o-m-l-i-n-s-o-n; God, I can't even pronounce his first name."

Ford said, "Me neither."

"Jessica M-c capital-C-l-u-r-e; my competition, I suppose?"

"Just a friend."

"You know, Doc, sometimes you're just a little too calculating—running background checks on friends. I don't want to sound critical, but isn't that a little compulsive—"

"Didn't you run my name through the computer, Sal? When we first met?"

"Touché; you win. You're as careful as I am—which is why the files say you were so good at your job, I guess." Then she said, "The first man, Mario DeArmand, sounds familiar. Should he?"

"Maybe. He's from New Jersey. The eastern seaboard area. Now he's a county sheriff in south Florida."

"And the other names?"

"I don't know much about them. That's why I'm calling. It's possible there's something that connects them all. If there is, I need to know what. I also need to know if any of them work for our government—work for it on any level."

"You're getting into a pretty touchy area there, Doc."

"But with the best of motives."

"Well, I'll do what I can. Shall I call you tomorrow or send the printout Federal Express? No, wait. Tomorrow's Sunday. I won't be in the office until Monday."

"The sooner the better. You can give me a summary on the phone, and then we can talk about anything else you want, Sally."

She was laughing. "I've already told you too much, Ford. After you left that night—what was it? four years ago?—I kept asking myself why I'd told you about my little diary. I've never told anyone else about it. My God, we hardly knew each other, and I trusted you with information that—"

"Diary? Don't know what you're talking about. As in dear diary?"

"See? My instincts were right. I knew I could trust you. And Ford? I check these names for you under one condition. You have to promise to take me to dinner within the next . . . three months. No excuses."

"By September. I promise."

"And you never break a promise, do you?"

"I've broken several."

"An honest man, I knew that, too. I gave you a very high mark for honesty. . . ."

Ford made six more calls, one to New York, the rest to Everglades County, Sandy Key. He tracked down the funeral home that was to take possession of Rafe's body and found out the body would be cremated, that there was to be no funeral, but there would be a private memorial service. Rafe's older brother, Harvey, had made the arrangements. He would be flying from West Virginia tomorrow, so the service would be Monday, 1 P.M. Flowers should be ordered from Sandy Key Floral Shop.

Unless the coroner worked weekends, it didn't make sense for them to release the body so soon, so Ford called the Everglades County Medical Examiner's office and got a man who said there was no one there right now. Ford said, "You're there." And the man said, "But I'm not the one to talk to."

"I need to know if the autopsy on Rafferty Hollins has been scheduled."

The man said, "Hollins? It's already been done. They did it this morning, right after they brought him in. At least I guess they did—all the paperwork's been finished."

"Can you read me the report? The official proclamation of death."

"You a friend of the family or something? I don't think they give out that sort of information."

Ford said, "It's public record. They have to give it out."

"The guy hung himself, I know that much. Death by asphyxia, I guess. But I don't think you're right there. They don't have to give it out. They never have before."

"Does it say death by asphyxia on the death certificate?"

"Look, buddy, there's no one here right now. The medical examiner plays golf on Saturday. You're gonna have to call back. Or try the funeral home, they might have a copy."

"If he plays golf, who did the autopsy?"

"How should I know? Doc musta come in early. Call the funeral home if you want to know anything else."

Ford called the funeral home again and got the same lady he had spoken with earlier. "No sir, we don't have a copy of the death certificate. We have no reason to keep a copy."

"But you have to have a copy before you cremate the body, right?"

"We don't do cremations on the grounds. Everglades Crematorium provides that service for all the funeral homes in the county. On a contract basis."

"Then why are you taking possession of the remains after cremation? That makes no sense."

The woman said, "I'm afraid it's state law, sir."

"Is that what you told Harvey Hollins, the deceased's brother?"

"Of course I did, sir. It was my obligation."

Ford said, "Lady, there's no state law that says a funeral home must be involved in the dispensation of a body. What you told Mr. Hollins was a lie, and you did it so you could get your kickback from the crematorium and your kickback from whatever florist you've cut a deal with on Sandy Key, and so you could carve out a little piece of Mr. Hollins for yourself. I suppose you told Mr. Hollins not to worry about choosing an urn, and that you would be happy to fill out all the insurance forms—if there are forms involved in this case—so you can carve yourself an even bigger piece."

The woman said, "I'm afraid I don't like your tone of voice, sir. In times of bereavement, most decent

people consider talk of money to be in very bad
taste—"

"Which is exactly why the people of this country pay
out more in a year to funeral homes than the government spends on providing them with police or fire protection. Lady, I'm going to make sure Mr. Hollins lets
me have a look at your bill. There better not be a charge
for embalming and the cremation fee better not be padded, and under no circumstances do I want to see your
deluxe model last-for-eternity bronze urn on the list.
Keep it fair, lady. . . ."

And the line went dead.

With a growing sense of urgency, Ford dialed Everglades
Crematorium. The remains of Rafe Hollins were being
disposed of much too quickly, and Ford had no idea what
he could do to stop it. What he did know was that, with
no body, there would be no way to prove Rafe had been
murdered—short of a confession. A man answered, and
Ford asked when Hollins was scheduled for cremation.

"Who wants to know? You with the family or something?"

Why was that always the first question? Ford decided
to take a chance. "I'm with the Florida Department of
Criminal Law, the governor's office. We're thinking
about red-tagging the remains pending an investigation
by our office."

"You're shittin' me—whoops. I mean, you don't want
us to do it?"

Ford said, "That's exactly what I mean. If we decide
to go ahead with the investigation, we can have the pa-

pers to you by . . . Tuesday," trying to buy some time so he could . . . what? Contact some newspapers; maybe get a good investigative reporter interested. With luck and the promise of publicity, there was a chance the governor's office might actually be involved by Monday afternoon . . . a slim chance.

The man said, "Who's this speaking?"

"Captain Lewis, FDCL."

"Hang on just a minute, Captain Lewis."

Ford sat listening to the silence, thinking. Even if the guy fell for it now, there was no way they'd hold the body through Monday on the strength of a phone call. But that, at least, would give him tomorrow, Sunday, to get something going; an extra day. No one in government worked weekends.

"Captain Lewis?"

Ford said, "Yes."

"I'm real sorry, Captain Lewis, but I'm afraid you're a little late. They just ran him through . . . cremated him, I mean. Came out 'bout ten minutes ago. But look, we did everything we're supposed to do. Called the medical examiner, got approval just like the law says; observed the forty-eight-hour waiting period—"

"Forty-eight hours? They didn't find the body until late yesterday. And the medical examiner wasn't even in this morning. He plays golf."

That set the man back; made him even more nervous. "All I know is, we got a call direct from the sheriff, and around here that's as good as the medical examiner. The sheriff does that sometimes; fills in when Doc Carter is busy or out of the county. He said everything was in order; said for us to go ahead. You got any more questions, maybe you should talk to him."

Ford said, "You're sure the body's gone?"

"I caught them before they put the ashes in the pulverizer but, yeah, it's gone all right."

"Then maybe you can tell me a couple of things. What's the death certificate say about the cause of death?"

"Well . . . wait a minute, we got a copy here someplace. I got the coroner's tag. That good enough? On the tag it says asphyxia due to hanging; be the same on the certificate unless you want me to read it direct—"

"Any notations about whether photographs were taken or fingerprints made?"

"Well . . . no, but they usually do that. They don't have to, but it's normal procedure—"

"Who ordered the cremation?"

"The family, probably . . . wait a minute—they got that written right here on the tag, too. That's kinda weird. Usually the order comes in separate, not on the medical examiner's tag. But it says here cremation by request of Mrs. Helen Burke Hollins. That's the guy's wife, I guess. Maybe his mother. You want us to put a hold on the ashes? Pieces of bone now, mostly. You promise to get the papers to us by Monday morning, we can do that."

Ford said, "No. You can release the ashes."

He had one more call to make, an anonymous call, but that would have to be from a pay phone. He wanted to contact the FBI; give them what he knew about the boy. Just in case everything else failed. . . .

SIX

Ford idled into the marina to get his evening quart of beer. He was tired of the talk of death; felt like kicking back and taking a good, deep bite of life for a change. Several of the women doctors had returned, looking relaxed in beach clothes, shiny hair combed just so, standing there on the dock talking to Jeth. Ford pretended to study his mooring lines until Nicholes called him over and made introductions. There was one he liked: Dr. Sheri Braun-Richards. Short blond hair, nice athletic body, something solid behind the blue eyes and a smile that didn't strain.

Ford listened politely until he had established she wasn't one of the neurotic nonstop talkers or one of the man-haters who had girded herself in the flag of feminism, then struck up a conversation. She was a gynecologist from Davenport, Iowa. Had a confident manner and a quick sense of humor. Ford laughed at her stories because they were funny. And did he live all alone on the

gray house out there, the one built on stilts? Must be nice
hearing water lap all night long. She had always been interested in marine biology, but knew nothing about it, living in Iowa all her life. Ford could see the evening taking
shape; could see it in Dr. Braun-Richards's blue eyes.
Nothing overt, but not coy; aware that a subliminal process of selection was going on; aware that, because she
was on vacation, there was no time for the normal pre-
sexual proprieties. Ford liked that awareness. And he had
gone long enough without a woman.

"I think someone's calling you." She was pointing
at the marina office, amused that he hadn't heard Mac-
Kinley banging on the window.

MacKinley was holding up the phone. Ford said,
"Don't go away."

"We might be down on that big blue sailboat." Not
committing herself to stand there and wait, but making
sure he knew where she would be. That was good.

"I'll probably be going back out to the stilt house in
a little bit. You and your friends could stop out, look
around, maybe have a beer."

She knew what that meant but played right along.
"Sounds interesting. But I think I'd have to leave my
friends here. They met some people on the sailboat last
night." Getting better and better. Why hadn't he thought
to take a shower after work?

She drifted back into the circle of conversation, a
pretty woman in white knit shirt, cut-off shorts, with the
good legs of a tennis player. Ford headed for the office.

It was Jessica on the phone. She'd gotten his new
home number from information; tried and tried but it

was busy all afternoon. Then it wasn't busy, but he didn't answer, and she was wondering why he hadn't tried to call her. "Doc, I hope it's not because you're mad at me for abandoning you last night."

Ford said don't be silly, he wasn't mad—looking out the window, watching Dr. Braun-Richards.

"Well, I wouldn't blame you if you were. Benny came on like such an ass. Doing his Mr. Macho routine. Working in the art world, living in Manhattan, he has a thing about proving he's not gay."

Ford said he hadn't noticed; Benny had seemed like a very nice guy—enjoying the clean lines of Dr. Braun-Richards's body as he spoke on the phone; the soft facial contours, the way she laughed . . . a little bit of the college girl left in those cut-off jeans.

"Then maybe I can take you up on your offer to have dinner. A little late, but my treat."

"Dinner?" Ford had a redfish fillet and a mackerel in the refrigerator. He'd planned on cooking. "Dinner would be nice, sure. But I was going to hang around the marina tonight. Jeth said he might need a little help . . . with some things."

MacKinley looked up from his magazine, his eyebrows raised. He knew that Jeth didn't need any help.

Jessica's voice dropped, softened. "I'd like to see you, Doc. Just for a little while if I can. Please? There's something I'd like to talk with you about."

Ford watched Dr. Braun-Richards step onto the blue sailboat with the others, accept a drink from the owner. Ford said, "Well . . . sure. For a little while. You want me to come out now?"

"The sooner the better."

Ford said, "Now . . . ah . . . well, sure. For a little bit. I can tell Jeth to wait."

"Don't sound so anxious!"

Ford freed the lines of his skiff, aware that Dr. Braun-Richards was watching. Jeth was on the sailboat with the others, and Ford called, "I'll be back in about an hour."

Nicholes, who didn't know why he should care, called back, " 'Bout an hour . . . right."

The sailboat owner had his hand on Dr. Braun-Richards's shoulder, trying to show her something, and she turned away as Ford said, "I'll probably go straight to the stilt house when I get back . . . if you want to stop by."

Nicholes said, "In ba-ba-'bout an hour . . . right."

Jessica's house: ceiling fans, throw rugs on pine floors, rattan furniture, hatch-cover coffee table near the fireplace, two cats lounging on the Bahama couch, another atop the stereo, unframed paintings stacked in every corner, the odor of an old beach house mingling with the smell of paint supplies, incense, and cats.

When Ford pulled up to the dock, Jessica stood beneath the porch light leaning against the door frame, hip thrown out, hand behind her head, looking like a bus-stop blonde in a 1930s movie. But the hair was long auburn, and she didn't linger, meeting Ford at the steps, falling into his arms, hugging him. "Boy, I missed you." Then led him into the house, holding his hand. She was shaking.

"Are you okay?"

She swung down on the couch beside him, her hand coming to rest on his thigh. "I am now. I missed you, that's all." She was wearing faded jeans and a white T-shirt—braless, too, which made Ford take a breath because he could see her in the soft light of the lamp beside the couch. She said, "I feel like such a jerk going off and leaving you last night. You had something you wanted to talk about, and I could tell it was important, but I just left . . . and you're my best friend. For some stupid party so Benny could push my paintings."

"You didn't have fun?"

"A lot of smiling and nodding and everyone so superior, talking about Rauschenberg's latest breakthrough and the next political fund-raiser—my God, what happened to your face?" She was touching the scratch marks on his cheek tenderly, concerned . . . her own face becoming blurry to Ford's eyes at close range: Lombard filmed through a filter; a genuinely classic face.

"I took a spill at the marina. Tripped on the dock."

She kissed his cheek, then his lips, too, very softly. That was a new one. "You big clumsy lug. Yesterday it was vultures, today the dock. You need someone to look after you."

"Took the skin right off, huh?" Like a little boy with a scrape.

"I've got some antibiotic cream in the bathroom—" She was already standing. "You're sure you don't need it? Then some wine. Last night a very fat, rich man gave me a twenty-year-old Chardonnay that is supposed to be wonderful. He said he bought a case at auction, and I'd hate to even guess what it cost him."

"Wine," said Ford. "That would be nice." He would have preferred Old Milwaukee to old Chardonnay, but why be ungracious?

She went into the kitchen, patting each cat on the way. Ford stood, hands in the pockets of his khaki shorts, heard Jessica call for music and touched the digital buttons of the stereo until he found public radio: Dvorak, maybe, with a lot of timpani. Then he studied the paintings. Over the fireplace was a big print by Chrzanoska, a sole-eyed woman with a pearl headpiece, holding a cat over her bare breasts. There was something haunting in the woman's eyes, something that reminded him of Jessica . . . and he found it touching that she did not display her own work as prominently. Some of her watercolors were on the side walls: wading birds feeding at low tide; an old man in a wooden skiff; storm clouds approaching a lone mangrove island, everything frozen in an eerie bruised light. There was a canvas on the easel, too, something new, and he peeked beneath the paper dust guard to see a man wading the flats. The man wore only brief khaki shorts, his thigh muscles flexing as he lifted his leg to take a step, very wide shoulders, body hair covering the rib cage. An impressionistic treatment, but anatomically suggestive in certain details and oddly sexual. Only the hands, face, and some of the background hadn't been finished.

"You weren't supposed to see that. Not yet." Jessica stood holding the wineglasses, uneasy. He had never seen her embarrassed before. It changed her face; gave it a nice color. She said, "It's not done. I wanted to wait, get my courage up because . . . it's you."

"Me? I don't have a face."

"It's not done yet, silly."

"That's the way I look when I go collecting? And I thought I wore boots."

"Ah, Doc, please don't chide me . . . and don't smirk like that." She bumped him with her shoulder as she handed him his wine. "I've been trying to make myself paint what I feel, not what I see. I got into such a rut; that's what coming to Sanibel was all about. I don't know that I was ever really good, but I was successful; my first shows got great reviews. I'm just trying to find that thread again, the honesty that's in me. It's a hard thing to get back, honesty. Once you've lost it, it's damn hard to recover . . . and you've heard this speech way too much, over and over from me."

He had heard it. Jessica had been in New York only for a year before being embraced by some powerful critics who heralded her as the Renaissance stylist of American impressionistic gothic—whatever that meant; Ford didn't know. They said she was breaking old ground in a new way, and for a couple of years she could do no wrong. But then she fell from grace. In the eyes of the critics, everything she did was wrong and, worse, she had invested badly, spent lavishly; ended up in debt with a bunch of paintings that wouldn't sell. She had borrowed from her agent until her agent dropped her, and that should have been the low point, but it wasn't. For the next year she lived in a Greenwich Village flat sleeping all day, avoiding work at night, doing drugs in hip discos and fighting depression. She wasn't quite twenty-five. But then she somehow caught herself. She got a low job on some marketing firm's ladder, worked hard, lived cheaply, and paid off the debts. And saved enough to rent this working retreat on the island.

Jessica said, "You don't like it, do you?"

Ford looked at the canvas again. There was the man striding through shallow water, a wedge of mangroves and the bay behind him. A squall was coming, pushing a burnished green light, and the water was a roiled green with wind feathers in random streaks. It had taken great precision for her to capture that mood of randomness, that sense of the inexorable, yet she had controlled it so that the coming squall dominated the bay, but not the man. The view was from the man's side: revealing, powerful . . . somehow a little troubling, too, but not lurid. Ford said, "No . . . I like it, Jessi. I like it a lot. Am I really that hairy—"

"Oh, you men—as if that matters at all. And you're smirking again."

"I've never seen myself on canvas before."

"Why should I be so embarrassed about this? I just wanted to try and do something different, something strong. Show the male form in an attitude that wasn't cheap or glitzy. I'm an artist, for Christ's sake, and there should be no taboos—quit that smirking!" She was laughing, the tension gone. "Drink your wine and shut up. No, don't shut up. Tell me what was so important yesterday; the thing that made me feel like such a shit for going off and leaving you."

Ford said, "You said you had something to tell me."

"I do. But not now." She was sitting on the couch, looking over the lip of her wineglass. "It'll keep."

Ford said, "Did you know a man named Rafe Hollins?" then watched her carefully as she stared into his eyes for a moment before saying "No; no, I don't think so— should I?"

"I found your name in his address book. There was a telephone number, too, but with a New York area code."

It was an old number, disconnected. Ford had tried it.

She puzzled over that, sipping at her wine, then said, "Wait—is he a pilot?"

"He was."

She was nodding. "Okay; right, I know who you mean. A couple of years ago, when I was thinking of moving down here, I wanted to fly over the area in a small plane, really get an idea of where the best places to live might be. I called the municipal airport to see about a charter, and I ended up in one of those small helicopters they use to spray crops. I think the pilot's name was Rafe; kind of an odd name—I don't remember his last name—and he flew me around all morning. He didn't have to charge much, he said, because it was a company helicopter or something. Big guy; very nice looking in a cowboy sort of way, but a little too loud for my taste. And he did things to try and scare me. Flew very low; made sharp turns. I guess he thought it would impress me. It didn't."

Ford said, "That was Rafe. Did you ever see him again?"

Jessica said, "No." Then: "Why were you looking through his address book?"

"Yesterday afternoon I found his body on a little island south of here—"

"His body? You mean he was *dead*?"

"As in very dead. I wasn't sure it was Rafe at first. Vultures had been working on the body for a while, so it was hard to tell—"

Jessica had her hand to her mouth, incredulous. "That's why you came here in such a mess! And you were bitten! My God, Doc, don't be so nonchalant. Tell me what happened!"

So he told her about Hollins. Told her about high school, the phone call and finding him on the island, finding the gems; some of the rest of it, but keeping it simple while Jessica listened, making sad faces. "My God, that's awful. Just terrible. But are you really sure it was him?"

"I am now. I thought maybe Rafe had killed someone accidentally; someone he was supposed to do business with and, in a panic, tried to cover it up by planting his own wallet on the corpse. It would have been a dumb thing to try, but people often do dumb things when they're scared. It was Rafe, though. If he wasn't dead, he'd have gotten in touch with me by now. He needed me to help get his son back."

"What are you going to do, Doc?" Jessica was on her feet, looking for the wine bottle, truly upset.

Ford said, "There's not much I can do about Rafe. For some reason, someone in Everglades County wants his death to appear as a suicide. They may have had a hand in the murder, but I don't see sufficient motive. Rafe went through a nasty divorce, and a local judge got involved with his ex-wife, but they'd already taken his son and his money; why would they want his life? It's more likely someone on Sandy Key decided that Rafe was unimportant enough to sweep under the carpet, avoid all the bad publicity, and then they could still look for the murderer on the sly. That's what I hope happened."

"But there has to be someone you can call; someone who can find out for sure if he was murdered or committed suicide—"

"He was murdered. There's no doubt about it."

She said, "I know he was your close friend, Doc. But that doesn't mean he couldn't have gotten very sick; sick enough to take his own life." The gentle voice of reason, reminding him.

"You think I'm making an emotional judgment. I'm not. Take the suicide note. It said: I just can't take it no more; something like that. Illiterate; real hicky in big, rough block letters. Well, that's a role Rafe liked to play: the backwoods redneck role. Talked real slow, real southern, like he was dumb as dirt. But he only did it around people he didn't know very well, and always for a reason. He liked to use it to bait the self-important ones, the snobs. He'd start asking dumb questions, and these people would kind of look at him like a bucket of meat, and he'd keep asking questions, getting sharper and sharper but still with the hick accent, until he had made them look like complete asses. Rafe was a very bright guy. Articulate on paper. I went to high school with him."

"That's the only reason you think he was murdered? The way the suicide note was written?"

"No. But the note's part of it. It tells me Rafe didn't write the note. And it tells me quite a bit about who did. Whoever wrote the note didn't know Rafe very well, but they knew him—and probably on a business or professional level. Why else would he have played the redneck role other than to use it to some kind of advantage? In their conversation or conversations, Rafe wanted the person to think he was dumb. And they believed the act enough to try and mimic him on paper. So that leaves us with some reasonable suppositions: The person who wrote the note was involved with Rafe in some kind of business dealing. He was probably an American originally from the north, probably articulate, probably egotistical—all necessary for Rafe to make his redneck routine work."

Jessica was looking at him. "My God," she said. "The logical mind."

Ford was warming to the subject, arranging it in his mind as he talked. "Whoever wrote the note was the murderer or one of the murderers. That's the working hypothesis. Match it with some of the other things I saw on the island, and you come up with an even clearer picture. It was probably two men. They didn't known much about boats or knots, so they had to come in a very small boat—the kind that doesn't carry more than two people. The water's so shallow, they wouldn't have made it to the island otherwise. They beached at the same cove Rafe beached his boat; they weren't comfortable in the woods, and stuck around for a while after Rafe was dead, probably looking for something. The emeralds, maybe, but that's an assumption. They didn't find what they were looking for Thursday, the day they killed him, so they came back yesterday for another look. A big golden-silk spider had a web across the path from the cove, and someone had walked through it. Rafe was tall enough to hit it, but he wouldn't have—he grew up in the woods. The man who walked through the web was coming from or going to his boat; probably going, because he was preoccupied, wasn't watching. It only takes a golden-silk spider about three hours to completely rebuild its web, and the spider was a little more than half done when I got there.

"Another thing: Rafe thought he had no reason to fear the killer or killers. If they arrived before he did, he would have seen their boat in the cove. If they came afterward, he would have seen them coming across the bay. So they were probably there on a business deal. He wasn't taking social calls. And they were probably buying, not selling."

"Sherlock Holmes," she said. "You're almost scary, Ford. You know the color of the man's eyes? What he had for breakfast?" She was half serious. "You think they were there to buy the emeralds."

Ford said, "If they were, it knocks down an earlier assumption: that Rafe had taken the emeralds from the men who ultimately kidnapped his son. He wouldn't sell something he thought he needed to trade for his son. But it doesn't matter what they were there to buy and it doesn't matter what else I know. The death certificate says death by hanging. Even if the coroner took the time to find out what really killed Rafe—and I doubt if he did—the autopsy report will support the death certificate. The body has been cremated, so the killer is in the clear. If there's no body, there's no way to refute the autopsy."

"But couldn't the police test the ashes some way? You hear all about those police labs; they can tell everything from a little piece of carpet fiber, tiny things like that."

"After cremation—man or animal—the only thing you can test for in the lab is metal content in the bones. The metallic poisons, like arsenic, aren't destroyed by fire. I doubt if Rafe was poisoned, but, if he was, they wouldn't have used arsenic. Arsenic tastes bad. It has to be given in small doses over a long period of time."

"You're an expert of poisons, too?"

"No, but seventy-five percent of the aquarium fish bought and sold in the U. S. are originally stunned and caught through the use of poisons. All over the world they're killing the reefs by dumping cyanide just so collectors in this country can fill their tanks with pretty tropicals. It's come up in my work before; I know a little."

"So there really is nothing you can do—about your friend, I mean."

"I could get some kind of investigation going into the odd procedures of Everglades County, but it wouldn't clear Rafe. Plus it would just take away from the time I need to find a way to free Rafe's son. When I ran into him that time in Costa Rica, Rafe was looking for work. I gave him the names of some people. I thought they might help him. So, directly or indirectly, I played a part. I helped get him involved with the people who kid-napped his son."

Jessica said, "You can't blame yourself for that, Doc."

Ford looked at her for a moment. "Why would I blame myself? I meant that I'm one of the early links in a long chain; the one best suited to trace the events that followed. I've already contacted a guy I know in Masagua. He's on the National Security Affair's field staff—they're the ones who recommend what the CIA should or should not be doing. It's this guy's job to cultivate contacts, make surveys, assemble data; like a combination librarian and investigative reporter. The NSA sets up their people with cover jobs—they have him publishing a small English-language newspaper—and he pokes around the country, filing reports. He's looking for Jake right now. If the NSA guy can get him, I'll sell the emeralds and set up some kind of trust fund for the boy . . . maybe make sure he doesn't go back to his drunken mother."

"They're that valuable?"

"There are two; each about the size of a bird's egg."

She stiffened a little, showing her concern. "Tell me you're not keeping them at your place, Ford. You're too smart to keep something so dangerous."

"No one knows I have the emeralds. Besides, I put them in a place no one would ever look—down the mouths of some preserved sharks. In my lab." Ford took a drink of wine. All that talking, and he wanted a beer. He got up and went to the refrigerator.

As he came back, Jessica was saying it was so damn

sad such bad things could happen to people; really feeling it, her head on Ford's shoulder, and he could smell the
shampoo scent of her hair. The poor little boy out there
all alone. His father dead and a mother that probably
didn't care—her arms around Ford now, holding him.
Then she was kissing his neck, squeezing him, touching
her lips to his cheeks, and it was becoming something
else, no longer grief. Ford pulled away. "Whoa, what's
going on here, lady?"

Jessica looked up, eyes moist but smiling. "Sometimes
you're such a bastard for details; getting everything
straight."

"I thought we had an agreement."

She said, "Our experiment. That's why I called you."
Her fingers were on his thigh, then his abdomen, touching
softly, drawing designs. "I want it to end tonight." Like
a little girl, not looking at him.

Ford let her fall against his chest, slid his hands along
her ribs brushing the firm weight of her breasts . . .
thought of the painting, and almost said something
silly to lighten the mood.

He did not.

There would be no need for CBS, Ford was thinking,
not if every woman in the world looked just like this.

No need for television, lawyers, *Playboy*, toupees,
Doonesbury, war, or Dr. Ruth Westheimer. The end of
competition and contrivances: A good dose of natural
selection, that's what the world needed. Jessica's brass
bed was on the second floor. A quarter moon floated
above the bay and the window was swollen with filtered

light. Jessica lay naked on the sheets. Her hair was wild upon the pillow, lean legs as if carved from marble, nipples still erect, breasts pale white, full, rounded beneath their own weight, pubic hair iridescent in the moonglow, an amber tangle as if illuminated by internal light. Bioluminescence, it made him think of that.

Ford had his head upon her chest, looking toward her toes, toward the window. He could feel her breathing, feel her heart beat. He was looking down the soft curvature of her stomach, seeing muscle cordage and ribs flex with each breath, and he was thinking there was a finite number of times he would be with this woman and there ought to be a way to lock onto a moment such as this, to preserve it, but there wasn't. Never would be.

"My stomach's growling. But I don't feel hungry. Can you hear it growling?" Whispering, her eyes closed, Jessica had her fingers in his hair.

"Uh-huh. Like a mariachi band. Keeps playing the same song." Her voice was deeper, huskier in the quiet after-time, and he thought of Pilar Balserio. It had been like that with her, the change in voice. He'd admired Pilar for years, wanted her the whole time, but was in bed with her only once and then back to the States. Something that intimate, and no way to hold on. It left a yearning. . . .

"Did I scratch you? You don't need any more scratch marks, Ford."

"Minor cuts and abrasions, that's all. Well worth it."

"Didn't bite too hard?"

"Um . . . nope . . . everything intact."

"It's just that . . . it was the first time it ever happened with me. That release, like they write about. I used to think they were lying . . . or I was frigid. God, I thought my heart was going to stop. Like in *Cosmopolitan*."

"You're not frigid. I'll sign papers."

"You believe me . . . that it was my first? It really was."

Ford answered, "Of course I believe you," not sure that he did, but it didn't matter.

She was silent for a time, stroking his head. "You were mad at me last night for going to the party."

"No. I did some work. Tomlinson came over. I went to bed early. I wasn't mad."

"You haven't asked me anything about it, being with Benny. Are you sure you weren't upset?"

"That's your business, Jess, not mine."

She touched his jaw until he turned his head to look at her. "Sometimes I don't know when you're serious or when you're not. You're the warmest listener I've ever met. But then you talk, and it's that cold act of yours. I'll tell you anything you want to know, Ford. Anything." And sounded as if she meant it; as if she wanted him to ask her things.

Ford said, "Tell me how Benny tried to get you in bed," not because he wanted to know, but because it seemed like a safe question.

"You're so sure he did. I was surprised."

"He's a former lover. He came more than a thousand miles to see you. You live alone, he was alone. Tropical night with moon. And you were surprised?"

"Your logical mind, I forgot. We left the party early, about eleven, and he wanted to take me to his place. He just invested in a condo and he was all excited, said he wanted my opinion on how it should be decorated. I insisted he bring me home. Then he said he'd pulled a shoulder muscle or something. Executive boxing is the current fad in Manhattan; the ex-Ivy Leaguers go down to the club and slug it out over lunch. He's supposedly very good; it was an excuse for him to say he was, anyway. He wanted a massage; a rubdown, he called it. His shoulder hurt. But he had to take off his clothes to do it properly, and that's when I told him to leave. He got huffy, then he thought the he-man approach might work, force me a little. I threatened to slap him, I really did." She giggled, an odd sound of delight. "That really got him. He had already unbuttoned his shirt, and he looked so silly. He left right after that. Benny likes to show off those muscles. You two are such opposites; you and those baggy clothes. You, I had to picture in my mind; imagine. It was nice."

Ford was thinking about Jessica's porch light, but he said, "You're talking about the painting."

"Yes. Painting . . . from what I imagined. I hope you don't mind, Doc. I think it's the best thing I've done in a long time. But I'd do it differently now. Your back's wider, your body hair is lighter. You're nicer in real life."

Her hands were on his back now, sliding down, searching, and Ford rolled to his side. "Are we talking about the same painting?"

"Well . . . you have to allow me some creative latitude. Not much, though." Smiling as she found him, inspecting. "I've decided to call the piece *Sanibel Flats*. I thought about *Littoral Zone*, one of those marine biology terms. Doc—" The touching stopped now, but she was still holding him. "There's something else I need to tell you." An edge in her voice, as if she had put it off long enough.

"Umm . . . it's getting tough to concentrate." But listening carefully.

"I'm leaving for New York day after tomorrow. It was Benny's idea, but I think he's right. I need to circulate more. People don't just buy art, they buy the artist. There's a big show and an auction on Wednesday. It's a private show, but they'll let anyone in who looks like they have lots and lots of money. A few of my pieces are going to be included. I'll be back by Friday. Benny flew out this morning, made the reservations. I insisted on a Friday return. I just don't want you to worry about Benny and me. There's nothing there. Do you believe me?"

Ford said, "You have no reason to lie to me, Jessi," looking for a reaction that didn't materialize. Jessica kissed him and they didn't talk anymore.

Her nose touching the cool glass of the upstairs window, Jessica McClure watched Ford go down the porch steps, across the dark yard to the dock where moonlight broke free of the trees and showed him plainly. She liked the look of him, the shape of him and the way he moved, and when he stepped into his boat she could almost feel the weight of him on her; a good feeling both comforting and sensual, and she cultivated the feeling, reluctant to let it go, as she watched the little skiff carry him away.

"Why don't you stay the night, Doc?" asking even

though she knew his mind was made up; could tell by the methodical way he buckled his belt and found his shoes, but interested in what his excuse would be.

"Because . . . I don't want to."

That simple. It made her smile, the honesty of it. Maybe that's what she loved in him most—his honesty, or at least his frankness; and just thinking that surprised her a little.

What I love in him most. . . .

She *was* in love with him, though she hadn't said it to him, or even admitted it to herself. In love with him . . . the way he looked, the way he felt, the way his hard hands touched softly, softly, and the way he settled onto her couch, his distant, driven expression slowly replaced by a look of contentment as she lighted the candles and put on music. He was becoming home to her, and maybe she was becoming home to him—and perhaps that's what love was.

Jessica pulled jeans on over her panties, a baggy T-shirt, and went downstairs thinking about what it would be like to live with Ford, thinking she wasn't getting any younger, thinking of the way it might be: him out in his lab (a new lab in an old house they would buy and she would decorate) while she finished her own work, and they would take turns with the cooking (he was a good cook, that she already knew); two professionals with different work but one life, and she needed to start having children soon . . . and that was part of this new realization, that she was in love with Ford. Her biological clock was ticking away, and she needed to get started. She needed a husband. Ford liked children—he'd said so.

The way he talked about those poor Indian kids in . . . Guatemala, was it? . . . hunting in the garbage dumps for food. The memory had hurt him; she could see it in his eyes. He was a strange man in a way, and his coldness sometimes frightened her, but he would be a good father. And at night, when the kids were in bed, they could sit together outside on the porch, talking about future things, things they would do together, and about their past. . . .

Their past . . .

The thought of that crackled through her fantasy, shearing it at the foundations and scattering it like so many leaves.

You stupid, lonely bitch—mooning around like some soap-opera housewife.

Why the hell didn't Ford ever ask her any questions about it? That would have made it so much easier. Would have made it seem less like a confession. But that was wrong, too, and she castigated herself: *You call him out here to explain things to him, but instead you lie to him and hustle him into bed. He would have understood! He could help! Nothing surprises that man. . . .*

Jessica put the kettle on for tea, then walked back into the living room, patting each cat and whispering its name. She stood before the easel, flipped back the dust cover, and considered the painting. The wading man stared back at her, his faceless expression a pale void. She hand-cranked the canvas higher on the easel wings and began to prepare the palette cups, the smell of gesso primer and linseed oil coming strongly from the sketch box. But then the telephone rang.

Well, the big softy is calling to say good night.

Smiling, she went to the phone, picked it up, and her expression changed. She said, "What do you want?" Then: "Goddamn it, Benny, I'm done with all that. No more! Absolutely not! You said we had a deal!" She listened for a time, and her voice grew dull: "Okay . . . okay . . . okay." Then she said: "Don't ever call me this late again, you son of a bitch," and slammed down the phone.

The kettle was screaming, and she ran to the kitchen. She was trembling; she wanted to throw something, she wanted to curl up in a fetal position and bawl like a baby.

Instead, she turned off the stove and went back to the easel, forcing a coldness upon herself, knowing that the only escape, for now, was in the oblivion of work, thinking: *You've survived worse. . . .*

It was nearly 1 A.M. by the time Ford got back to the stilt house, dropping his boat off plane way early just in case the happy sea cow was around. The marina looked sleepy, all the lights shimmering and a few solitary silhouettes on the docks. He turned on the lights of the fish tank. There were the squid, back in among the rocks and the sea anemones. They looked a little pasty, lethargic. That worried him. He'd do a salinity check tomorrow. Check the oxygen content, too.

He went upstairs, put hot water on for tea, tuned in Radio Havana, stripped off his clothes. The fresh water supply was a wooden cistern above and beside the tin roof, heated by the sun. The shower was outside on the side deck, and Ford stood under the shower lathering, rinsing, lathering again. Singing a little bit, too: "Moon River" in Spanish; good old Radio Havana. He was just reaching for his glasses when he heard a noise, someone clearing a throat. And there stood Dr. Sheri Braun-Richards, looking starched and athletic, holding one hand against her face like a blinder.

"Hey!"

"My gosh, I thought for sure you had a bathing suit on or something." She was laughing, not looking at him.

"Hold it . . . I've got a towel here—"

"People don't do this sort of thing in Iowa, you know. Walking around naked, singing in the middle of the night. I think there are laws against what you do in Iowa. I'm almost sure of it."

"I just put it . . . someplace. Glasses all wet . . . wait; no, that isn't it—"

"It's okay, it's okay, I'm a doctor." Laughing harder, coming up the stairs. "Here—here's your towel," handing him the towel. She stared directly into his eyes as Ford dried himself, amused, but a nice touch of frankness. Ford liked that.

He said, "I have some clothes inside."

"That's one way to keep them clean. Very innovative."

"You and your friends stayed late. I was hoping I'd see you again, but I got held up." Already lying about Jessica. But he was just being friendly, he told himself, a good host, and there really wasn't any question of morality because he expected nothing from Jessica and she expected nothing from him . . . and now he was lying to himself, too.

Dr. Braun-Richards was saying "Two of my friends went back to the hotel. Another is on the blue sailboat . . . probably for the night. For the first couple of hours, I stuck around hoping to see your lab. Then I didn't have a ride. So I've been talking to Jeth. I've heard all about you."

Ford wrapped the towel around his waist, adjusted his glasses. "I can give you a ride. Or you can borrow my bike, my ten-speed." Which sounded as if he were trying to get rid of her; he could see it in her face. So he added, "But, if you're not in a hurry, I could show you around. I usually stay up late working."

Which seemed to make her feel better. "Jeth told me that. He said you're like a hermit out here. All you do is work in your lab and drink a quart of beer every night. Sounds like a nice life to me, Ford. Oh yeah, he told me something else; told me several times, in fact. He said you never take any time for fun, not even women." Giving that a wry touch, aware of what Jeth was trying to do. "He said you're just too involved with your work. I admire that kind of dedication, but Jeth says you need to relax more. The people at the marina worry about you. Yes, they're very worried about you, Doc Ford."

Jeth the matchmaker; a dangerous avocation for a man who stuttered so badly. Ford was rolling his eyes. He said, "I'm very touched," already computing his recovery needs, all considerations of morality abandoned. After the multiple sessions with Jessica, he wasn't sure his body was up to it, and it wouldn't do to disappoint a doctor. She'd diagnose some kind of structural infirmity, intellectualize it. He said, "Come on. I'll show you around," trying to buy some time.

He did, too, and had a nice talk. Dr. Braun-Richards asked good questions, showed the right interest, had a nice way of listening: smiling, nodding, always a step ahead but willing to wait. When Ford offered again to drive her back to the motel, the doctor said, "I'm not going to be shy about this," sounding a little shy just the same.

"Oh?"

"You're going to make me say it? Okay. I'll say it. I leave for Davenport tomorrow, back to the same old routine. But tonight I'm still on vacation. Tonight I'm with a man I like; a man who doesn't live in singles' bars, wear gold chains, patronize women, or seem like the type I'd need to read a blood test before feeling comfortable kissing him." The shyness was gone, and she was closer now, touching his forearm, looking up at him. "I like you, Doc. And I'm in no rush to go back to my motel room."

Ford glanced at his watch. Not even two hours' rest. He kissed her gently and felt her breath warm in his mouth. Then she was in his arms and she shuddered as he touched the small, sharp point of her breast, firm beneath the material of her blouse, but didn't understand at all when he said, "I'm in no rush either. . . ."

Two-thirty A.M., and Dr. Braun-Richards said, "You're looking mighty proud of yourself, Dr. Ford," yawning, stretching catlike, as sweaty as if she had just finished five sets at the club.

"What? Naw, not really." Feeling like he should kick the floor and say *Ah shucks*.

"You've got that kind of smile."

"Well, naw, not really." Staring at her, liking the way she was prettier without clothes; a woman who seemed more at ease naked, comfortable with the animal skin.

"I wish I would have met you a week ago."

"That would have been nice. A whole week."

"But we've got all night."

"All night . . . all night?" Ford caught his smile before it disappeared, just in time. "But you probably have to be up early—"

"I don't have to be anywhere until noon." She was sitting up on the bed, reaching for him . . .

Ten minutes later she was saying "Well, it happens," trying to sound warm, understanding, but sounding clinical nonetheless. "When a man gets into his thirties—"

Ford stifled a groan.

"—a man gets into his thirties, his ability to respond can gradually decline. It's absolutely nothing to worry about. There have been case studies done."

"Not like tonight, there haven't."

"What?"

"I said don't be so anxious to leave."

"I just thought you might want to get some rest." Like he was a doddering old invalid.

"I have some beer around here someplace." Now standing naked in the dull light of his little refrigerator, letting his eyes wander over the contents, really taking his time, looking all around the beer.

"I've read that vitamins can help."

Diet Coke. Mayonnaise. Half a tin of anchovies. Four bottles of lab chemicals that had to be refrigerated. And that mackerel wasn't looking so good anymore. If he ever got a minute to himself, he'd dump it. "Beer has vitamins," he said.

She came up behind him, wrapping her arms around him, as he finally took out a bottle of beer. "It's a food," he said.

"Hmm," she said as she slid her head under his arm.

"Lots of vitamin B. Or A. One of those." He took a drink.

"Hmm," she said again.

"Did you know that Viking sailors signed onto boats almost strictly on the basis of the quality and amount of beer the captain was taking? They didn't ask what countries were going to be plundered, or how long they were going to be gone. Just what kind of beer and how much."

"The Vikings discovered America," she said.

"They also invented the pants fly."

"I see," said Dr. Sheri Braun-Richards.

"But who remembers?"

"That's not what I see, Ford." Snuggling closer to him now. "I was premature in my diagnosis. That food of yours works."

Ford said, "Oh?" Then: "Oh!"

He put down the beer.

SEVEN

BOMB BLAST KILLS MASAGUAN PRESIDENT

Masagua City, Masagua (AP)—Don Jorge Balserio, president of Central America's poorest and most embattled country, was killed yesterday evening when a bomb exploded outside the Presidential Palace. Five members of Balserio's notorious Elite Guard were injured in the blast, two critically.

Three Masaguan left-wing revolutionary organizations and one ultra-right-wing guerrilla group have all claimed responsibility for the bombing. Masaguan officials, however, suspect one of only two groups: the Masaguan People's Army or a lesser-known guerrilla organization that calls itself El Dictamen. Neither group has claimed involvement.

The Masaguan People's Army has long been at odds with Balserio's administration. Its leader, Juan Rivera, threatened Balserio's life publicly after the last election. Rivera, who openly models his dress and flamboyant style after Cuba's Fidel Castro, retreated to the mountains with his followers three years ago.

The ultra-leftist group El Dictamen is reportedly an offshoot of Peru's Chinese Maoist terrorist organization, Sendero Luminoso, or Shining Path. It has been linked to numerous acts of terrorism throughout Masagua and the rest of Central America. In English, "El Dictamen" means "The Judgment."

Balserio was elected president of Masagua in a controversial election that, according to some critics of American foreign policy, was orchestrated by the Central Intelligence Agency. Balserio was returned to office for a second term in an equally controversial election. He had seven months remaining in his second term, and was expected to run for reelection . . .

Ford sat on the dock reading the newspaper. He rarely looked at a newspaper. Didn't understand the nation's habit of clubbing itself each morning with a list of tragedy and doom before trying to go cheerfully into the day. Like arsenic, it had to have a cumulative effect. But he had bought this thick Sunday edition to see if there was more to read about Rafe Hollins. Rafe was there, an obituary: two tiny lines of type and information about the memorial service. And—surprise—Balserio was there, too: second page, international section with a file photo. Balserio, with his thin black mustache and black hair protruding from beneath the general's cap, looked like a Miami coke dealer at a costume party. That's just about the way Ford remembered him. An extremely tall, pompous man, shrewd, brutal, and superstitious, who had nothing but contempt for the people he ruled.

Ford hadn't liked Balserio. Pilar despised him. She married him when she was twenty-one, abandoning an already brilliant academic career at the Universidad de Costa Rica to fulfill a marriage contract arranged by her father. The wealthy families of Central America still did things like that. When Balserio ascended to the presidency, Pilar found herself in a role familiar to many women in many cultures: She was smarter than her husband, more sympathetic, better at dealing with people and details, yet was relegated to looking pretty at social functions. Instead of becoming bitter, though, Pilar got involved. She kept up on what each branch of the government was doing and gradually made herself indispensable because she was the only one in the Presidential Palace who did know. By Balserio's third year in office, Pilar had the administration working smoothly and with purpose. The generals loved and admired her, so the military remained loyal to her husband. The people of Masagua were enjoying the improved housing and medical care. For the first time in four hundred years, the country was at peace, and Balserio was quick to take the credit.

But Balserio finally heard the whispers, though long after everyone else in Masagua: He was just a puppet, the rumors said, his wife the puppeteer. He acted at her bidding. There was only one thing the *presidente* wouldn't and couldn't do for this great lady—which is why she had never conceived, borne a child. Furious, Balserio notified his department heads that they were no

longer to discuss matters of state with his wife. She was
banished from the government, though she remained in
the palace . . . and in Balserio's bedroom, where she still
did not conceive. The government began to fall apart;
the people began to react to the increasingly brutal
treatment they received at the hands of Balserio's men.
Balserio answered with more brutality, and the tenuous
peace was gone.

Now this.

Ford folded the paper and stood. MacKinley came by.
"You're looking a bit sleepy today, Doc. Didn't get our
eight hours last night, did we now, cobber?" Smile,
smile. Ford had heard the same thing from Jeth Nicholes
and J. Y. Lavender, one of the local sailing instructors.
Sheri Braun-Richards had left an hour after first light,
walking down his rickety stilt house dock for all the
early risers to see.

Sunday or not, he made phone calls. He tried an old associate of his in Washington, D.C., Donald Piao Cheng,
but didn't get an answer.

Major Lester Durell of Fort Myers-Sanibel Municipal
Police Department was home, though, getting ready to
go play golf, he said. Durell had been a senior when Ford
was a sophomore, played on the same baseball and football teams. Ford had dropped in at Durell's office once
not long after his return to Florida: modern office with
blue carpeting, a collection of ceramic pigs in police
uniforms on the shelves, framed commendations and a
diploma of his bachelor of science degree from Florida
State University's School of Criminology on the wall. It

wasn't the cop office you see on television. It was the office of an organized executive, competent in his work.

Ford was counting on that.

He asked Durell if he was going to attend the memorial service for Rafe. Durell hesitated, as if he hadn't really planned on it, then said, "Sure, M.D. If you're going. You trying to make this into a sort of reunion thing? Get a lot of the guys together to give Rafe a send-off? If you are, I'll warn you right now that most of them are gone, moved away. Either that, or so rich on real estate they're at their summer homes in North Carolina."

Ford said, "I'm not interested in a reunion, Les. I want a chance to talk to you privately and thought it might be a convenient time."

"Privately?" Said with a falling inflection that communicated suspicion; the cop defense system was suddenly in place. "About what?"

"About Rafe. Not just privately, confidentially, too. I know you can't agree to something like that on the spur of the moment, so I thought I'd give you a day's warning."

"Maybe I can give you an answer right now. I'm an officer of the court in uniform or out of uniform. That's the law. I'm going to have to hear a lot more before I can guarantee confidentiality. By then, Doc, you may have already told me too much. Do you still want to see me tomorrow?"

"I'll risk it . . . maybe for half an hour or so after the service? Oh, Lester—one more thing. If there was one investigative reporter in the area you would genuinely hate to have after your ass, who would it be?"

"I've got nothing to hide. None of them bother me."

Getting colder, more remote. He and Ford hadn't been close friends. Ford had the impression it wouldn't matter if they had.

"But if you had done something, and there was one reporter—"

"What's this all about, M.D.? You got yourself in trouble? Or are you trying to play amateur detective? People watch TV, get the impression they can snatch clues out from under the noses of the pros, solve the puzzle, live happily ever after, which is utter, utter bullshit. It doesn't work that way and, from what I remember of you, you're too smart to think it does."

"I didn't mean to make you mad, Les."

"Then don't try to manipulate me."

"I wasn't manipulating. I want the name of a good investigative reporter. I can get it from you or from someone else."

"You're thinking Rafe was murdered. That's what this is all about, isn't it?"

"Yes."

There was a silence followed by a sigh. "There's a guy on the area paper, Henry Melinski. Henry S. Melinski, that's his byline. Weighs about a hundred forty pounds, but he's got these blue eyes like an assassin. He doesn't scare and the bastard hangs on like a pit bull. If I'd done something wrong—which I haven't—I think I'd move to Pago-Pago or someplace if that bad boy got on my trail."

"What about the Miami *Herald*? You know anyone there?"

Lester Durell said, "Before I do any more volunteering, I think we need to have a talk first, Doc. I'll see you tomorrow." And hung up.

Ford worked around the lab for a while, then tried Donald Piao Cheng in D.C. again. This time Cheng's wife answered, wanted to know when're you coming by to visit, Doc?; said they always had a spare bed; said you won't believe the change that's come over Donald. "He's outside jumping rope, can you imagine?"

Ford tried to imagine. Cheng was maybe five eight, weighed two hundred pounds, smoked cigarettes. He worked for the U.S. Customs Department; a Type-A personality who couldn't slow down. Precise, driving; work, work, worry, worry, worry; everything right by the book. Ford couldn't imagine.

But then Donald got on and said he'd quit smoking, was down to 175 and wasn't going off the diet till he weighed 160. Ford said that was great, and he'd called to ask a favor. Cheng said, "Name it. As I remember, I owe you one very big favor and two or three small ones." With Donald Cheng, it wouldn't have mattered who owed whom because they were friends.

It took Ford a while to describe exactly what he wanted. When he was done, he added, "I don't want to mislead you, Don. I haven't told you everything."

"No kidding?" Cheng said dryly. "I was afraid you were being unintentionally inscrutable."

"It's necessary. I wouldn't do it if it wasn't."

"But what's so important about a painting you want me to go clear to Manhattan to bid on it? Not that I'm not happy to help."

Ford said, "It was painted by a friend of mine. I like it. I'd like to own it."

"My God, if the artist is a friend of yours, why don't you just tell her; buy it from her?"

"Because that way she'd feel obligated to give it to me. She needs the money."

"*Jeez.* Mister white knight on a horse. I try to tell Margie what you're really like, and she says, Oh, he's got such a good face, such nice eyes, you're just jealous of the way he looks, Don, and he's so good with the kids. You quit NSA for six months, now you really are a nice guy? And an art lover, no less."

From the phone in the lab, Ford could see two paintings on the walls: a stilt house at low tide by Wellington Ward and palm trees on a beach by Ken Turney. He said, "I know what I like," which would have made Jessica roll her eyes. "And I've been gone a year, not six months. You understand, I'd like you to be there for the whole sale. This painting might come up early, or maybe real late. I want to make sure you're there for the whole thing."

"In other words, they might try to sell something illegal toward the end of the show, and you don't want me to miss it."

"That's not the sort of thing you should hear from me."

Cheng said, "Okay, okay, the whole thing. Manhattan. Kids dye their hair purple there. Walk around with great big radios."

"Your hair used to be down to your shoulders. Margie showed me the photos. You went to Woodstock and slept with Ivy League girls who felt guilty because you were a downtrodden minority. You told me that. You wanted to return to China and communicate with the bones of your ancestors."

"I may; I still may do that!"

"Hey, Don, there's one more thing."

"I was sure there would be at least one more thing."

"I have the chance to invest with this importer who says he's going to buy a lot of Mayan artifacts in Central America, then bring them back and sell them at a huge profit—"

"That's a transparent lie, and I just want you to know that I know it."

"I hoped you would. Anyway, I wanted to know what the laws are against that sort of thing."

"There are about seventeen years' worth of laws against that sort of thing. Twenty-seven years if we really want to come down hard. There's the National Stolen Properties Law and the National Receiving Stolen Goods Law—U.S. Codes twenty-three fourteen and twenty-three fifteen if you're writing it down. Then there's the smuggling statute, USC five forty-five, Paragraph B—"

"That tells me what I want to know."

"No, you're trying to tell me what I should know. Right? Diplomatic language; putting some very odd stuff between the lines, here, Doc, and I want an explanation when I return with your painting."

"Then you'll do it?"

"I'll miss my run. I usually run in the evening. I'm getting in shape for Boston. But, yeah, I'll go. And I'll dress very nice, just like you said."

"There's one more thing, Don—"

"You've already had your one more thing."

"Is this going to be considered a big favor or a little favor?"

"Why is it I get chills just hearing you ask that?"

"Because you know, even after this, you still owe me a big one."

Ford leafed through the phone book until he found a number for Melinski, Henry S. It didn't say B.J. after his name: bachelor's degree in journalism. In a few years, it probably would. Journalists were taking themselves awfully seriously these days. He dialed the number and let it ring ten times before hanging up. Well, that was okay. It might be better to wait until Sally Field called him with more information.

What he was trying to do was get the right organizations in line; to nudge them in the right direction. It was the one hope he had of securing justice for Rafe Hollins. Lester Durell had said stories of the successful amateur detective were utter bullshit, and Ford knew that he was right. The odds were impossible because, on a formal business basis, people didn't deal with people anymore, they dealt with beings Ford thought of as Bionts. In the literature of natural history, a biont was a discrete unit of living matter that had a specific mode of life. In modern America, to Ford's way of thinking, a Biont was a worker or minor official who, joined with other Bionts, established a separate and dominant entity: the Organization. A Biont was different from an employee. Ford was seeing fewer and fewer employees around. The Biont looked to the Organization as a sort of surrogate family; depended on the Organization to care for him in sickness and in health, to provide for his recreational, spiritual, and social needs. The Organization was an organism, much as a coral reef or a beehive could be considered an organism, made up of individual creatures working for the good of the whole. When the Organization prospered, so did the Biont—a sort of professional symbiosis, with loyalty built in. A Biont might grumble about his host in private, but just let an outsider try to sneak in, ask for information, arouse suspicion, or endanger the Organization, and all the unit members would unite like a shield to rebuff the intruder. Ford thought of the way Aztec ants rushed to attack anything that happened to touch their hosting Cocoloba tree. He thought of killer bees.

There were too many organizations involved: the sheriff's department of Everglades County, the medical examiner's office, Sealife Development Corporation on Sandy Key. An outsider might be able to wrangle a small bit of information from one, but the hope of assembling incriminating data from all three was absurd. What he could do, though, was try to use the organization-organism theory to his advantage. In nature, all organisms filled the dual role of predator and the preyed upon. Big things attacked smaller things. They picked up the scent, stalked, and fed.

Ford was now assembling bigger predators. He was throwing out the scent.

EIGHT

He had work of his own to do.

He still needed more sharks for that order from Minneapolis Public Schools, and he wanted to check the salinity and oxygen content of his fish tank.

Sharks, first.

He put rods and cast net in his skiff, then decided to take his fly rod, too. On the grass flats at the mouth of Dinkin's Bay, just across from Jessica's house, he threw the cast net and put a couple dozen pinfish—small bait fish—into his live wells. While he was catching bait, Jessica came out onto the dock and waved. Ford could see that she wanted him to stop, but he did not. Instead, he ran out onto Pine Island Sound, then cut southward toward the causeway that connected Sanibel to the mainland. When the water shoaled to five feet, he began to drift. Using a light spinning rod, he caught six small blacktip sharks, enjoying the way they jumped: dark projectiles on a pale sea. Then a school of ladyfish moved in, feeding in such a frenzy that he lost several baits without a shark strike.

He put the blacktips on ice, then ran north toward St. James City on Pine Island where, in 1885, W. H. Wood stayed. Wood was the New Yorker who, fishing in Tarpon Bay, caught the first tarpon ever taken on rod and reel. Ford landed three more blacktips and, drifting all alone on a vitreous glaze of sea and sky, sweat dripping down his nose, released several spotted seatrout.

Then he noticed something in the distance—something glittering, energized, rolling across the calm like a boat wake: a school of tarpon coming toward him; a dozen or more fish moving in a tight pod. Their big tails were throwing water; their chromium scales threw sunlight. Ford picked up his fly rod, stripped out line to cast, and stood on the bow of his skiff waiting, his pulse thudding, his mind stilling, concentrating, as he gauged the path of the tarpon and the point where his fly might intersect with them. They were big fish: six feet long, most of them, rolling and diving in a frenzied carousel, gulping surface air before ascending, blowing bubbles, their huge horse-eyes vivid with life but devoid of emotion; primeval fish that were wild with purpose but as mindless as rays of light.

Ford stood watching, loving it.

Then they were close enough. On the surface, the tarpon were silver with dark backs that paled in gradations of blue. As they dove, their bodies became golden beneath the tannin-stained water. Ford released the hook he was holding, catapulting the blue-and-white streamer fly forward. He hauled with his left hand and shot out thirty feet of line on the back cast. Then he released the line on the fore cast, and the streamer fly seemed to carom off the sky. Then it slapped into the side of the boat . . . because he was standing on the line coiled upon the deck.

Boy, oh boy . . . Calling himself names as he tried to untangle himself. So much for grace under pressure.

He straightened the line with a roll cast, then went through the ceremonies of false casting, trying to pick out another fish. This time he casted cleanly, but the adrenaline was in him and he casted way too far: eighty feet, and the plastic line smacked the belly of the rod as if it could have gone another fifty. Ford began to strip in quickly so that the streamer might still intersect with his chosen tarpon. But then an unseen fish materialized through the murk: a flash of gold like refracted light; a momentary vision of a gigantic scimitar turning by his lure. His line jolted, then tightened. Ford lifted the rod, feeling a great weight like a snag, his eyes focused on the triangulation point of rod and line and bay. There was a microsecond of calm; an oleaginous swirl. Then the water erupted into an incandescent whirlpool as the tarpon broke through the film of water, its mouth wide, eyes wild, shaking its head: a huge, animated form that froze for a moment in midair, silver on blue, then tumbled into the water with the percussion of a refrigerator falling from the sky.

Ford was soaked . . . the fish was running, taking line . . . his reel strained with the whine of precision machinery that was being pushed beyond the limits of lubrication, as if the damn thing might overheat and disintegrate in his face.

The fish jumped a second time, way, way in the distance, the suction-clatter of impact reaching Ford's ears a moment after it had already reentered the water. Then the tarpon was running again, but not as fast. Ford touched the reel's spool, applying pressure, and the bow of the skiff swung slowly around, as if drawn to the tarpon: the inanimate in pursuit of the inexorable.

Now it was fun. The strike of the fish and the first jump were always the most fun, but, in the moment of their occurring, the shock was too close to terror. He would enjoy that moment later, when his legs stopped shaking, when his motor reflexes returned, when he didn't have to remind himself to breathe. Now, though, he could relax a little and take inventory. The line was his conduit to the fish; a sort of sensory filament that joined him, for a very short time, with that which he admired but could never truly be a part of nor fully understand. That's what he liked best about it. By putting his fingertips on the line, he could feel the fish, almost as if he were touching it. The tarpon was shaking its head. Now the great tail was surging, banging the line as torque increased . . . now it was ascending, stretching the line so that it whined in the summer calm, and Ford could feel it all, one creature connected to another.

He played the fish for about ten minutes, though it didn't seem that long. It would take another, say, half hour to actually land the fish, but Ford didn't want to land it. He was too familiar with the end-game: the way the tarpon would veer toward the boat listing to one side, come up and make a deep belching sound like a blown horse, its gill rakes grayish from exhaustion and its muscles saturated with lactic acid from the long struggle. Even though he could have revived the fish, that final scene would have ruined it for him, so he pointed the rod tip at the tarpon, cupped the reel with his palm, and let the leader break at the tippet. Popular literature said the hook would corrode away within forty-eight hours—a ridiculous figure that he didn't believe. Ultimately, though, the hook would rust out and, in the meantime, the fish would have no trouble feeding.

The tarpon jumped once more, a strong jump, and was gone.

Tomlinson said sure, he understood what Ford was doing; dormitory chemistry had been his strong suit, and the only difference here was you just measured the precipitate, didn't swallow it or smoke it.

Ford said, "Ah," feeling that the Winkler Titration Method of determining oxygen content in water had somehow just been slandered. "You've got it figured out already, huh?"

Tomlinson was combing his fingers through his long blond hair, peering at the 300-milliliter flask Ford held in his hand. "What's to figure out? You fill the flask with water from the fish tank. You add the manganese solution, then treat it with an iodine base. Why else would you do that but so the manganese can combine with the oh-two to form a stable oxygen-manganese complex? Hell, Doc, a guy would have to be dumb not to see that."

Ford had been doing the test for years, and it still wasn't clear to him why the manganese required iodine. He said, "And that cloudy stuff in the flask, the precipitate, how would you measure that to determine how much oxygen is in the water?"

"That's supposed to give the oxygen content?" Tomlinson looked puzzled. "How the hell can that be? It's not proportional, man. Situation like this, you got to deal in proportions. Need something else; a little kicker in there to free the iodine. What, you going to titrate a disproportional precipitate? Like barking up the wrong fucking tree, you ask me."

"Well, you have to treat it with sulfuric acid first—"

"Right! Now how damn obvious, and I didn't even think of it. Got the ol' thinking cap on backward today, man—"

"And that dissolves the oxygen-manganese complex—"

"For sure, you don't have to say another word. Gives you free iodine in an amount proportional to the original amount of dissolved oh-two. Then you titrate it; probably use some kind of starch to make it easy to measure."

"Well, starch, yeah, you can use starch—"

"Converts the whole business to iodine; probably a real pretty color, too, like violets or roses; you know, flowers. Goddamn, Doc, you know your business. I'll give you that."

Feeling dumb, Ford said, "Experience. I've been doing it for a long time." Feeling mild shock, too. This was Tomlinson the drug casualty talking?

Normally, about this stage of the Winkler Titration Method, Ford referred to his notes so that he got all the steps straight. Now he forged on from memory so as not to disillusion Tomlinson . . . and maybe to save face, too. When he was finished, he looked up from his calculations and said, "There's plenty of oxygen. Seven parts per million, which is high, but not too high. I've been testing the pH right along, and it's fine. So that leaves salinity, the amount of salt in the water. Cephalopods are very sensitive to changes in salinity."

"I bet you got some kind of meter to test that."

"There's a thing called a refractometer, but mine's still on back-order. There's another way to determine salinity, though—"

"Hey! Couldn't you just figure out the density of the water? That ought to give you the salt content."

Ford smiled patiently. "That's a common mistake. Don't forget that water temperature has an effect—"

"Cross-graph it, man. Figure it all out on intersecting curves. Of course water temperature has an effect on density, that goes without saying."

Ford said, "Right. I'm sorry I said it."

They were sitting on the upper deck of the stilt house, Tomlinson talking away while Ford watched the moon drift out of the mangroves. He liked Tomlinson and he liked to hear him talk, but now he was mostly thinking about his fish tank, why he couldn't keep squid alive. Salinity had checked out at twenty-four parts per thousand, which was exactly the same as the salinity of the bay in which he had netted the squid. What could be wrong?

Tomlinson was saying "Look at those big boomers down there, swimming round and round," staring into the shark pen at the three cruising shapes. "They got my mind in gear again, man. You and those sharks got my brain working for the first time since I left school." He lifted the bottle of beer to his lips. "I don't know whether to thank you or file charges."

"Huh?"

"Check it out: Yesterday I spent the whole day doing research. The whole day. Really humping it, too. Taking notes, cross-referencing, listening to Iron Butterfly." He took another drink. "Didn't take a whiz for about three hours straight."

Ford heard enough of that to ask "You find out why sharks in Africa swim counterclockwise when they're in captivity?"

"What? Naw, I should have checked on that; I coulda. This woman I know lives up on Captiva Island, she's got a computer. One of those laptops with a ten-meg hard drive and a telephone modem, so you can dial into these massive data banks, find out everything on just about any subject. But it wasn't sharks I was researching, it was the religious history of the Maya. The story you told about the freshwater sharks got me interested. Pagan deities, man. Ancient ceremonies. The influence of ancient religion on a specific modern culture. It's all part of philosophy and world history, my two chosen fields. Decided it was time for me to get back to work."

Ford was listening now. "You find much material?"

"A shitpot full, that's all. Coulda filled books, only this chick has a modem that receives at twelve hundred bauds and a crummy little printer that will only print at six hundred bauds. Don't you hate to borrow junk like that? Result: I couldn't print at all. Had to take notes like a crazy man. The old memory isn't what it used to be. Age does that, you know."

"Age," said Ford. Tomlinson was late thirties, tops. "Right."

"You said you worked in Masagua, but you ever hear much about the history: the Maya and the Spaniards and all that? It's crazy, bizarre; a fucking philosophical gold mine."

Ford knew some of the history, but he said, "No. Tell me."

"Religious and racial genocide, that's what the Spaniards were into, man. This conquistador, Pedro de Alvarado, marches into the area now called Masagua with just over four hundred men. He's met by one of the two main tribes there, the Kache. The Kache were mostly farmers, hunters; working class, blue-collar types today. The Kache had about fifty thousand warriors, but they took one look at Alvarado with his long blond hair and decided he's the white god of Mayan mythology, Quetzalcoatl. Weird, huh?—the prophecy of a white god before they'd ever seen the Spaniards. Makes you wonder how much those Vikings got around. So the Kache surrender to Alvarado without a drop of blood being spilled." Tomlinson looked at Ford and held up two fingers. "Important points for later reference: The blond god Quetzalcoatl, and the Kaches were too scared to fight."

"Got it," said Ford.

"The next tribe Alvarado decides to conquer is the Tlaxclen, way up in the mountains. The Tlaxclen have their workers, but they're mostly priests and architects, the keepers of the calendar. They're the descendants of the Maya who built the pyramids; the ones who invented the calendar. Remember—the classic period of the Maya was over by the time the Spaniards got there. Nearly all knowledge of glyph writing and pyramid building had been lost, but the Tlaxclen still knew the ceremonies; still knew the calendar."

"I've heard about that calendar," Ford said. "Pretty complicated. It started fresh every fifty-two years."

"Uh-huh, right. The Tlaxclen called that final year the Year of Seven Moons. Poetic damn people, weren't they? The Kache and the Tlaxclen traded, intermarried, got along just fine. Every year, on the summer solstice, both nations met in a really big ritual called the Ceremony of Seven Moons. It was what my old philosophy profs would have called a classic artifact of union. See, the Tlaxclen used this ceremony to hold the people together. Like what the Holy Grail might be to Christians, or like the sacred pipal tree where Sakyamuni got enlightenment and became Buddha. Something that kept things tight.

"Every year, a hundred thousand Maya or more participated. Very mystical; very complex. The Tlaxclen priests were the keepers of the faith because only they knew the incantations and how to read the signs."

Tomlinson looked at Ford. "But maybe you know this stuff already, having lived there."

Ford said, "Keep going. It's getting good."

"Oh, man, it gets better and better. See, the Mayan fascination with time, numbers, astronomy was all related to their dependency on agriculture. It was their religion, trying to predict the weather, trying to control the growing seasons. Appease the gods; stuff like that. Scratch any religion, and you come up with the day-to-day fears of its followers. The Maya were nature worshippers, worshippers of the seasons. Hell, supposedly the only time they copulated was in the spring. The Aztecs sacrificed as many as twenty thousand people in a single day, but the Maya didn't go in for that. Even before killing an animal, they had to whisper the prayer 'I have need' to explain themselves to the gods. Piss off the gods, and they'd send bad weather, destroy the crops."

Ford said, "So Alvarado attacked the peaceful Tlaxclen priests."

"Right. But here's the clincher: He forced about ten thousand Kache warriors to go with him and help fight. Maybe the Kache still thought he was Quetzalcoatl. No one knows, but they followed him. It was a long march into the mountains; took them several days to get there, and Alvarado only carried enough food for his own men. The Kache warriors were starving, and Alvarado told them they had to eat the bodies of their enemies. Can you picture it? The Maya weren't pacifists, but they weren't murderers either. Now they were being forced into cannibalism. It was bloodbath time. Human butchery. A monk traveling with the army described in writing how children were killed and roasted in Alvarado's presence; how men were murdered just so their hands and feet—the tenderest parts—could be eaten. When Alvarado confronted the Tlaxclen priests at this mountain lake—"

"Ojo de Dios," Ford put in. "That's the name of the lake: God's Eye."

"The Eye of God, yeah—jeez, I love the names people give stuff down there. Anyway, when Alvarado got to the lake, the Tlaxclen sent out six thousand warriors. They wore cotton shirts and feathers and blew conch-shell trumpets to make sure they didn't take this Spanish geek by surprise. Honorable to the end, man. Six thousand spears against armored soldiers on horseback and ten thousand Kache warriors. Bummer odds, but the Tlaxclen still fought. When the priests saw the slaughter, they began to throw their religious artifacts into the lake. Stone calendars and tablets. Legend says there was a big stone star chart with emeralds marking constellations. They didn't want Alvarado to have them; that would have been sacrilege, man.

"Apparently this lake is real deep, and the stuff was never found. Alvarado looked, too. He'd heard about those emeralds. People have searched ever since, but no luck—probably because there were a bunch of earthquakes in the years following the conquest.

"Anyway, the Tlaxclen were enslaved. So were the Kache, for that matter. But because the Kache had helped the conquistadors, they were of a slightly higher rank than the Tlaxclen. The Kache were given better food, better jobs; they were given the bulk of the land when the Spaniards pulled out. Hell, the Spaniards didn't want it. No gold in Masagua, right? So the Kache became the ruling, upper class. Now, you'd think the Kache would've treated the Tlaxclen pretty good. Like out of remorse. But they didn't. It's one of those perverse quirks of human nature that we end up hating people who have seen us humiliated. Plus, the Tlaxclen had added to the humiliation by fighting the Spaniards, and the Kache despised them for it. They became even crueler than Alvarado."

Tomlinson was combing his fingers through his hair, excited. "Do you see the significance of all this, Doc? Goddamn, it's as amazing as it is tragic. Within the space of a couple of weeks, the two-thousand-year-old social and religious foundations of an entire people were destroyed. The Kache had been defeated by a handful of men, surrendered without a fight. They had not only murdered their brothers, but they had eaten the corpses. Humiliation like that doesn't just last for a few years, it lasts for generations; hundreds of years.

"The Tlaxclen went from high priests to slaves, and at the hands of their own people. The Ceremony of Seven Moons—the thing that had always united them—was lost, then Catholicism was forced on them. But here's the thing that interests me—" He slid forward in his chair. "One of the Tlaxclen priests decided the religion and the ceremonies of his people should be recorded. This priest was a smart dude, man. He saw what was going on around him, and he knew this wasn't just some minor defeat his people had suffered. It was for all time. So he confided in one of the Spanish monks.

Musta been a couple years after the conquest; one of them, you know, had to learn the other's language. And this monk wrote it all down. Of course, even the Tlaxclen had probably lost the secrets of Mayan glyph writing by this time—this was way after the Mayan Classic Period, like I said. But, from what I read, the monk may have gotten the whole story, step by step, on the ceremonies, religion, philosophy. Everything. He compiled it into a book, ink on parchment, called the *Kin Qux Cho*. I translate that as *Rituals of the Lake*.

Ford looked at him. "You can read Mayan?"

Tomlinson seemed slightly offended. "Goddamn, I spent the whole day poring over that stuff. Who wouldn't pick up a little? Besides the written Mayan was translated into phonetic archaic Spanish; it's maybe two hundred words, and those are mostly nouns. What's to learn?"

"Oh," said Ford. "That's all it is." He knew only a handful of people familiar with written Mayan, and only one who could read archaic Spanish—Pilar. He said, "And I thought it was hard."

"You want something hard, try reading those Mayan glyphs. It's gonna take me at least a week just to figure out their damn calendar. They had three different systems: the Calendar Round—that's the fifty-two-year cycle—the Sacred Round, and the Vague Year, all computed on a vigesimal count, which is a snap, but everything over the number ten is in glyphs, which is a bummer, man."

"Now you want to learn how to read Mayan glyphs? I don't get it, Tomlinson. What's the point?"

"The *Kin Qux Cho*, man. The book, that's the point.

It was written four hundred and fifty years ago, but no one even knew what it was until about eight years ago. Some graduate student discovered it while going through the archives there in the museum, but the damn Masaguan government immediately took control of it. No one's had a look at it since. No one knows for sure what's in it; it's all speculation. See, the way I see it, the descendants of the Kache probably still run the country, the upper class—"

"They don't think of themselves as Kache or Tlaxclen anymore, Tomlinson—except for maybe some of the mountain people."

"It doesn't matter what they call themselves. They're still Kache, and they still must have one hell of a sense of shame about what happened to them. Why else would they put that book under wraps? Why else would they be so afraid of their past? Do you see the damn irony, Doc? It hit me yesterday when I was out on my boat meditating. Sitting there drifting, watching the sunset, and all of a sudden, *bam,* there it was. These people are acting out the whole conquest scene over and over again. Like punishing themselves in utter damn humiliation. The fighting, the revolutions, killing their own kind—just like when Alvarado came. And they're still following the white god, Quetzalcoatl, only now Quetzalcoatl goes under a couple of names, like the Soviet Union and the good old U.S. of A." Tomlinson was nodding, feet moving, pleased with himself. "What a study, man. Parallel the religion and philosophy of pre-Alvarado Maya with the Maya of today. Take pure data four hundred and

fifty years old, juxtapose it with current data. See what
little quirks survived. Genetic memory, man, don't sell
it short. That stuff runs deep in an isolated race. Find
out if they haven't incorporated some of the old religion
in with their Catholicism—"

"Oh, they have, they have," said Ford. "I've seen it.
They burn candles before old Mayan carvings. They
hold crucifixes but chant in Tlaxclen."

"See! It's all falling into place, Doc. Meeting you,
hearing about those sharks, my brain coming back to
life. It's like preordained, man. Don't doubt for a second that everything in this world happens at exactly the
right time. It all falls into place, just waiting on us to
come along. I know." Tomlinson looked at the horizon
and sniffed. "Karma's my business. Now I just need to
get my hands on a copy of that damn book."

"You make it sound like it won't be easy." Speaking
as if uninformed, but Ford knew that it wouldn't be easy.
Now, in fact, it might be impossible.

"Maybe not. But academicians stick together, man.
Flash the right credentials, see the right people. The
Masaguan government will have to release that book
someday."

"If the government has it."

"What? I had all the latest data on the screen yesterday, man. Supposedly they keep it in the Presidential
Palace, locked up. Like a national treasure, proud enough
to show it off, but too ashamed to let anyone translate
it. You know something you're not telling me?"

Ford had hardly touched his evening quart of beer,

but now he took a long drink. He knew something, but he wasn't going to risk telling Tomlinson. Not yet. He knew the *Kin Qux Cho* was no longer in the Presidential Palace. He knew that Pilar Santana Fuentes Balserio had been the graduate student who, eight years before, had discovered the significance of the book. And he knew that it was Pilar, working with an accomplice, who had stolen it.

It happened the night before he left Masagua. He had been the accomplice.

NINE

Harry Bernstein didn't call Monday morning from Masagua, but Ford got a nice surprise from Sally Field: a package, Federal Express, with computer cross-checks on every name he'd given her. She must have gone into the office immediately after he called and worked on her own time. A nice gesture, worth a lot more than just a dinner. Ford took the package inside and sat down with iced tea to read.

Almost everyone in America over the age of twenty-one is listed in some computer bank somewhere. Check those data centers one by one and they might produce a line or a paragraph. Access the facilities Sally had at her disposal, though, and even an innocuous law-abiding wallpaper salesman would produce half a page. Her sources were the best in the world, the sum of intelligence resources and data centers from around the globe.

Mario DeArmand was no wallpaper salesman. There were two pages of him, staccato nonsentences and figures. Before he became sheriff of Everglades County, DeArmand had been involved in pyramid schemes. Herbal Foods; Rags-to-Real Estate—two scam corporations disguised as multilevel marketing companies. They bought late-night television time to drum Herbal Food distributorships and their get-rich-quick real estate courses to poor schmucks who never stopped to think: If these people are making so much money selling health food and real estate, why do they want competition from me?

DeArmand had been investigated for tax fraud, mail fraud, and conspiracy to defraud the public, but had always found a way to buy his way out. When the quack food business got too hot, DeArmand and his partners pooled the rich profits and bought an island in Florida: Sandy Key.

That brought Ford to a sheaf of papers with information about Sealife Development Corporation. Sally's computer sources had provided a list of stockholders, lien holders, board members, and the board members of Sealife's parent company, Seaboard Marketing Unlimited. Most of the data was useless—but not all of it. It provided him with the link he was looking for, the connection through the maze work.

The most reassuring information was on Tomlinson. Tomlinson did, indeed, have a doctorate from Harvard— this after graduating summa cum laude, a year at the Sorbonne, and spending two days in the Suffolk County jail for refusing to pay more than a thousand dollars in parking tickets. His family had also had him committed to Cook County Sanitarium for six months—why, it didn't say. More important to Ford, Sally had noted at the bottom of Tomlinson's dossier: *Never worked for us or anyone else here.*

If Sally was right it meant Tomlinson had not been sent to Florida to keep an eye on him.

Ford needed someone smart and clean. But was Sally right?

When he could wait no longer for Bernstein to call, he got in his pickup truck and headed for Sandy Key and Rafe Hollins's funeral. He drove across the causeway, then turned south onto U.S. 41, a six-lane Cuisinart where bad drivers from all over the nation gathered to tailgate and rush only to wait impatiently at the next light; unhappy travelers as driven as their automobiles. Here was the asphalt essence of everything bad Florida had to offer: a fast highway of Big Macs, furniture warehouses, trailer parks, disco drunk factories, and used car lots with pennants sagging; an unbroken strip of tacky, plasticized commerce stretching two hundred miles from Tampa to Naples, jammed with traffic that slowed only when sirens screamed and ambulances came to strap the broken and bleeding onto stretchers and cart them away.

Ford hated it.

He endured the rush for about six miles, then turned east onto a back road. Then for thirty miles it was pastureland, phosphate heaps, and cypress heads rising cool in the distance. Crossbred Brahman cattle stood swatting themselves in the heat while vultures hunched on wires above, awaiting road kill. This was backcountry Florida: sun-bleached sawgrass and sulfur swamps, citrus groves and oak hammocks; land of stars and bars, country music and four-wheel-drive cowboys. Ford drove along at a pleasant 55, arm out the window, waving at anyone who seemed friendly, drawing his arm in when dumpsters screamed past leaving their haze of phosphate dust. Then he turned west again, crossed Highway 41 with its smell of hot asphalt and hamburgers, and for twenty miles it was trailer parks or stucco apartments and fields of smoldering slash pine where the bulldozers had come in and scraped the land bare, making room for more apartments, more development.

Years ago, he had traveled this road many times, but now he recognized nothing. He was not surprised. Florida wasn't just growing, it was exploding. People were moving into the state at a rate of about a thousand a day, seven thousand new residents a week, packing their lives into U-Hauls, turning their backs on the dying industries of the Midwest and heading sunward. The gush of transplants was making a few developers happy, making a bunch of investors and lawyers wealthy, but making fools out of just about everyone else. The love of money kept people in the development trade yammering for more zoning changes, and the fear of money inspired local commissioners to grant the changes. Never mind that the demand on Florida's already waning water supply was increasing by about a half-million gallons a week. Never mind the number of cars on the already jammed highways was increasing by about twenty thousand a month. And never mind how out-of-control growth was affecting schools or impacting on the environment because, hell, all growth was good; growth meant money—just ask the elected officials struggling to make their towns into carbon copies of Miami. Too few public servants had the foresight, or the courage, to say what was really true: that allowing growth to be self-limiting was the very worst form of carrion-feeder economics. It was a get-it-quick-before-it-rots philosophy that promised long-term disaster even more surely than short-term profits. Only three things limited growth naturally: crime, decay, and overpopulation. Most politicians didn't have the courage to say it, and too many voters didn't give a damn because Florida wasn't their state anyway, not really. Wasn't anything their grandkids were going to be stuck with. They were really New Yorkers or Hoosiers or Buckeyes; just happened to be living here for a while, that's all. Besides, Florida was just an old whore who was going to be picked clean no matter what, so why not get in line, make some quick money?

Above the distant palms, Ford saw the horizon change. Noticed the swollen, tumid blue of the sky, and he knew the sea was there; would have known even if he had not traveled this road before. Then he came to the bridge . . . not the old swing bridge he remembered, but a new, arching concrete monster that carried traffic high over the bay and down onto Sandy Key. From the top of the bridge, Ford could see the whole island: a long cusp of beach with casuarina midlands that had been chopped into a gridwork of canals and then smothered with a stalagmite jumble of condominiums and the bleak geometrics of planned housing. A sign at the base of the bridge told him this was the handiwork of Sealife Development Corporation.

Ford wasn't impressed. He remembered Sandy Key from high school—a few fish shacks and a lot of empty beach—but that's not why he didn't like what he now saw. It had nothing to do with nostalgia. Ford seldom thought of high school or the years he had lived on Sanibel; never longed for what too many people remembered as those carefree teenage days. He much preferred adulthood, living in the present, and had little patience with the nostalgia freaks, people who escaped the obligations of Now by living in the rosy Then of their imaginations. The only reason he had returned to Florida was because of the bull sharks and the chance to open Sanibel Biological Supply. He had expected change. The west coast of Florida was attractive and people naturally gravitated to attractive areas. But Sandy Key hadn't just changed, it had been chopped up, reconstituted, and stamped from a mold. This wasn't change, it was greed; unimaginative greed, at that.

Ford drove through the sterile downtown area, immune to the tacky Polynesian façades and cutesy boutiques. He took the address from his sports coat pocket and found Sandy Key Funeral Home: a beige stucco box on a sodded lot with palm trees.

There were a few cars in the parking lot, and Ford stepped out into the heat.

Some place for Rafe Hollins to end up.

Nine people showed up for the memorial service, all men. Knowing Rafe, Ford would have been less surprised by a room full of women. He had hoped for a chance to see Rafe's ex-wife not that he thought she could or would tell him anything. Just wanted to see her; see the woman Rafe had chosen only to end up hating. He recognized most of the men. Former high school teammates, counter-culture Sixties' expatriates who had weathered the Age of Aquarius, the Drug Culture, and Beatlemania without noticeable scars, probably because they hadn't paid any of it much attention. They looked like businessmen or commercial fishermen, but their faces still had the weird beach boys light: good-timers who had joined the establishment without being ingested by it. They didn't look too happy now, though. Just uncomfortable.

Major Lester Durell of Fort Myers-Sanibel Municipal Police Department was there. Ford nodded and got a curt nod in return; the defenses still up. Someone touched him on the back, and Ford turned to see Harvey Hollins. Harvey was five years older than Rafe, just as tall and much wider, but without Rafe's grace and good looks. Harvey had always been the plodder. Bright, but slow in speech and deed. He had a thick pug nose, the Hollins cleft chin, and dark, dark eyes set beneath a heavy brow, and Ford could see that his eyes were red. He was taking Rafe's death hard, looking like a big, sad child in the black suit a size too small for him.

Harvey said, "He woulda sure wanted you here, Doc," taking Ford's hand in his, shaking it warmly. "Boy, you two were a pair. Never saw one without the other, and those jokes you used to play made me so damn mad. Like when you melted down that Ex-Lax and slipped it

into my candy bar. Man, I coulda killed you two—"
And caught himself, realizing what he was saying.

Ford said, "It's okay, Harv; I know. I'm sorry we had
to meet like this. You need any help? I'll take over if
you want."

"You already helped, Doc. That bitch of a funeral
director cornered me when I first came in. Wanted to
know where my friends got off questioning her ethics.
I didn't even have to ask what friend; knew it was you
right away. You and your double measure of gall. Too
much, I used to think. But I figure your questioning her
ethics cut four maybe five hundred off the bill, which
will go to little Jake when we find him."

Ford said nothing, just stood there looking into the
big man's red eyes.

"Rafe didn't kill himself, Doc."

"I know, Harv."

"There's only one reason my brother woulda killed
himself. That's if he'd let something happen to Jake."

"I'm sure Jake's fine. Like you said, Rafe wouldn't let
anything happen to his own son. He'll show up."

"He loved that boy more than anything. We didn't
talk that much after I moved. People move, grow apart . . .
even brothers. I've been asking myself why in the hell I
didn't call him more. When we did talk, it was young
Jake this, young Jake that. I have two daughters, so I
know how a man feels about his children. Rafe wouldn't
have killed himself. I'd bet my last dollar on it."

"I think you're right, Harvey."

"Do you, Doc? Do you really?" His expression was

so filled with gratitude that Ford had to glance away. Harvey said, "I told all the other guys that, and they just sort of stared at me, feeling bad but not believing it. I told Les Durell and he acted like he didn't even care. And we played ball together."

Ford said, "Durell has to act like that. He's a professional with a conflict of interest: You guys are friends. He can't show favoritism, even if he's interested. He's got to be tough on himself and doubly sure of his facts. He heard what you said, though, you can be sure of it."

"You really think so?"

"You knew him better than I did. What do you think?"

"Well . . . Les was always smart. And not too easy to read. Mostly I asked him to help find Jake. Rafe's dead; there's no bringing him back. But we've got to find that little boy. You know what Les said? He said he'd make sure all the proper authorities had been contacted. The proper authorities. Even when I told him I'd offer a five-thousand-dollar reward, my whole savings, that's all he would say."

Ford said, "I'm sure everything possible's being done," feeling like a jerk for not being able to say any more.

Harvey didn't even seem to hear him. "Just the thought of it, Doc. . . . The idea of a Hollins child out there all alone, no one to look after him, not even knowing his daddy's dead, maybe waiting for his daddy to come back—" Harvey turned suddenly, looking at the wall until he regained control. He cleared his throat and said thickly, "We better get in there. The service is about to start."

The funeral director—out of spite, probably—had put Rafe into a green glass vase. The kind for long-stemmed roses, but with a lid on it. They'd put the vase on a rostrum between two candles, and Ford sat in the back row, wondering what a really cheap urn looked like. Organ music was being piped into the room, seemed to be seeping in through the walls with the smell of refrigerated flowers and thick drapes. There was a man in a dark suit sitting beside the rostrum. Ford hoped it wasn't a minister, but it was. The Reverend Somebody from the Sandy Key Baptist Church. He looked like a television evangelist with his chubby face and sprayed hair. The minister kept glancing at Harvey and smiling, as if to reassure.

Rafe had been raised as a Baptist, Ford remembered, but hated church and organized religion by the time they met in high school. It seemed unlikely that he had changed during the intervening years, so it seemed just as unlikely that the Reverend Somebody had known Rafe at all, let alone well enough to memorialize him. Just so long as he didn't give a sermon. But he did.

Ford settled into his seat, ready to tune out the slick, shallow performance to come. But, surprise, surprise, the sermon was neither slick nor shallow. The Reverend Somebody turned out to be a thoughtful man and an honest speaker. No, he hadn't known Rafe. But he knew about pain, and he knew about loss, and he spoke about the things he knew with sincerity, a clarity, and a sense of humor that had every man there sitting up, listening. By the time he was done, Ford felt better about Rafe and better about funerals, but foolish for having stereotyped the minister so glibly. Presupposition was a disease of the lazy or terminally oblivious, and he had been showing symptoms of both lately.

When the minister finished, the men milled around talking, pretending to be unaware that no one seemed to know exactly what to do next. Harvey stood in the corner, staring at the urn: a *what now?* expression on his face. Ford touched him on the elbow and said, "I have a boat back on Sanibel. You're welcome to use it. Maybe spread the ashes around Pine Island Sound. Rafe would like that."

"Yeah, well . . . that would be nice, only my plane home leaves Naples at four. I can't afford to take any more time off work, and it's a pretty long drive back to Sanibel." Harvey looked at him. "You could take them, Doc. You were his best friend."

"I will if you want."

"Or, I was thinking, with all these guys here, it might be nice to take care of it right now. While they're still around. They all played ball with him, they knew him better than anybody else."

Ford said, "The beach is only about three blocks from here—"

"I was thinking maybe North Cut. That's only a mile or two, and the tide rips through; carry him right out to sea. One night, when we were kids, Rafe caught a thirty-pound snook there using a white bucktail tipped with shrimp. Man, was he happy."

"I'll tell the guys to follow us."

"Doc? There's something else you can do . . . if you don't mind too much."

"Name it, Harvey."

Harvey was looking at the floor, uneasy. "Could you carry that . . . that vase with you? My nerves are all messed up today, and I just know I'll drop the damn thing and break it."

"I could drive you both."

"Naw, I feel like being alone for a little bit. If you don't mind."

"We'll meet you at North Cut," Ford said. "I'll take care of everything here. Take your time."

He told the other men where to meet, then found the funeral director. On the phone, she had sounded as if she was in her fifties with blue hair and a sour, pinched face. She was actually in her late thirties, had the hair of a Woodstock groupie, and a sour, pinched face. Ford said, "I'd like to take care of the bill now," taking cash from his pocket.

The woman was standing behind a plastic desk and her expression told Ford that she recognized his voice. "The deceased's brother has already made arrangements for that," she said primly.

"He's made arrangements to pay, or to make payments?"

"Mr. . . Ford was it? I really don't see—"

He said, "Dr. Ford," cringing at the childishness of demanding the prefix, but dealing with a woman like this seemed to require it.

"I really don't see that it's any of your business, *Dr.* Ford."

"Let's pretend you don't have any say in the matter."

"He's already signed the papers. Arrangements have already been made—"

Ford leaned over the desk a little. "He's made arrangements to pay off the bill in monthly installments at—what?—twenty percent interest? But now I'm going to give you cash, and you're going to mark the bill paid and you're going to give me a receipt. You have to accept cash, lady, for any outstanding debt. It's the law. Even if it means missing all that nice interest."

Fuming, biting her lips, the woman pulled open a drawer, flipped through files, and pulled out the statement. "I'd prefer a major credit card. It would make it easier for our records."

Ford said, "I don't use credit cards."

The woman slammed the drawer closed. "I'm not surprised."

TEN

Rafe was in the pickup, riding right there beside him through the heat and traffic, and Ford couldn't resist the urge to open the urn and have a look: some brown and gray stuff, about the same texture as cat litter, but a whole bunch of bone shards, too. Seemed to be way too many bones to be properly called ashes, and then Ford remembered the man on the phone, the man at the crematorium, saying they'd cremated the remains but hadn't pulverized them, and should they put a hold on that?

Apparently they'd put a hold on the pulverization just to be safe, or had forgotten because the process had been interrupted. Which wasn't great news. Now Harvey was going to have to see his brother's bones spread along with his ashes; bits of fingers, tibia, ribs easily recognized. And Ford had thought the worst was over. . . .

North Cut was a deep-water pass that separated Sandy Key from the next barrier island. It was narrow, only about a hundred yards wide, and the tidal current ripped through like a river. Ford carried the urn down onto the beach where Harvey and the other men were standing. They were an odd-looking group in their dark suits, standing uneasily in the sun as vacationers strolled by and while, down the shore, teenagers threw a Frisbee for a big Chesapeake Bay retriever.

Harvey took a breath and said, "Well, I guess we ought to get it done. What you figure, just sort of pour the ashes in the water? Tide's going pretty good; nice outgoing tide. Take my brother right out to sea."

Ford was holding the urn in his right arm, but he shifted it to the other side, away from Harvey, and removed the lid so that Les Durell and a couple of others could peek in, but Harvey couldn't. Ford said, "We could do that, Harv. Or . . . I guess there are a couple of other ways to do it, too."

Durell was looking in the urn, then he looked down the beach at the dog. The danger of dumping all those bone shards in the water with a retriever around was obvious, and he said quickly, "Yeah, Harvey, maybe we ought to think of another way."

Harvey looked perplexed, but a little irritated, too. "What other way? You guys have a better way, just come out and tell me. Damn it, I wish we'd brought that minister. He was a good guy. He'd of known how to do it."

Bern Horack, who was a couple of years older than Ford but had graduated a year behind him, said, "Maybe you should say a few words, Harv, then we could throw the whole jar in. Like a burial at sea." He was staring at the retriever, giving it an evil look. "Unless you boys want to excuse me for a minute, while I find a club—"

Ford cut in, saying "How about this, Harvey? We could walk past the urn and each take a turn throwing some of Rafe's . . . ashes . . . into the water. It might be a nice way to say good-bye. And each man could have a moment of silence to think about Rafe, remember him the way he was."

The look of evil on Horack's face faded. "Reach in there . . . with our hands?"

Harvey was nodding, oblivious to Horack, relieved. "That's a good idea, Doc. I like that. These are the best friends Rafe ever had. Your way would make it real personal." He looked at Ford for a moment. "You were his best friend. You start. I'd like to just watch for a bit."

Ford placed the urn at the water's edge and stood in silence for a time. Then he reached into the urn and took a piece of bone with the ashes, hoping to set a precedent. He threw overhanded, far enough out into the pass so the tide wouldn't bring the bone back, pretended not to notice the ashes that blew back in his face, then stepped away so the next man could take his turn. It was a moving thing to see—at first. But there were a lot of bone and ashes, and only ten men. It would take three, maybe four full passes to get rid of everything, and Ford was already beginning to worry the heat and the grimness of the task would destroy what, at best, was a delicate mood. But then he noticed something . . . something in the way the men were throwing. The moments of silence were becoming shorter and the throws longer, each man trying to throw a little farther than the other, but without showing extra effort. They were watching until the shards hit, too, leaning to the right or left, depending on how they curved. Even Ford had to admire how the wind caught the chunks of bone, making them veer like wild curveballs or screwballs. The veil of competition finally burst open when Horack, on the fourth round, took a piece of rib, crow-hopped like an outfielder, and hurled it halfway across the pass, then turned around beaming. "Let's see you bastards beat *that!*" And then looked at Harvey Hollins in a dawning agony, remembering where he was, what he was doing. "Boy, Harv . . . I'm sorry. I got kinda wrapped up; plus Noel Yarbrough there was hogging all the really big pieces, and . . ."

Harvey, though, was smiling. Then he was laughing; laughing and sniffing at the same time, wiping the tears away. "I know, I know. Did you see that thing break?"

Relieved, Bern Horack said, "Even when Rafe was pitching regular, he never had better stuff in his life. Like it dropped off a fucking *table,*" then worried about that for a moment, but Harvey was still laughing. So was everyone else.

Les Durell said, "Why don't you and I take a little walk," looking up at Ford, this broad man with a boyish face but piercing eyes.

The others were heading toward a bar down the beach, and Ford yelled to Harvey that they'd be there soon, then said to Durell, "Let's go."

They walked for about a hundred yards in silence before Durell said, "You got me all the way down here. So talk."

"I remember you as being more cheerful. It was that much trouble to come?"

"Right; cheerful. I'm normally very cheerful—when I'm not being forced to act like a cop. You're forcing me. Not that I'm sorry I came. It was probably the nicest service I've ever been to; the only one where I've ever laughed, anyway. But I've been going to too many of them lately. That's how you can tell you've reached middle age, by the way: Your friends start dying."

"Rafe didn't just die."

"So I've heard."

"But you're not going to pay any attention to Harvey or me?"

"In this state, about two thousand people every year take the suicide cure for insomnia. How many times you think the loved ones go running to the police, saying it had to be murder because so-and-so wasn't the type? I'll pay attention when I hear something worth listening to."

"Just the facts, ma'am, huh?"

"That's right. I like facts. Numbers are easier to deal with than people. Law enforcement is tough enough without getting emotionally involved."

Ford said, "Okay, Les, I'll give you the facts. I have information that proves someone—probably one or more people in the Everglades County Sheriff's Department and the medical examiner's office—tampered with, suppressed, or ignored evidence in the investigation of Rafe's death. The information I have also strongly suggests that he was murdered."

"Yeah? So tell me."

"That's the catch. If I give you that information, I'll be confessing to a felony."

"That's just great; just goddamn great. You and Rafe were smuggling drugs together, weren't you?"

"I only saw Rafe twice since high school. I wasn't smuggling anything."

"Right, oh sure. Rafe with his big house and big cars, flying in and out of the country. You think I didn't know? Every morning I woke up, I expected to see his name in the paper, arrested by the feds. I was very damn glad he didn't live in my county. I hate arresting friends. I've done it."

"Which is a subtle warning to me."

"I didn't mean it to be subtle."

"I'll give you the information, but I'd like it to be in confidence."

"I can't promise that, M.D. I'm sorry."

"Then I'm going to tell you anyway."

Durell held up an open palm. "Before you do, let me give you another warning. More facts and figures. Every five hours or so, someone in Florida ends up on the business end of a knife or some cheap handgun and gets murdered. A couple thousand known murders a year, and a fourth of those never even come close to being solved. Never mind about the bodies we don't find that end up scattered across the 'Glades or shoved under some mangrove root someplace. Those poor bastards go into the books under missing persons. You've read how tough it is to pull off the perfect murder? Well, that's pure bullshit. A perfect murder happens every day in this state; every single day. And it's not because the law enforcement agencies aren't competent, or that cops don't work their butts off, or don't care."

"If you're trying to make a point—"

Durell stopped, turned, and looked at him. "The point is, your information better be very good. If it's not, you could confess to a felony and get absolutely nothing in return. Murder isn't that easy to prove, and murderers tend to make themselves real hard to find. Think it over before you tell me anything."

Ford had already thought it over. It took about ten minutes to give Durell the entire story. He spent most of that time describing how determined Rafe was to get his son back from the Masaguan kidnappers. The only thing he left out was what he'd found in the tree trunk. Durell's expression went from pained to suspicious to thoughtful. He was silent for a time, then said, "Tell me again why you thought it might not be Hollins. At first, I mean. You went too quick over that part."

"Just small things. The watch was on the left wrist, with suntan marks to match. There was identification in the wallet, but nothing current."

"So? Lots of left-handers wear their watches on their left wrist, and he'd spent so much time out of the country maybe he had no current I.D."

"I know, Les, I know. I was just trying to tell you step by step how my mind was working when I found him. The point is, if he was alive, he'd have gotten in touch with me by now."

Durell was quiet again, receding into the cop mind; big-shouldered man in a suit, out of place in the heat of a Florida beach. He said, "I come up with four or five different scenarios; reasons for you to make up a story like this. But none of them seem to fit what I know about you."

"It's because I'm telling the truth."

Durell was nodding, still thinking. "The jerks who run Everglades County, this little island kingdom, have been riding toward a fall for a long, long time. Maybe this is it. But why would they want a murder to go in the books as a suicide?"

"Bad publicity."

"It's possible, but I don't buy it."

"Rafe used to work for Sealife Development; put them down as employer when he bought his last house. I have a copy of the computer records back at my place."

"What'd Rafe do for them?"

Ford said, "I don't know; some kind of flying, probably. But one of the last things he said to me on the phone was that he had to meet some guys from Sandy Key. Maybe he had something on them and was trying to leverage it into cash. Or maybe he tried to sell them something and they decided to just take it."

"Some guys from Sandy Key?" Durell said. "That doesn't narrow it down much."

"Les, I worked on that body for twenty minutes and it seemed a hell of a lot longer. I tied the feet and hands so there would be no mistaking it for suicide. But they called it suicide anyway and, less than twenty-four hours later, cremated the body. Somebody is trying to cover up something."

Durell was nodding, thinking, saying "Okay, okay. . . ."

Ford said, "Then you're convinced?"

"I'm convinced you tampered with evidence and that DeArmand's bunch got a little too cute trying to smooth it over."

"Rafe was murdered and you know it."

"What I know is, there's almost zero chance of proving it now. But the governor's office might like to hear about DeArmand and the Everglades County Medical Examiner's office. Dereliction of duty, criminal negligence, failing to hold a body forty-eight hours. You drop the right bomb and sometimes all kind of creatures start crawling out. Even killers."

"I've collected some data on DeArmand. None of it is incriminating by itself, but, taken as a whole, it shows he's crooked and slippery . . . and dangerous. I've got stuff on Sealife Development Corporation, too. And the registration numbers from the boat I found on the island that day. I'll put it all in a letter and send it to your office."

Les Durell was looking at him, not reacting, a steady look of appraisal. "You know what I'm worried about? I'm worried about you. Some guy who thinks he's clever enough to bang around playing detective, manipulating people, making way too much noise. If DeArmand suspects someone is interested, he's going to cover his tracks so quick that even the governor's office won't be able to seal his records or get subpoenas out fast enough. And I don't want to spend a lot of time, do a lot of work, knowing someone is going to screw it all up making amateur mistakes."

Ford shrugged. "I guess you'll have to take it on faith that I won't."

"I take God and the Democratic Party on faith, not you. Within an hour of you calling me, I'd done computer checks through the Federal Crime Information Center, the FBI, and a couple of others. Missed my tee-off time, and you know what I got for my trouble? Almost nothing. Bare bones stuff. You did your military training at Naval Special Warfare Center in Coronado, California. So I take that to mean you were a navy SEAL. You got a couple of college degrees while in uniform, so I take that to mean the navy invested extra money in you for a reason. You scored real high on your Civil Service exam and left the navy for no apparent reason. And that's it, buddy boy. I've run checks on priests that gave me more."

"I've lived a quiet life."

Durell said, "You think if I hadn't figured out what kind of quiet life, I'd be wasting my time talking to you right now? I don't know why Sanibel Island attracts so many retired CIA agents. You guys have meetings, put on dances? And there's another thing."

"Oh?"

"Yeah. Maybe you didn't think of it, but if De-Armand's bunch *was* involved in the murder, they're going to be wondering who got to the body first and messed up their nice suicide. They're going to be wondering who called it in. They might even be looking for the guy."

Ford said, "I didn't work for the CIA."

"You're better off me thinking you did. Being an admitted felon and all."

"The next time we have a dance," Ford replied, "I'll make sure you and your wife are invited."

Ford stopped at the beach bar and had a beer with Harvey Hollins, Durell, and the rest of the guys, then left them there, old teammates hooting it up and replaying lost games. It was the way all funerals should end. Across the asphalt parking lot, his truck shimmered, saturated with midday sunlight; the door and steering wheel hot enough to cauterize flesh. He rolled down both windows and shifted to speed, his soaked shirt cooling in the wind off the road. He had Rafe's address book out. There were a couple of places Ford wanted to see.

The main street was Ocean View Drive, a slow business district four-lane: True Value Hardware, Burger King, Island Doctors Clinic, Cobb Cinema; everything built of concrete block, low to the ground. Sealife Development Corporation offices were just beyond, not quite to Sandy Key Mall, a one-story building behind a two-story façade: broad lawn, a fountain with American and Canadian flags, a parking lot dividing the main building from two model homes. DELUXE VALUE AT MIDDLE CLASS PRICE. Billboard signs with open-house banners. There was a car in the lot, so Ford pulled in and a salesman in one of the model homes told him the corporate office was closed, being Monday—Sunday was their big day—but if Ford wanted a deal on a house or condo, now was the time to buy. Was he interested?

Ford said he was—wishing there was some way to get inside the corporate building to see what kind of bric-a-brac the corporate elite used to decorate their offices.

The salesman wanted to know if he was interested in a beach condo. They had one or two new units, a very few used units. Or, if Ford wanted something a little higher priced, they'd just listed a split-level executive house on the seventh green of the country club. "Our Thomas Jefferson model," the salesman said. "Rarely available." Ford asked if he had a photo of the house—he'd be willing to follow him into the corporate build-ing, if the salesman wanted to unlock. The salesman said no, he might have one back in the files and, when he went to check, Ford lifted the Realtors Only listing book and glanced through it. In the few minutes the salesman was away, Ford counted more than a dozen Thomas Jefferson executive models for sale. Every other listing was a beach condo.

Real estate sales seemed a little stagnant on Sandy Key, and Ford wondered if Sealife Development was having financial trouble.

He tried a few more ploys to get into the main build-ing; none worked. If he wanted to check the office shelves for pre-Columbian art, he'd have to come an-other day.

Just off the main street, he found the Everglades County Sheriff's Department: three floors of brown stucco with mirrored windows and a chain-link lock-up out back where several white-and-green squad cars glit-tered in the sun. At the desk, he asked the stern woman in uniform and holster harness if Sheriff DeArmand was in. If he had been, Ford had already decided he would ask about employment. He wasn't.

What Ford was trying to do was get a feel for the place, a sense of the organization. He had fifteen single-spaced typed pages on Sealife Development back at his lab, but he wanted to flesh out the impression. He wanted a physical understanding of what he was up against. He bought a city map at a 7-Eleven and, using Rafe's address book, found DeArmand's home: a huge split-level version of the Thomas Jefferson executive model built on a sodded half-acre plot that butted up against a line of gray melaleuca trees that separated it from the golf course.

Ford slowed. Three cars in the drive: a new station wagon, a red Corvette, and a white, unmarked Ford squad car. DeArmand and wife seemed to be home. Ford considered stopping; thought about asking directions—"I'm looking for a Jefferson model on the seventh green"—but decided that was just a little too cute, too risky. He turned at the circular dead end, then headed back out to Ocean View. At a pay phone, he found the address for H. B. Hollins—it wasn't in Rafe's book—and drove to the other end of the island looking for 127 Del Prado Place: a white ranch house with two palm trees, an overgrown lawn, and a faded Honda Accord in the drive.

The bell didn't work, so he rapped on the door . . . waited . . . rapped again . . . waited . . . then followed the sound of thudding rock-n'-roll and the smell of chlorine to the screened pool behind the house.

The pool water was the color of lime Jell-O, and a

woman there lay on her back in a lounge chair, pale pink thread of bikini bottoms tracing the curve of her buttocks, pink bra top in a tiny heap beside the chair, heavy breasts taut in the heat beneath a viscous coating of oil, arms stretched behind her head to form a pillow, eyes closed.

Helen Burke Hollins, Rafe's ex-wife, was spending this quiet afternoon at home.

Ford had to speak loudly over the music. "Hello? HELLO?"

The woman stirred lazily, reached for the drink on the table even before opening her eyes, saying "Come on in, babe—you're way early."

Ford opened the screened door and stepped into the muted sunlight, replying "Rafe's funeral didn't last as long as I thought."

Focusing her eyes, she said, "What?" Then: "*Hey!*" as she snared the bikini top and pressed it against her breasts, saying "Who the hell invited you in, buddy?"

Ford said, "You did," trying to smile as if embarrassed, averting his eyes. "I didn't realize you were . . . not dressed. I'm really sorry, Helen. I had no idea."

She had the top on now, squirming to get herself placed just so, standing to face Ford. "Who the hell are you, anyway? How do you know my name?"

Ford was still smiling at her—the kindly stranger who had done a dumb thing. He started as if to answer, then said, "Man, Rafe was sure right. You sure are pretty," as if a little in awe. Which was a lie. Helen Hollins had mousy bleached-blond hair, a chubby little-girl face with thin pouty lips beneath the pink lip gloss, a bulb nose, and a thick layer of brown belly fat that rolled over the elastic of her bikini bottoms. From the way Rafe had talked, Ford had expected better. But the lie softened her; he could almost see the hostility drain from her face. She said, "You knew Rafe?"

"Yeah. We were friends back in high school, then we did some work together down in Masagua. I thought I'd stop and see if you needed anything. I thought you might be at the funeral."

"Not goddamn likely." She was back on the lounge chair again, sitting, taking a gulp from the tall glass and shaking a nearly empty pack of cigarettes. "You must not of talked to Rafe lately if you thought I'd be there. We didn't part on what you'd call the best of terms. The bastard."

Ford said, "Oh. I'm sorry. Rafe always spoke so highly of you. . . ."

"That's a laugh."

"Well . . . I didn't know. I hadn't seen him in more than two years, then I flew back into town just in time for another friend of ours to tell me about the funeral. It was quite a shock."

Exhaling smoke through her nose, using her thumb to flick at the filter of the cigarette, she said, "What did you say your name was?"

"Rafe used to call me Doc."

"And you worked with him down there in Central America? You know what he did?"

Ford said, "Same thing he did for Sealife Development, right?" Playing it coy, as if he knew the whole story.

That made her snort. "He sure as hell didn't make the kinda money he was making spraying mosquitoes for a bunch of spics."

"Different pay for different payloads, Helen."

"And that's what you do? You fly?"

"No. There's money to be made other ways down there."

She liked that, the inference that he had money; staring at him, her eyes moving from his thighs to his face in appraisal, she began to smile. "Rafe was the type to always pull out the high school yearbook, brag about the good old days. I remember your picture. The handsome one. Rafe used to mention your name. Told me all about the wild things you two did." She let that hang in the air for a moment before adding "He said the girls purely loved you two. Said *you* had something to offer."

Ford said, "Well, Rafe was always one to exaggerate."

In the long silence that followed, her eyes took on a sloe, sleepy look, never leaving Ford's eyes, and for the first time, Ford could feel more than see what Rafe had meant that morning on the phone.

That's what she does to guys. . . .

A bead of sweat fell from her nose to her chin, then down onto her left breast, and she wiped it away with a slow massaging motion of her right hand. Ford felt a stirring in his abdomen, and he watched her meaty thighs squeeze, then spread slightly as she said, "Hey, I'm not being much of a hostess. Let me get you a drink or something. Gin and tonic? A beer?"

"Tonic and ice would be fine."

She was standing, not bothering to adjust the suit now

even though a blood-pink half circle of areola peeked over the thin bikini bra. "You don't look like any Boy Scout to me. Maybe just a splash of gin? Or maybe something you don't put in a glass."

"No thanks. I've got a long drive ahead of me."

She had a high, girlish laugh. "Long, huh?" and was off across the deck, wide hips swinging on the pendulum of narrow back, thigh fat echoing the impact of bare feet on cement, sliding the glass doors open without closing them behind her.

Ford released his breath, then laughed softly at himself. *Loosen your belt, boy, and get some air to your brain.*

In his life, Ford had met four, maybe five women who had affected him in exactly the same way; women with that same quality of animal sexuality, a sexuality so strong that it bypassed the conscious fabric of awareness and struck some deep visceral chord. It had little to do with beauty. None of the ones Ford had known had been model material. They had been tall and gawky, lean and sharp, or ripe and doughy like this one, Helen Hollins.

Rafe had said, "She smells like she wants it."

From inside the house, the music changed from heavy metal to mainstream rock as the woman switched stations and lowered the volume, then called out, "Hey, you—Doc. Give me a hand in here."

Ford stepped through the Florida room into the refrigerated chill of air conditioning, his eyes trying to adjust to the darkness. Plush carpet, heavy drapes, the chemical smell of synthetic fiber mixed with the odor of soiled clothes thrown on the couch and coffee table. Suburban decor beneath a layer of dirt. Then she was standing before him with that same sleepy look in her eyes, a bottle of tonic water in her hand, but giving him all her attention. "Can't get the damn thing open."

Ford took the bottle, opened it with an easy twist of the wrist, trying to keep his eyes off her but not succeeding, and she said, "I know—am I cold or just glad to see you?" as she turned, brushing her hand across the front of his pants, and that quick she was in his arms, her mouth on his, stripping off the bikini top as if Ford just couldn't do things fast enough, her nipples sharp, hard projectiles against his shirt. She was whispering "God, laying out there in that sun, with all that oil on me, God, how I need it," but Ford was already pushing her away, holding her by the shoulders, his own sexual wanting replaced by a growing revulsion.

He said, "Rafe said something about a little boy. You sure you have time for this?" hoping that would jolt her out of the mood.

It didn't. "He's gone, babe. Just you and me in this great big house," and she was back in his arms, touching him, touching herself, mouth open . . . but then a banging sound came from outside, the sound of a car door shutting. "Oh, shit, it's Robert!" and she was hurrying to get back into her bikini top. "Hey . . . you—"

Ford interpreted the blank expression. "Doc."

"Yeah, Doc. Why don't you walk on out by the pool, have a seat. I was expecting this friend of mine, only—" She was walking toward the front door, glancing at the small gold watch on her wrist. "—only the shithead's early."

Ford took the bottle of tonic and strolled back to the pool. He could hear the muted conversation coming from inside, then the woman led a man out onto the deck: a tall man, early thirties, with a tennis player's body to match the tennis shorts and sports shirt. Neatly styled brown hair, glasses, bookish face, and a cold look of disinterest until Helen said, "Robert, Doc and Rafe used to work together down there in Central America."

"Oh? Doing what?"

From the screened pool door he was about to open, Ford could see a blue Porsche in the drive. The judge who had railroaded Rafe had driven a Porsche; Judge Robert Alden, if his computer printouts were correct, a sizable stockholder in Sealife Development. Ford decided to take a chance. He said, "We were in the antique business," and got just the forced nonreaction he was hoping for.

"Ah, well . . . that must be exciting." Suspicious, but not willing to pursue it.

Ford said, "Depends on who you deal with," and stepped out into full sunlight as Helen took his arm, saying "Hey, wait—I'll walk you out."

At his truck, she glanced back at the pool, then held her mouth up to be kissed, but Ford touched his finger to her lips. "You'd better save some of that for later." Which she misinterpreted, winking. "The guy's kind of a dud in the sack, so give us an hour or so to talk, huh? We've got some business. Then come back and the two of us can get some real exercise."

Ford shut his door, started the truck, and smiled. "Don't bet your firstborn on it, lady."

He was being followed.

The white car had come out of nowhere; must have been doing over a hundred, then slowed when it got on his truck's rear bumper. Looking in his rearview mirror, Ford recognized the white unmarked squad car and knew that the driver must be Sheriff Mario DeArmand. Image of a big, swarthy face, no hat . . . carrying a passenger with him, too; a man, but Ford couldn't make out the features.

Judge Alden must have gone straight to the phone.

Ford assembled a plausible story in his mind, expecting to be stopped.

But DeArmand didn't stop him; just followed half a car length off his bumper, giving him a message, then slowed and turned away as Ford crossed the county line.

Late that afternoon, Ford worked in his lab, finishing up the order for Minneapolis Public Schools, hoping the phone would ring. Once he had looked upon phones as little plastic invasions of privacy just waiting for an opportunity. Now he seemed chained to the damn thing.

When he finished injecting the last shark, he laid them all out in a row on the stainless-steel table, savoring his handiwork. Like a carpenter reveling in his tongue-in-grooves, he felt kind of proud. He put the unpackaged specimens in laminated barrier bags, added formalin, sealed the bags, and boxed the whole lot. Then he typed out an invoice—Sanibel Biological Supply's first—and taped everything nice and neat, ready for mailing.

It was after dark by the time he finished, and he decided to try Henry S. Melinski, the investigative reporter. It was possible—maybe probable—that Durell could get the governor's office interested in the malfeasance of Everglades County officials on his own. But Ford knew that while political appointees sometimes acted out of a sense of the righteous, they acted faster when publicity and righteousness were combined.

Melinski wasn't at the paper, so Ford tried the home number again. This time, Melinski answered. He sounded bored; real bored and hard to impress. Yeah, he knew about the suicide on Tequesta Bank, so what? Sure, it was murder—this guy Hollins murdered himself, right? Not joking, but not serious either; a man who had to deal with a lot of cranks on the phone.

Ford said, "An anonymous caller told the police where to find the body. I was the anonymous caller."

Which knocked some of the boredom from his voice, but Melinski still wasn't impressed. So Ford told him that what he saw on the island and what the Everglades County Sheriff's Department concluded didn't match up, and now he was pretty sure the governor's office, probably the Florida Department of Criminal Law Enforcement, was going to investigate. Melinski said, "Pretty sure they're going to investigate? To me that means you probably had a couple of martinis, decided to call Tallahassee so you could act like a big shot, and the secretary you reached at CLE was polite. What's this pretty sure bullshit? You're wasting my time, mister."

"Major Les Durell didn't think I was wasting his time. He's the one who's going to contact the governor's office."

There were a couple of beats of silence. "Durell's in on this?" Impressed, but not wanting to show it.

"You'd better ask him. Or you could wait for him to call you."

"That'll be the day. When it comes to giving information, that guy's so tight you couldn't yank a pin out of his ass with a Land Rover. The question is, if Durell's involved, why do you want to let me in?"

"Because Rafe Hollins was a friend of mine."

"So what? Friends send flowers. They don't call reporters."

"The governor's office investigates criminal matters, not civil. And Hollins got a raw deal the whole way around. The judge who presided at Hollins's divorce hearing is having an affair with Hollins's ex-wife. Judge Robert Alden. It may have started before the hearing, I don't know. She's a drunk and a drug user, but she got full custody of their son. Plus all the money. Hollins kidnapped his son after an eyewitness described to him how this judge hit the boy and bloodied his nose. The boy, by the way, is eight years old. The eyewitness called the police, and I'll give you one guess how that went."

"I don't need to guess. I know some of those wormy bastards on Sandy Key. They stick together . . . which is why we never hear about it when one of them slips up."

"They slipped this time. Like the way they handled Hollins's autopsy and cremation. Plus what I saw on the island."

"What did you see on the island?"

"I can't tell you. Major Durell said if the people involved suspected they were under investigation, the case would be ruined. I was sort of hoping you'd just concentrate on the way Rafe was railroaded in the divorce. When that boy's found, they sure as hell shouldn't give him back to his mother."

"Do you remember who you're talking to? I'm the reporter you called. You can trust me."

"Durell said specifically not to trust any reporters with the information. He said they'd print it way too soon, blow the whole thing—"

"Listen, buddy, I don't need some mystery voice or some Eagle Scout cop to tell me how to do my job. I've held more stories and hung more corrupt assholes— Hey, Durell didn't mention me specifically, did he?"

"Well, your name came up."

"That son of a—"

"He said he didn't want you looking over his shoulder."

"His *shoulder*? Well, it's a little bit late for that, chum. Let me tell you what I think. I think you and Durell are involved in a conspiracy to withhold state's evidence. There's a Sunshine Law in Florida, sport. Everything, and I mean *everything*, is public record. So you can tell me now, or I can hear it when you're on the witness stand, sweating out a felony charge."

"You don't know who I am."

"*Shit*. By tomorrow afternoon I'll know your shoe size."

"You can't trace this call—"

"Durell will tell me, Einstein. You think he's going

to deny it after all I already know? He's tight, but he's not dumb."

"Hey, look, I don't want to get in any trouble. I just want to help Rafe. But if you're not interested in the way he was railroaded—"

"Do you have ears? Can't you hear? I'm interested, for Christ's sake. The corrupt judge, the druggie ex-wife, the father who wanted to protect his son so much that he was driven to kidnapping. Shit, it's great. But I want it all. And I want it all now."

Ford was leaning back in his office chair, feeling sneaky—and not pleased with the feeling—but he really had no damn choice. Crosby, Stills, Nash, and Young were on the stereo doing "Wooden Ships," nice and soft. Ford started wagging his feet in time with the music, saying "Well, if you really think I should . . ."

Within minutes of hanging up, Ford's phone rang. It was Les Durell. Ford said hello, then said, "Les . . . Les . . . Les . . . Les, let me have a chance to explain—" Then he gave up and just listened for a while, then he said, "Les . . . I hope you don't have a blood pressure problem—" Then he listened some more.

Durell said, "I thought it was understood you wouldn't tell anyone else, damn it! Now I'm going to have that— that vulture on my ass! What I ought to do is just wash my hands of the whole business."

Ford said, "Take a breath, Les. Take a big breath. Even you need to breathe."

"I just can't believe you told Melinski. Just the damn stupidity of it!"

"The power of the press, Les. If Melinski's good, he can expose things the law can't touch and he can print evidence the courts would never entertain—"

"He could blow the whole damn thing by writing too soon!"

"He was your choice. You recommended him. I got his name from you, remember?"

"Like choosing my own poison. I don't like being tricked, Ford!"

"You weren't tricked. I don't work for you, Les. I'm a private citizen who can do what he damn well pleases. What pleases me is making sure the people who set up Rafe get squeezed and squeezed hard—"

"And I don't like being cornered! You know damn well I've got no choice but to follow this thing through now. Melinski knows all the terms: suppression of evidence, dereliction of duty, failing to arrest a confessed felon—*you*. If I don't find a way to hang DeArmand and his crew, that reporter asshole is going to spread my nuts above the fold right there on page one. You knew that. That's why you did it. At least have the decency to admit it."

"Okay. I admit it."

Durell groaned. "He's going to be goosing me along, second-guessing me every step of the way—"

"Do you really think he's dumb enough to print too soon?"

"That's not the point—"

"Come on, Les. Do you think there's a chance he'll break the story before you're ready?"

Durell was silent for a moment. Then he said, "No.

He's a pain in the butt, but he's good. God, do I hate to admit that."

"Then you really don't have anything to worry about—if you do your job. Besides, all you have to do is collect enough evidence to convince the governor's people they should get involved. That shouldn't be too hard."

"Ford, do you have any idea how lucky you are you're talking to me on the phone and not face to face? I mean it. Do you have any idea?"

"I truthfully do, Les. I believe you'd take swing at me if you could."

"I'm going to do a lot more than that if this business somehow turns sour. If I get hurt in any way, I'm going to drag you right down with me."

"My word against yours, Les. But yeah, you could make it unpleasant for me. That's why I chose the smartest cop around."

"Christ, flattery no less! The worst that can happen to me is I lose my job. But you, you'll go to prison. You can count on it."

"I'd prefer not to go to prison, Les. Don't let me down."

Buck Bernstein sounded tired; sounded too weary to be mean. Even over the bad trans-Caribbean connection, Ford could hear the rumble of passing trucks and muted sirens. Things were getting wild in Masagua.

"Balserio's dead, man. You hear? Standing outside the palace with about ten of his Elite Guard and a bomb went off. In his briefcase. You've never seen such a mess

in your life. They still haven't found all the dude's med-
als. Some of them probably still up there in the air,
haven't hit the ground yet."

"You know who did it?"

"Nope, not officially. Between you and me, though,
we think it was his own people. His two top generals
have already taken control; declared martial law, got soldiers and tanks everywhere. Our people are sort of sitting back, waiting to see which of the generals we should
sit down and deal with. Meantime, the guerrillas are out
there like a bunch of jackals, all of them plannin' the
best moment to sneak in and try to steal the prize."

"And you've got elections coming up in the fall."

"Shit, don't even mention that. Things crazy enough
down here."

"What about the boy, Buck? The eight-year-old, Jake
Hollins?"

"You expect miracles; you think I've had time to
track the kid down, all the stuff going on now?"

"You didn't find out anything?"

"Give me a break, man. I got it maybe narrowed
down a little. And you expect any more with me sittin'
in the middle of a fucking war zone, you're crazy. What
I did was try to find out who was dealing with the kid's
dad. Figure whoever was dealing with the kid's dad
probably took the kid. That make sense?"

"It's a place to start anyway."

"Two places to start, man. He was flying for two
groups. This guy, this dead friend of yours, he about six-
three, two forty; a big guy with brown hair and one of
those dented chins?"

"Yeah, that sounds like him."

"Good. Didn't call himself Hollins. Called himself Rafferty; had a couple different passports, which is par for the course. Did some flying for your buddy Juan Rivera, the commie you got all the baseball equipment for. Hey, Ford, you really give them uniforms that said 'Masaguan People's Army' on the front? In Dodger blue?"

"That's what Rivera asked for, that's what he got."

"Then it's no damn wonder they give me your job, tell you to get your ass out and not come back for two years. Giving shit to the fucking communists."

"What was Hollins flying for Rivera? It could be important."

"Just guns far as I can tell. And he didn't do much of that. Rivera's been around for quite a while. Likes to use his own people. Maybe some drugs, too, but that's not Rivera's style."

"He said it wasn't drugs."

"If I was a friend of yours I'd lie, too. Knowing what a sneaky shit you are."

"Who else was he flying for?"

"Probably Julio Zacul, that bad man. When that bomb killed Balserio, I figured right off it was Zacul. Sendero Luminoso, those maniacs. Shining Path. They moving up from South America faster than killer bees."

Ford said, "I know."

"Just the way Zacul'd do things, though. He likes to leave a real mess. Put all the women and children from a whole village in a church, lock the doors, and set it on fire. That's the kind of thing make him smile. But how would he get the bomb into Balserio's briefcase? No way. Had to be an insider. My sources tell me your buddy was flying in guns for Zacul. Small weaponry, grenades, shit like that. Nothing real big, and just occasional, so he wasn't high priority. Another couple of months of it, though, and the FBI woulda nailed him anyway."

"That's all he flew for Zacul? Just guns?"

"None of them carry just guns, you know that. They fly in with guns. They fly out with a money crop."

"What was the money crop?"

"Maybe drugs. But maybe something else, too. Zacul's got a thing for artifacts. You know, Mayan stuff. Carved heads, stone calendars, shit like that. Those things sell for big bucks up in the States. Zacul's always been into that. That's what my source tells me, anyway. Has his own private collection hidden out there in the jungle, and sells off the stuff he doesn't want. Has his men do the excavating. Zacul likes to use it to help play the crowd."

"What?"

"You know, when someone's around who can help him. He plays the Mayan Indian bit trying to take back his land of his ancestors. Shit, the guy's from Peru, pure Castilian far as we can find out. Not a drop of Indian blood in his body. But the act still gets him a lot of supporters up there in liberal land. Movie-actor types, like to have their pictures taken with outlaws. They put on benefits, send U.S. dollars. Makes them feel real caring, politically aware. The dumb asses."

"I don't suppose you could give me the name of the source."

"You suppose right. Not until I get the negatives from those photos, anyway."

"Did your source tell you where Zacul and his men are camped?"

"Up in the mountains, just like your buddy Juan Rivera. Where all those bastards hide out. That's who you figure has the kid? Zacul?"

Ford said, "It seems to fit with the story the boy's father gave me."

"Then I'd write him off as dead. Zacul doesn't like you gringos, even the young ones, and he's about as crazy mean as they come."

"I still want you to try and find him."

"*Me?* I got all the information I could, damn it. Don't play these bullshit games with me. I'm gonna have a war to deal with here in a few months or one real nasty election, and I don't have time to run around looking for some kid who's probably already dead. You're gonna have to come down here and get him yourself."

"I'm not allowed to return to Masagua for another year, Buck. You'd have me arrested at the airport."

"What kind of asshole do you take me for?"

"You don't really want an answer to that, do you?"

"I want those negatives, Ford."

"Then find the boy, Buck."

ELEVEN

Ford went outside, into the darkness, down the steps to the dock that sided the shark pen. He had two boats, the eighteen-foot flats skiff and an old twenty-four-foot flat-bottomed trawl boat that he used for dragging up tunicates, seahorses, small fish, and other specimens. He had felt tradition-bound to name each of the boats, but had come up with nothing that didn't sound cutesy or egocentric. He considered *Beagle II* for the trawl boat; maybe *W. H. Wood* for the skiff, in honor of the man who landed history's first tarpon. But when the guy came to paint the names, neither name seemed right, so he had had *Sanibel Biological Supply* stenciled on the sterns of each, and left it at that.

With its nets and outriggers folded above, the trawl boat looked like some huge, gloomy pterodactyl as it swung experimentally on its lines in the calm night, bow tied to the dock, its stern anchored off. Ford checked the lines of the trawl boat, then stepped into his skiff, touched the trim button, and lowered the engine. He idled across the bay toward the dim shape of Tomlinson's sailboat in the distance.

Dinkin's Bay was a backwater, far off the course of normal boating traffic, so Tomlinson showed no anchorage light atop the mast, but his cabin light was on. There was music, too; weird discordant notes of a wooden flute curling out of the cabin, floating over the dark water like mist. As Ford drew closer, though, the music stopped and the silhouette of Tomlinson, wearing only shorts, appeared on the cockpit.

"Hello the boat!"

"Hey . . . Doc, that you? Hey, this is great. Come on aboard." It was beer time anyway, Tomlinson said, and it was real nice getting company for a change, almost like Christmas sort of, and he'd just finished playing along with Shuso, playing the Japanese bamboo flute.

"Shuso?" Ford had followed Tomlinson down into the cabin of the sailboat and took a seat on the settee berth. There were neat rows of books, brass gauges on the bulkhead, and the cabin smelled of damp wood and coffee and diesel fuel.

Tomlinson rummaged through the ice locker, found two bottles of Steinlager, then slid in behind the dinette table. "The Zen Buddhist, Shuso. You never heard of him?" Like he might have been talking about Boston leftfielder Mike Greenwell or Brian Wilson. "Started his own Zen sect. Uses the traditional *hotchiku*, a plain bamboo flute, to express the true feeling of Zen, like haiku; you know, poetry."

"Ah," said Ford. "That Shuso."

"Right. Trouble is, Shuso never found a suitable student to carry on his form of Zen. No one willing to dedicate their life to the *hotchiku*. It's been pretty sad. Makes him kind of a tragic figure, really." He handed Ford the flute he had been playing—a long unvarnished length of bamboo with twelve neatly awled holes. "Figure I might take a little trip to Japan, maybe in the fall, pop in on this great man and surprise him. Let him know I'm on the trail; see if we have something karmic going. I have a feeling I'm just the guy he's looking for. Shuso's getting pretty old. He could kick off at any minute, you know."

Ford tasted his beer; really good beer, from New Zealand. "No, I didn't know. But it's kind of coincidental you should mention travel—"

"No offense, Doc, but I don't happen to believe in coincidence." Tomlinson had accepted the flute back and was touching the holes dreamily, playing it in his mind. "Everything that has happened, everything that will happen, it all exists in this single moment, endlessly surfacing and submerging; natural order, perfect law. The word coincidence is an invention that defines our own confusion better than it describes a unique occurrence."

"Oh," said Ford. He believed in coincidence and he believed in confusion; had had too much experience with each not to believe, but he hadn't come to argue philosophy. "Well, anyway, traveling, that's what I came to talk about. The son of a friend of mine is in trouble. Down in Central America; Masagua. He's been kidnapped by smugglers, probably revolutionary guerrillas, a group called the Shining Path. I'm leaving tomorrow to try and get him out."

Tomlinson looked at him for a moment. "You're not joking about this, are you?"

Ford said, "Nope."

"Sounds dangerous, man. The Shining Path, I've read about those people. But I thought they were in Peru."

"Peru, then Colombia, now putting down roots in Central America. My friend is dead and there's no one else to help his son, so I feel like it's sort of an obligation. The kid's only eight years old."

"Right! For sure, man; you gotta do it. The grand gesture: one brave man walking into the Valley of the Shadow—hell, no other choice for a moraled human. Fuckin' A." Tomlinson finished his beer, then hurried to the ice locker to get another, ducking beneath the low bulkhead. "You're probably going to be killed, huh?"

Ford said, "If I thought that, I wouldn't go."

"All by yourself, trying to steal a little boy away from a bunch of zapped-out Maoists who'd boil babies just for a change in menu."

"You're not making this any easier, Tomlinson."

"Huh? What? How do you mean."

"My friend called me just before he died to ask me to help get his son out. He said he needed at least two men to make it work. He was right. To free the boy, it's going to take at least two guys. To make some kind of exchange, or set up some kind of diversion. I won't know how to work it until I get there."

Tomlinson said, "Yeah?"

Impatiently Ford said, "So?"

Finally the light dawned. "Me? You're asking me to go?"

"Yes," said Ford. "I am. You said you're interested in the Mayan culture, well, this trip should take you right through the heart of it."

"Goddamn, I'm flattered. I really am!" Tomlinson was beaming. "This is the first time anyone's ever trusted me to do something important!"

Ford didn't like the sound of that, but he said, "It may be dangerous."

"For a little kidnapped kid? Hell, I don't care."

"Illegal, too. I don't want anyone to know we're in the country, so that means sneaking in. Usually it can be done with a bribe, but if we get the wrong official it could be trouble. I just want you to know what you're getting yourself into."

"Trouble? You call that trouble?" Tomlinson's head was bobbing up and down, excited. "Misplaced papers, bad I. D.'s, sitting in tiny rooms while guys in uniforms rant and rave about insufficient data—that's been my fucking *life*, man. That's no trouble. It's like old home week to me."

"Just so long as you know—"

"I wouldn't miss it! Don't you see all the little karmic links? Me looking at those sharks of yours, asking one dumb question, but exactly the right question. Getting interested in Mayan history, doing all this research. It's like Lachesis and Clotho drew us a personal road map to the future; Kismet City, man."

Ford didn't know who Lachesis and Clotho were and wasn't about to ask. Tomlinson said, "You are officially absolved of any responsibility, as of this moment. No shit." Said like a holy proclamation.

"You're certain?"

Tomlinson crossed his heart. "Scout's honor. When do we leave?"

Ford hadn't even made the reservations yet. "Tomorrow; I'm not sure what time. I'll call and find out tonight, then stop over in the morning. We might be gone for a while; keep that in mind. Maybe a week, maybe three."

"Hell, three weeks or three months, I still only got two pairs of pants."

That was good. Ford liked traveling with people who packed light.

He left Tomlinson's, jumping his skiff to plane, and ran through the darkness across the flats, picking up the canted wooden posts marking the channel that funneled to the mouth of the bay. Pelicans and cormorants flushed in mass off the rookery islands as Ford slid past, gray shapes ascending through the light of a waxing moon. Jessica's house seemed even smaller in darkness, its windows aglow within the shadows of the casuarina pines, and Ford could hear music coming through the screened door as he tied off his skiff. People singing in Italian, a tenor crying to a lofty soprano; some kind of opera.

"Anybody home?" Ford could see Jessica working in the next room. Concentrating before the easel, chewing at the end of her brush, she wore jeans and dark blue T-shirt, hair woven in a tight braid down to the middle of her back. "HELLO?"

She started, turned and focused, then smiled. "Hey, get in here. I'm pissed at you," talking as if she were kidding, but with an edge to her voice, as she found the stereo and turned down the music, then came and gave Ford a strong hug but no kiss. "You could have at least stopped this afternoon and said hello. Or asked me to go out collecting with you."

Ford said, "I thought you would be packing."

"Right. I throw a few things into a bag, and I'm packed. A New York auction doesn't require a fashion statement. And I'm only going to be gone a few days." She took his hand and pressed it against her cheek, then let it fall as if sensing his mood. "Hey, what's going on here, Ford? You mad about something?"

Ford followed her across the room as she motioned for him to join her, saying "I came to say good-bye" as they sat on the couch.

"I wish I didn't have to go."

"Me, too. I'm leaving for Masagua tomorrow. I'm going to try and get my friend's son back."

She said, "Oh," not liking the sound of it, and began to pick at the paint that stained her fingers, not looking at him. "Why do you have to do it? Why can't you just call the police and let them take care of it?"

"We already talked about that."

"I don't want you getting involved in all this. I was hoping you were upset about what happened Saturday night."

"About us being together? Why would I be upset about that?"

"Not us." She turned, studying his eyes. "I mean you and the woman who stayed with you. The blond woman. After you left me."

That was a surprise, and Ford didn't try to hide it. "News travels fast around this bay."

Jessica said, "No, I was out for a ride on my bike yesterday morning and saw her leaving. Very pretty, Ford. I hoped that's why you felt bad." When Ford did not respond, she asked: "Do you?"

"No."

"Would you have told me?"

"Not unless you asked."

"Are you in love with her?"

"No."

She said, "Oh. Well, I guess we didn't make any commitments, did we." Getting icier and icier.

"No, we didn't."

"I don't want to be a bitch about this, Ford. I'm no priss. But it hurt. I thought Saturday was special." She had been sitting close to him, her shoulder touching his, but now she moved it away.

"It was very nice."

Jessica said, "Well, at least we've always been honest with each other."

And Ford said quickly, "Have we?" holding her eyes until she finally looked away.

She said, "I don't think this is a good night for either one of us. Maybe we should talk about it when we get back."

Ford said, "Just one question: That marketing firm you worked for in New York—are you still associated with those people?"

In a small voice, she said, "No."

"But your friend Benny is, isn't he? Benjamin Rouchard; one of the stockholders."

"You checked up on me, too, huh? Did I pass? Or is this just midterm?"

Ford didn't react to the anger in that. "I came out to tell you it's a bad time to be involved with them, that's all. I'm not prying. I don't want you to get hurt."

She was quiet for a moment, as if allowing the anger to fade. "I'd rather not go into something when neither of us has a lot of time. It would be one thing if you could stay the night—" Throwing that out like an invitation. When Ford made no move to accept, she added, "But you won't, will you?"

Ford said. "I haven't even made reservations yet. And I have to pack."

"Then I'll walk you to your boat," as if calling his bluff, and Ford followed her out of the house. But at the dock she stopped him once more. "Doc?"

"Yeah, Jess?"

"Doc. . . ." She held the end of her braided hair in one hand, fidgeting with it, not looking at him. "Doc, why do you come out here? Why did you like seeing me— before Saturday night, I mean?"

"Companionship, I guess. We have fun together."

"I know, but what else?"

Ford thought for a moment and then tried to answer as honestly as he could. "I like the way you look; I like the way your mind works. I like coming into your house at night when you're playing classical music, and you have candles burning. It's nice."

She smiled slightly, still not looking at him. "Doc, when we were together I almost told you that I was falling in love with you."

Ford waited, saying nothing, then touched his finger to her chin, tilting her head. He kissed her gently, held her in his arms for a moment, then stepped onto his skiff, immediately disturbed by the sense of relief he felt, the feeling of freedom that small distancing created in him: her on the dock, him behind the wheel, already touching the key. He said, "Be careful in New York, Jessi."

Ford and Tomlinson caught a commuter flight from Fort Myers to Miami, then flew LACSA into San José, the course taking them in just close enough to the Mosquito Coast so that Ford could see the dark haze of what was probably the eastern shore of Masagua. His cheek against the cool Plexiglas window, Ford played the child's game of wishing he had superpowers, X-ray vision, so he could peer through the miles and find a frightened little boy . . . and Pilar Balserio, too.

Then they were dropping down through the clouds to see this great glittering city surrounded by mountains; a city that, from fifteen thousand feet, looked a little bit like Atlanta, but without the Yuppie housing. Ford began to pick out the familiar landmarks of San José: the National Theatre, the lines of cars on Calle Central, all the nice parks looking cool and green in the clear mountain air. Then the plane jolted, tires screeched, and, to the roar of reverse thrust, the hundred or so people aboard, most of them slightly tipsy with all the complimentary wine, settled a little as their sphincter muscles relaxed, the cheerful mood of traveling replaced by the communal awareness of survival, and they applauded the good landing.

"I didn't expect this, man, no way." Tomlinson was looking out the window at the city, a little wide-eyed. "I thought it would be like a grass runway. You know, with cows and stuff running to get the hell out of the way of the plane." It was one of the few observations Tomlinson had made during the entire two hours, which was a relief to Ford. No chattering, and that was good, too.

"Plenty of grass runways around. We may see a couple before we're done."

"Far out. I'm for it."

Then they were off the plane, each with his carry-on bag, their only pieces of luggage: Tomlinson looking taller in his faded jeans and T-shirt, a canvas backpack swung over one shoulder, standing in line with all the shorter Costa Ricans. Ford had ticketed them under the names of Johnson and Smith. Then, on a different airline, had booked himself into Guatemala City two days later and under his own name: a flight he would not take, but that might fool someone watching the reservation list. Bernstein, for instance. He had arranged for Jeth and MacKinley to share the responsibility of feeding his animals, and mailed the data search materials to Les Durell and Henry Melinski. Into each envelope, he had added a typed, unsigned note that read:

I believe that a person or persons with the Everglades County Sheriff's Department, working with members of Sealife Development, have been involved in a smuggling operation. In this operation, munitions and weaponry obtained through the auspices of the Sheriff's Department are being sold for cash or traded for valuable pre-Columbian artifacts to a guerrilla army in Masagua, Central America.

At the immigration desk, Ford presented a bogus passport, Tomlinson his real passport. Both were passed without question.

Outside the terminal, the air was cool; bruised clouds shrouded the volcanic mountains: rainy season in Central America. Tomlinson said it felt like Colorado, only no SAVE ASPEN, SKI VAIL bumper stickers and no BMWs. "Really weird, man." They took a cab to a garage on the west side of San José where Ford rented a Toyota Land Cruiser, then drove into the heart of the city, through the wild fast traffic on Calle Central, past the modern skyscrapers and neat *tiendas*. The sidewalks were crowded— crowded with pretty secretaries and with men who looked like they'd just come in from herding cattle, with school kids in clean uniforms; everyone rushing, but smiling, too. On street corners were fruit carts, the smell of sliced mangoes and pineapples mixing with mountain air and the bakery smell of San José in the late afternoon.

"Great," Tomlinson kept saying. "I love it." Looking out the car window, really enjoying it.

They got two rooms at a small hotel downtown, the Balmoral, and just as Ford was about to get in the shower, Tomlinson knocked on the door and poked his head in. "What we do now, boss?"

Ford said. "We get some sleep. Tomorrow morning we head out early, north to Masagua."

"Do you have a plan yet?"

"I wish I did, but I don't. Sorry."

Tomlinson stepped into the room, slouched into a chair. "Just gonna kind of wait for things to happen. That's cool. But you said something about an exchange, right?"

"Yeah, it's one possibility. The boy's father took something from the guerrillas. They want it back. Maybe we can work out a trade."

"You have what the kid's father took?"

Ford threw his backpack onto the bed and took out the small cloth bag, scattering the emeralds and jade carvings onto the bedspread. "I hope this is what he took."

Tomlinson whistled softly. "Man, these things are *beautiful.*" Holding the small green owl, then the parrot under the light, touching the stones to his cheek, appreciating the smoothness as a child might. "And these are emeralds, right? They gotta be." He was peering into one, as if gazing into a microscope. "These things gotta be worth a fortune. I've never seen stones as big as—" But then he stopped talking as his eyes widened, a light going on. "Hey! Like the story I was telling you about the Kache and the Tlaxclen—the stone star chart that used emeralds to mark the constellations. These dudes could have found it!"

Ford was nodding. "Let's hope so."

"*Why?*"

"Because it tells me where they probably are: the lake, remember? On the Pacific Coast."

"Right. Hey, maybe they found some of the other stuff, too; pieces of the temple. Man, no wonder they want this stuff back."

Ford said, "That's what we're counting on. See, once we locate the guerrilla group, I figure our best bet is to stay in the nearest town and send a messenger into the hills. Tell them they can have the artifacts if they bring us the boy. Do everything right out in the open, in view of the public. That would provide the only safety factor we're going to get."

"Sounds simple enough."

"Yeah, but what if the boy's already dead? They're going to want the stuff anyway, and they're going to come looking for us."

"Oh yeah, right."

"Or what if they take a look at what we have and tell us it's not all there? Maybe they expected more."

"More? Your friend had other stuff, too?"

Ford sat looking at Tomlinson, wondering if he should tell him everything he knew, everything he suspected. The computer check had said he was clean, but Ford decided not to risk it, to keep things compartmentalized for now. Besides, wasn't it possible that Sally Field, the friendly D.C. secretary, had been asked to help set him up? It wasn't the first time Ford had considered that possibility. With her, work always came first—she'd said as much more than once.

Christ, now you're becoming paranoid.

Ford said, "I don't know, Tomlinson. We're just going to have to take it as it comes. Remember: We've got karma on our side," smiling, trying to humor him.

Tomlinson said, "Right. *Right.*"

Ford read until 10 P.M. He'd heard Tomlinson go out just after nine and now he rose, slipped the latch on the door, and found Tomlinson's backpack beneath the bed. He went through it carefully, but all he found of interest was a passport that showed the man had traveled in Europe and Japan. There were no entry stamps from South America or Central America, but that meant nothing. The passport could have been faked, or he could have a second or a third passport back on his boat. Or in a safety deposit box in Boston. Or D.C. Duplicates were easy enough to get.

Ford returned to his own room, changed into fresh cotton slacks and a blue chambray shirt, then left his room key with the desk clerk.

He had a ten-thirty appointment with Rigaberto Herrera, a former CIA operative and longtime friend, at a bar called the Garden of Eden. He'd made the appointment from Florida the night before, giving Rigaberto a list of things he would need. They had spoken again by phone after Ford's arrival.

The Garden of Eden was a big white aristocratic house—gables, verandas, and wrought-iron fences—

built on its own grounds at a time when San José was still a small colonial town. The city had grown up around it. The house had been converted into a garden restaurant with a dance floor inside and a funky little bar, but mostly it was a whorehouse, the classiest in San José. One of the names Ford had found in Rafe Hollins's address book was Wendy Stafford. According to Bernstein, Stafford now worked at the Garden of Eden—which didn't surprise Ford. He had known the woman years ago. They'd slept together a couple of times, back when she was a Peace Corps volunteer, a rich American girl with an itch to help the less fortunate, ripe with guilt and eager to make restitution, but who somehow seemed destined to be swallowed up by the very darkness from which she wished to wrest others. Ford had met many Wendy Staffords in his travels: American princesses who sought out the jungle on a lark, but who soon found themselves entangled beyond any hope of escaping.

He walked past the American Embassy where he had worked for a short time, up the *calle*, through the little park, and there was the house, the Garden of Eden, with pale lights in the windows and trees throwing shadows. The doorman nodded at him, then he was inside, feeling the eyes of the women on him. Costa Rica produced some of the most beautiful women in the world, and the Garden of Eden offered the most beautiful women in Costa Rica: girls in their late teens and early twenties with long black hair and dark, dark eyes; girls who, back in the States, would be film actresses or models, but here were dressed in bright dresses or tight jeans and blouses, working their way out of poverty and enjoying it, judging by the smiles on their faces. But Ford had always been skeptical of those smiles. During the six months he worked in San José, he had become friendly with a couple of the girls. Though he sometimes paid them, he never slept with them—not that it would have been an indignity to him. He had slept with women of far lower moral fabric who were of supposedly much higher social stature—women who were whores by nature, not by occupation. He had never slept with a girl from the Garden because, Ford told himself, he didn't want to add to the desperation that he guessed was the framework of those smiles. Pure egotism on his part, as if he could make some slight difference.

It was Tuesday night, a slow night, and most of the tables were empty. The three-piece jazz band played "Satin Doll" while, overhead, ceiling fans stirred the tumid air. Several of the girls at the bar tried to catch his eye, clinking the ice in their glasses. Another girl stood alone on the dance floor, a particularly striking brunette, swaying softly to the music. She smiled at Ford, a sleepy smile, and beckoned with an index finger, wanting him to join her. He shook his head slightly, then walked across the room to the veranda, and there was Rigaberto, a five-foot six-inch hulk in sports jacket and tie, sitting beneath a tree at a white wrought-iron table.

"Am I late?" Smiling at his old friend, then joking about his weight and the gray in his black hair and mustache, joking about him sitting alone in a house full of women.

"You are laughing, but my wife was not laughing

when I told her I was coming to this place. Out in the jungle, out with the guerrillas, that would be all right. But not a whorehouse. She fears more for my morals than my life. Would you like something? A beer, perhaps."

The waitress brought Ford a Tropical, good Costa Rican beer in a dark bottle, and Ford said in Spanish, "Is the woman here? I did not see her when I came in." Liking the dignified tone his formal construction of the language added.

Herrera had already checked. "She's working tables out in the garden. As a waitress. It is something that the older girls do. They do not stay so busy with men."

"Did she recognize you?"

"Why would she recognize me? It was you she knew. But I am not so sure you will recognize her. To such a woman, the years are not kind. Would it matter so much if she saw me?"

Ford said, "No. I just don't want to frighten her. It is important that I speak with her."

"Concerning the little boy you seek?"

"Yes. Several years ago the boy's father was in Costa Rica looking for work. He asked me for some names, and hers was one of the names I gave him. At that time she had certain connections, and I thought she might help."

Herrera looked at the glass of beer he had hardly touched. "Yes, she had connections. At that time."

Ford said, "Shall we go to the garden and order a meal?"

The Costa Rican shook his head wryly. "At this

moment my three beautiful little daughters are asleep
and my wife is sitting in the bed, watching the clock."
He shrugged. "Women, they do not understand a matter
between friends. But I will stay long enough to finish
my beer and make certain I have brought all the
things you requested." He put a leather briefcase on the
table. "The photographs were not so easy to get; especially the photographs of Julio Zacul. They were
taken several years ago, when he was a student at the
university. I enclosed one each of the other three important guerrilla leaders, including Juan Rivera. But you
know him, of course."

"Yes," said Ford. "If Rivera has the boy, there should
be no problem. Other than getting into his camp. But I
doubt if he has him. I suspect it is Zacul."

"That is too bad. I have heard stories about him."

"As have I."

Herrera said, "Getting the passports and the working
visas, of course, was not difficult. You must paste in
your own passport photographs, but I have included the
yellow masking. It is a plastic film you must strip away
and stick over the inside jacket."

Ford said, "I am familiar with it," as he opened the
briefcase, then he looked up quickly. "Rigaberto, there
is a gun in here. I asked only for a knife."

Herrera was smiling. "I am relieved that you know
the difference. It is a forty-five-caliber automatic; a
Browning. I've included a box of cartridges and two
clips. Each clip holds seven rounds. There is, of course,
a knife, too. A military knife with a hollow handle that
holds fishing line and such things."

"You are very thoughtful, Rigaberto, but I don't think I'll need a weapon. I hope not, anyway. Besides, one pistol against the guerrillas who have the boy—"

"It was not the guerrillas I was thinking about when I decided to give you the gun, old friend. It was because of the man who travels with you. I did not like what you told me about him. I checked as best I could with the people I know here, and, while it is true none of them knew of this man, it all sounds very suspicious."

"Yes," said Ford. "That is why I asked him to come along."

"I do not understand, but if it is a confidence you do not wish to share—"

Ford said, "It is possible there are people in my government who think I stole a certain artifact from the Presidential Palace in Masagua. It is possible they sent this man to find out if I was involved. But since I spoke with you, I was told by a good source that the man is a civilian."

"Plus you were not involved."

"Of course not."

"It is important, this artifact?"

"In the proper hands, it is the one thing that might help unite the people of Masagua."

"Then it is very important, indeed. And is this artifact still in the proper hands?"

"It was when I left Masagua. Now I am not so sure."

"Then that makes me worry all the more for your safety. For such a thing, one life means nothing." Herrera's dark eyes became cold. "If you like, I will return to my home and call another friend of mine—Rudolpho

Romero, the middle-weight fighter who once fought in Madison Square Garden. Rudolpho and I will visit this man who travels with you. In a very short time we will know exactly what his intentions are. My wife would understand a thing such as that. She would not mind."

Ford said, "No. I'll find out in my own fashion."

"I do not think it is wise entering Masagua with a man you cannot trust. Forgive me, old friend. You are intelligent in many ways, but there are other ways in which you are not so learned. I think Rudolpho and I should have a discussion with this man."

"I'm not so sure you would learn anything, even if he has been sent after me. He is very smart. Perhaps he is very shrewd, too."

"Rudolpho's fists are wiser than the wisest. And I suppose this superman is bigger and stronger than you, too?"

"No, but smarter, perhaps. In ways."

"Then do this for me: Find out his intentions before you get to Masagua. Afterward it may be too late."

Ford said, "I will. I'm not looking forward to it, but I will."

Herrera stood abruptly and held out a big hand. "Then I will wish you luck with the lost child you seek and the artifact you did not steal. And remind you that you need only call for help, from anywhere in Costa Rica or Masagua, and I will come. I am not one to forget the kindness of old friends." He smiled. "But, next time, let it be in the jungle. Not a whorehouse."

Ford saw Wendy Stafford stiffen as he walked into the Garden's dining area, a cobblestone patio with trees and

Japanese lanterns, and took the table recently cleared by
her. She vanished for a time and he began to wonder
if she would send another waitress, but then she reap-
peared. She wore jeans and a white apron over the baggy
T-shirt, her long blond hair looking frizzy and unkempt,
and Ford guessed she had lost ten or fifteen pounds since
he had seen her last. She had once had one of those
healthy, heavy, square-jawed faces of a type often seen
on the campuses of certain private colleges: the face of a
daughter who'd gotten a full dose of her successful,
athletic father's genes. But now her face was drawn and
lined, no longer pretty but still handsome, and her blue
eyes darted here and there, alive but different.

Some of the American princesses lost themselves
because of love. Or because the promiscuity had gotten
out of hand and, in their own minds, made it impossible for them to return. Or because of drugs.

With Wendy Stafford, Ford decided, it was drugs. Or
maybe all of the above.

In Spanish, she said, "May I take your order?" then
looked at him, pretending to focus, pretending to be surprised, and said in English, "Marion? Marion Ford?
My God, it's you, isn't it!"

"Hello, Wendy."

"It *is* you!" Really playing it up, as if they'd met on
the street or something. "Imagine meeting you after all
these years. And here, of all places!" Giving the laughter
a prim tone, chiding him for being in a whorehouse,
letting her order pad drop onto the table as if her job was
a secondary consideration; a society girl who was still
above it all.

"You're looking well."

"Oh, no flattery, please. I'm a mess. I've been over on the Caribbean coast all week, working with the Miskito Indians, and you know what the conditions there are like. Then one of the poor girls who works here called me just as I got back to San José and asked me to fill in for her. What was I going to say?" Talking way too fast; a girl who had become very good with the quick lie; the blue eyes still darting, refusing to lock onto Ford's.

"I need to talk with you, Wendy. Privately."

"Now, you mean?

"Tonight, yes."

She picked up the order pad again, giving it meaning. "But that girl I told you about. I have to work for her. If it was just me, I'd leave right now." She laughed. "I mean, I'd have never even been here. But I don't want to get her into trouble."

Ford took a bill from his pocket, a fifty, which was more than twice what the girls charged, and slid it onto the table. "Maybe if you gave the floor manager this, he'd understand."

The woman stared at the money for a second, pretending to be slow on the uptake. "You mean . . . like I'm really one of the girls? Like you're paying for me?" The nervous laughter again. "Well, it might work. Like I'm one of the whores. Wait until I write Daddy about this. He'll be furious." A thirty-year-old woman still talking about her daddy as she took the money from the table, then stopped, thinking. "Do you just want to talk for a short time, Marion? I mean, if you want to pay for the whole evening, I think the girls charge more. From the way I've heard them talk, anyway." Lying smoothly as Ford took out another fifty, she said, "It'll go to my friend, of course. I just don't want to get her into any trouble."

"Still thinking about everyone but yourself, Wendy."

Ford watched as she crossed the deck and tried to hide herself in the shadows of the trees, giving the money to the floor manager then quickly stuffing her cut into the pocket of her jeans. Then she was back, pushing her hair from her shoulders as if she'd just gotten out of a fast boat, saying "Well, he fell for it. I've been bought and paid for. It's something my grandchildren will laugh about."

Outside, the air was balmy and the woman paused to light a cigarette, inhaling deeply, then said she didn't want to go anywhere for a drink, maybe her apartment would be better since it was so close, and Ford knew it was because the management would be checking up on her, making sure she wasn't doing a party for the price of one man.

The apartment was only two blocks away, a one bedroom walk-up above a butcher shop. He expected the place to be a mess, and it was: bed unmade, clothes thrown on chairs, and a cat meowing for food as they came in. The cat gave him a quick mental picture, a surge of Jessica, but he pushed it from his mind. There were posters on the walls, political posters calling for equality and to save the wildlife, and the air conditioner spackled into the wall had a condensation problem, peeling the paint away with rust streaks. The place smelled of the bad air conditioner and of the butcher shop below.

"Drink?" She was at the refrigerator, looking in, her face appearing somehow younger in the bleak light.

"No thanks, I'm fine."

"You won't mind if I do. God, the way they work us down there. Even on a slow night." Then looked at Ford quickly as she took out soda water and let the door swing shut. "The way they work the girls, I mean. I don't see how they stand it." After tapping out another cigarette as she poured a tumbler half full of rum and added the soda, she took the chair across from him.

Ford said, "Three years ago I gave a friend of mine your name. He was a pilot and looking for work down here. His name was Rafe Hollins. He may have called himself Rafferty."

The abruptness of that made her take a drink, and she gave it some time, calculating, as if trying to remember. "I don't know, Marion. The name sounds familiar, but I'm not sure."

"Your name was in his address book. This address, so it had been updated. He said you told him why the Department of Immigration didn't have me listed as a temporary resident."

She smiled, leaning back with her cigarette. "Marion Ford, secret agent man. So how are things going at the ol' CIA? Invaded any small countries lately?"

"You were wrong then and you're wrong now, Wendy. I never worked for the CIA. Now I don't work for the government at all."

"Then why the detective routine? Why so free with the big bills if you just wanted to talk to me? Some people might consider that offensive, ol' buddy."

"Not if the questions are strictly business. Rafe Hollins was a friend of mine. He was flying Mayan artifacts into the States and making one hell of a lot of money at it. But he's dead now and it leaves a nice little void. I'd like to pick up where he left off, only I don't know who his contacts were. I thought you might be able to help—for a price, of course."

"Rafe's dead?" She reached for her drink again, not hurt by the news but surprised.

"Then you did know him?"

"He came to see me. It was interesting, having someone come to me using your name as a reference. At first I thought you might be trying to sneak in one of your CIA buddies on me. But then I figured he would have never used your name if he was. Besides, he just wasn't bright enough—not that your organization only takes sparkling intellects."

"Rafe was no genius." Playing along with Hollins's hick routine, finding it useful. "But even if I was involved with the CIA, why would I send an agent to court you?"

"Oh, come on, Marion. Don't play dumb. I've always been involved with the cause—" "Cause" said as if it should be capitalized; swirling her drink as she peered over it, starting to feel important and letting her guard drop just a little as the rum began to take hold. "You had to know that. You knew I was trying to get information for my people; that's why you told me so little. Why do you think I slept with you those times? Like a game." This said with a nasty edge that she seemed to enjoy.

Ford shrugged. What he remembered about it was Wendy getting sloppy drunk, groping his leg under the table while fighting not to slide out of her seat, that's how ready she was. He said, "No, I didn't know. But it doesn't matter now."

"The cause still matters, Marion. The revolution. It matters to me." But the mechanical tone in her voice told him that it didn't; not really.

"And money doesn't?"

"My family's wealthy, don't you remember?"

Ford did a stage survey of the apartment with his eyes. "It looks to me like your family cut you off a long time ago, Wendy. And I'm here to make you a fair business proposition. If you provide me with names and locations of Rafe's contacts, the people who were providing him with the artifacts, I'll give you five percent of the net for the first year, two percent for the next two years. That should come to something like a hundred thousand over the three-year period, cash. Just for information. Tonight."

The blue eyes weren't darting now. "This doesn't sound like the Marion Ford I remember."

"We all change, Wendy. I got real tired of being one of the have-nots. Of taking orders from other people, cleaning up their messes while they cashed in. Idealism starts to seem a little childish if you get kicked around enough."

She said, "Whew, you don't have to tell me, buster," and Ford knew that he had hit the mark; watching her as she stood, stretched with the weariness of it all, then crossed the room toward the bottle. "A hundred thousand just for telling you Rafe's contacts?"

"And where I can find them. The information has to

be good. It has to be accurate. Later on I may ask you for one or two other favors, but nothing big. Logistical stuff."

"How do I know you're not still working for the Company? Maybe this is a scam so you can get me to help you smoke out my comrades up in the mountains."

"For one thing, I didn't quit my job. I was asked to resign. I was in Masagua and they decided I was trying to help Juan Rivera more than their puppet Balserio. They were right. Check around if you don't believe me." Which was a lie, but Ford knew she would never get around to checking.

She considered that for a moment, wanting to believe him, wanting the money. "My God, the All-American boy helping a communist. Maybe there's hope for the world after all. But so far I haven't heard you mention any advance. Just the promise of money, like I'm supposed to trust your fair bookkeeping."

"I'll give you . . . five hundred tonight, and send you another thousand if your information turns out to be good." Standing as he counted out the bills, putting them on the table in a stack in front of her.

She looked at the money, touching her tongue to her lips, as if she were hungry. Ford wondered how much heroin five hundred would buy in Costa Rica. Or cocaine. Yeah, cocaine: no track marks on her arms. In Costa Rica, it would buy a lot of cocaine.

"Do you have a map?" she asked.

"I have several maps. What country?"

"Masagua, of course."

Ford took out the good topographical map that

Herrera had provided and spread it out over the money. She hunched over the map, touching it with her index finger, concentrating. "Have you ever heard of Julio Zacul?"

"I've heard of him. That's the guy you're worried I might sic the marines on?"

She looked up at him, still thinking of Zacul, a brief look of pure hatred. "For that bastard, you can call in the marines, the gurkhas, anybody you want. After what he did to me. The bastard. I was worried you were after Rivera."

"It sounds like you know Zacul pretty well."

"I should. I lived with him for three months. Followed that son of a bitch everywhere. I did things for him . . ." She shivered slightly. "Things I can't believe I did. Things he made me do. He's sick, Marion. An animal— if you're one of his women, and there aren't too many of those. He prefers your type—or boys."

Ford felt his stomach turn, *one of his boys*, not wanting to hear any more but still listening. She went on a quick talking jag, close to losing control, telling him about this man she hated and why until Ford finally took her arm, calming her, and said, "Show me where he is, Wendy. Point to it on the map."

She downed the last of her drink, throwing her head back as if it were medicine. "It's just that I've never been the same since I was with Zacul. Bad things have happened to me. Like a curse. The things he made me do seem like a crazy bad dream now. Like those Mexican girls in the cheap films. The animal." She was still shaking.

Ford said, "Then you won't mind making some money off him."

"No, I won't mind at all. But I'd rather see him dead. When you find him, though, watch yourself. Rafferty flew authentic artifacts out for him, but Zacul sent a lot of fake stuff, too. He has his men make it. The first stuff he offers you will be fake. Just a warning. He'll judge what you know by the way you react to the first stuff he offers."

"Zacul was the only one Hollins was flying artifacts for?"

"I don't know. How should I know? But probably, yeah. He was the only guerrilla I know who dealt in that sort of thing. On a big-time basis, anyway."

It didn't take her long to describe how to get to where Zacul was probably camped. Ford knew that section of mountains very, very well. She kept saying Zacul would have her killed if he found out. Ford pumped all the information he could out of her, about the way Zacul arranged his camp, his routine, how best to deal with the man on a business basis, because now he was admitting to himself what he hadn't wanted to admit before: Julio Zacul had Jake Hollins.

As Ford folded the map to go, the woman stood up, swaying slightly, a little drunk, and leaned against the bathroom doorway, her head tilted to one side. "Do you have to leave so soon?" Trying to look seductive, but looking sad and defeated instead. "I was going to take a shower. A nice long, hot shower. Maybe you'd like to join me. I can wash your back. You've already paid for it, you know."

Ford said, "I can't, Wendy. I'm in a hurry," after repressing the urge to say "Maybe another time—when I'm feeling real dirty."

He was glad he didn't say it. As he opened the door, she was sitting on the couch four rums gone, knees together, arms pressed over her breasts, and she said in the voice of a dazed little girl, "I'm not pretty anymore, am I, Marion?" Crying, too, but not making any noise; looking straight ahead, her eyes glassy.

Ford set the satchel on the steps, went to her, and kissed her tenderly on the forehead. "It's time for you to go home, Wendy. You should take that money and buy a ticket home."

"They'd never take me now, Marion. On the phone Daddy said—"

"On the phone is one thing, Wendy. He can't look into your face and refuse you."

"Do you think so, Marion? Really?"

"I want you to call tonight, Wendy. Will you do that?"

She had still made no reply when he closed the door behind him.

Tomlinson was calling "What? What? Who *is* it, man?"

And Ford, standing outside Tomlinson's room, said, "Let's go. It's time to get going."

"It's morning already, man?"

"Close enough."

Tomlinson swung the door open. He was wearing salmon-colored long johns—long johns? Yep—standing there with his scraggly hair and beard, digging a fist into his eyes. "Christ, Doc, it's till dark outside."

It was just after midnight, 12:08 A.M.

"You know what they say: Early bird gets the worm."

"Feels like I just went to sleep."

Ford said, "I've got the Land Cruiser all loaded. I'll meet you in the lobby in fifteen minutes."

"Far out, man. Far out. Up with the farmers. . . ."

TWELVE

On a rhumb line it was 150 miles to the border of Masagua, but the mountain roads of Costa Rica, though they were good roads, followed no line. They followed rivers through the high cloud forests, and Ford drove while Tomlinson slept beside him, the lights of the vehicle tunneling through fog into the darkness. After three hours the terrain began to change. The rain forest began to draw in, thicken, and the road narrowed, like driving through a cave. He had to use the wipers to clear the windshield of condensation and, with the windows down, he could smell the cool hollows and the tannin-stained rivers. He could smell the jungle and knew Masagua was near.

Then there was a sign that said it was ten kilometers to the border station, and Ford slowed until he found an old logging trail and turned off the road, bouncing and jolting. He shut off the engine and pushed the door open so that the dome light was on. The chirping of frogs was like one long scream in the darkness.

Tomlinson stirred, awakening slowly.

Ford reached into the backseat and unzipped the leather satchel. He took out the forty-five-caliber automatic and waited. He waited until he was sure Tomlinson was awake, then he punched in a clip, slid the breach back, and watched Tomlinson's eyes flutter and finally open wide, seeing the pistol.

"Holy shit!"

"Take it easy."

"What's with the gun, man? There fucking tigers around here or something? Restless natives?"

Ford said, "We need to have a talk, Tomlinson."

"Talk, yeah, sure." Getting as far from Ford as he could, his back against the door, not frightened but nervous with a pistol between them in the narrow confines of the Land Cruiser. And trying hard to wake up quickly. "Christ, watch it, that thing could go off. You got bullets in there?"

"Just seven. The border guards are up ahead. About six miles."

"Border guards . . . I thought we were going to bribe the bastards. Hey, Doc, I got to be frank—I don't like this gun business. And bullets, too. Guns give me the heebie jeebies."

"But we need to have a talk. I keep wondering why you're so quick to follow along, Tomlinson. I keep wondering why you don't ask me more questions about this trip." Holding the forty-five in his right hand, not pointing it at Tomlinson but keeping it between them.

"Questions?" Looking really uncomfortable now, Tomlinson had begun to tug at his hair, as if he were trying to come up with a quick question or two. "Well, you're an awfully early riser—I was going to ask you about that, but we all have our quirks." He paused, looking at the pistol . . . then at Ford. "That's what this is all about? You want me to ask more questions? I mean, we can definitely work something out in that regard. It's your vacation, man. I'll try to help brighten it up any way I can."

Ford studied him for a moment, doubting if anyone so smart could be so vacant. He said, "I didn't come for a vacation, I came to get the boy."

Tomlinson nodded quickly, anxious to understand. "I know, I know. Little boys are nature's gentlemen. I was just joking about the vacation thing. You know, trying to lighten things up."

"There's something else you should know. One year ago I helped steal the *Kin Qux Cho* from the Presidential Palace in Masagua."

That made him sit up. "The *book*, man. You stole the book that has all the old Maya ceremonies in it? Rituals of the Lake? *You?*"

"That's right, me."

"Come on, now you're joking, right? Like April Fools, only it's not—hey, maybe it is April. I've been losing track—"

"It's no joke, Tomlinson, and this is no game."

"Goddamn, Doc, you're really serious, aren't you?" Tomlinson was looking at him, the slow smile turning into delight. "You, a thief; who in the hell woulda thought it? There are depths to you, man. Stuff I never guessed was there. And you really know where the book is? Damn, I'd give anything to see that book."

Ford rested the gun on the gear shift console, within easy reach of Tomlinson. "You'll never get much closer. It's only about three miles from here, hidden away. But I can't let you see it." Then he left the gun there, taking his hand away, letting the lie settle; turning away, as if looking out the window, but watching Tomlinson.

"Hell, man, if you say you can't, you can't. Just seems a damn shame, me being a scholar, that's all. Maybe I could see it later?"

"No. No way. Sorry. I think you'll be a help getting the boy. But I can't let you get involved any more than that."

Tomlinson was assuming an expression, contemplating, but he had still made no move toward the gun. Ford said, "I've got to take a whiz. Be right back." He stepped out into the jungle and the car door swung shut so that now he could see only Tomlinson's outline. He stood behind the vehicle for a time, watching as Tomlinson slowly leaned forward, reaching for the pistol. Ford crouched slightly and, in three steps, was at the passenger's side. He pulled the door open, but before he could do anything Tomlinson swung the automatic toward him . . . holding it with two fingers, like it was a soiled diaper, and said, "Doc, I'll help you with the boy, but first you've got to agree to something." Ford stood motionless, waiting, as Tomlinson added, "You've got to agree to put this thing someplace where I can't see it. Bad vibes, man; very bad vibes. It really disturbs the fucking thought processes. And take the bullets out, too."

"You want me to hide the gun." Ford's heart was pounding, the adrenaline really pumping through him, even though the automatic contained an empty clip. Empty weapon or not, it would have gotten nasty had Tomlinson tried to force him to retrieve the book.

Tomlinson said, "Right. I hate to be so firm, but this business about shooting border guards is just asking for bad karma. You shoot a border guard and, next thing you know, the whole trip is going to start getting weird. Take my word on this one." Tomlinson was holding the automatic by the barrel, wanting Ford to take it.

Ford said, "Tomlinson, let me just ask you outright: Did the CIA send you to keep an eye on me?" as he accepted the gun back.

"The CIA?" Acting as if he were giving the question serious consideration, but in a patronizing way, like dealing with a crazy man. "Ah, no-o-o-o, but it would be an easy mistake to make. Could happen to anybody."

Ford stared at him for a moment. "You don't work for them, do you? You really are exactly what you appear to be. Amazing."

"See what happens when you think about killing border guards?" Tomlinson said kindly. "It sets all the negative ions in motion. Really destructive stuff, man. I've got some books you should read."

"Okay," he said. "All right. I believe you."

"See, we all got auras, man—these sort of electrical fields around us, only you can't see them—"

"Auras, right, uh-huh." Relieved, Ford put the automatic back in the briefcase, gathered himself for a moment, then took out a fake passport as Tomlinson rattled on.

"These auras are made up of ions; positive, negative, you know, basic physics man."

"Right. Hey, give me your passport for a second."

Saying, "Now, normally you have a real positive aura. I mean *the best*. That's why people are attracted to you." Tomlinson fished his passport out of his back pocket and handed it to Ford. "The moment I met you, I thought, 'Now this guy's been down some unmarked channels. A real karmic hipster.'"

Ford said, "Gee, thanks," as he used a knife to cut the photograph from Tomlinson's real passport and then trimmed the yellow masking to size. Tomlinson was watching now, interested, saying he was real impressed the way Ford did that, as if he'd done it before, and don't be hurt about his asking no questions, he'd ask a lot more from here on out.

The border guards waved them through with a quick glance at the passports, more interested in collecting the tourist tax, which Ford knew they would pocket, and getting back to sleep. There was a village beyond: tin-roofed shacks and shabby bars, then more jungle. The roads were bad now, rock and mud. It was the rainy season and the bridges not washed away were bare planks thrown across gullies. Twice Ford had to get out and sound the depth of a creek before driving through it. Then Tomlinson decided that should be his job, wading into the next creek up to his beard before calling back they'd have to find a better place to cross. Between creek crossings, Ford told Tomlinson the truth about the *Kin Qux Cho*.

"Then you really don't know where it is?"

"Not for sure."

"Then why did you lie to me, man?"

"It was a test, for God's sake!"

"Goddamn, some test. Next time just send me a telegram saying my parents got blown up by Iranians or something, but leave the guns at home."

"I had to be sure."

"That sort of thing is bad for the heart. I almost wet my drawers."

"Okay, okay, just drive."

Tomlinson drove in silence and, after a long time, asked, "Did that woman, Pilar what's-her-name, really do that to you? *Coitus interruptus*, armed-guard style?"

"Just afterward. Almost like she pressed a button beside the bed. I didn't even have time to get my clothes."

"What a bitch, man."

Ford said, "No. She had her reasons."

"You're sticking up for her? You must still be in love with the lady, man." When Ford did not answer, Tomlinson said gently, "It'll pass, Doc. It may not seem like it now, but it'll pass. I know. I've been through it."

Ford said, "I'd like that."

Much later, replying to a long monologue by Tomlinson, Ford asked, "And that's when they institutionalized you?"

Tomlinson said, "Yeah, they had to. It's hard to believe now, but for a while there I was what you might call insane. . . ."

The half moon was waxing, but the jungle seemed to lure in, then absorb all light, so that the frail moon above only emphasized the darkness. The roads became narrower, pale ribbons in the overhanging foliage, ascending, always climbing, and at the top of each ridge the forest spread away in striations of silver mist with shapes of gigantic trees protruding through the haze. Sometimes, on a far mountainside, Ford could see lights glittering in tiny coves: campfires of Mayan villages. The fires touched the air with woodsmoke long after they had receded into the gloom. Ford took the wheel as the eastern horizon paled and the sun, still unseen, illuminated the high forest canopy with citreous light.

At 10 A.M. Ford said, "I think we're almost there." He had been following one of the maps, marking their progress, while Tomlinson sat peering out the window, pointing at monkeys and wild parrots.

"This guy Zacul's camp?"

"No. A place where we can get breakfast. A little village called Isla de Verde. I want to see someone else first."

"You know best, man. I just hope they sell corn flakes. I have corn flakes every morning."

Isle de Verde had once been an agricultural outpost, a settlement of people drawn into the forest so that they might get rich tapping chicle trees and selling the sap to U.S. chewing gum manufacturers. No one ever got rich, and when the manufacturers found a synthetic chicle, which was cheaper, the agricultural outpost became just an outpost, a clearing in the jungle with bamboo huts and plywood *tiendas* where stray dogs dozed in the road. As Ford drove down the mud street, people turned from their work to watch, then turned away again, showing no expression. Unlike the more traditional Maya of the higher mountains, the villagers here wore Latino clothing: simple white pants or pastel skirts, light blouses and scarves. But the high cheeks, dark eyes, and earth-toned faces were unmistakable: pure Mayan.

In a village such as this, merchants did not need signs because everyone knew what was to be bought and where. The place where a meal could be purchased was a simple bamboo chickee with a tin roof and bottles of beer and Coca-Cola on display in the front window. Ford knew of the restaurant because he had been in Isla de Verde several times before, but coming always from the north, not the south. He parked the Land Cruiser beneath a tree where two sway-backed horses and a goat grazed.

The proprietor—a slender man with the knowing eyes of a priest—acknowledged Ford with the slightest of nods, remembering him but saying nothing, motioning them toward the smaller of two tables in the tiny room. "You would like coffee? Or perhaps a beer?" Standing there with a towel over his forearm like the maître d' of a great hotel.

Ford said, "Coffee, yes. And a meal. A breakfast, if it is not an inconvenience."

"It is my great pleasure."

"Perhaps there is something else you could do for us."

The proprietor shrugged, a noncommittal gesture. "If it is possible."

Ford took a piece of paper from his pocket and handed it to him. "I would like this message delivered to a friend of mine. A man who lives in the hills. I will pay you and the messenger for your trouble, of course."

The proprietor took the paper, glanced at the name on the outside, then stuffed the note in his pocket as if it were a matter of indifference to him. "I will bring the beverages," he said, then walked quickly to the kitchen.

Tomlinson said, "I hope he brings a menu, too."

Ford said, "I don't think they have menus here. I can check if you want."

"You guys lose me, the way you jabber away in Spanish like that. I've got to learn the language, man. I've got to learn those glyphs better. I've got so damn much work to do on this project of mine, it's great. You know, stimulating." He looked at Ford. "No corn flakes, huh?"

"I wouldn't get my hopes up."

"Did you already order?"

"You pretty much take what he brings you. It'll be good, though."

It was, too: fried plantains, eggs, black beans, rice, and thick slices of bacon. Tomlinson didn't eat the bacon—he didn't eat flesh, he said—but he ate everything else. Then they went for a walk, past the neat houses with their swept lawns, down to the river where they watched children playing in the sun while their mothers washed clothes on the rocks, knotting and beating the clothing as women had for a thousand years.

Ford never saw the messenger the proprietor sent, but an hour later, four men on horseback rode into the village towing two saddled horses behind. They wore T-shirts, not uniforms, but each carried an automatic rifle and the lead man said to Ford, "You are to come with us, *señor*."

Ford said, "We have a vehicle. We can follow."

"No, *señor*. You are to ride with us. It is his wish."

Tomlinson said he'd never been on a horse before and Ford said it was a little like being on a sailboat, only drier—but Tomlinson, upset by the weapons, did not smile. They rode single file into the mountains, then stopped on a ridge above a shallow valley. Below lay the shapes of tents hidden among the trees and a huge clearing covered with camouflaged netting. Tomlinson whispered, "What they hiding under there, man? Artillery? A landing strip, maybe?"

Ford said, "Watch. Watch the soldiers. They're rolling the netting back now."

There was part of a grass runway covered by the camouflage. So were two mobile units of antiaircraft artillery, old Yugoslavian M65s from the looks of them. Mostly, though, the camouflaged netting was being used to hide a baseball diamond.

THIRTEEN

Dressed in khaki fatigues and cap, his black beard showing splotches of gray, Juan Rivera stood outside the HQ tent and threw his arms wide apart, smiling as Ford rode up. "Do my eyes deceive me? Is it the great Johnny Bench? Is it the ugly Yogi Berra? No . . . no, it is my old comrade Ford come to help us in our time of need." Joking with Ford, but performing for the men around him, too, which was Rivera's way: a showman, always speaking to a crowd even when there was no crowd to hear.

Ford said, "It's been a long time, General Rivera," enduring the guerrilla leader's bear hug, but relieved, at least, that Rivera hadn't had him arrested. With things the way they were in Masagua, there had been no way for Ford to know in advance how he would be received.

"You and your friend are hungry? I will have a meal prepared—"

"We ate in the village, General."

"Then you are in need of a bath. Or sleep, perhaps? You have traveled far—"

"A bath would be nice, but later. After we've talked."

"A woman, then?" His arm thrown over Ford's shoulder, leading him toward the headquarters tent, Rivera was speaking confidentially now, making a show of being a host who anticipated all needs. "Finding a healthy woman in this time of many diseases is not such an easy thing, but I have several here you may find pleasing. Volunteers, dedicated to the cause." His wink was both humorous and wicked. "I have been accused of choosing my volunteers for their beauty, not their brains, a thing I will not argue."

Ford said, "You are widely known for your taste in women, General, but I'm not in need right now. Thanks anyway."

Rivera stopped and put his hands on Ford's shoulders. "You are fit, then? You are well?"

"I'm just fine."

"And your friend? Forgive me, but I am wondering why a man such as you is traveling with this . . . this hippie." Meaning Tomlinson, who was back with the horses. The people of Central America still distrusted the long-haired late Sixties wanderers they remembered as ne'er-do-wells and bums, and Rivera, Ford could see, wasn't eager to extend his hospitality.

"He's a business associate. He's fine, too."

"Then you require nothing?"

"I would like to talk with you—"

"Hah! It is always business with you! It is a bad thing, a very bad thing to think of nothing but work." They were inside Rivera's tent now: a high room of canvas with Coleman lanterns hanging from wooden supports and sandbags piled chest high around the inside perimeter. Ford stood while Rivera went behind a great metal desk and began to rummage through a box, but still lecturing. "You should use me as your example, Marion. I am about to lead my army into a great revolution. I am about to assume command of my beloved country. I have a thousand things to do; ten million people depend on me, but I make sure that I take the time for recreation." Rivera took something from the box and placed it on the desk: a pale-gray uniform, folded. A baseball uniform. Then he added a hat and a catcher's glove to the pile. "This hippie friend of yours, does he play the game, too?"

"You want to play baseball? Now?"

"In honor of your arrival. Unfortunately, my best team is out on maneuvers—yes, even my finest players bear arms for the cause. We will make do with reserves and scrimmage my third team, me pitching, you catching. This hippie friend of yours, do you think he is a player of quality?"

"I doubt if Tomlinson's ever touched a ball, but I really don't think—"

"Ah, then he will not need a uniform. He will play on the opposing team. It is only fair that the third team be handicapped in some way since my own team is not at full strength."

Ford said, "Juan, I haven't played since the last time I was here—" Dropping the formal address with only the two guards outside the tent to hear.

"Tut-tut, Marion, no excuses. I have something to show you. Something new. Very important!" Rivera lowered his voice, sharing a secret. "It is a new pitch, my friend. A pitch I have developed which, I say in all modesty, no hitter in the American major leagues could touch. But I am anxious for you to judge. You, my favorite catcher, will evaluate this pitch of mine fairly."

"The reason I'm here, Juan—it can't wait while we play nine innings."

"Just seven, then. A short game." Looking at his watch, smiling through his beard, Rivera said, "Did you know that the Giants of New York once drafted Fidel as a pitcher?"

Fidel as in Fidel Castro, and Ford did know because Rivera mentioned it every time they met. Rivera continued, "Do you realize that no American major league team has ever made me—probably the greatest pitcher in all of Central America—even the smallest of offers? Does that not seem odd?"

Ford said, "We've talked about this before, Juan. I think it's because major league scouts shy away from war zones."

"It is purely politics," Rivera countered severely. "The capitalist dogs of your country have conspired against me so that I may not spread my influence through fame earned playing your national sport." He looked at Ford, calculating. "Do you still count the manager of the Royals of Kansas City as one of your friends?"

Ford said, "He managed the Royals' Triple-A team and now he's with Pittsburgh, in the majors. Yes, we still stay in touch."

"In the major leagues?" Rivera wagged his eyebrows, impressed.

"Yes. Gene Lamont. A third-base coach."

"Then I will leave it to you to judge this new pitch of mine. If you are excited and feel it necessary to contact your friend who coaches in the major leagues, I will not object. But I warn you, I am no longer interested in their offers—though, even at the age of thirty-seven, I feel certain I could win twenty games."

Ford played along. "But General, if this new pitch is as effective as you say, I will feel obligated. The game of baseball makes certain demands upon its fans."

Rivera was stripping off his shirt, showing his massive hairy chest. "Perhaps. But I warn you again, their offers are a matter of complete indifference to me. I live now only for the revolution."

"The Pirates of Pittsburgh will be disappointed. As will the Dodgers of Los Angeles."

Rivera stopped undressing, one leg still in his pants. "It is possible that your friend might communicate the information to the Dodgers of Los Angeles?"

"Both teams are in the National League, and you know how baseball players love to talk."

The guerrilla leader considered this for a moment, then threw his pants into the corner for his orderly to pick up. "If the Dodgers of Los Angeles are to be disappointed, you will leave it for me to disappoint them. You will communicate only what you see. It is not necessary for them to know I live only for the revolution and would refuse their offer anyway."

Ford said, "As you wish, General Rivera," and

followed one of the guards to his billet, where he suited up.

Monkeys watched them warm up. They came down out of the high forest canopy, a whole tribe of howler monkeys hanging from the lower branches, babies clinging to their mothers' backs, big males swinging by their tails and throwing small green mangoes, imitating the players.

"That one monkey has a better arm than I do," Ford said to Tomlinson. Tomlinson was playing catch with him, handling the glove and throwing better than Ford had expected. He was pretty smooth; he'd played the game, which was another surprise.

Tomlinson said, "What I don't understand is why you get a uniform and I don't." Like a child slighted, and now he was throwing harder as if to prove he had talent enough to deserve the gray double-knit suit with MASAGUAN PEOPLE'S ARMY emblazoned in blue on the front. "I played in high school, man. I played two years in college. I mean, this was my sport before I got interested in substance abuse."

Ford said, "I'll give you my uniform if you promise not to get any hits off Rivera. No joke. Strike out if you can. But don't make him mad by getting a hit. We want to get this game over with fast, and then I'm going to have to ask him for a favor."

"It's just that it seems a little arbitrary, putting me on a team without uniforms just because he doesn't like long hair. It's not in keeping with Marxist-Leninist philosophy to choose a ball team that way. How can the guy pretend to be a communist?" As if he hadn't even heard

Ford. Still indignant, still throwing hard, Tomlinson was already being drawn onto competitive avenues, and Rivera wasn't even on the mound yet.

"I'm surprised a Zen Buddhist could get upset about a game."

"The Buddha woulda been a baseball fan, believe me."

"Ah."

"Baseball is more than a game, man. It's a ceremony."

"Oh."

"All the people who have ever played baseball are linked by virtue of having dealt with predictable game situations in unpredictable ways, each person trying to resolve random events within an orderly sphere of balls, strikes, and outs—"

"Boy oh boy."

"Plus there's the scorebook: a historical document more accurate and succinct than, say, the Old Testament. All these thousands and thousands of scorebooks all over the world forming an unbroken ceremonial chronicle far more detailed than, say, Ireland's Book of Kells—"

"Tomlinson, all we want to do is finish the damn game without offending Rivera. He's a baseball fanatic. He takes it very seriously."

"Well, I'll try . . . but I'll feel like a heretic."

Tomlinson didn't have to try too hard to look bad, nor did anyone else on the opposing team: a ragtag bunch of teenagers and men in khaki who played with enthusiasm but not much skill.

Rivera could pitch. He'd lost some velocity on his

fastball, but it still moved; still tailed in on right-handed hitters. He had a fair curve, a split-fingered sinker, plus his new pitch, the one he said he had invented, a one-fingered knuckleball he threw side-armed so that it broke like a screwball. He presented an imposing figure on the mound, too: six feet tall, probably two twenty, bushy black beard and in full uniform except for the fatigue cap he always wore, lighting a fresh El Presidente cigar between each inning. In a potential strikeout situation, Rivera would call Ford out to the mound. "You probably do not realize it," he would say, "but this man at the plate hits as well as the great George Brett." Ford would look back to see some stringy kid who didn't look old enough to drive. "Watch how I handle *Señor* Brett." Then he would kick back and strike the kid out looking. Another hitter was as good as Pete Rose. Another was as powerful as Mantle. Tomlinson reminded him of the great DiMaggio. Rivera struck them all out, using the knuckleball, lost somewhere between fact and fantasy like a child playing alone in the backyard, winning the World Series in the last of the ninth on this remote jungle field.

Doubling as umpire, Ford moved the game along as quickly as he could, giving Rivera every close call. But he still found pleasure in being behind the plate, calling pitches, blocking low stuff, talking to the hitters. The knuckleball was hard to handle, especially on third strikes, and his concentration drew him deeper into the game, like a kid again, for Tomlinson was right in a way: a world seen through the bars of a catcher's mask is timeless, unchanging, and for those few innings Ford became a creature whose life had been interrupted by nothing more than twenty-five years of passed balls and stolen bases. Better yet, he hit two singles and a double, driving in three runs.

Going into the top of the seventh, Rivera had walked four but had a no-hitter going, and Tomlinson came up with two out.

"It's rally time," Tomlinson was saying, swinging three bats like he meant business. "No more Mister nice guy. Rivera has a ten-run lead and one little hit can't hurt."

Ford said in a low voice, "He'd be happier with a no-hitter. Let's try and keep the general happy."

"Doc, I got my own integrity to consider. I really think I can tee off on this guy."

Ford thought for a moment, then said, "Okay. Maybe you're right. Hit away."

Tomlinson did, too; caught a tailing fastball fat and drove it deep, but not deep enough. The centerfielder tracked it to the camouflage netting, which had now become the outfield fence, leaped and made a nice catch, stopping the home run and saving the no-hitter. Rivera seemed to love the moment of suspense more than anyone; got Tomlinson in one of his affectionate bear hugs, leading him back to Ford at homeplate, saying "It took the great DiMaggio to solve the mystery of my fastball, but even he did not solve it entirely!" delighted with the last out of his no-hitter. Ford told the general he had pitched a superb game and that he was anxious to communicate the information to his friend with the Pittsburgh Pirates, but first he had important business in

Masagua. And Rivera, who was speaking English to
Tomlinson, talking baseball, said to Ford in Spanish, "If
there is any way I can hasten the completion of your assignment, you need only ask. You did not tell me this
hippie friend of yours is not only a great baseball player
but also a student of the game. He knows almost every
statistic for all of those who have pitched for the Red
Sox of Boston!"

Four hours later, after Ford had bathed and eaten
and slept, he walked out of his tent to see Rivera and
Tomlinson—both of them in uniform now—still talking baseball, sitting beneath a tree while howler monkeys rattled the limbs above.

Rivera said Ford's plan to rescue the kidnapped child
might work, but it was also very dangerous. "You do not
know this man Julio Zacul. You do not understand him.
If he does not believe your story he will have you killed.
You will get no second chance. I am not a selfish man
but, if you are killed"—Rivera made an empty, open-
handed gesture—"who will tell the third-base coach
with the Pirates of Pittsburgh about the great no-hitter
pitched by me?" Smiling, but not kidding; actually concerned about Ford's scouting report.

They were sitting at a table outside Rivera's tent. The
sun was behind the mountain and they talked in the
fresh wind of the coming daily rainstorm, speaking in
English for Tomlinson's benefit while orderlies took the
dinner dishes away. The camouflage netting had been
rolled from the clearing and several hundred of Rivera's men performed marching drills, their foot cadence

echoing through the trees. Rivera watched his men as he talked, taking pleasure from their discipline, taking pleasure in the cigar he had just lighted.

He said, "Julio Zacul could have been one of my most gifted lieutenants—not most trusted, mind you. Most gifted. He came to me straight from the University of San Cristobal in Peru, an outstanding engineering student who said he was prepared to give his life to the revolution. This was six, perhaps seven years ago. Yes, this is the way he looked in those days." Rivera picked up the photograph Herrera had provided Ford, studied it for a moment, then spun it back onto the table. The Julio Zacul of college days looked neither like a guerrilla leader nor a killer. He had a lean, aesthetic face that was slightly feminine with long lashes, high soft cheeks, and dark eyes that looked neither fierce nor menacing, just bored, as if he wanted the photographer to hurry up and finish. It was one of those gaunt, good-looking faces out of an Arrow Shirt ad; a young man already in control who was anxious to get started; anxious for more.

Rivera said, "He has changed since then, of course. He is heavier by seven or eight kilos. His hair is longer, almost to his shoulders, but still very black. He has a scar here." Rivera touched his cheek, making a crooked line. "But he still has that soft look, like a child or a girl nearing her readiness. Though I am a man of the world, it is a thing that always bothered me, that softness in his face, like a young woman. He came to my camp with a half-dozen of his friends from the university, all enthusiastic about the revolution. He was so obviously the leader that I immediately trained him as an officer.

Within six months he commanded his own company with these six friends as his subordinates. They lived together, Zacul and these men. That they were more than friends soon became evident, but, as I said, I am a man of the world and such relationships trouble only small minds. Zacul led his company brilliantly, though neither he nor his subordinates were courageous fighters. They preferred the techniques of terrorism, the coward's way. I would have banished him from my camp when I first realized this, but I had no choice. I needed men." Rivera looked at Ford. "You may remember that six years ago was a time of much fighting, much ugliness in this country."

Ford said, "Yes. I was in South America at the time, but I remember."

Rivera nodded as if he could hold Ford responsible, but chose not to. "It was during that fighting that I began to hear stories about Zacul and his men. War is not a pretty thing, and all of us involved in war have done things we would rather not discuss. Someone once said that an immoral act is anything we feel bad about afterward. That is not true. I have often felt bad after doing things that needed to be done. In my mind, an immoral act is anything that makes us feel shame. I have never been ashamed of the things war demanded I do. I have felt bad about them, but I have never felt shame. But there were things that Zacul and his men did that made me feel ashamed. Many things—in the way he tortured prisoners, in the way he dealt with the women of the enemy, in the way he dealt with the enemy's children. When I finally confronted him with these stories, he laughed at me. He called me a weak old man. He called me this in front of many of my people." Rivera signaled to the orderly, handed him his empty coffee cup, and asked for beer.

Ford was trying not to smile. "What happened after you hit him?"

Rivera shrugged. "You are right. I did hit him. He has the look of a woman and he is a coward, but his men were watching. There was a fight, of course. His men stayed out of it because my men would have killed them. It was a long fight and very painful. Zacul left with the scar I have described. It was nearly a week before I could hold a baseball. I was surprised to hear later that he lived." Rivera looked at Tomlinson. "He was not a fan of the game. He refused to play because he said the game originated in the United States."

Tomlinson had been following along attentively. "Hell no, a guy like that wouldn't play. This Zacul sounds like the original conehead to me."

Rivera said, "I have not seen him since that day, nor his six friends. It is a matter of pride that very few other men followed him. His soldiers hated him. He used fear to command. Since that time, though, he has gathered many other troops so that now the strength of his army equals mine. Zacul is the only reason that I am not now sitting in the Presidential Palace in Masagua. I know I must first defeat him. He knows that he must first defeat me. We both wait like great cats, gauging the other before we stalk the prey. I am confident, though, that my army will prevail. We have always performed with honor on and off the field of battle. But Zacul does

not know the meaning of the word. Fate will play a hand,
do not doubt. We will emerge victorious. Soon I will live
in Masagua City, in the Presidential Palace. I will be the
servant of my people."

"As a communist," Ford said. He was not smiling
now, holding the fresh beer the orderly had brought.

Rivera did not reply for a moment. Then he said,
"Have you watched my men marching? Have you seen
how they are armed?"

Ford had, of course, noticed. Many of them carried
Soviet weaponry, but older arms: AK-47s with the
scythe clips and wooden stocks, plus odds and ends of
other eastern bloc ordnance.

Rivera said, "There was a time when the Soviets gave
me their full support. Now it is Zacul's men who carry
their new weaponry. I do not know how he won their
attention, but it doesn't matter. Other than that, I will
say no more to you about my intentions. Understand,
you are my friend, but you also once worked for a
government that may even now be planning my destruc-
tion. Perhaps you still do."

That raised Tomlinson's eyebrows; he looked at Ford
quizzically as Ford said, "No, I don't—but you have no
way of knowing for sure. I understand that. But your intentions are important because, in asking you to help,
we'll also be helping you. I don't care anything about
politics. You know that. But I'm not politically unaware."

"If I enter the Presidential Palace," Rivera said carefully, "it will not be as a puppet. Besides, communism
is dead in the Soviet Union. Perhaps it is dead all over.
It is a truth that brings me great sadness." He paused.

"This much I will tell you even though I truly do not see how you can be of help."

"I think I know where Zacul's main camp is."

"So you have said. But it is a thing I often hear. Besides, why do I need to know where Zacul hides when he and his army know so well where my camp is?"

"Your plan is to wait until he attacks you?"

Rivera made a sweeping gesture. "Look around and you will see my plan. Look around and you will see the mountains that protect us. On each mountain we have built an observation tower. In each tower is a man with a radio who communicates with my headquarters. If Zacul tries to attack us here, we will destroy his army as it conies up the mountain. And he surely will try to attack. He is an impatient man."

Ford said, "You're the one who spoke of his intelligence. You think he'd try such a thing if he felt he would fail? When he comes, he'll be prepared. Maybe his friends, the Soviets, will provide him with planes and helicopters. The mountains aren't going to help you much if Zacul has enough helicopters."

Rivera sat silently for a time contemplating his beer. He had plainly already considered the possibility, and it troubled him. Ford said, "Zacul knows you're a patient man. He knows you'll wait. But every day you wait, you give Zacul more time to prepare for a successful assault on your camp."

Rivera looked at him. "It is possible."

"It's probable."

"Yes, probable. So what do you propose as an alternative?"

Ford took out the map of Masagua, the one with
Zacul's probable camp location marked, and spent fifteen minutes outlining two specific strategies. When he
was done, Rivera remained hunched over the map. Tomlinson stirred uncomfortably when Rivera said, "You
are not talking about a battle, here." He looked at Ford,
and spoke in Spanish. "This is an assassination."

Ford could not sleep that night; could not sleep, probably, because he was anxious to be gone. He was anxious to find out if Rafe's son was still alive, anxious to
be done with this business in Masagua so he could get
back to Sanibel, his stilt house, his work, and the life
that he had once hoped would be simple and without
encumbrances. That simple life, the one recommended
by Thoreau, was an unrealistic goal, though—not that
he had ever wanted it; not really. He had wanted a sim-
pler life, not a simple life, but now even that was proving impossible. In a modern world, only a person who
was absolutely selfish could live an absolutely simple
life, and only a hermit could live free of the personal
and moral obligations inherent in taking one's own existence and the existence of others seriously.

Tomlinson would have something to say about that;
yeah, Tomlinson could spend an hour talking about the
obligations of existence.

Ford stood in the darkness beneath a huge guanacaste
tree. He wore khaki fishing shorts and the blue chambray shirt. It was cool after the evening rain. The moon
was up, and there was the smell of burning wood: the
cooking fires of the soldiers. He had a small flashlight,

and he walked from the line of tents toward the dense foliage bordering the cloud forest. There was a copse of wild plantain trees, with their large bananalike leaves and bizarre, colorful inflorescences, growing above a pool that was the confluence of several mountain rivulets. Touched by the flashlight's beam, each big leaf became a separate and living entity, each leaf the possible host or habitat of a variety of insects and animals, and Ford studied the leaves, trying to relax. The best way to see the jungle, he knew, was from above; the best way to learn about it, though, was from below, one leaf at a time, because each plant was a microcosm of the great green whole.

By crouching he could see up and inside one of the plantain leaves, and there was a colony of small bats roosting: disk-winged bats, their leathery wings pulsing with the regularity of lungs. The sudden light stunned them for a long instant and then they were gone in a panic, their eerie shapes silhouetting against the moon. The leaf that had held the bats leaned out over the water, and Ford placed his foot at the edge of the pool so he could get a closer look. There were beetles feeding on striations of the leaf, some kind of heliconia-feeder, but Ford didn't know which kind. Nearby, frogs began to trill again, and Ford used the flashlight to find them: red-eyed and brown tree frogs. It was the mating season, and several of the females had smaller males clinging to their backsides. That made Ford search for something else, and it didn't take him long to find the glutinous deposits of frog's eggs stuck to the undersides of the leaves. Some of the eggs had already matured into tadpoles, and the viscid masses hung in the light like icicles, dripping life into the water below . . . where two—no, four—cat-eyed snakes waited, feeding on the globs of tadpoles in a frenzy.

Ford watched the snakes feeding, taking an odd pleasure in knowing that this same drama was going on all around him; the same cycle of copulation, birth, and death; the same earnest theater being played out by jaguars, dung flies, tapirs, leaf-cutter ants, crocodiles, boas, and men throughout the millions of acres of jungle darkness.

A twig snapped behind him and Ford turned to see Juan Rivera standing in the shadows. He was bare chested and smelled of soap, as if he had just finished showering. Behind him, the face of a teenage Mayan girl peered out through the flap of Rivera's tent. She called the general's name softly, but her voice had the flavor of a command.

Rivera held up one finger as if asking her for a little more time, then looked at Ford. "*Women*," he said; one of those flat declarations that, even in formal Spanish, communicated a matter beyond control.

Ford switched off the light; switching from one world to another. "A new wife, General?" He stepped away from the water and walked until he was beside Rivera.

"Ah, Marion, you should not make sport of me. I have only one true wife, the mother of my children, the woman I love. But out here in the jungle one must find comfort where one can. This girl who waits for me in the tent—" He nudged Ford, whispering like a confession. "—she makes demands of me. Unrealistic demands.

Then has a way of smiling when I cannot fulfill her every whim that makes me furious. I have threatened to send her back to her parents in Masagua City. Many times I have threatened this, and I am not a man who makes threats lightly." He lowered his voice even more. "But in some strange way her smile makes me even more determined to please her. Is that not odd? She makes demands of me and sometimes even presumes to tell me how to run my army. There is a demon in that little girl, I tell you. A demon, and she is bossy, too. So many times I have had to remind her who is the general and who is the simple village girl. Even then she just smiles. Yet I let her stay."

Ford said "*Women*" in the way it was always said— not sure he meant it; not so sure he didn't.

"What man of the world does not know it?" Rivera looked at Ford, shaking his head as if the burden of this unknowable thing was understood now that they had shared it. "But you, you are still not married, Marion?"

"No, not yet. Perhaps one day. I would like to have a child."

"Do you know why I think you have never married? I think it is because your heart belongs to one you cannot have." A statement that would have sounded sappy in English, but which came off as fatherly in Spanish.

"My heart belongs to one I cannot have?" As if the whole idea were too dramatic to be taken seriously.

"It would not be so surprising if you had listened closely to the gossip when you lived here. There was much talk about Pilar Balserio, my friend. No, do not give me that evil look. It was not that kind of talk. It was the talk people make when they admire a person. It was well known that she ran the government for a time. People loved her for the good things she did; for her kindness and her wisdom. Even though her husband forced her into seclusion, the talk continued. It was said she went to live in the convent across from the Presidential Palace. It was said she went there not because of her husband, but because she had fallen in love with a foreigner, a gringo, a man with hair the color of Quetzalcoatl's."

Ford said, "You never seemed like the superstitious type to me, Juan. Nor a man who gives credence to Mayan legends."

"I am not superstitious. Nor have I ever believed someone from outside our country will come to save us—but I am a Maya. I am a student of our culture, as is Pilar Balserio. The old stories are important even if they are not true. I remember that she spent many months doing research at a Mayan site by a lake in the mountains." Rivera was smiling. "You only recently mentioned the name of that lake; the lake near which you feel Zacul has his camp. Yes, Eye of God, that is the lake's name. She lived on the lake at about the same time you and I first met. Remember? It was before your government sent you to work in Masagua City, and you lived on the shore of the lake in that thatched cabana, the one with the stone cooking place and the dock where we drank beer. You said you were there to study the sharks."

"I was studying the sharks."

"You also fell in love with Pilar Balserio. No, do not

deny it. I felt very dense when I heard the rumors later. When you two were together those few times, I saw no sign of love in your faces. Usually a man can tell. Even when the woman is married."

"That was a long time ago, Juan."

"Yes. But with a woman such as that, the heart scars but it does not heal. It makes me sad, thinking of your predicament. For you, of course, there has been no other woman."

Ford was chuckling. "You are a romantic, Juan. All of you Latins are romantics. Even you Maya Latins. There have been plenty of other women."

"Women for the body, yes, but maybe not for the heart. Not a woman who makes you furious with her smile like my little demon Teresa who waits for me in the tent. Not a woman, Marion, you will let stay."

"You're getting nosy in your old age."

"Is it that I am nosy or because I am right that you evade the question?"

"I have no reason to evade anything. If you really have to know, there was one. A woman in Florida. An artist. She is as pretty as Pilar and almost as intelligent. A woman to share children with."

"Your Spanish is too good for you to make an error in tense. You said there *was* a woman."

"Perhaps there still is. I'm not sure. Not yet."

"If you are unsure, then you must try and speak with Pilar while you are here. You must not let the opportunity pass. We are men together, and I tell you to do this thing. Such opportunities are rare. It is possible that you may never get a chance to speak with her again."

"I've checked with the people I once worked with, and no one knows where she is."

"You did not check with me."

Ford wasn't sure he wanted to pursue it, but he felt the old longing and he heard himself say, "I would be interested in anything you might know. There are reasons I need to speak with Pilar; reasons that have nothing to do with love."

Rivera's head was bobbing, nodding, saying I-told-you-so with his expression. "I thought you would be interested. First let me explain that I cannot tell you how it is I know the things I know. Let's just say I've heard it from the people of the mountains. They are my people and have no reason to lie to Juan. It was from these people I heard that, in the weeks after you left, Pilar went once again to that lake in the mountains to continue her investigations. You knew that there was supposedly once a great Mayan temple built on a hill above that lake?"

"Yes," said Ford, "I knew."

"And there was a great ceremonial calendar that, in some way, was lost. A very valuable artifact. It was covered with emeralds."

"I have also heard of the calendar."

"I have been told that Pilar went back to look for this calendar—not because of the value of the emeralds, but because it played some important role in the ceremonies of our people, a thing called the Ritual of the Lake. She made certain discoveries on that lake, but if she found the calendar I cannot say. She had a camp there with workers, but the camp was attacked by robbers and Pilar was badly beaten by these men."

Ford took a deep breath, held it, then released the air slowly. "Robbers," he said, but he was thinking of Zacul.

"They stole things. They killed some of Pilar's people and they beat her. I've heard they beat her quite badly. Nuns found her and took her to a convent to heal, and there she remains. Or so I have heard."

"Then she may be dead for all you know."

"Do not get angry at me, old friend. I am only the messenger, and it is not an easy thing to tell." Rivera shrugged. "Is she dead? I think not. I have heard rumors of nuns, nuns from that convent, traveling the country and talking to the people. They have been telling people what happened to Pilar. They have been telling the people that they must do a certain thing. They have been telling the people they must come to that lake in the mountains on a certain night in June, the night of the summer solstice. The nuns even sent an emissary to the village below, Isla de Verde, to tell these few people. Perhaps that is how I came to know."

"Did they tell you why the nuns want them to go to the lake?"

"There can be only one reason. Pilar wants the people to unite behind her. She wants control of Masagua. If she was not so widely known for her goodness, for her kindness, some might even suspect her of placing the bomb that killed her husband." Rivera's tone of voice did not suggest if he suspected her or not.

Ford said, "Then she has become your rival, just as Zacul is your rival."

"It is difficult to think of such a woman as a rival. Now my only rival is Zacul—and, of course, the generals who are presently in control. The other factions are weak. Ultimately they will back him or they will back me."

"Then you will help me?"

Rivera made a gesture with his hands, a gesture of finality. "No. I'll not risk my men on a premature attack."

"We would need only two commando squads attacking from different directions. All we need is an avenue of escape. In return, Zacul would be eliminated."

"Yes, I know—sever the head and the snake dies. But who would do it?"

Ford said, "I think you know."

Rivera studied him for a moment, then said, "To be frank, I believe Zacul will have you and your hippie friend killed the moment you show any curiosity at all about this child you seek. It is a source of admiration that you would risk your own life for a boy you do not know."

Ford said, "Then you overestimate my resolve. It would be nice to rescue the child, but I won't pretend that I'd trade my life for his. As for Tomlinson, I've decided it's too dangerous for him to go. It would be useful to have him, but I cannot accept the responsibility. Not after what you've told me. Could he remain here with you for a few days?"

"Of course. He is a scholar. And I would like to pitch to him again."

"Then I will leave in the morning, before Tomlinson is awake—"

"Juan? Juan?" A girl's petulant voice interrupted, and

both men looked up to see the small figure in a long white shirt, hands on hips, dark hair hanging over heavy breasts, silhouetted by the light from within Rivera's tent. "I am getting very sleepy, Juan. Waiting for you is causing this pain in my head."

"Then do not wait! Go to sleep!" Rivera called back, sounding angry for her interruption, but he was already moving away from Ford, toward the tent. To Ford he said, "*Women*," and sounded slightly embarrassed as he added, "These pains in her head are a worry to me. I must go now. But I will have two men waiting to escort you back to the village."

"Thank you, General."

"Such pains in the head are not normal for a young girl. And only the touch of my hands will make the pain go away. It is a mystery, no?" Still embarrassed, still explaining himself, General Juan Rivera of the Masaguan People's Army disappeared into his tent.

FOURTEEN

A quetzal bird flew over, a red-chested male trailing its green tail feathers like a yard-long banner. The quetzal dropped down out of the jungle shadows, flew hard across the clearing, then banked abruptly toward the rising sun and burst into iridescent flame, sunlight still clinging to the bird's wings as it faded from sight.

Two of Rivera's soldiers were waiting, and Ford swung onto the saddle and nudged his horse. They rode from the camp straight up the mountainside to a ridge to begin the series of switchbacks that would take them around the peak to Isla de Verde. Ford stopped for a moment on the ridge, looking down into the camp. Rivera's men were stirring in the fresh morning light, tending their cooking fires. Dogs trotted here and there scattering chickens while a couple of other early risers saddled horses.

Ford wondered how Rivera had fared with his teenage mistress. He doubted if the pain in her head had lasted long; doubted if it would ever last any longer than it took to get Rivera to do exactly what she wanted. That made him smile, thinking of Juan being bullied by the tiny girl.

The two soldiers waited; when Ford nodded, they kicked their horses into a lazy walk. They rode for twenty minutes before one of the soldiers stopped suddenly, holding up his hand like a cavalry officer. In Spanish, the man said, "Do you hear something? Did you hear that?"

Ford sat listening; sat listening to the rustling silence of deep jungle; sat listening to saddles creak and their horses blowing air; sat listening . . . and then he heard it, too: voices behind them. The two soldiers quickly slid off their horses and led them into the jungle, weapons raised. Ford sat alone on the trail, feeling ridiculous, then got off his horse, too.

The voices had come from the switchback beneath them, so it was nearly ten minutes before the men came into view: two more riders on horseback. Ford guessed the soldiers were going to wait until the men were past, so he crouched down, but then he saw the men clearly, and he stepped out onto the path because one of them was Tomlinson.

"Goddamn, Doc, I didn't think we were ever going to catch you." Pulling his horse up like Randolph Scott, but looking like Joe Cocker, Tomlinson was grinning as if they hadn't seen each other in a month; a reunion smile. "I kept telling these cowboys we had to hurry— you know, like *vamos*. But these horses got minds of their own, man."

Ford said, "Now that you've caught us, you're going

to have to turn right around and go back. Didn't Rivera give you my message?"

"Yeah, man, sure; he gave me the message. You said it was too dangerous. This Zacul dude was better organized than you thought, and I had to stick around and play baseball with the general. Some message. You coulda told me personally, you know."

"I can't take responsibility for your safety, Tomlinson. I knew there would be some danger involved, but I didn't know how much until I talked to Juan. I'd appreciate it if you stayed here for a few days—or I can drop you off at the next town. You might be able to rent an old truck or something, but I'm not sure."

Tomlinson was shaking his head, not accepting any of it. "Bullshit, man. I'm going with you. This is the chance of a lifetime, and you think I'm going to miss it? My shot at being a bodhisattva. Besides, there's that kid to think about."

"You have nothing to do with the boy."

"Which just shows you don't know what bodhisattva means."

"Right. And I don't want to know."

"The kid and I are both caught up in a big dharma, man. You, too. None of this is accidental, Doc—"

"I don't want to hear any more of this stuff, damn it."

"Most people fear death. Me, I'm tuned into the only one valid fear: missing life—"

"Tomlinson—"

"I'm just telling you how I feel. I'm going with you, Doc."

"I'm telling you I can't be responsible for your safety."

"Hey, whose asking you to be responsible? You want to know why you can't be responsible for me? I'll tell you why."

Ford listened for a moment to what was to become another lesson in philosophy, then cut him off saying "Okay, okay." He was getting back onto his horse

Tomlinson said, "I'm way past twenty-one and I can make my own decisions."

"I said okay!"

"I knew you'd come around to my way of thinking, man."

"Just no more of that ping-pong karma Buddhist talk. It gives me a—pain in the head. And don't say I didn't warn you if things get rough."

Tomlinson kicked his horse up alongside Ford's. "You know what I think about danger? I think if you're walking on thin ice anyway, why not dance?"

Ford said, "Tell that to Zacul when we find him."

They drove 150 miles over bad roads, down through the central plateau of Masagua with its grazing cattle, its solitary gauchos, then west toward volcanic peaks, which sat on the horizon like stalagmites piercing smoke-colored thunderheads near the edge of the sea. Beyond the volcanoes, Ford knew, was the lake, God's Eye.

They stopped once for a breakfast, then again in Utatlan, the only town of size between Masagua City and the Pacific. Utatlan had been founded by the Spaniards in the 1500s, and it still looked like something out of a postcard from Castellón with its whitewashed haciendas and donkeys pulling carts down red brick streets.

Ford said, "Don't have far to go now, bubba."

The streets were crowded and he was driving slowly, arm out the window, taking pleasure in the look of the town and its people. Women in traditional Mayan dress, bright skirts and embroidered blouses, balanced water jugs on their heads while men in mauve-striped panta- loons and white straw hats sat by fountains selling the wares they had brought down from the mountains. "We can get some supper here, and I need to make a phone call. I guess we ought to think about spending the night, too. It'll be dark in a couple of hours."

Tomlinson was looking at the small notebook he car- ried. He was reading, leafing through the pages, then comparing his notes with the map he had spread over his knees. He had been going over his notes for the last half hour.

Ford said, "It may take me a while to get my call through. I have to call the States. You want to go ahead and find a place to eat?"

Tomlinson made no reply. He was reading, concen- trating.

"Did you hear me? You want me to try and make my call, or do you want to order some food first?"

Tomlinson looked up suddenly, like he was surprised Ford was there. "Hey, you know where we are?"

"Sure I know where we are. We're in Utatlan. It's an interesting little town, but watch your step. The people are clannish, and you're a gringo in a country about to have a revolution—don't forget it."

"No, not that. Do you know where we *are*? This is it, man. This is the place!"

"What place? What are you talking about?"

"The fifteen hundreds, man. When Alvarado conquered the Kache and the Tlaxclen. He came from the north with his horsemen down through the central plain to a Mayan trading center built on the branching of two rivers. That river we came across was the Azul. And that river up there—" Tomlinson was pointing at a rocky riverbed ahead where green water flowed past women washing clothes on the bank. "—is called the Sol." Ford translated without thinking: the River of Blue; River of the Sun.

Tomlinson said, "This is the place where the Kache surrendered to Alvarado without a fight. This village, Utatlan. This is where the whole damn sad story began. Hey, pull over there by the river. I want to look at something."

Ford waited in the vehicle while Tomlinson got out, and then Ford got out, too. While Tomlinson looked at his map and looked at the mountains beyond, Ford began to lob rocks into the river: small round rocks good for throwing, but his arm was sore after the game yesterday. "See the valley way, way over there just below the clouds?" Tomlinson was pointing again. "That must be the mountain pass where Alvarado made his forced march with the Kache. It was probably all jungle back then. Had to be a hell of a tough trip. Made them kill other Maya just so they could eat. That's the route they took when they went hunting for the Tlaxclen. The lake where you expect to find this Zacul character is just beyond those mountains, isn't it?"

"Right. About another twenty miles on the map. A heck of a lot farther by mountain road."

"And that's the lake where the Tlaxclen priests lived?"

"So the story goes."

Tomlinson was nodding, smiling, pleased with himself. "See how it's all fitting, man? It's like some magnet is drawing us. Right down the path. Can't you feel it? Doc, I can close my eyes and hear the conquistadors' horses coming. I can hear their damn armor rattling. The Kache probably waded this river to get a closer look at this wild-looking Spaniard with long blond hair dressed in metal. Alvarado had to seem like someone from outer space to them, riding an animal they'd never even seen before. It's no wonder they thought he was a god. And they maybe stood right where we're standing now watching him and his little army coming with absolutely no idea in hell that the culture of a hundred generations would be destroyed within just a few weeks." Tomlinson's eyes opened. "There's something about these hills, man; something about this country. The jungle holds onto things. It absorbs events. Five hundred years is just a blink of the eye in country like this, and things echo for a long, long time. Go ahead. Try it. Close your eyes and listen."

Ford said, "I'll let you do the cosmic listening. I've got to make a phone call."

"Suit yourself, man, but it's all still right here. A place like this, lost spirits linger."

They drove toward the heart of the town, then parked and walked because the streets were narrow and filled with people and slow-moving carts. Thursday was market day in Utatlan, a big event for all of the people who lived in the surrounding mountains; a day of bartering and drinking. The main street dead-ended in a plaza bordered by shops and old stone buildings. In the center of the plaza was a small park with a fountain, a few trees, and several stela—standing stone slabs covered with Mayan hieroglyphics. Traders had set up their booths in the plaza, and everything was for sale: live chickens, goats, wild mountain fruit, hardware, bolts of handwoven cloth, baskets of herbs, coffee beans; all these smells blending with the smoke of small cooking fires and the sharp odor of incense.

Forming the back of the plaza was a stone cathedral, four hundred years old, cracked by earthquakes, its stone steps scooped by the comings and goings of a million souls. Men in pantaloons and colorful shirts marched up and down the steps swinging censer cans of burning copal leaves while their women knelt on the floor inside the church lighting rows of candles and burning small offerings to gods known only to themselves. The mumbled chants in guttural Mayan added a percussion backdrop to the noise and wild laughter of the marketplace, and the smoke pall drifting over the plaza swirled in the cool mountain sunlight.

"The Catholic priests let them do that? Burn offerings on the floor of the cathedral?" Tomlinson's head was turning this way and that, trying to take in everything at once as they moved through the crowd, both of them a head taller than the earthen-faced Mayas who glanced up at them, expressionless. "Any way you slice it, that's paganism, man. According to the church, anyway."

"The priests leave town on market day," Ford said.

Tomlinson laughed, like it was a joke.

"No, I mean it. In these mountain villages, the priests physically leave town on market day. It's their way of pretending not to know about the religion the Indians practice. If the priests tried to put a stop to it, the Indians wouldn't show up at mass on Sunday. So the priests compromise by ignoring it. The one thing they won't let the Indians do is sacrifice live animals inside the church. Most of these little towns have some secluded spot for sacrifices. A place with an altar, a cross, and usually some kind of stone Mayan deity figure set up. When the Indians want to make a blood offering, they go there."

"Catholicity. I like that. My respect for the church just went up a notch, man."

"I'm sure the folks in Rome will be relieved to hear."

"Hey, I've got a right to judge. I was raised in the church, man; furthermore, I liked it. When I was a teenager, I wanted to be a monk; live in an abbey and sing Latin songs."

"That I believe."

"But then I found out about the Beatles."

"I believe that, too."

"Catholicism is great. They got a franchise everywhere."

"Uh-huh." Ford had stopped. "That little restaurant with the veranda look okay to you?"

"Sure, anyplace is okay with me. As long as they got beans and rice."

"Then why don't you go on in and order for us and I'll try and find the public phone."

"I'd bet long odds there isn't one. This little town is still in the bronze age, man."

"You'd lose. When Pilar was involved in the government, she saw to it that every village with a population of more than five thousand had at least one public phone, a public health facility, and a school."

Ford left Tomlinson at the restaurant and headed off through the crowd alone. He had to stop three people before he found one who spoke Spanish and could tell him where to find the phone. It wasn't a phone booth with neon lighting. The public phone was inside a house where a short fat Mayan woman sat in attendance. She dutifully noted Ford's call, accepted coins in payment, contacted the overseas operator and told her that the call was to Washington, D.C., person-to-person to Donald Piao Cheng, collect. The operator said it might take a while to get the call through and the Mayan woman assured Ford she would send a runner for him when the call was completed.

Ford ate rice, red beans, and boiled chicken at the little restaurant and drank Masaguan beer served in a liter bottle with a ceramic top. Tomlinson was saying he was anxious to get back to the plaza and take a look at those Mayan stelae, and Ford said he could take his time because they would spend the night in Utatlan. He didn't want to chance stumbling onto Zacul's army after dark and getting shot before they could find a messenger to forward their offer of an exchange. Tomlinson said that was good; he needed a break from all that traveling. Ford said it wasn't going to be much of a break because they were going to spend their free time going over how Tomlinson was going to react to the questions Zacul would surely ask him.

"Damn, man, we went over and over that stuff for the whole six hours it took us to get here."

"If we had six days, Tomlinson, it still wouldn't be enough time. If Zacul isn't absolutely convinced you're an expert on pre-Columbian artifacts, he's going to kill us. It's as simple as that. No judge, no jury, no trial. He'll just take us out and shoot us."

Tomlinson, finishing his beer, said, "I don't know what you're so worried about, Doc. I bullshitted my way through Harvard on all kind of subjects I didn't know."

Ford said, "It's just that Harvard has a different grading system. With Zacul, it's strictly pass or fail."

The Mayan woman sent a boy to get him, and Ford followed the boy through the market to the little house and picked up the phone. Donald Cheng was waiting. "Doc? Jesus Christ, Doc, you sound like you're about a million miles away. What's that echo? You in a plane or something?"

"No, at the base of a mountain. In Masagua—which is strictly between you and me. Did you get to the auction? Tell me you went to the auction, Don."

"I went to New York. I went to the auction. That painting you described to me never came up for sale—not that I'm surprised."

"You didn't leave early—"

"Just to make a phone call. I had to go out and call an agent friend of mine with New York Customs. And I bet a hundred bucks you know exactly why."

Ford said, "Oh?" and then waited.

"You said the guy holding the auction, this Benjamin what's-his-name character, Benjamin Rouchard, might be a little shady. Well, he's at least a little shady. Along with paintings, this guy was selling stuff he shouldn't have been selling. Jade carvings of jaguars, parrots, these weird little stone statuettes with nasty-looking faces and great big schlongs. He had about a dozen pieces on the block and a couple hundred more in the back room. I guess he was moving it out slow; didn't want to flood the market. You know what some of that crap sold for?"

"A lot," said Ford.

"Yeah, it's very popular with interior decorators these days. Pre-Columbian art is illegal, expensive, and bizarre, which makes it chic. One of the statuettes went for just under ten grand. And there was no documentation on any of it. No bills of sale, no statements of provenance, no shipping manifest, nothing. Smuggled goods. We're going to get one of our experts to verify the stuff as authentic, but I think it's real. That's why the high rollers come to his auctions. They know Rouchard sells only the real stuff. All Aztec."

"Mayan," said Ford.

"Hah! Caught you, you bastard. I knew you knew. That's why you pumped me about all those laws. Why didn't you just come out and tell me?"

"You're about to find out, old buddy."

"If it has something to do with that woman artist, you wasted your time being tricky. She was just an innocent bystander as far as we're concerned. We nailed Rouchard and we're checking his records to see if we can pull in any of his partners. But we don't want the woman—unless you count the way some of the guys were drooling when they looked at her. Which I guess explains why you suddenly became an art lover."

"Rouchard is in jail?"

"Oh, hell no. He's out on bail, first offense and all."

"Which means he could be out of the country by now."

"He could be. It's not like he was smuggling in coke or heroin or something. But it's the sort of arrest we like to make to keep our neighbors to the south happy. Lets them know we care about preserving their rich and colorful history and all that shit. As if I care personally, but it's illegal and this guy was doing it in a big way, so I'm glad you steered me in even if you did it in your own weird, convoluted way."

Ford looked at the Mayan woman sitting there looking out the window, listening to him but not seeming to understand. He pressed the phone closer and said, "I want to know what else you found there, Don. It's important. There's one particular thing I'm looking for—"

"So now we're getting down to it: the real reason you didn't want a well-organized bust walking into that auction. You want something. Now it's becoming clear—"

"I do want something. It's a manuscript. Very old, written on parchment with no end boards and not very long—maybe forty, fifty pages in script; archaic Spanish with rough illustrations, hand drawn. I don't know for sure that Rouchard had it, but if he did, he may not even have known it was valuable. He'd probably want some expert to appraise it before he tried to figure out how to peddle it. It may have been in that back room with the other stuff. Or his home. Did you find anything like that?"

There was a long silence before Cheng finally said, "Well, yeah. I think maybe we did. I'm pretty sure we did. One of the agents showed me something like that. There was so much stuff I didn't look at any of it too closely, but I remember seeing—"

"I want it, Don. I need that book. I need it in a big way."

"Doc, I can't do that. You know I can't. That stuff all has to be catalogued and tagged as evidence. When we're done with it, it'll be returned to the rightful country if provenance can be established. That's the way the antiquities act reads."

"You made the bust late last night, Don. You mean to tell me your people have already catalogued all that stuff—"

"You know damn well we haven't. We didn't even get the search warrants signed until late this morning. That's why you sent me to an art auction and not a bust, isn't it? You were buying yourself time just in case this book you wanted happened to be there—"

"That's exactly what I was doing. I didn't want to have to ask you to take an article already catalogued and tagged as state's evidence. That would be against the letter of the law, Donald, and I knew what your answer would have to be. But now that manuscript—if it's the piece I need—is just sitting in a room—"

"Yeah, a room that we've legally sealed."

"Right. But the article hasn't been catalogued so it's not yet considered evidence."

"Ah, shit, Doc, you're really reaching. You must really want that manuscript."

"I do. I'll tell you why later, but I need it just as soon as you can get it to me. You still owe me a big favor, Don. Do you remember why?"

"You know goddamn well I remember. I will always remember."

"I'm calling in that favor now. But you have my word that I won't sell the manuscript for profit and that it'll be returned to the proper people in the proper country."

"Meaning Masagua."

"Yeah, Masagua."

There was another long silence. Donald Piao Cheng was a man who did everything by the book, followed every letter of the law, and this wasn't coming easily. "Well," he said slowly, "we've got plenty of other stuff on the guy. Like I said, there are a couple hundred pieces boxed in that room. And the really important evidence is the stuff he'd already auctioned off."

"I appreciate it, Don. I really do."

"But Christ, you don't want me to try and get it to you while you're out of the country?"

"I wish you could. But you can't. Not safely, anyway."

Ford asked Cheng to describe the manuscript in more detail and then, convinced that it was the *Kin Qux Cho*, gave him the address in Florida to which he should have it couriered.

FIFTEEN

Men in the gutters were being peed upon.

At first dark, the Mayan men put down their copal censers and picked up bottles of *aguardiente*. They had been drinking all afternoon but, with the start of the festival which always concluded market day, they began to drink in earnest. The Maya were not loud and jolly drinkers, nor did they drink in violent packs. These small men in striped pantaloons were intensely alone as they drank, gulping straight from the bottle, throwing their heads way back. They drank as if it were a punishment, as if seeking oblivion. When they finally fell, their friends rolled them into the gutters for, traditionally, it was the duty of the women to rouse their sons or husbands and get them home. But the women would not bother to try until late that night or the next morning, and so now the village dogs sniffed the fallen and, with great ceremony, lifted their legs to pee.

Ford sat on a bench in the plaza watching the dogs,

watching the activity while Tomlinson kept up a running commentary on the glyphs he was tracing from a stone stela. Torches illuminated the plaza, but Tomlinson had to use a flashlight to decipher the nuances of etchings which had survived nine hundred or more years of weather. This was Tomlinson at his best, taking written materials and cross-referencing and crosschecking them against a memory and intellect that, considering his past, should have long since been rendered just one more warped record from the generation of Flower Children.

Tomlinson was saying, "Figuring out the date of this thing is a real bitch, man. You have no idea; no idea at all. See this?" The stone stela was about two feet taller than Tomlinson, and the main figure—a profile of some long-gone Mayan chieftain or god—was bordered by hundreds of blocks of intricately carved figures. "These here are the calendar glyphs. You read them in blocks of four, the first glyph in the top line, the first glyph in the next line, then the second glyph in the top line, and the second glyph in the next line. So on and so on, like that. See this thing that has four petals like a flower? This was their figure for zero. Problem is, the Maya saw time as an unending march into the future. Zero can mean the beginning of something, but it can also mean the completion. But see how the flower petal is affixed to this thing here, that kind of looks like the head of a bat? In glyphs, a bat face means very tired; the end of something. Then you have these three bars and four dots. That's the number nineteen, almost like Roman numerals. So this block of glyphs is telling a kind of story: that something came to an end or began during the nineteenth *katun. A tun* is a three hundred sixty-day year; a *katun* is twenty of those years; so the nineteenth *katun* would be . . ." He was actually doing the math in his head. ". . . three hundred and eighty years before or after something. You following me so far?"

Ford said, "Nope." He was watching people in the market form a loose semicircle around the steps of the Catholic church, readying themselves to participate—as they did each week—in a dance which had become ritual in the isolated Mayan villages of Central America, the Dance of the Conquest. This was no spontaneous dance inspired by the bottles of *aguardiente*. It was an articulate drama, refined over hundreds of years, that depicted the coming of the conquistadors. Each village supported its own small industry dedicated to carving masks and sewing costumes, with each new generation serving its apprenticeship.

Why the villages of Masagua continued to perform the dance, Ford did not know.

There were about a dozen dancers, and he watched as they filed down the street, shaking their rattles, already lost in the identities of the masks they wore. The conquistadors had angelic faces, painted blond hair, blond mustaches, and each bore a close-lipped smile that resembled a mannequin's leer. Some of the conquistadors were strapped into cloth horses. But the masks depicting the Maya, as through some strange act of self-flagellation, were grotesque caricatures of humanity, more demon than man.

The Maya on the street showed no emotion as they parted to let the actors pass.

Ford said over his shoulder, "You need to watch this, Tomlinson."

Tomlinson was still concentrating on the glyphs. "You don't see why learning to read these dates is so important, do you, Doc?"

"No, but I don't have to see it. You're the one who's going to have to convince Zacul."

"What I'm talking about goes beyond Zacul, man. I'm talking about my work; I'm talking the *Kin Qux Cho*. Do you realize no one has completely figured out the Mayan calendar? Scholars know even less about the Mayan writing system—pretty amazing when you consider that the people who devised the glyphs and the language are still around. You know why I think it's so important to crack the code?"

Ford said, "No. But you're going to tell me anyway—"

"It's because the figures carved into these stones go to the very damn heart of why these people seem . . . like such lost souls. Don't they seem that way to you? Kind of remote? Kind of lost?"

Still watching the dancers, Ford nodded.

"See, even if a group of people can provide itself with all the basic physical needs—food, fuel, and water—they still have to devise a method of dealing with the existential problems of existence before they can be properly called a civilization."

"No lectures on existential problems, Tomlinson. I don't like it when you do that."

"That's not what I'm talking about. I'm talking about why figuring out their writing system is so important. The Maya were an agrarian people. The existential events they had to deal with were floods, earthquakes, drought, and disease. Their way of making these random tragedies into an orderly pattern was to carefully record not only the success or failure of the current growing season, but also to make detailed predictions about future growing seasons. Gave everything symmetry, see? It all has to do with numbers, man; with these glyphs. They are the key to the foundation the whole damn civilization was built on. The Maya were fanatics about numbers. It was their religion. Take away the religion, you've got a lot of lost souls." Tomlinson was beginning to sound a little angry, but he was still squinting at the glyphs, trying to read them. "And you say once you've got the book, you're not going to let me see it—"

"I said we may not have time."

"It's just that I think you could be a little more willing." He abruptly folded his papers, slapped his notebook shut, and plopped down on the bench beside Ford. "No offense, Doc, but I personally think you've been an asshole when it comes to that book. If you don't care about academics, you ought to at least think about these people."

Ford was smiling. "Getting a little frustrated trying to figure out those glyphs, Tomlinson?"

"Damn right. Cross-eyed and crazy. Almost over-fucking-whelming. I mean, people have worked on this stuff for years and still don't understand it."

"Have a beer. We'll have a long talk about the book—but later."

"That's another thing. You're always giving me beer. You never drink more than three a day, but you act like

I've got no willpower at all." Tomlinson had already taken one of the liter bottles from the paper sack beside the bench, and now he took a long drink. "Hey, why are all those people wearing costumes?" As if he'd just returned to earth and opened his eyes.

The dance had already begun. The actors wearing the grotesque masks were alone before the onlookers, doing a slow, strange shuffle, weaving like reeds in the wind. Through the nature of the choreography, the dancers gradually seemed less and less to depict the ancestral Maya than forms of essential, malevolent spirits. They jumped and shouted, shaking their rattles. Small children who watched put their hands over their faces and slid behind their mothers, frightened.

As Ford shared with Tomlinson what little he knew about the dance, the conquistadors broke through the crowd—and that was the way to describe it, for they brushed the onlookers aside in a sort of abbreviated trot, as if on horseback while the Maya in their grotesque masks threw their hands up, writhing, terrified. Then began a series of choreographed assaults by the conquistadors. The battle lasted for a long time and it seemed as if the conquistadors were exorcising demons rather than defeating a people, and once again Ford had the impression of self-flagellation, of the Maya punishing themselves for an event that had occurred on this very ground four hundred years before.

Then the conquistadors danced alone, thrusting their cherubic masks forward, which seemed to emphasize the leering smiles as they slowly, slowly adopted the shuffling, weaving step of the demons they had just vanquished, then quickened the cadence until they were twirling around in a frenzy like a people gone mad.

Abruptly the drums and rattles were quieted and the dancers filed off again.

The villagers did not applaud.

"I'll be damned," whispered Tomlinson. "That dance made the Spaniards look like the good guys . . . but in a weird sort of way."

"I know what you mean," Ford said. "But I can't put my finger on it either. Their ancestors are portrayed as demons, but the conquistadors, in some subtle, backhanded way come off as being even more demonic."

"Maybe it's those masks. Those masks with their painted blond hair and those weird expressions give even me the creeps."

Thinking of the men lying drunk in the gutter and of the wandering stray dogs, Ford said, "Maybe it's the masks. But maybe it's something else, too."

Tomlinson said he wasn't sleepy; said he wanted to go out and have one more beer and maybe have another look at the glyphs.

Ford told him not to stay up late, they'd be leaving at four, an hour before sunrise. Like a camp counselor talking to a kid. He also told him to be careful.

Tomlinson said, "I specialize in being innocuous, man."

And Ford replied, "Don't kid yourself. Everyone in town knows we're here. Just stay out of trouble."

The best hotel in Utatlan was the only hotel, a two-story roadhouse built for the field hands of some long-gone coffee plantation. The outside walls were adobe, the rooms whitewashed. There was one shower stall and the toilet was downstairs, a cement slab with a hole augered through. Ford sat outside the hotel for a while watching huge Central American moths beat themselves against the lighted windows. He remembered a story he'd heard in the Amazonia region of Peru. On one night of each year, the story went, jungle moths would gather and fly toward the light of the full moon.

At 8 P.M. he showered then went upstairs. His bed was military issue and the springs sagged beneath his weight. The last time he checked his watch before falling asleep, it was 8:45 and Tomlinson still wasn't back.

He was involved with a dream when he heard the noise; a clattering, thunking noise, like a bunch of kids running up steps. The noise slid into his dream, then became a part of the dream. He was dreaming of sharks—the big bull sharks he kept penned off his lab on Sanibel. It was not unusual for him to dream of the species he happened to be studying, and to Ford it was a sign his subconscious was at work on conscious problems—the only significance he would ever ascribe to dreaming.

But the sounds didn't fit properly with the dream. The only way the bull sharks could be making that kind of thunking noise would be if they were banging into the pen, but the pen was built of plastic-coated wire, not wood, plus that sort of behavior was inconsistent with what Ford knew about sharks in captivity.

Then he was sitting up in the darkness, his pulse thudding, aware that someone was banging against the door. Not knocking—banging—someone throwing his shoulder against it. He swung out of bed, found his bag, and began to fish around in the darkness, looking for the pistol. But then the door crashed open and the silhouettes of three men stood in the wedge of light, two of them holding short-barreled shotguns.

The middle figure, the one not holding a weapon, said in English, "Don't do anything stupid. You come with us. You resist, we kill you here." A nervous voice, uncomfortable with the language.

Ford said, "What the hell's this all about? You can't come barging in here! I'll contact the American Embassy in Masagua City—"

"We are not dumb Indians, *señor*. We know what you are and what you are not. You will not contact anyone unless you dress quickly. You come with us! Now!"

The light came on, a bare overhead bulb on the ceiling, and Ford stood before the three men. Two of them wore green military fatigues; young, stocky men with dust-colored skin and blank expressions, holding weapons. They addressed the third man, the one doing the talking, as Colonel Suarez. Suarez wore civilian clothing, dark slacks and a loose dark shirt. He was shorter than the others, but bigger through the chest and arms; older with hairy hands and huge forearms. The shotguns were pointed at Ford's legs, then lifted toward his chest as Suarez approached him. "Did you hear me, *señor*? I told you to get dressed." Ford said nothing, just stood there in his underwear as Suarez, almost as if in slow motion, cocked his fist back and hit him hard in the face, knocking him to the floor. "When I tell you to do something, *señor*, do it immediately. Is clear?"

Ford's sat up and touched his jaw, his cheek. There was no bleeding and he wondered why it hurt so badly. He had been hit before and it had never hurt like that, but then he realized it was probably because the punch had come as such a surprise. There was no adrenaline in him to dull the pain. He got slowly to his feet, trying to keep his distance from Suarez. He said through the pain, "It's suddenly very clear."

"Good," said Suarez. "You will now get dressed while my men search your bags—if you do not object, of course." The man smiled slightly, a little nervous, but showing a set of very white teeth as Ford pawed the nightstand looking for his glasses.

They paid little attention to the cloth sack containing the jade, but they took Ford's pistol, knife, their passports, Tomlinson's notebooks, and his sheaf of traveler's checks. They also took the money from Ford's pants, but they didn't check his belt where most of his cash was hidden. The men put everything but the pistol and the money back in the bags, then secured them.

Tomlinson. Glancing at his watch, Ford wondered what had happened to Tomlinson. It was 2:35 A.M. and Tomlinson should have been back long since. Maybe they had him, too. But why?

When he was dressed, Suarez pushed him roughly into the hall, hurrying him along. The two men carried both his backpack and Tomlinson's. Obviously, he wouldn't be coming back to this room. It was as if they were cleaning up the evidence, and that scared him.

Ford was aware of faces in cracked doorways peeking out. In Masagua, people had learned not to interfere with armed men in uniform, and they pulled their doors shut quickly. They were turning away from his abduction, refusing to see it, just as stragglers on the early morning streets of Utatlan refused to see.

They took him down an alleyway that stank of urine, unlocked a door, and shoved him into a room. It was a tiny room with a single kerosene lamp on a wooden table. Ford steadied himself as his eyes adjusted, and there, slumped in a corner, was Tomlinson. Tomlinson's face was caked with blood, both eyes shut. For a moment Ford thought he was dead and felt the same vacancy of emotion, the same sense of waste, he had experienced upon finding Rafe Hollins. But then Tomlinson opened one swollen eye, smiling through the blood, saying "I screwed up, man. I really screwed up."

Behind Ford, Suarez said in convoluted English, "Your friend was very happy to find someone in the Cacique Bar he could talk with. He is a talker, this friend of yours. He told me you had come to Masagua to find Julio Zacul. Such a coincidence, no? that I am closest friend to General Zacul."

One of the soldiers pulled the door shut and locked it as Suarez said, "Now we discover exactly why you want to find my friend."

SIXTEEN

Ford was forced to sit at the table and Tomlinson was lifted into the chair beside him as Suarez took the two passports and studied the photos. Still speaking in English, he said, "William Johnson, this is your name the book says, and your city is from New York. Is correct?"

When Suarez spoke English, he sounded like someone's funny uncle, and none too bright. But it was a device; a deception that Suarez was shrewd enough to use, and Ford knew he had to be careful. He had no idea what Tomlinson had told them, or why he had told them anything, so he stuck with their original story—but aggressively, wanting to lead Suarez, not follow him. He shook his head. "No, the passports are fake. My name is Ford. His name is Tomlinson. I had the passports made in Costa Rica. You should have figured that out just by looking at them."

The frankness of that raised Suarez's eyebrows. "Perhaps the passports are real. Perhaps the names you give me are lies."

"Look inside the passports. There will be a Masaguan stamp, but none from Costa Rican customs. That's where we came from, Costa Rica. If you don't believe me, take a look at the contract in the vehicle we rented in San José."

"You entered illegally Masagua?"

"That's right, we did."

"So quickly a confession! Perhaps you will admit as quickly that you are agents sent by the Agency of Central Intelligence to find General Zacul. You and the other fucks come to try and destroy the movement. Murderers!"

"Murderers?" As if he were shocked at the suggestion; amused, too, but Ford wasn't smiling. "Look, we don't work for anyone but ourselves. You can believe that or not, but you had no reason to beat my associate. I mean, take a look at him. Does he look like a CIA agent to you? If you're not going to use your heads about this, at least use your eyes."

Suarez turned away from Ford as if musing, then swung unexpectedly and hit him with the back of his hand, almost knocking him out of the chair. "This partner you have wouldn't cooperate. This partner failed to understand our seriousness, just as you apparently do not understand."

There was blood on Ford's face now, a slow trickle coming from his nose, and he wiped it away knowing he had to show outrage, not fear, if they were to live long enough to meet with Zacul. "Your questions would be a hell of a lot easier to understand, Suarez, if you told us who you are. For all we know, you could be outlaws. Or the police. Or maybe government forces trying to destroy the general yourselves. Tell us why we should talk and then maybe we'll be more willing."

Suarez leaned over him, and Ford smelled the sharp stink of tobacco on his breath. "You must talk or we will kill you. Is cause enough?"

"It's a cause, but not a good reason. If you really are a friend of Zacul's, that might be a good reason."

"I will ask the questions here."

"Ask all you want. I'm not going to feel like doing much talking, though, unless you give me some answers first." Suarez took that musing attitude again, preparing to slap him, and Ford said quickly, "Look, we're not CIA agents. Can't you get that through your head? You can beat us all you want, but we're not going to admit to that because it's not true. In fact, it's just stupid. I personally don't give a damn who runs this country. The communists or the right-wingers, it's all the same to me. I'm here because I'm a businessman; strictly for profit. We have a business proposition to make General Zacul. That's why my friend was making inquiries. If you know Zacul, you can help us and I think we can help you."

Tomlinson leaned forward to speak, but caught Suarez's look of warning. Suarez wasn't going to let him say anything to help guide Ford's answers, and Tomlinson sat back, giving a sad shrug, as if to say again he was the cause of this.

Suarez said, "It is a thing of ease to claim you are businessmen, but a difficult thing so to prove."

"Would a CIA agent who doesn't speak Spanish go in to a public bar and ask the whereabouts of someone he wanted to spy on? Do you come across that many dumb CIA agents? We're here because we want to do business with Zacul. But first we have to find him. Why in the hell do you think I had the fake passports made? I didn't want our own customs people to be able to trace us from Costa Rica into Masagua. I didn't want them speculating about why we were here."

Suarez studied him for a moment, thinking, then said in Spanish, "Your associate said you came because you wanted to sell General Zacul weaponry. If it is true, I believe the general would be interested in talking to you. But you have made no mention of weapons."

It was an obvious trap, a soft offer to draw him into a lie, but Ford didn't fall for it. Replying in Spanish so as to suggest to Suarez he had no reason to communicate with Tomlinson, Ford said, "I am surprised my friend would invent such a story. It's not true. Maybe you frightened him into telling a lie. There is only one reason we are here: to arrange to buy pre-Columbian artifacts. The only reason. We had planned on paying American dollars, but if Zacul wants to work out some kind of trade for weapons, we can discuss it. Frankly, though, I don't know a thing about weaponry. I have an associate in Washington, D.C., who has some connections, and since he's one of my principal backers he might be able to help." Getting that information out in the open in case this was all because the Mayan woman had talked about his phone call; wanting to defuse the implications before Suarez had a chance to mention it.

It was a wise decision.

"Ah, yes, your friend in Washington, D.C. I heard of a call you made. It was a collect call, I believe. Very long." Adding the last in a tone that implied he knew what was said in the conversation.

He didn't know, of course. The Mayan woman obviously hadn't understood his conversation with Cheng. If she had, Suarez would have probably killed them immediately. "He's a business associate," Ford said, "and he lives in D.C. So what? That doesn't mean we're government agents."

"He must be a very important associate for you to call him from such a remote place."

"I called to ask him about an auction that was held in New York last night. Some artifacts were auctioned off, and I wanted to see how the bidding went. Such things are only worth what people are willing to pay, and so far they're willing to pay a lot. I was checking the current market to see what kind of money we could offer Zacul."

Suarez nodded and took a few steps away from the table. As he did, he picked up Tomlinson's notebook and began to leaf through it. He paused, studying the tracings Tomlinson had taken off the Mayan stela, and Ford sensed Suarez was beginning to soften a little. The notebooks were a strong piece of corroborative evidence. In English Suarez said, "Why this man did not tell us you have come to buy artifacts? Why did he refuse to speak?" He was nodding at Tomlinson.

Through his swollen mouth, Tomlinson croaked, "I thought you were a cop, man. Smuggling that stuff is illegal. Christ, I didn't want to go to jail."

For a moment, Ford thought Suarez was going to laugh, and he decided to press while the going was good. "General Zacul used to deal with an American named Hollins, but who was known here as Rafferty. He had a fake passport—"

"Hollins?" Suarez dropped the notebook and leaned over the table again, pushing his face close, and Ford saw for the first time that the colonel wanted to kill them; as if killing them would pose fewer problems than dealing with them. "Yes, we were aware of this man's real name. How is it you know of this man?" Talking in fast, strident Spanish.

"Hollins was an acquaintance of mine. My associates and I helped him market some of the stuff he transported for Zacul—"

"Then you know where this man is now? You know the whereabouts of Hollins?"

Even though Ford knew that Zacul wanted Hollins, the intensity of Suarez's voice startled him. They wanted him, all right, and they wanted him badly.

"Yes, I know where he is. He's dead."

"Dead?"

"Murdered. Check in my bag, the shaving kit, and you'll find a couple of newspaper clippings about it."

Suarez began to pull things from the bag, took out the clippings and read them anxiously. "It says here that he committed suicide—*suicida*, no?"

Ford shrugged. "I don't think so. He lived a dangerous

life, and I think he probably made some kind of mistake; trusted the wrong people. But it doesn't matter. Hollins is gone. That leaves General Zacul with no one to market his stuff. That's why we're here. I got to Hollins's body about an hour before the police. I found a little metal box the murderer had overlooked. There were interesting things in the box, particularly a notebook with his list of connections. That is how I found Zacul's name."

Suarez lunged forward suddenly, taking Ford by the shirt and shaking him. "What else was in the box? What else, do you hear me? Tell me now or I will have my men shoot you this instant."

Ford pulled slowly away from the man, no longer frightened, no longer worried about Suarez killing them—because he had Suarez, really had him. He said, "Some of the things are in my backpack; your men overlooked them in their first search. Some jade carvings, amulet-sized, and two emeralds. I brought them as a token of good faith."

"What else?"

What else? The emeralds weren't enough, and Ford knew he'd have to play his hole card. He said, "An old manuscript with a lot of writing I· didn't understand," watching the man's eyes.

"The book," Suarez said in a low voice, but very tense. "Describe the book to me."

Ford smiled. "You're interested in the book?"

"Yes!"

"Let's see. . . . It didn't have any covers on it. About thirty-five, forty pages long. Dark ink with some draw-

ings in faded red and gold. That's about all I can remember."

"You still have this thing?"

"I have it. But I didn't bring it with me. Not to Masagua, anyway."

"Where is it?" Suarez was hunched over him, his fists
clenched, as if he wanted to pull the information from
Ford's throat.

Ford leaned back in his chair and folded his hands
behind his head, comfortable but not wanting to push
the advantage too far. "I've done enough talking for one
night, Colonel. My friend needs medical attention. And
I could use some sleep. If you want to hear any more
about the book, you'll have to take me to Zacul."

Suarez gave him a long, cold look. After a few moments he said, "Very well. You will ride with us," but
Ford got the impression that Suarez saw this as only a
temporary concession. Ford knew that, barring interfer-
ence from Zacul, Suarez would kill them.

Ford shook his head. "We'll follow you in our own
vehicle. It'll be easier for us to get back that way."

Suarez pulled a snubnosed revolver from the back of
his pants, cocked it, and leveled it at Tomlinson. "It has
already been decided. Do you wish to argue more?"

Ford got no chance to sleep; nor did he get a moment
alone with Tomlinson. Suarez locked them in the room
with a guard, then returned an hour later to lead them
through the streets of Utatlan to a clearing beside the
River of the Sun where four transport trucks waited.

It was 4:30 A.M.

Three of the trucks were filled with boxes of food and other supplies—Suarez had come to town for market day. The back of the fourth truck had room for the dozen or so guerrillas, and that's where Ford and Tomlinson rode, sitting in the open truck among crates of bananas, papayas, and live chickens.

The last thing Suarez told the guerrillas before starting the caravan was if the gringos tried to escape, shoot them.

The trucks made their way across the western valley, throwing a dusty wake in the darkness, while behind them the twinkling lights of Utatlan were absorbed by the low dark hills and then the fiery haze of a slow sunrise. The fresh light was harsh, and it touched the peaks of the volcanos that lay ahead in abrupt striations of light and shadow, showing wedges of mountainside. Two of the volcanos were active, and the roiling smoke, normally gray, was transformed into iridescent orange by the sunrise. The smoke flattened above the coned peaks in a great swath of rust.

Ford and Tomlinson rode in the far corner of the bed, nearest to the cab. They hadn't spoken more than a few words to each other because the soldiers sat on the other side, just a few feet away. The soldiers probably didn't understand English, but Ford wanted to take no chances. Not now; not when they were so close. But then the trucks began a long series of switchbacks as they entered the volcanic ranges, and the noise of the shifting gears and straining engines blotted out all other sound, so Ford slid down closer to Tomlinson and nudged him with his foot. "You asleep?"

Tomlinson had his head pillowed on a sack of beans,

his long legs draped over more sacks, and his eyes were closed. "What?" He sat up and stretched a little, touching his face experimentally. "Naw, had to open my eyes anyway to see who was kicking me."

"Sorry. I guess you've been kicked enough for a while."

Both of Tomlinson's eyes were black and his face was streaked with iodine from the first aid kit Suarez had given Ford. Looking around, he said, "Hey, you catch those volcanos up ahead? Weird-looking, man. Like something out of an Edgar Rice Burroughs novel. Like you expect to see dinosaurs and winged reptiles and stuff. Cave men eating raw meat, maybe."

"Sounds like you're feeling better anyway."

"I feel like hell, man." He tapped his head. "In here I feel like hell."

"I can bang on the cab and tell Suarez to give us some more aspirin."

"Pills aren't going to help what I feel. It's what those guys did to me. The way they humiliated me. They hit me with their fists and they kicked me in the nuts. They . . . they made me cry, Doc. I pissed my pants and they made me cry like a baby. That sort of shit shouldn't happen to a human being." He put his head down, not able to shake it off, the abasement.

"It's okay, Tomlinson."

"It's not okay, man. You told me to be careful, but I had to go and open my big mouth to that asshole Suarez. Hell, he seemed like a nice guy. Kind of dumb and harmless. Next thing I knew, he was kicking me down the alley. Now I've screwed up your plans."

"Not too loud. Keep your voice nice and relaxed, like we're talking about the weather or something."

"Well, I did screw it up, didn't I? No more messenger going into the mountains for us, no more clean exchange. And they're probably going to kill us."

All of which was true.

Ford said, "I'll think of something. We'll just have to play it by ear. One thing we can't afford is for them to catch us in a lie. Our stories have to match. That's why I need to know what you told Suarez in that room. Everything."

Tomlinson blinked at him. "I didn't tell him anything, man. I zoned out while they were beating me. I had no reason to tell them because I didn't feel a thing."

"Look, Tomlinson, it's all right if you talked. It's nothing to be ashamed of. You said they humiliated you—"

"Not by beating me, they didn't. Hell, they degraded themselves, not me. It's what they made me feel that was so damn humiliating. It's what was going around in my brain while I was zoned out. You know what they made me feel? Hatred, man; hatred like I've never felt before. Hatred for all the cruel, unfeeling, unthinking sons of bitches in this world, and I wanted to kill them. I mean, I actually wanted to take a gun and kill the bastards because they were enjoying it. I could see it in their faces, kind of grinning while they kicked me, Suarez most of all. Hell, it was like a trip to Disney World for that buggy fucker. Hatred does a number on the bladder, I found that out. But I didn't tell them a thing, not one damn word."

"That's why you feel humiliated?"

"Sure."

"You feel bad because of the way you reacted." Incredulous, as if Tomlinson were a cross between Audie Murphy and E.T.

"Yeah. You know why? 'Cause I still got that feeling in my head. I can't get rid of it. I close my eyes and I see Suarez grinning and kicking, and I want to take a gun and give him one right here." Tomlinson, looking miserable, touched an index finger to his nose and pressed his thumb down.

Once they were in the mountains, the caravan made several stops, pulling off the road near clusterings of thatched-roof huts on the hillsides. At each stop, a couple of soldiers came straggling down, Maya teenagers, mostly, looking too small for their camouflage fatigues and shiny AK-47 Soviet assault rifles. These boys were the substance and sustenance of war in Central America, leaving their mothers to carry weapons made in countries they knew nothing about and would probably never see; fighting battles against their own kind in which each side functioned as little more than mercenaries on their own land. The young guerrillas would swing up onto the already overloaded trucks, neither smiling nor speaking; resigned to something, but Ford had never quite understood what was at the core of that resignation. He doubted if he ever would. Then someone would whistle and the caravan would rumble onward again as the teenage soldiers blinked stoically in the wind.

Two hours from Utatlan, they reached the peak of the

306 RANDY WAYNE WHITE

lowest pass and there was the lake, God's Eye, bright blue and almost perfectly round from that distance, glittering like a mirror amid the dark hills which surrounded it. Beyond a vent in the hills was another pale-blue void that Ford knew was the Pacific Ocean.

Tomlinson was looking, too. "Boy, there's no describing that, is there? Like a picture you see on a calendar, only you hate to see something like this on a calendar because it spoils it some way."

Ford said, "See that village? It's Tambor. I used to live down the shoreline from there, about a mile. I had a little lab set up."

"Where you studied the sharks."

"Right. For about eight months."

"I'd like to get a look at ol' *Carcharhinus leucas*." Using the Latin name, but not sounding affected—something only Tomlinson could do.

"Just don't get in the water to do it."

"Man-eating fish, huh?"

"They're not as quick to attack as the Maya say, but they can be pretty aggressive. They act differently than sharks in saltwater, too. For one thing, their growth's been stunted, possibly because of overpopulation, possibly because of the fresh water, but mostly because of the limited food supply. The lake's more than a thousand feet deep in some places, but the sharks have to feed near the surface because that's where the food is: fish, birds, turtles, stuff like that. They take what they can get."

"I'd feel safer in the water than I would with that bastard driving."

"Yeah, well, you probably would be safer. Once I watched these guys trying to row a horse across the lake on a makeshift bamboo ferry. The ferry dumped and the horse went in the water. I was in a boat, so I got a good look. I hadn't seen a shark all morning, but within a minute of that horse hitting the water, they were all around. The water's so clear you can see them from a long way off."

"Goddamn, they ate a whole horse?"

"No. That's the point. They never touched it. The horse made it clear to shore with these five-footers cruising all around. But the way those fish vectored in the instant that horse hit the water was impressive. I don't believe in the legends, but I don't want to test them either."

Tambor was bamboo, thatch, plywood, and tin, too rustic to be tacky, too well traveled to be quaint because it was the only village on the lake built on the main road. Ford looked to see if he recognized anyone as they drove through, thinking that, if they stopped, he might somehow be able to get a message to . . . who? Rigaberto Herrera, maybe. Ford couldn't think of anyone else who could help.

He didn't recognize anyone on the street, though. And the caravan didn't stop. It turned east up a mud logging trail, the trucks grinding along in low gear, twisting and sliding for nine or ten miles past a series of camouflaged bunkers. They were following the perimeter of the lake toward the sea, and, at each checkpoint, guerrillas stood with their machine guns and made sloppy, bored salutes. Finally the forest thinned and they ascended onto a broad plateau a hundred feet or so above the lake and about a mile from the Pacific, but still hidden by the hills behind and the forest beside. Then they came to a clearing: Zacul's main camp, almost directly across the lake from Tambor.

Ford had spent time on this section of shoreline, but he didn't recognize what he now saw. What was once thick jungle had been cleared and pushed back. Zacul had installed a permanent camp, using fiberglass housing shells that were camouflaged to blend with the high green forest canopy. There was a big open cook house, kettles boiling. There were open-air messes and a parade ground, too. Ford guessed there were facilities for five hundred or more men. The rest of Zacul's forces, as were Rivera's, would be spread around the country as a sort of civilian militia. Sitting not far from the parade ground beneath gray webbing was a Soviet gunship, its blades folded like wilted petals, rockets clinging to its underbelly like eggs on a gravid crab. There were artillery bunkers, too—antiaircraft ordnance, Ford guessed, but the artillery was covered and he couldn't see it clearly. The whole camp had a sterile look; a place of raw earth and fresh paint, as if the bulldozers had only recently finished their work.

Protruding from the jungled hillsides, in stark contrast, were wedges of gray stone blocks buried beneath earth and vines that were now being torn away by men working on scaffoldings.

Tomlinson noticed and nudged him, excited. "Those are pyramids, man. Even covered by that hill, you can see the shapes."

Ford said, "Yeah, I think so."

"I thought an earthquake supposedly took all that stuff. Look at it, man. It's not supposed to be here."

Ford did not reply. He had suspected that this was where he would find Zacul, suspected it when he heard that Pilar Balserio's archaeological camp had been attacked by robbers.

Zacul and his men had been the robbers and it was here they must have assaulted Pilar and taken the book that Rafe Hollins would later steal from them, the *Kin Qux Cho*. Now Zacul and his men were continuing the work that Pilar had started, uncovering the lost temples of the Tlaxclen Maya.

When the trucks stopped, they waited for the soldiers to get out; then Ford jumped to the ground. He took a few steps, looked to see if anyone was watching, then squatted and picked up something small and black, as shiny as quartz. He handed it to Tomlinson.

"What's this, man? An Indian arrowhead? Naw, it's a—"

"It's a shark's tooth," Ford said.

Tomlinson was staring at the ground. "Hey, they're all over the place. There's one; there's another one. A big one, too—"

"Don't pick it up. Just keep walking."

"What are sharks' teeth doing up here, man? We must be a mile from the ocean and at least a half mile from the lake. A lot higher, too."

"It's because we're standing where the lake used to be."

"Huh?"

"The earthquakes didn't cover the lake, they moved it. That's why no one ever found anything looking in the lake."

"I'll be damned!" Tomlinson couldn't resist, and picked up another shark's tooth. "Yeah, right—I get it. The whole bottom shifted." He turned to Ford. "But how did you know? Did Pilar tell you?"

Ford said, "No, I told her."

They were herded across the parade ground to a fiberglass structure about forty feet long and fifteen feet wide set apart from the other, smaller huts. Two guards with automatic weapons lounged outside, and they watched blankly as Suarez snapped open the padlock. "Your hotel while you are our guests." Grinning like a comedian, Suarez made a sweeping gesture with his arm. "But do not get so comfortable. I am sure General Zacul will want to speak with you soon. Tomorrow, yes. Or the next day." He had made a joke in English and was laughing.

Inside, daylight filtered through a grating at the far end creating a dusky darkness that emphasized the heat and the stench. Ford was aware of movement inside, of other shapes hunched close to the ground. Then his eyes adjusted and he could see that the shapes were human; people chained to the walls, sitting in the stink of their own offal, no longer bothering to swat at the flies that buzzed in a translucent veil around their faces.

Most of them were men, but there was at least one boy, too. Ford stood breathing shallowly in the foul air, studying the child chained beneath the grating. The boy was using his free hand in play, trying to build a tiny house of twigs but without much success. The house fell when Suarez slammed the door, locking them in. The boy began to rebuild the house again, but it fell once more. Finally, with a moan of frustration, he knocked the twigs away and buried his face against his arm.

He did not cry, though, and his silence was more chilling than any scream.

The boy was Jake Hollins.

SEVENTEEN

Tomlinson was saying "You know why I like traveling with you, Doc? Because you steer clear of all that tourist-trap stuff. No Days Inns or Ramadas for you, man. Places you go, a guy doesn't have to worry about that troublesome holiday traffic." His voice slightly higher with a nervous edge, Tomlinson was frightened and had to talk.

They had found a space on the ground as close as they could to the boy without making it obvious that they had an interest in him. Outside the temperature was probably 84 degrees with a cool breeze from the mountains. Inside the fiberglass hut, though, it was like a sauna, and Ford's cotton shirt and pants were already soaked. If the heat was bad, the stink was worse, plus there were the flies.

Now Tomlinson was trying to be funny.

"Then there's all the interesting people we've met,

and now you even found us a place to stay for free." He patted the ground like it was a pillow. "Don't think I don't see the wisdom in a vacation like this. Nothing shakes off those nine-to-five blahs like a good dose of hepatitis."

Ford was watching the boy, studying him out of the corner of his eye. Physically, Jake Hollins was a mess. His long brown hair hung matted over a grimy face, and his Miami Dolphins T-shirt was as mud-caked as his jeans. He had shown some interest when he heard them speaking English, turning toward them with a face that emanated a glow as brief as a firefly's, an expression of pure hope. But he had quickly withdrawn again, sliding down into a curious sitting fetal position, rocking back and forth as Ford had seen blind invalids rock. The boy had wanted the face of his father, not the stares of more strangers.

Now Jake Hollins didn't seemed to hear them at all; seemed, in fact, oblivious to everything around him. After ten or twelve days in this hellhole, Ford guessed, oblivion would be a welcome escape. Especially for a sick child—the boy clearly had a bad case of dysentery, judging from the mess around him. He looked feverish, too, staring out from dark eyesockets like an animal peering from a cave. It was the one painful ingredient in the whole initiative that Ford hadn't anticipated: They couldn't tell the boy they had come to help him. Not right away, anyway, not until Ford was convinced Zacul or Suarez hadn't planted an observer inside the jail. They couldn't take the chance of Zacul discovering that the child's life was a potential bargaining tool. And, from the look of him, Jake Hollins might not last much longer without some word of hope.

Ford took a deep breath, sighing, and Tomlinson seemed to pick up on what he was thinking, saying "I wish there was someone else in this dump who spoke English. No offense, Doc, but you haven't exactly been a joy to talk with lately."

The boy just sat there, still rocking. Didn't even look up.

Ford slid closer to the boy as he pretended to stretch. Then he began to collect the twigs Jake had been playing with, taking care to keep the pile right in front of the boy. Tomlinson said, "See, Doc, you've got the advantage here. Conversationally speaking, I mean. You can speak Spanish, so you can talk to anybody you want. But me, I don't speak anything but English, so I've got no one else to talk to."

The boy still did not react.

Ford began to lay the foundation of the house. But he laid it out crooked so that the next level of twigs didn't quit fit, and the next level fell.

Tomlinson said, "You aren't much at building boats either."

Ford said, "It's a house," as he began to lay the crooked foundation again.

Then someone else spoke, a soft voice from halfway down the room saying "You are Americans, no?" Leaning forward to make himself known was a slightly built man sitting in white underwear and covered with mud, but with a formal expression on his face, as if he were at a cocktail party and about to make introductions. "I hope you do not mind that I try my English on you, but lately—" He shrugged, oddly embarrassed. "I so seldom get the chance to be using it."

"We're Americans," Ford said.

"Ah, yes, I thought so by your accents."

Tomlinson said, "Not that it makes any difference around here. General Zacul seems to treat all prisoners as equals."

The man shook his arm and the chain made a rattling noise in the dusky light. "Not completely equal. You are to be here only a short time. Me, I have been here for . . ." He stared at the ceiling as he calculated. "I have been here for nearly a month. Perhaps longer. They would have chained you if you were to be here like the rest of us. Since the floor is earth, they are afraid we will dig out."

"You're considered criminals, then. That's why you're here?" Glad for the diversion the man was creating, Ford got to the third level of the house before the twigs fell this time. Once again he started to rebuild on a crooked foundation.

"Oh, yes. Every person here has committed a crime. We are all very desperate criminals." The man sounded so weary that the sarcasm in his voice wasn't easy to read, but it was there. "The person sitting across from me, his name is Fredrico. Fredrico's crime is that he sold some vegetables to a group of government troops. Fredrico has been here even longer than I. Two months, he says. And that boy sitting by the door, his name is Jesus. Jesus is not yet eighteen years old, and his crime

is that he refused the attentions of one of General
Zacul's advisors, a Cuban officer named Arevilio.
When Jesus's parents learned that a man tried to take
their son to bed, they naturally contacted the authorities. For their crime, they were murdered. For his
crime, Jesus was brought here. Someday Zacul or Arevilio or one of the other officers will come and seduce
the boy again, for it is their way. Until that time, he will
stay here chained with us. Or they will take him to the
little wooden shed near the cliff to await execution."

The man was sitting there in the filth, speaking softly,
talking about outrages but not sounding outraged, just
tired.

Once again Ford's house fell.

The man said, "The man lying near the door, his
name is Creno. Creno's crime is that he is a Miskito
Indian. Normally, the soldiers of El Dictamen shoot
Miskito Indians on sight, for that is the wish of General
Zacul. But Creno has not been shot because he apparently saw something that he should not see. What this
thing was, Creno has been kind enough not to tell us.
But because it is possible that Creno told others about
this thing he should not have seen, General Zacul has
ordered that he be tortured each day until he talks. Only
after talking will he be shot. It is a thing you call irony,
no? Normally, one is threatened with death if one does
not cooperate. But Creno faces certain death if he does
cooperate. So he has endured these many weeks. Three
weeks, I think. Yes, more than that. He has been a great
inspiration to us. But, as you can see, he cannot last
much longer."

Creno was a tiny man with straight black hair who lay naked, face down on the ground. There was a random grid of red welts on his back and buttocks, whip scars, probably. He had not moved since their arrival, just lay there panting in the heat like a wounded animal.

"What about you? What's your crime?" Tomlinson asked.

"My crime is that I am a physician. I could have opened a practice in Masagua City after internship, but I chose instead to spend a year practicing in the rural areas of my country—to pay a debt of respect to my own people. About a month ago this army attacked Pochote, a mountain village they suspected of helping another guerrilla group here, the Masaguan People's Army. Zacul's soldiers burned the village, but that is not the worst thing he did. He assembled the men of Pochote and offered them the chance to join his army. He asked for volunteers, which was Zacul's way of tricking them for, of course, none of the men volunteered. He had burned their village, you see.

"There were forty-three men in that village over the age of fourteen. Zacul and his lieutenants cut the testicles off all forty-three of those men. They stripped the men, tied them with ropes, and used no anesthetic. It took all night. When I arrived two days later, the floor of that place was like a charnel house. It was black with blood. I tell you, when Zacul goes to a village now and asks for volunteers, *all* the men step forward. That was his intent when he tricked the men of Pochote. I have heard him joke of it."

The doctor continued, "I learned of the atrocity and

traveled two hundred miles to help those men. Several had bled to death; two had committed suicide. Those who survived were already badly infected when I arrived, but I had brought medicines and set about trying to treat them as best I could. Several days later I was arrested. Four times they have taken me to a room and beaten me. Each time I am asked to sign a paper which says that I agree to serve as a medical officer in Zacul's army. I am not a strong man. In fact, my classmates considered me to be a coward. So I was surprised and rather proud that I did not sign that paper during the first torture session. Of course, they did not beat me badly. They are desperately in need of a physician, so I'm sure they treated me more gently than the others you see here, such as Creno. But I began to take strength from the courage of poor Creno and I survived the second beating. Now I have survived four, and it has been three or perhaps four days since either Creno or I have been beaten." The young doctor leaned farther forward, anxious as a child as he said, "You, obviously, are not considered criminals by General Zacul. I will not ask why you are here, but perhaps you have even spoken with the general. Perhaps you know him as a man in some way. Do you think it is possible that he has given up his efforts to force us by torture? Do you think it is possible that we might some day be released?"

Ford was reaching to reconstruct the foundation of the twig house for the seventh time when a small white hand reached out and stopped his. Jake Hollins was staring at the pile of twigs, but watching him peripherally.

There was an expression on his face: impatience, Ford decided. As if to say *Can't you adults do anything right?*

Ford liked the expression on that small, grimy face with its cleft chin; recognized something in the light of those dark-brown, gold-flecked eyes that he had once admired in Rafe's. As Tomlinson and the young doctor continued to talk, he and Jake Hollins began to build the house together.

Ford did not answer the physician's question.

Three A.M., and Ford was whispering, "A boy who lived in Tambor used to bring me sharks' teeth. Hundreds of them, some of the biggest and best I've ever seen. I finally convinced him I'd still buy the teeth if he showed me where he was finding them. He brought me here."

Both Tomlinson and Ford were lying on their stomachs, gripping the steel stake to which Jake Hollins was chained, trying to twist it free. The stake was driven through the chain, through a heavy grommet built into the fiberglass, then deep into the ground.

The boy was asleep, knees drawn up to his stomach, lying on his side.

Ford said, "The question was obvious: Why so many sharks' teeth a half mile from the lake and nearly a mile from the sea? They weren't fossilized; nothing to suggest a prehistoric drop in sealevel. It gave me something to think about, and, believe me, you live alone in a place this remote, you treasure little mysteries like that.

"At about the same time, I met Pilar. While her husband was on a tour of Europe, she had rented a little cabana about a quarter mile from my lab and lived alone. We met on the beach, and gradually—very gradually—became friends. I began to help her in her work, and she began to help me in mine."

"And that's how you fell in love with the *Presidente*'s wife, man. I can see how it could happen."

Ford said, "Balserio wasn't president then but, yeah . . . that's how it happened. Pilar and I had some great talks sitting outside that cabana at night, just the two of us. She was about as desperate for company as I was at first, but then it became more than that. We weren't lovers; not completely, but I guess I was in love with her—as close as I've ever come to being in love, anyway. Twice she said that she loved me, and a woman like that doesn't use the word loosely."

They were twisting the steel rod back and forth, working it like a crossbuck saw, and it was beginning to move. Tomlinson said, "A guy like you, he's got to be in prison before he opens up. I think you ought to consider this a kind of therapy; make it into a positive thing."

"Uh-huh, right. Pilar's the one who told me the story about the Kache, the conquistadors, the calendar, the earthquakes; all of it. The problem she was working on was what happened to the calendar. If the legends were correct, the calendar should have been someplace in the lake. It's a hell of a big lake and it's deep, but it's only really deep toward the middle and, considering all the people who have looked for the calendar, someone should have found it. At that time, Pilar was plotting constellations for the fifteenth and sixteenth centuries, doing a lot of complicated math and trying to figure out exactly where the Tlaxclen priests would've had to mount the calendar to reflect the light of a certain major constellation. She had settled on Orion as the constellation because it had seven bright stars and, in Tlaxclen tradition, the last year of the calendar was called the Year of Seven Moons. This event only happened once every fifty-two years—"

"I know, I know," Tomlinson said impatiently. He was sweating, working hard but trying not to look like he was working in case anyone was watching. "Christ, I'm the one who told you."

"Oh, yeah . . . Anyway, she kept coming up with the eastern shore, where we are now. But so had a lot of treasure hunters, and this was the only section of the lake that had really been thoroughly searched, even with all the sharks. That's when it came to me, sitting outside the cabana with Pilar one night. The earthquakes that came after Alavardo's conquest either drastically reduced the level of the lake or altered its position. Where we are now was once underwater, that's why all the sharks' teeth. If the Tlaxclen priests had really pushed the calendar into the lake, it would not be sitting beneath the jungle a half mile or more from the shore."

"Not bad, man. I bet Pilar loved that idea."

Ford had both hands on the stake and slowly worked it out of the ground. "Pilar like the idea. She loved me."

"So why did she leave you?"

Ford slid the stake back into the ground and patted earth around it. "That's a mystery I never solved."

EIGHTEEN

Late the next morning there were voices outside the stockade. The door was pushed open and an unfamiliar figure stood staring in, lean in the bright column of light which jarred through.

It was Julio Zacul.

He peered into the darkness for a few moments, trying to see, then turned away as if the effort was undignified. To the guard he said, "Bring the Yankees," and disappeared from the wedge of light.

Ford patted Jake Hollins's leg, telling him to stay put, to hang on. The boy seemed to understand as quickly as he had discovered upon waking that the stake which held his chain was loose.

Now, as then, he said nothing; just blinked brown eyes at Ford.

Zacul was waiting for them, standing with Colonel Suarez in the shade of a wide guanacaste tree. Both wore fatigues and Suarez had something in his hand, something Ford couldn't see, which he held to his nose before handing it back to Zacul. Now they were both lighting cigarettes: Zacul, tall and lean with stars on the epaulets of his shirt, leaning toward Suarez's lighter, his hand cupped around the flame. It was the face from the photograph, older, heavier, but still with that pointed expression: skeptical, judgmental. But there was something different in the eyes now—a glassy look without emotion, like illness. Ford guessed him to be twenty-eight or twenty-nine, six three, two hundred pounds, but with the softness of someone who had grown up inactive and indoors. All the little nervous mannerisms added to the impression of hyperactivity: the way he tapped his fingers incessantly, bloomed his cheeks out as he tasted the cigarette smoke, shifted from one foot to another, talked in sudden bursts. The black hair was combed straight back, shiny with combing, and the face was gaunt, handsome and cruel with the sickle-shaped scar pale on the pale skin of his left cheek. He had a long chin and a strong, straight nose, like a beak. An automatic pistol rode low on his hips in a gunbelt studded with ammunition clips, and Ford had the impression he wore it that way for style, the way another man might wear an ascot.

"Your sleep was good, I hope." Suarez was grinning at them, still enjoying his bad jokes in English.

With Tomlinson a step behind him, Ford stopped just inside the circle of shade. "Maybe you think it's funny, Suarez, but I'm not accustomed to sleeping on the ground with a bunch of criminals. Listening to them crap their pants all night, *Christ*. That's not the way I treat people I want to do business with." Wanting to show displeasure, but not too much, hoping to get a quick reading on what Zacul had planned for them.

Zacul spoke, talking quickly; a man on power overload needing a vent. He said, "The colonel wanted to show you how we treat people who endanger our cause. Bad people. People who lie to us or try to trick us—as a warning. But perhaps he could have chosen a better way. Yes, I'm sure he could have chosen a better way." No introductions, speaking formal classroom English, Zacul gave Suarez a brief look of reproach that Suarez accepted for the fiction it was. They wouldn't have been put in the stockade if Zacul hadn't wanted them there. "He has told me," he continued, "of your business proposition. I am interested. My army and my political organization will soon rule all of Masagua but, for now, we must also be capitalists. We must make money where we can to finance our great cause." Saying this mechanically as his dark eyes searched Ford's face. "This man Hollins, he was a friend of yours, correct?"

"I did business with him a couple of times."

"As did we. I found him a good man, a trustworthy man." The eyes were still boring in on Ford.

"Maybe we're talking about two different men. The Hollins I knew was a thief and a cheat. He got exactly what was coming to him."

"You did business with a man you didn't trust?"

"I make it a habit not to trust anyone I do business with. I don't expect them to trust me so why should I trust them? I like things right up front, goods and money on the table. Don't confuse me with Hollins."

"I confuse you with no one. But Hollins is still in my

debt in certain ways, just as it is true we owe him certain things. I wanted to know if you were aware—"

"Any debts between you and Hollins have nothing to do with me. I'd rather not even hear about it. I'm offering you a new deal entirely—and probably a better deal, too."

"That will be for us to judge, not you."

"So judge. We will pay you forty percent fair market value for quality stuff, and pay you cash in American dollars. Half up front, half after sales. Because we plan to distribute through auction houses in L.A. and Miami as well as New York, we'll have wider distribution, and that means we'll buy a lot more product and still keep the prices up. We'll assume all risks, absorb any losses. All you have to do is provide the product, a landing strip, and the men to load it onto our plane."

"You are talking only about artifacts."

"Why? You have something else to sell?"

From the expression on Suarez's face, they obviously had something else to sell.

Ford said, "If it's what I think it is, we'd be willing to handle it, but in a small way. We'd job it out, not do the actual transporting ourselves. That's too dangerous. The Coast Guard looks for drugs. Pre-Columbian art is a whole lot safer."

"You seem very sure of yourself for one so new to this business. Perhaps it is because one of your associates works in Washington, D.C., that you expect few losses? He is an important man, this man?"

"Let's just say we won't have any trouble from U.S. Customs."

Zacul's expression was noncommittal, but his gaze

shifted as he inhaled deeply on his cigarette. To Tomlinson he said, "And you, you are an expert on Mayan culture?"

Tomlinson jumped slightly, nervous, but that was okay. It fit the part he was playing. "I'm an expert on Egyptian culture, an Egyptologist. I'm a new student of Mayan culture. There are similarities that, you know, are real interesting—"

"I brought him to help me identify and appraise pieces," Ford cut in. "He's here on a contract basis now, but maybe on a percentage deal later."

"Because you do not trust me?" Zacul said, smiling slightly.

Ford allowed himself to smile, too. "And I don't expect you to trust me."

"You told Colonel Suarez certain things. Should I trust that those things are true?"

"Like what?"

"He told me of this book you say you have. It is possibly a thing I would like to have for my personal collection." Said in an offhand way, Zacul acted as if he didn't much care one way or the other.

Ford said, "Colonel Suarez gave me the impression it's very valuable. I thought it was worthless until we talked to him," watching Suarez flinch—and enjoying it.

Zacul said, "Colonel Suarez knows so little about so few things." Suarez actually seemed to shrink, slowing as they walked until he was two steps behind.

"How much do you think the book's worth, General?"

Zacul shrugged while his nervous fingers tapped double time. "In dollars, not much. Not to a collector. But I am a student, and it's a thing I would like to have."

"Then I'll give it to you as a gift when I return for the first shipment. A present of good faith. It's in Costa Rica now. Safe."

Zacul liked that, Ford could see it in his face. "Very generous, but since I'm to have it anyway, why not tell me where it is so I can send a man to bring it? That way I can begin my study of it immediately, and, of course, it would finalize our business agreement."

Playing along, Ford said, "I'm going to have to think about that one, General. After the treatment we've received, I mean—"

Zacul nodded, looking at Suarez, that same expression of reproach, the same act. "Colonel, these men should have been treated as guests, not as criminals. This man has been beaten. Not by you or your men, I hope?" Speaking in English for their benefit.

Apparently it was a familiar role, and Suarez didn't bother to hide the smirk. "It seemed a necessary thing at the time, General."

"That is not the way I wish to run my army. A man must be judged fairly, not in some bar in Utatlan. I am very disappointed. From now on, these men will be treated as my personal guests. And you may consider yourself confined to quarters for the rest of the morning."

Suarez saluted smartly, then ambled off toward the lakeshore where he began to give orders to soldiers who were unloading boxes from several small boats.

Zacul was already bored with them. His attention wandered; he dropped the fake formality and kept lighting cigarettes. He had more important things to do than play host to two profit whores—Americans at that. That was fine with Ford. It meant he believed their story. That he paid them any attention at all was an indicator of how badly he wanted the book.

They had followed him through the camp to the hillside where men on scaffoldings were digging out the remains of at least one great pyramid, maybe another, though Zacul said it was too soon to tell. He led them up stone steps, like gray dominos, then through a low postern. It was cool inside the temple and smelled of earth and bat guano. There were vines growing out of the walls.

"There have been many earthquakes since the time of the conquistadors," Zacul told them. "You can see how this temple has been damaged. But in its historical value, I think this find equals that of Tikal in Guatemala. As *presidente*, I have proclaimed it a national preserve, the Julio Zacul Park of Kings, in honor of our great revolution and the Maya people. There will soon be tours on those small carts such as you have in the United States."

As president? Tours on small carts? Something behind those glassy eyes had lost a hinge, was swinging back and forth through reality. The guy was already living in the future.

Tomlinson was on his tiptoes, studying the wooden lintel above the entranceway, saying "This is *zapote* wood, as strong as iron but it lasts longer." Speaking to Ford but to convince Zacul he knew what he was talking about. "Take a look at this, Doc—" He was touching a small carving that had been etched outside the frame of the lintel's intricate glyph-work. The carving was very old, roughly done, and graphically obscene. "It's a graffito. The Mayan workers loved graffiti. Probably close to nine hundred years old. I bet it used to drive the priests crazy."

"More than a thousand years old," Zacul put in sharply, not contesting Tomlinson's expertise but to establish his own as superior. He looked at Ford. "This man calls you Doc. As in doctor?"

"That's right," Ford said, but offered no further explanation. He told Zacul he hoped the lintel would be included in the first shipment; said he felt they could auction it for thirty, maybe forty thousand dollars. Zacul said it would be worth at least eighty. He said it in a way that left no room for discussion. Zacul told them the lintel would be cut out of the doorway and ready for the first plane.

Zacul led them down the hill, not commenting on the other digs going on near the main temple. He spoke to his men in a barking Spanish, filled with slang and profanities which illustrated his personality more clearly than his formal English. Some of the work areas were screened from sight by awnings and an odd smell drifted from them: ether and gasoline. Once, when the general walked away for a few moments to speak with a worker, Tomlinson whispered, "Cocaine kitchens. Smell the fumes? They make the stuff right here."

Ford nodded. It was something Tomlinson would know by smell.

As they finished the tour, Zacul still had given no indication they had found the calendar or were even looking. But Ford knew they must be close. They had already salvaged at least two of the emeralds—the stones he had found back on Tequesta Bank. Ford wondered if they had found any more since Rafe's theft.

The question was soon answered.

Zacul led them to a clearing in which a great canvas awning had been raised and encircled with concertina wire. Two guards stood at the entrance holding assault rifles while, inside, several men wearing rubber gloves worked over vats that were probably filled with acid. Beyond the work area was a large storage site studded with Maya stelae, large and small, like a graveyard. The folding tables were covered with stone carvings and ornate pottery. At the rear of the area was another one of the portable fiberglass huts, this with a third guard standing at the door.

Ford guessed the concertina wire and the extra guard had been added after Rafe's last visit.

Zacul told Tomlinson to look all he wanted; asked him to give him an idea of what some of the smaller stelae might be worth. The question was too innocent, implying a lack of expertise that Zacul would have never admitted even if it were true. It was a test; the test Wendy Stafford had warned him about back in Costa Rica, and now it was up to Tomlinson.

Tomlinson walked slowly along the stone rows, stopping here and there, squinting at glyphs, touching some of them. He seemed to pay special attention to the first row, a dozen stones no higher than his thighs.

Finally he said, "Stelae this size are the easiest to sell. They're portable enough for people to display them easily in their homes, but still big enough to be impressive. Real works of art." He was squatting, one hand on a stone, looking at Zacul. "I guess the median rate for one of these stela might be nine grand; probably average around eight if you spread them around, market them right."

Ford winced at the expression on Zacul's face. "Then you would pay me approximately four thousand American dollars apiece for those stones?" Like he was springing a trap.

Tomlinson stood. "It's up to Dr. Ford what he pays you, but I couldn't recommend he pay more than a couple hundred or so apiece. The stones in this row are copies. They're good copies, but it still adds to the risk. I'm just telling you what they'd sell for if we found the right buyers. It would be dangerous, though. If collectors got word Doc was pushing bad goods, it could mess up his whole operation. He'd make money up front but he'd lose in the long run when word got around."

Ford was so relieved he had a hard time manufacturing the proper indignation. "What are you trying to pull here, Zacul? I offer you a fair business deal and now you try to push off fake stuff on me. I don't like that. It's bad for everyone concerned."

Zacul was anything but meek. "You said you don't trust me? Well, I don't trust you. It is an easy thing for two men to say they have come to my camp to buy artifacts. They might come for other reasons and have absolutely no knowledge of what it is they're pretending to buy. I test in my own way—" Now he looked pointedly at Ford. "—and you will not use that tone of voice with me again." He let the stare linger before saying to Tomlinson, "How did you know these pieces are counterfeit?"

Tomlinson's expression was thoughtful, like a professor waiting to elaborate. "For one thing, I had the advantage of seeing them all together. The glyph patterns are similar and the stones are all approximately the same size. A buyer wouldn't have that advantage, but someone who really knew what they're doing might notice that they're made of aggregate, not pure stone. They've been poured into a mold, like cement, before you had your people antique them. Then there's the glyph of the moon goddess repeated four times on each of them. On the first glyph on each stone the nipple of her left breast is convexed where the mold has been pitted. A small convexity like that wouldn't have lasted a hundred years, let alone a thousand."

Zacul nodded slowly. "I will have my men tend to it. Come, I wish to show you a few more things."

Zacul kept his best stuff inside the fiberglass hut. There were fireproof drawers filled with jade amulets and carvings. In one, Ford got a quick look at another large emerald before the drawer was slammed shut again. Rafe hadn't taken them all, or they had found more. The best piece was a mosaic, a life-size human mask made of several hundred intricately worked jade shards. The mask had the humped Mayan nose and haunting, hollow eyes, like a skull. Zacul said a similar piece had recently been sold on the black market to a museum for $140,000 and wanted to know if Ford had any connections with museum curators. When Ford said he did not, Zacul told him to cultivate some. It was a flat statement, neither an order nor a request. He added, "American museums are able to pay more than most private collectors, and they are experts at legitimizing the provenance of illegal imports. Not long ago an American curator was fired by her board of directors for notifying the customs authorities after being offered a particularly valuable but stolen gold monstrance from Colombia. Some museums value art more than they value the law."

"I didn't read about that," said Ford.

"It's because nothing was written about it. But I know that it is true. You can be sure other curators know of it, so they may be even more anxious to bid on this mask. You will investigate the possibilities."

"At the same percentage we've agreed upon? You can bet I will."

Zacul pushed the drawer that held the mask closed. "We have not yet agreed upon a percentage," and walked away.

They followed him back through the camp, hurrying to keep up. He showed them another fiberglass hut where he said they would sleep, then stopped outside the screened kitchen adjacent to the huge open cooking area that sided the main mess. Inside was a young man in an apron, stirring something in a small pot. He was beaming at Zacul but not making eye contact, sweating over the stove. Zacul said, "This is the officers' kitchen and my personal chef, Oscar. He will prepare your meals, show you where to bathe, and tend to anything else you may need. Tell him what you want and he will provide it. I will have your luggage returned to you, minus any weapons you may have been carrying."

Ford said, "Does that include the two emeralds and my jade?"

Zacul eyed him coolly. "Those things were stolen from me by your friend Hollins. But I'll allow you to sell the jade. As a gesture of good faith. The emeralds I will keep."

Ford considered protesting but, instead, simply nodded his acquiescence.

Zacul said, "You have free access to the camp that lies between the road and the sea. You may go to the beach, but do not stray near the dig site, into the sector near the bluff, or down the road that leads to Tambor. My men have orders to shoot on sight, and they will not hesitate."

Ford said, "We were hoping to leave tomorrow, but first I'd like to get the percentages down, maybe draft an agreement—"

"You wish to pay me cash? American dollars?"

"Sure . . . what else?"

"The man we knew as Rafferty paid in weaponry. I'd hoped you'd have his connections."

"We might be able to work something out—"

But Zacul was already walking away, not listening, giving orders to Ford over his shoulder. "Your associate will leave for Costa Rica tomorrow by truck. You will not. You will stay with us until he returns with the book you so generously offered to give me. At that time we will discuss percentages and logistics. As of

now, the terms you have offered sound agreeable—
with the exception of special items, like the jade mask."

"But Tomlinson doesn't know where the book is—"

"Then you will tell him." Zacul's dark eyes took on
that penetrating look; wild, near the borders of control.
"You will not leave here until I have it."

Julio Zacul returned to his quarters, ignoring salutes,
ignoring the garbage heap these peasant soldiers had
allowed his camp to become, eyes focused only on the
doors that were quickly opened for him, until he threw
himself on his bed, his face wet, his veins burning, his
brain fighting a gray deliquescence, that woozy feeling
of reaching critical mass on the cocaine express.

"Suarez! Suarez, you shit-heel! *Suarez!*"

He closed his eyes, breathing deeply while his heart
pounded in his ears, then he opened his eyes, allowing
his vision to blur within the symmetric zone of the ceiling fan overhead. What would Guzman think if he saw
him now?

A dark thought, and Zacul cringed as it lingered.

Abimael Guzman Reynoso, that great man; Guzman
who had told them all that to triumph over the capitalists,
they must not fall victim to the weaknesses of the capitalists: no alcohol, no tobacco, no drugs, no sex; nothing
that was pleasurable until they had eliminated the can-
cer, cut it out and killed it. Of course, Guzman himself
had chain-smoked cigarettes and bedded many of his
students—young women and men—but that was all right.
Guzman was the swordsman; they were the sword.

Zacul had been seventeen when he left the house of his wealthy father to attend the University of San Cristobal in the department state of Ayacucho, in the mountains southeast of Lima, Peru. It was there he was assigned to Guzman's philosophy class; it was there he fell under Guzman's spell.

There were already rumors about the man. It was well known he was an ardent Chinese Maoist; it was not well known that, by his careful recruiting of fellow professors, he had gained control of the university. Sendero Luminoso, the Shining Path, had already been founded, and Guzman's philosophy—that capitalism could be eliminated only by killing without conscience—was soon its only curriculum.

"Terror," Guzman had told them, "is our only weapon. In the end, the people we terrorize will get down on their knees to thank us."

Zacul, always a good student, had also always been a moody, solitary boy. That changed when he met Guzman and was accepted into Sendero. His first assignment (and that's what Guzman called them—assignments) was a raid on the village of Lucanamarca. It was a summer morning in February when Zacul and twenty others, armed with rifles and axes, entered the village looking for an informant. The villagers, who were mountain peasants, insisted they knew nothing of an informant. Zacul had watched transfixed as the leader of his group ordered all the women and children of the village into a church, then set the church on fire. As mothers tried to push their children through the windows of the burning building, members of *Sendero* used their axes to kill the children. It was a horrifying thing to watch, yet it had also filled him with a strange elation; a tingling in the spine. Zacul had drawn closer to the blazing church as if drawn by a magnet, when suddenly a village woman skidded around a corner to face him. She was as surprised as he by the confrontation, her eyes a study in pure terror, and Zacul had continued to walk toward her as she backed away . . . back, back, back, her hands thrust outward, and then she had dropped to her knees—not at all what he had expected. Instead of fighting for her life, she had simply knelt there, her eyes looking up at him, body slack, knees slightly spread in complete submission, her face very pale but calm. The first time he swung the ax, his aim was bad, and the blade cut through her shoulder. She had kicked some, yet the expression in her eyes was unchanged—as if she had awarded her body to him, completely to him, and Zacul had never felt such a sensuous rush of emotion in his life. Once again he had swung the ax, burying it in the top of her head and, though the feeling of pleasure lingered, the climactic emotion faded with her last breath.

He and his comrades killed more than sixty people that day; eleven by his own hand, and each produced in him that same wondrous feeling. Later Guzman personally congratulated him, then took him to bed—a strange night of pain and pleasure that ended with him sobbing in Guzman's arms. Zacul moved very quickly up the Sendero ladder after that. He was among the first assigned to take the movement out of the country. Masagua, Guzman had told him with tears in his eyes, was ready for the new generation.

On the bed, Zacul rolled onto his side, still breathing heavily. "Suarez, you pig. *Suarez*. Get in here!"

There was a tap at the door and Suarez came in quietly, as a nurse might enter the room. "I'm sorry, Julio. I was only just told that you were calling." He had opened a plastic bottle and was tapping out small blue capsules into his palm. Zacul grabbed three and swallowed them quickly, then lay back again, already feeling better, knowing the pills would soon do their job. He said, "The two Yankees—do you trust them?"

Suarez said, "Of course not. But the large one, he knows something of the book. That is clear."

"Tomorrow you will arrange for a truck to take the hippie to Costa Rica. If he produces the book, we will deal with them. We need the money."

"If he doesn't?"

Zacul didn't answer. Instead he said, "And this child we have; the son of that whore Rafferty—he is no longer any use to us."

"Then we should no longer keep him as a prisoner?"

"The prisoners—that's another thing! I'm sick to death of their stubbornness and their filth. I can smell them when I walk to the lake. This camp is becoming a pigsty, I tell you. We have been patient enough! I have my limits!"

"Of course."

"We'll shoot them this afternoon."

"Very well."

"*I'll* shoot them."

"The boy, too?"

Zacul sat up, feeling the first sweet edge of the medicine entering his bloodstream. He thought for a moment, and said, "No. This evening, when I'm done with the prisoners, you'll bring the boy to me."

"Certainly."

"Then you and I and the other officers will have a special dinner. A small celebration."

Suarez said, "I will notify the cook."

Ford said, "I'm looking for frogs."

Tomlinson watched patiently as Ford, on hands and knees, crawled along the path, pushing over rotted logs, which immediately swarmed with ants or termites.

Finally Tomlinson said, "I'm the last one to rush a student in his work, but don't you think we ought to figure out a way to make Jake part of this deal before you do any more collecting?"

"That's what I'm doing. That's exactly why we need to find this frog. A bright-red tree frog. You could help, you know. You have any cuts or anything on your hands?"

"No."

"Good. We need a bunch of them."

They had bathed from buckets inside their hut and changed clothes while the chef, Oscar, fried fish fillets for their lunch, corvina in garlic sauce. It was among the best fish Ford had ever had, but Tomlinson had refused it, choosing to have the cooks in the main mess ladle out a plate of red beans and rice for him.

Now they were halfway down the jungle trail that led to the Pacific, already beyond the high bluffs at the southern perimeter of the lake. They had told Oscar they were going for a swim in the ocean. They told him to tell the general if he saw him. From the expression on Oscar's face, the chef clearly hoped he would not see the general.

Ford said, "You know what Zacul wants, don't you?"

Tomlinson was already kicking over logs, making a halfhearted search. "Yeah, he wants the book and he wants to sell us a lot of artifacts at inflated prices and make a ton of money. That's what I mean: Couldn't we work the boy into the deal some way?"

"How? The book's in New York. It won't even get to Florida for another day or two—and I'm not positive about that."

"Oh yeah."

"We've got to get the hell out of here tonight, Tomlinson. We've got to grab the boy and go. If you get in that truck to go to Costa Rica tomorrow, I'm never going to see you again, and you'll never see me, because they'll kill us both."

"Right. *Shit*." Then Tomlinson said, "Hey, is that one?" A small red frog jumped out from beneath a log . . . sat blinking in a ray of sunlight . . . then jumped again.

"Grab it."

Tomlinson hunched over the frog, then hesitated. "These things don't bite, do they?"

Ford lunged and caught the frog, then quickly gloved it with the tail of his shirt to protect his hands. He held it up so Tomlinson could see. The frog was only about three inches long, iridescent scarlet with black flecks at the dorsum. "This is one of the *Dendrobates*," Ford said. "In South America, they call it the poison dart frog because it secretes a poison through its skin that the natives use on their arrows. It's an alkaloid poison, potent as hell."

"You're going to shoot Zacul with an arrow?"

Ford was transferring the frog to his pocket. "I'm not sure what I'm going to do. We have to create some kind of diversion to get Jake out, so I thought if we could catch enough frogs to get a couple of tablespoons of the poison, we could sharpen some sticks and somehow surprise the guards—"

"That sounds pretty chancey."

"I know, I know. They'd shoot us before the poison had time to take effect. Hell, I don't know . . . I'm desperate, and that's the first thing I came up with. But the officers are the key. The soldiers around here aren't loyal to Zacul. They obey him out of fear. Take a look at the camp. Discipline's sloppy; beer bottles everywhere. With the officers out of the way for a while, maybe we could get the boy and make a break for it. Maybe if we could get the poison into their food—"

"I'm not too crazy about that, either."

"I'm open to suggestions." Getting a little tired of Tomlinson's second-guessing.

"You're talking mass murder, man. I'm no fan of Zacul's, and if he really butchered those villagers like that doctor said, then the bastard should be committed. But I'm not going to have a hand in killing. Couldn't we just trick Zacul into coming into Tambor with us and hope we can find someone to help us?"

"Like who?"

"You said you knew people there."

"Yeah, I do—peasant people who are terrified of anyone in uniform. We're not going to find any help there."

"Maybe Rivera heard about us being kidnapped. He has people in Utatlan; informers, you said."

"We can't count on Rivera. Face it, Tomlinson, we're going to have to find our own way out. For now, you can help by looking for more frogs."

"I don't know, man."

"The poison won't kill them. It'll just make them sick for a while. Maybe paralyze them for an hour or two. And that's only if I can find a lighter so we can roast the poison out of the frogs, and only if the poison doesn't taste so bitter Zacul and the others won't eat the food." Sighing because now the plan sounded even weaker.

Tomlinson stood looking at him calmly. "You're telling the truth?"

"I wouldn't ask you to help if I wasn't."

"Okay, okay—let's flush out some more of those little bastards."

But by the time they came to the lagoon on the jungle side of the long rind of white beach and sea, they had found only one more poison dart frog. They would need at least a dozen, maybe more.

Discouraged, Ford began to wade the shallows of the lagoon. It was a clear-water bay with plenty of tidal transfer so the place was alive with tunicates, purple and gold cushion stars, club-spined sea urchins, bright sea fans, and all the scurrying, feeding, fecund life of a Pacific tidal pool. The bottom, he noted, was white sand and eel grass, and resting in or moving slowly over the bottom was a large population of gray and black fish with large flat heads and big incisor teeth—a genus known as *botete*. They were slow moving; so docile that they could be caught by hand. When they did decide to move, they propelled themselves with their tail and lateral fins like wind-up fish in a bathtub. Around more northern shores, fish related to the *botete* were called box fish or puffers or porcupine fish. It was one of the most prevalent fish in Pacific backwaters, and Ford wasn't as surprised to see so many as he was surprised that he hadn't thought of them before.

Now that he had noticed them, he wondered if he should continue looking for poison dart frogs.

"What's going on up there?" Tomlinson was standing in the shade of a mangrove, hands on hips, his back to Ford.

Ford followed Tomlinson's gaze to the bluff above the lake a half mile away. From where they stood, with volcanoes seeping pale smoke in the background and the lake pouring a silver waterfall into the jungle below, the bluff was a spectacular sight. But Tomlinson wasn't enjoying the view. There were men on the bluff. Soldiers, but other men, too. Several of the men were naked. One wore baggy white shorts. All of them walked oddly, and Ford realized it was because their hands were tied behind their backs.

"Hey, what are those guys going to do?"

Ford said nothing, just watched as the soldiers lined the men on the high ledge above the lake. He knew what they were going to do.

Tomlinson said, "That one soldier's Zacul, isn't it?

Yeah, that's Zacul. See how he moves—like he's got batteries in him. He's a cocaine freak, man. I could smell their kitchens up there by the digs. Gas and ether. You can always spot a coke freak." Then Tomlinson said, "Oh, my God."

Zacul was standing in front of one of the naked men, his right arm held straight out. The naked man was small with long black hair, and Ford guessed it was Creno, the Miskito Indian. Zacul's arm bounced and Creno tumbled backward off the bluff, hitting the rocks like a rag doll before disappearing behind the trees, into the lake.

A couple of seconds later, the echo of a gunshot reached them.

Ford began to walk slowly toward the bluff, as if ready to charge Zacul—as if that would help. "You don't see the boy up there, do you? Anyone Jake's size? That guy in the white underwear is the doctor, but I don't see any kids—"

Tomlinson said in a whisper, "My God, he shot another one. He's going to shoot them all."

Ford stopped walking. "Yeah, I think he is."

The prisoners were on their knees now. Or on their bellies, trying to squirm away. Zacul shot them in the head one after another, and soldiers came behind him to kick eight more bodies off the bluff. Amazingly, some of the victims kicked wildly as they fell, still conscious despite the head wounds. Then the only one left was the young doctor, but Zacul kept the gun at his side. The doctor was on his knees, rocking back and forth, and Zacul seemed to be talking to him. Ford was about to say "He'll sign that paper now," but didn't have the words out when the doctor got slowly to his feet, hesitated, then took a long step and threw himself off the ledge. He fell freely for a microsecond then hit buttocks-first on a jagged rock outcrop before tumbling down the wall and out of sight.

Tomlinson released a long breath, like a groan of pain.

Ford said, "We can't let Zacul or anyone else know that we've seen this."

Tomlinson dropped to his knees in the sand, head down, and made a deep primal grunting noise: a sob.

Ford twisted a branch off a mangrove tree and began to strip off leaves. From his pocket, he took the two small red frogs, released them, then waded into the lagoon. With the branch, he penned a *botete* then flung it up onto the beach with his hands. He caught six more before he realized Tomlinson was standing in the water watching him, his face still pale. "You want me to help, man?"

"No."

"I don't know what you're doing, but—"

"Just walk down the beach and pick up some shells. Some nice pretty shells so we can show them to that maniac if he wants to know what we were doing down here. But stay away from this lagoon unless you want me to lie to you again. . . ."

NINETEEN

Ford caught ten of the fish and worked on them in the shade of the mangroves. Their skin was as leathery as melon rind and he used a sharp stick, ripping them open from the anus. But then he found a couple of razor clams that were better for cutting.

Ford laid back the bellies of the fish, then cut out the small livers and gall bladders as carefully as he could. Several of the fish were gravid, and he added a few of the eggs to the pile.

Tomlinson came up behind him, throwing a shadow. "I've seen people eat those kind of fish. Or fish kind of like that, I'm almost sure. In New Jersey they call them sea squab. I think they were called fugu fish in Japan. They keep them alive in the markets." There was the timbre of relief in his voice, as if Ford couldn't be planning anything that bad.

"Do you know what they call people who eat fish from this family?"

Tomlinson shook his head. When Ford said, "They call them fools," Tomlinson turned without comment and walked away.

Ford tore a piece from his shirt, wrapped the entrails, then threw the dead fish far out into the lagoon.

They followed the path back toward the camp and stopped where it swept closest to the bluff. They were above the lake and could see some of the bodies still floating. The young doctor was facedown, his arms thrown out, his legs submerged and spread. The water was clear and very blue, and it added to the impression that the doctor had somehow been frozen in freefall, trapped in blue space.

They could see something else, too: dark torpedo shapes that appeared small from that distance, spiraling up through the shafts of sunlight which pierced the depths. They were sharks; dozens of them. When the sharks broached and listed to feed, the corpses bobbed like corks, trailing rust-colored stains that marked the trajectories of the feeding fish: red contrails on the pale void.

They stood watching for a short time, saying nothing, then Tomlinson said, "He went brave, that doctor. I wish his schoolmates could have seen him. The man was no coward. Jumped off the cliff rather than work for Zacul."

Ford suspected the doctor had probably jumped out of fear of being shot, but either way it had taken courage. He said nothing.

Back at their hut, Tomlinson piled the seashells outside the door as Ford said, "I'm going to pay a visit to

the chef." Tomlinson, who still looked shaken, very
weary, said he would come along; that he might be able
to provide a diversion. When Ford said he couldn't,
Tomlinson insisted. "Look, man, what we saw upset me,
okay? But I'm not an invalid."

"Then what you can do is try and find a leverage
bar—a strong limb or something—we can use to pry up
the lip of the stockade. Hide it in the weeds. We may
need it tonight."

Tomlinson said, "I feel like I'm going to throw up."

Ford said, "In the next few hours there's going to be
a lot of that going around."

Oscar was alone in the officers' kitchen, peeling potatoes. He looked up expectantly when Ford came through
the screen door. Was there something the *señor* required? Some way he could be of service? Ford said
that he had come because the fish prepared for his lunch
was superb; that he wished to watch a master at work if
it was possible.

Oscar beamed, looking down at the pile of potatoes.
"It is true," he said in Spanish, "that I once trained in the
very best kitchens of Masagua City. But out here, with
these limited facilities, my work has suffered," looking
rather sad as he made this sly request for reassurance.

"Artistry shows even when the materials are inferior,"
Ford offered. "I cook only as a hobby, but I know that
much."

That quick, Ford had the run of the kitchen. Oscar
wanted to show him everything; to make all the diffi-

culties he endured known. His stove was fueled with wood. It was fine for boiling and frying, but how could one bake properly with such a system? Bread was difficult; cakes a disaster. But did the general and his officers understand these difficulties? No, but they expected perfection anyway. Then there was the problem of proper utensils. How could he provide superior fare when he was forced to use the cookware of peasants? Ford listened sympathetically as he worked his way between Oscar and the stove.

There were several two-gallon pots bubbling on the fires, and Ford lifted the lids one by one. One pot held red beans. Another held several chickens being rendered for stock. In a third, spiny lobsters, whole clams, and a fish head simmered in an oily broth. The beans would have served; the fish chowder was ideal. Ford inhaled deeply, as if in ecstasy, and put the lid on the counter. "Bouillabaisse!"

"What?" Momentarily confused, Oscar had to look in the pot himself to see what Ford was talking about.

Ford said, "Truly, you are a master. Who would have expected to find such artistry in the jungle?" Then he hesitated. "But perhaps I'm wrong. Perhaps it isn't really bouillabaisse, for I see you are using clams—"

Oscar held up his index finger; an exclamation. "I use them because our bouillabaisse is not the weak soup of the Mediterranean! This is ocean bouillabaisse, as delicate and as strong as the sea itself. I use mollusks as well as crustaceans, plus good fresh corvina. You will see! I will serve you this for your dinner."

"If you're sure General Zacul and his officers won't require it all. I don't want to deny my host."

"They would eat it all if I let them, the"—Oscar was about to say "pigs," but he quickly amended—"for they are having a party tonight. The Cubans especially appreciate fine seafood, as does the general. They have complimented me personally."

Ford pointed to the enlisted men's mess where soldiers in T-shirts stirred huge pots cooking over open fires. "Do those men also know the secret of your bouillabaisse?" When the chef turned to look, Ford dropped the *botete* entrails into the soup and he began to stir with the ladle.

"Those men are peasants. They cannot even cook beans properly. I will serve you and your associate the soup for dinner."

Ford scooped a ladle and smelled it. "You think there's enough?"

"Tonight I will eat beans like the peasants so that the soup may be eaten by one who appreciates artistry."

Ford put the lid back on the pot. "A sacrifice you won't regret, Oscar."

When Ford returned to the cabin, Tomlinson was inside pacing back and forth, back and forth, He looked up when the door opened and said, "They took him."

"What?"

"They took him—the kid! They took Jake!" He was running his fingers through his hair, frantic. "Not five minutes ago I saw Suarez pushing him down the path. That *dick*."

"Where? Toward the cliff?"

"Naw, the other way. Toward the main building."

Ford said, "Maybe they were taking him to the shower or something," not because he believed it, but to calm Tomlinson.

"*Come on.*"

"Wherever they took him, we can't do anything about it now."

Tomlinson stepped in front of him, his eyes intense, breathing too fast, hyperventilating. "Whata you mean we can't do anything about it? We got to; *those bastards!* I've had just about enough of this shit, Doc. I can't take much more; I mean it. I keep seeing those guys falling off that cliff. I close my eyes and I see that little doctor hitting the rocks. You think I'm gonna let that happen to that little kid? No way, man; no fucking way." And he pushed past Ford and started out the door.

Ford grabbed his arm. "What are you going to do?"

"I'm going to talk to Zacul, that's what I'm gonna do. I'm going to try and talk some sense into him. He's got no reason to hurt that child. He's got no reason to hurt us either. I'll make him see that!"

Ford pulled Tomlinson back into the hut. "I can't let you do that."

"Let go of my arm, goddamn it!"

"I can't let you—"

Tomlinson yanked his arm free, yelling "You son of a bitch, you got us into this; and now you won't let me get us out!" He lunged for the door again, but Ford caught him by the shirt, swung him around, and slammed him into the wall.

"Tomlinson? *Tomlinson.* I want you to take some deep breaths. Nice and easy." Speaking softly, trying to get through the shield of paranoia; trying to reach the man inside. "You're not thinking clearly. You understand?"

Tomlinson was looking at the floor, trembling, refusing to meet Ford's gaze.

"There's nothing we can do now. If we try, Zacul will kill us all. Each and every one of us. You know that."

Tomlinson nodded slowly, then something broke in him and he began to cry softly. He pulled away from Ford, went to his cot and sat down, his face buried in his hands.

"We'll be okay, Tomlinson. We'll make it. We're all going to make it." Speaking with confidence, but not feeling it, Ford opened the door of the hut and went outside to sit beneath a tree.

Half an hour later, Tomlinson came out. He looked scraggly and very tired. He stood above Ford, saying "I really freaked out, man. Sorry."

"Don't worry about it."

"It's like a disease."

"Yeah, well . . . like you said: We all have our quirks."

"I can't believe shit like this goes on in the world."

"Every hour of every day it goes on. Someplace."

"People back in the States don't realize, man. This is like something out of a movie."

"No. You've got it backward. Life back home is like something out of a movie. That's what people don't realize."

"You think the kid is dead?"

"I haven't heard any shots."

"I hope not, man. I really couldn't take that. I'd be ready to cash it in right here."

What Ford was hoping was that Jake Hollins wasn't hungry, or didn't like fish. . . .

Oscar served them in their hut an hour after sundown. When Ford asked if the general had enjoyed the meal, the chef straightened himself, saying grandly "The general can wait while I serve a man who is a true gourmet," rolling his r's, which gave the French word an earthy sound.

Tomlinson and Ford touched their spoons to their lips and raved about the soup, though they did not taste it. Pleased, Oscar complained more about the bad cooking conditions, made more excuses for the poor food, and got more compliments from Ford.

When the chef was gone, Ford said, "Don't eat anything."

Tomlinson stopped with a spoonful of beans in mid arc. "I thought you said it was just the fish chowder."

"He could have used the same ladle. He could have poured some of the soup into the rice to spice it up. We don't know what he did. Don't eat anything."

Tomlinson put his tray on the ground and leaned toward Ford. "What the hell is in those fish gizzards?"

Ford said, "You really want me to answer that? Don't you assume some responsibility if you know?"

"Yeah, but I'm not hypocrite enough to refuse to listen now."

Ford said, "If that's the way you want it," and began

to scrape the food off onto the ground behind the cots.
"Those kind of fish, puffers, are found in warm waters
all over the world. The flesh is okay as long as it's been
cleaned properly or if the fish hasn't been injured during its life cycle. But only fools take the chance because
the liver, the gall bladder, some of the other viscera con-
tain a crystalline alkaloid. If you eat an injured fish,
you get sick no matter how carefully it was cleaned. I've
seen it happen."

"That's all that happens? You get sick?"

Ford made no reply.

Tomlinson pressed. "You mean you've seen people
die, that's what you're saying." Tomlinson was beginning to slip back into the pattern of shallow breaths
again, getting anxious.

"No. I've never seen it. But I watched a physician save
three people from dying once. He had the knowledge
and he had the right antidote. Without it . . ." Ford
shrugged.

"You're not telling me what I think you're telling me?
You're not going to kill all these people, are you, Ford?
You know the antidote, right?"

"I remember the name of the drug and the dosage."

"But what makes you think they have the antidote
here?"

"Nothing—I haven't given it much thought."

"Even if they did, you wouldn't offer it to Zacul."
Stated flatly in disapproval.

Ford opened the door and put the plates outside. "It's
too bad the general forced that doctor off the cliff. He

would have helped. In a way, Zacul killed himself and didn't even know it."

The oil lamp was out, but Ford was still awake. They were both dressed, lying on their cots. He said, "Muscarine. That's the poison. It took me about an hour this afternoon to remember the name. I kept thinking mascara, like the stuff women wear. It's also found in certain mushrooms, only I don't know which kind—the poison, I mean."

Tomlinson said, "Next time I read some label with natural herbs and spices, I'm gonna be less enthusiastic." Then he said, "Sshhhh. What's that?"

There was the sound of a door slamming and loud voices. There was panic in the voices, and Ford felt the panic vibrate within him, adrenaline mixed with elation. Tomlinson said, "Someone's coming," and Ford swung his feet off the cot, waiting.

There was the heavy thud of footsteps outside: not the sound of someone running, but of someone trying to run, dragging his feet and stumbling. Then there was a banging on the door, rattling the whole fiberglass structure. The door flew open before Ford could get to it, and there stood Julio Zacul. The flashlight he carried was pointed at the ground, bathing him in a grotesque light. He wore only pants and his gunbelt, no shoes. His chest made shallow lunges, desperate for air, and he was bent at the waist, his free hand thrown across his bare abdomen in an attitude of pain. His face was contorted, oily with sweat, and his eyes were wide and wild as he said, groaning, "Something very bad has happened. Something very bad. You are a doctor, no? You must help me."

When Ford just stood there, Zacul reached out to grab him and almost fell. Holding onto Ford's shirt, he repeated, "I need help! You are a doctor?"

Ford took Zacul's wrist and pushed the hand away. "I'm a doctor. So is this man. But we're not physicians."

Zacul moaned.

Ford said, "I thought we met a doctor when we were in your stockade. Why don't you get him?"

"No, no, he is gone. He can do nothing." Zacul's speech was labored, each word an effort. "I'm sick, can't you see that? We are all very sick. You must have some training. Do something!"

Ford took the flashlight from him and took him by the arm. "Do you have any medical supplies in camp?"

"Yes. A few. In my quarters."

"Then take us to them."

Ford and Tomlinson half carried, half followed Zacul across the grounds. The moon was over the mountains, three-quarters full, and by its light Ford could see that many of the soldiers had left their posts, gathering the way some people gather at car wrecks, fascinated with tragedy but nervous, too, standing in small groups, whispering.

"I am going to be sick. Let me go." They let Zacul fall to the ground and the soldiers shifted uncomfortably as they watched their general bark at the earth and wipe his mouth with the back of his hand.

Ford heard one of the soldiers mutter, "See? He is

dying. I have heard that some are already dead." But when Ford looked at the soldiers and nodded, they pretended not to see, averting their eyes.

"Let's go, Zacul. Let's get you inside."

Zacul and the other officers were billeted in a separate compound, a fenced grounds where a two-story block and wood house was surrounded by several fiberglass huts. Zacul led them into the main building, through a dark room with metal desks and the sharp acidic odor of a printing machine. The next room was much larger, an officers' mess and recreation room. There was a pool table, a bar with cheap plastic chairs, and, all around the room, dozens of candles had been lighted. There was the smell of incense, too; it was like walking into a brothel.

Judging from the magazines strewn around the floor, a brothel was closer to being what the room was used for. Tomlinson considered one of the magazines for a moment, then kicked it closed with his foot, a grimace of distaste on his face.

From somewhere a radio blared loud Latin music and on the long dining table were liquor bottles and smoldering ashtrays. Several of the bottles had been overturned and the gray carpeting below was stained. There were also two small bowls filled with fine white powder on the table. One of those had spilled, too, covering the table like talcum. Ford saw all of this peripherally, for the men who lay on the floor dominated the wreckage in the room.

It had been a party some would not live to remember. There were six men—no, seven. They wore only pants or were naked. Some sat staring blankly at the wall, trying to breathe over their thick, distended tongues. Others writhed on the carpeting in their own vomitus: eerie, contorted figures in the flickering light. Others lay deathly still, their knees pulled toward their chests, their eyes opened and fixed, but still breathing. Ford recognized Suarez as one of those still alive. He was on his knees, salivating uncontrollably. Only one uniformed soldier tended the men, wiping them with cloths. The others, apparently, had fled.

Ford asked, "Are the medical supplies in here?" Zacul, taken by another spasm, pointed at a box on the wall. As Tomlinson helped lift the box off its brackets, Ford whispered, "Start looking for Jake. He's got to be around here somewhere. And grab a weapon if you get the chance."

"No guns, Doc. Sorry, but no way."

"Goddamn it, Tomlinson—" But the man was already gone, rushing off to search the building.

Ford put the box on the table, unlatched it, saying to Zacul in a louder voice "It looks like you guys got hold of some bad cocaine, General."

"Yes, yes, that's possible. Is there something for the pain? I can't stand the pain anymore."

Ford went through the supplies quickly. "There's no medicine in here, this is a first aid kit. I can't do anything with this."

Zacul yelled to the lone soldier who soon returned with an even bigger metal box. Ford put it on the table and opened it. The kit was Soviet issue, labeled in several languages and very well equipped. The drugs were packaged in groups according to specific need: shock, bacterial disease, cardiac arrest, field anesthesiology. Ford opened three of the anesthesiology packages, separated the syringe kits, and placed six vials of atropine sulfate on the table. He hesitated, then took out one vial of normal saline solution. "There are things here that'll make you feel better, General, but I don't know how to treat for cocaine overdose. I'm going to need help for that."

Zacul groaned again.

"Is there a doctor in Tambor?"

"No."

"Is there a phone in Tambor? A place I can call a hospital and get some advice on how to treat you?"

"Yes! That is what we must do. Go to Tambor!" Zacul was hunched on the carpet, his head between his knees.

Ford was drawing saline solution into one of the syringes, holding it up to the light. "Is there someone around who can fly those helicopters?"

"The Cuban, Arevilio. He is our trainer. The others are away in the city."

"Tell someone to find him."

Zacul called to the soldier again, demanding that he bring Arevilio immediately. But the soldier shook his head and pointed to a motionless figure on the floor. The Cuban appeared to already be dead.

Ford said, "I'm going to have to drive you. We'll need a truck and I'm going to need someone else who speaks English. If I get an American doctor on the phone, someone is going to have to ask him questions while Tomlinson and I work on you and your officers."

"There is Colonel Suarez—"

"Suarez is sick, too." Talking as he loaded the other syringes with atropine sulfate, Ford then injected the saline solution into Zacul's arm.

The saline solution was a placebo; it would have no effect. Atropine sulfate was the antidote.

Zacul was coughing, rubbing his arm. "Is it so necessary? I'm too sick to think. Why do you make these demands!"

Ford said, "It's necessary unless you want to die. Someone else who speaks English."

When Zacul only groaned in reply, Ford finally just came out and said it: "What about the little American boy who was in the stockade?"

Zacul raised himself to his knees and seemed to focus for a moment. *"What?"*

"The boy, Jake Hollins—where is he?"

Through the bleary eyes came a sharp look, and he asked, "How did you know he was no longer in the stockade?" and Ford realized he had stumbled badly.

"I thought I saw Colonel Suarez release him."

Zacul said, "Yes, of course—the boy could help," speaking very carefully, in a way that made Ford uneasy. "He's here. In my quarters—there, with the hippie now."

Tomlinson, looking grim, was leading Jake Hollins by the hand. The boy had been bathed, his clothes washed, and he looked very small walking beside Tomlinson. His chin was down, like a shy child at a circus, and his head moved timidly as he took in the chaos around him. Ford knelt, touched the boy's arm, and the boy looked up at him and said, "Whelp, that lil' house of ours got wrecked again," with a southern accent that was nice to hear after so much Spanish.

Ford said, "We'll build a better one," before glancing at Tomlinson. "Is he okay?"

Tomlinson was glaring at Zacul, his face pointed, really angry. "You're a good argument for euthanasia, you know that, Zacul—" But, before he'd even finished the sentence, Zacul had grabbed the boy, holding him by the throat, his pistol out, barrel pressed against the child's head.

"This is what you came for, isn't it? I don't know why I didn't see it before!" Then he was on his feet, still holding the boy, eyes glazed but lucid enough to say "You're not going to leave me here. If you make any move against me, I'll shoot the boy. You are going to take me to Tambor. You are going to find help for me—" talking in surges between deep gulps of air while the boy, already crying, called to Ford, "I don't like this man! Make him let go!"

'Ford had his arms out, holding Tomlinson back, and when Tomlinson tried to call out, *"But you've already been given the antidote—"* Ford drove his elbow backward and heard Tomlinson gasp with pain. If Zacul found out Ford knew the antidote, they'd all soon be dead.

Ford said, "Okay, Zacul. We'll take you to Tambor. Just don't hurt the kid."

TWENTY

Soldiers were running. Ford couldn't figure out why. They were running through the mud in the moonlight, glancing over their shoulders as if something were chasing them. Some of them were shooting, too, firing wildly toward the road that led to Tambor.

Ford had been standing on the porch. His glasses were fogged from the smoke inside and he cleaned them on his shirt, trying to see what it was the soldiers were running from. But when the shooting started, he dropped to the ground, as did Zacul. "What in the hell's going on here?"

Zacul just groaned and held tight to the boy. He was having trouble breathing. His tongue was so swollen that it was difficult for him to speak. When he did speak, it was in a ranting Spanish—part delirium, part fear—but his pistol never wavered.

Now Ford could hear more shooting, like strings of firecrackers popping in the distance. Then there were three explosions in quick succession, each closer than the other, the last hitting a fiberglass hut not far from the stockade. The explosion shook the ground and threw Roman candle streamers through a roiling ball of white smoke into the high trees. There was a momentary pause, then another explosion that whuffed as if drawing air before several fuel tanks ignited in an orb of white fire that crackled in the wet leaves behind the compound.

Through the smoke came more soldiers, more of Zacul's troops. They were yelling: some in pain but most out of fear.

They weren't just running, they were fleeing; trying to escape this unseen force coming from the road to Tambor.

Ford got to his feet, pulling Zacul with him. "Let's get the hell out of here."

Tomlinson, a step behind, called, "Are we being attacked? I don't understand what's happening."

Ford, who could make no sense of it either, didn't answer. They covered fifty more yards before Zacul stopped, gasping. "No more, I can run no more. I'm *very* sick. Please have my orderly find us a truck." As if his orderly hadn't run with the others.

Ford said, "We try driving to Tambor and we'll die for sure. Someone's army is coming down that road and I bet they'd love to get their hands on you."

Zacul said, "Then we'll take a boat, that's what we'll do . . . take a nice boat on the lake away from the noise of all these cowards." His mind wandering in delirium.

Crouching beside him, Tomlinson whispered, "Why

isn't he any better? You gave him the shot. Those guys inside started to breathe easier almost right away." Tomlinson had stayed behind to give the injections before catching up.

"Maybe he's just unlucky."

"Two of them were already dead. I think I saved Suarez, though."

"You would."

Tomlinson caught his arm. "You didn't give it to Zacul, did you? The antidote."

Ford said, "I think we'd better keep moving."

Tomlinson still held his arm. "Why don't you answer me? You didn't. You didn't give him the shot!"

Ford pulled his arm away easily, looking into Tomlinson's eyes. "I said we'd better keep moving."

More mortar rounds were coming in now, some exploding as they hit the tops of the trees. Diesel fires had spread from the trucks to some of the living quarters. The smell of melting fiberglass mixed with the stink of burning rubber and black smoke swirled in the cool wind coming off the lake.

Ford called, "Let's go!" and they made it across the parade ground, into the trees before Zacul collapsed once more, pulling the boy down with him. He was having more cramps, really hurting. He kept waving the pistol around. He wanted to know why the medicine wasn't working. Ford said he had to give it more time. Zacul said he couldn't stand the pain much longer and maybe he should kill the boy now; kill everyone now. Ford, crouching from the mortar fire and the gun, lied, "At least you're looking better, General. Your color's coming back."

When a mortar round cut the top off a tree about fifty yards away, Ford pressed his face against the ground as leaves and chunks of limb smacked the mud around them. Zacul raised his head and began to scream "I order you to stop! I order you to stop this minute!" getting crazier as he got sicker. What was keeping the man going?

The boat dock was down a steep hill and extended about forty yards into the lake. The dock was very wide, commercial grade, and built of huge timbers high off the water. Two flat-bottomed barges were tied to it and one small skiff. There was a high outcrop of rock and mud where a bulldozer had cut the road to the lake, and Ford told Zacul and Tomlinson to stay under the ledge while he got the boat ready.

The shooting was getting closer now. Looking up the hill, he could see soldiers silhouetted by the flaming buildings. These soldiers weren't running, they were stalking, taking their time. Using grenades, too, judging by the sound. And shooting at anything that moved, which was the way of jungle fighters.

Ford sprinted down the dock and dropped to his belly, inspecting the boats. He considered taking one of the barges. A barge would offer more protection against the incoming rounds, but it would be like steering a semi and slow, too. It was about four miles across the lake to Tambor, and he didn't want to spend an hour getting there. At the end of the dock was a skiff, and Ford crawled out to have a look. It was a wooden boat with a high sharp bow, about eighteen feet long with a forty-horsepower Johnson on the transom. It wouldn't be fast, but at least they could get it up on plane. He slid off the dock and climbed down a wooden ladder into the skiff. There were two plastic six-gallon fuel tanks in the stern. One was nearly full, the other empty. He threw the empty tank into the water before checking the rubber fuel line, making sure the bulb was primed. Then he pulled the starter rope and the boat lunged, almost throwing him into the water. Someone had left the damn thing in gear. He punched the shifting lever into neutral, then tried again. It took him three more pulls before the engine caught, throwing blue smoke in the moonlight while the whole boat trembled.

Ford climbed back onto the dock and began to run toward the rock outcrop. Halfway to shore, something detonated the water beside him and the wash almost swept him away. He fell and skidded along the planking. He lay there for a few moments, then got shakily to his feet. His ears were ringing and his hands tingled. He was wet, but it seemed to be water, not blood. Tomlinson was coming toward him, herding Zacul and the boy to the boat.

Another mortar round hit and the wedge of rock under which they had been hiding disintegrated into a great plume of debris that came raining down into the water, clattering onto the dock. Ford covered his head, yelling "They see us! Get into the boat!" But he didn't say anything more, just crouched there looking—stunned by what he saw.

The dock was aglitter with pale-green light, a light that refracted abrupt facets like the shimmer of broken glass or shattered ice. The source of the light was scattered across the dock like gravel and some of the bright orbs drifted down through the clear water, tumbling with the brief incandescence of meteors.

Emeralds.

Tomlinson went running past him, kicking more of the stones into the water. Ford made no effort to grab the stones but just watched, transfixed. Then he heard a grunting noise, like gagging, and Zacul was standing in front of him. Zacul wasn't looking at the dock, he was staring at something else, and Ford followed his gaze upward. There, in the smoking hillside, were more emeralds. They were embedded in a great jagged wheel of stone that protruded from the earth. Even though one large chunk of the stone had been sheared away, it was still huge, maybe twelve feet in diameter, bigger than seemed possible. Emeralds sparkled on its surface like sequins, making odd designs that Ford knew were constellations.

"The calendar," Zacul whispered. "After all this, I've finally found it." He turned, letting his pistol drop to his side, and Ford immediately yanked the boy away from him, yelling hoarsely: "Run! Get in the boat!" expecting Zacul to whirl around with the pistol. He didn't. He stood looking at the great calendar, bent slightly at the waist with pain, but oblivious to everything else.

Suddenly he turned to Ford, his eyes wild. "You will help me. Some of the stones are falling into the water. Help me pick them up!"

From down the quay, Tomlinson yelled, "Come on, Doc! We're waiting!"

Ford said, "You're on your own, Zacul. We're leaving."

Zacul pointed the gun at him, "Not now! Not yet!" his face so crazy with pain and greed that Ford knew he was about to shoot.

Ford bent, picked up several emeralds in each hand, and pushed the stones into his pockets obediently, then lunged suddenly, hitting Zacul with his shoulder. Zacul backpedaled, tripped, and landed back first on the planking. He lay on the dock fighting to breathe, but he still had the pistol and Ford kicked him hard in the ribs as he lifted it to fire. The explosion and the sudden vacuum Ford felt near his ear were simultaneous, like an electrical shock. His legs collapsed and he dropped down onto the general. Zacul clubbed him behind the ear with the butt of the pistol and managed to roll away, using his free hand to scratch at Ford's eyes. Ford locked his hand around Zacul's right wrist and used his open hand to punch the man's elbow inward. Zacul screamed with pain, as if he'd touched something hot, and the gun flew out of his hand, skittering across the dock. Ford crawled after it, picked it up, and, crouching low, swung it toward Zacul's face. "Rafe Hollins would want me to shoot you, Zacul."

The guerrilla leader was up on his knees, palms pressed outward. "Don't kill me, you can't kill me. Don't you see? We'll have money now, lots of money! You can't kill me."

Ford said, "I already have," just before Zacul made a

desperate lunge at the pistol. Ford could have pulled the trigger; he didn't. Instead, he batted the weak body away, and Zacul's momentum carried him off the dock and into the black, black waters of the lake.

The sharks should have gotten him. Maybe they did. Ford didn't wait around to watch.

He could hear Zacul yelling as he ran for the boat, then an abrupt scream like death itself, but Ford didn't hear anything more because another mortar round hit the dock behind him and suddenly he was flying . . . tumbling through space and into a void which was as black as the eye of God itself.

TWENTY-ONE

If it was a dream, it was like no dream he'd ever had.

Before him was an oblong space swollen with pearly light. The light came through in rays as well defined as laser beams, touching his face and his body with mild warmth. The area of incandescence dominated his view and filled the room—for he seemed to be in some kind of room, though he didn't turn his head to be sure. He could look only at the light, drawn to the refulgence like the jungle moths he sometimes thought about, the creatures that gathered one night of the year to fly toward the full moon.

Maybe I'm dead. . . .

He didn't like that. He didn't like that at all—not that he feared nonexistence, but more because of the implications of being bathed in celestial light. His pragmatic side rebelled at that, like the victim of a cosmic joke.

Something moved beside him, and he still did not turn his head. A shape came into view, gliding toward the source of the light. The shape sprouted arms, reached up, and the light was suddenly dimmed, as if curtains had been drawn. Then the thing with arms turned toward him and he could see that the shape was that of a woman; a woman dressed in white but with long black hair, though he couldn't see her clearly for his eyes refused to open completely. His eyelashes were a veil and he watched her glide toward him in soft focus. She reached out and he felt her fingers touch his face.

"Ford? Won't you please wake up? Ford, you dear ugly man."

Ford felt he should struggle to answer, for now he recognized the voice and the voice fit the face. But he didn't struggle. He tried to speak but, when no words came, he simply lay there feeling oddly complacent and very tired, an observer, not a participant. He was having a dream and this woman was part of the dream, Pilar Balserio.

Now both of Pilar's hands were on his face and she was leaning over him. She kissed his lips softly. "Do you know what the doctor says? The doctor says that sometimes people in a coma can hear everything. He says they have to be reminded that to get better all they have to do is open their eyes. So now I'm telling you: Wake up, Ford. Please. Come back to me now because there are things you should know and I must leave in just a few hours. Ford?" She waited as if expecting a response, then said, "I may never have the chance to speak with you again."

A reply formed in Ford's mind, though his lips still refused to transmit words. But he felt that that was all right; that she would understand. Couldn't she see that he was smiling?

There was a rustling noise, a sudden feeling of warmth, and Ford realized Pilar was lying beside him, her arm over his chest, holding him tight, her mouth against his ear. She was trembling; trembling and whispering into his ear so that it was as if her mind was speaking directly to his mind.

"I'm frightened, Ford. I've done so many bad things, but it hurts me most to know that I've hurt you. I want to tell you about those things—not because I want to share the guilt but because you are a rational man. You have a right to know. I won't add confusion to the pain I have already caused you. The night before you left, the night we made love . . . I'm the one who arranged for the guards to knock on my door at that hour. That's why you had to run. I knew that once I had loved you, really loved you in the way I wanted, I wouldn't have the strength to make you leave me once more. But it was necessary. It was necessary for my work. For my country. For my people. So I arranged for the guards in advance, not trusting myself. Does that make you hate me, you ugly man?"

Ford wanted to stir, to hold her, but he just lay there feeling the words. How could he hate her now for what he had already guessed?

"There is more you should know. I should tell you about the book. You brought it to me once, and I feel that someday you will return it to my people again. You understand my meaning; I'm sure that you understand. The book was stolen not long after I had finished translating it. It was taken by a man who cared only for the power it would give him. He wanted it as an artifact, a thing to show the people and help unite them in his drive for power. My people revere such artifacts and would attach great importance to the person who possessed it. But this man was a devil and I'm glad that you had a hand in killing him." Avoiding the general's name, but speaking of him with disgust while, in Ford's mind, the image of Zacul's face, those insane eyes, flashed for a moment, then faded as Pilar continued to talk.

"The book was a disappointment to me, Ford. It held no answers, it told very few secrets. But in ways— strange ways, ways that you would laugh at—it predicted the future of my people. It is because of the book that I knew so clearly what I must do. Other things became necessary. Some good things, some terrible. I arranged for my own husband's death. I murdered him. I am a murderess. I confess to you what I can confess to no priest because you, as no one I have ever met, are like me. You are a rational person and you know all the pain that that implies; all the loneliness. I killed him for the greater good, but I still feel the guilt, Ford. I wish you could talk to me and make me feel better. I wish we could talk as we did those nights on the beach. Did you know that the first time we sat talking was the first time since childhood that the loneliness in me disappeared? It was as if I had been waiting for you—you, a great ugly gringo older than me. Who knows why such things happen? But I could feel your words in my soul."

Then she lay silent for a long time, holding him. Ford could feel her soft breast on his arm; the thudding of her heart moved through him. His mind began to drift as he tried to focus on the expanse of light again, and he would have thought she had disappeared were it not for her steady heartbeat. Then she said, "There is something else I would like to tell you, Ford. But I can't because my life isn't my own. Do you know what makes me angry? My life has never been my own." She stood and leaned over him and Ford felt her lips on his. "I love you, Ford. I will always love you. . . ."

Then the dream was gone.

So why were there angels singing?

Dis manibus sacrum, ad astra per aspera . . .

Singing in Latin, their voices blended and wind-soft.

Cras amet qui nunquam amavit quique amavit cras amet . . .

Ford could feel the resonance of the chant seeping up through the floor, through the walls, surrounding him like a veil or the spirit of life itself.

Then he was sitting up, blinking his eyes. Before him was the oblong form which had once burned with light. It was a window, gray with the dusk beyond. The crown of a palm tree drifted into view, then drifted away again, rocking in the wind. Thus he knew that he was on the second floor. He knew that he was alive. But he could still hear the haunting cadence of the Latin chant.

Adeste, fideles, laeti triumphantes . . .

He was in a small room of wood and stone. The walls were whitewashed but not decorated. There was a dresser with a ceramic water basin and a silver crucifix. He lay in a simple bed with wooden footposts and beside the bed was a door. The door was open and the sound of women's voices came floating through.

Ford's brain scanned for an explanation, trying to figure out where he was, why he was here. Then he remembered Zacul and the explosion, and he decided that he must have been injured. In a slight panic, he took inventory of his limbs. His arms, his legs were in place, but his head hurt. He touched his head and found that it was wrapped with gauze. But there was only one small tender spot, toward the back, where the bandage was heaviest, and that was a relief. He tried to swing his legs off the bed but felt a sudden thrust of pain in his groin. Momentarily frightened, he threw back the sheet and looked beneath the long white nightshirt he wore. A catheter tube had been inserted into him. It was an unattractive thing to see, his member shriveled as if trying to hide while ingesting this sterile plastic tube, but there was no apparent injury. There were scissors on the table beside the bed, and Ford snipped the Y-prong. While water drained from it, he took a deep breath and pulled the tube out.

"*Ye-ouch.*" Swearing softly and already feeling better for the sound of his own voice.

Ford got to his feet slightly dizzy but strong enough. He followed the walls down the hall, the stone floor cold on his feet. When the singing grew louder, he knelt and looked through the stone portals that promoted air circulation, common in the old buildings of Central America. In the room below was a domed circular chamber designed in the old days for acoustical effect. There were nuns in the room, their heads bowed, hands folded. They wore white habits and veils, walking slowly and in step around the perimeter of the room as they chanted.

He was in a convent. But it wasn't cloister *La Concepción*, the convent outside the Presidential Palace in Masagua City. He had never been here before; he recognized nothing outside the window. He padded quietly back to the room trying to figure out what he should do. Where was Tomlinson? Where was little Jake? There was no closet in his room and he got down on his knees hoping his clothes might be under the bed. They weren't. As he got to his feet he bumped into the nightstand. Something tumbled off and crashed on the floor: a ceramic water pitcher. Ford stayed there for a moment, his buns hanging out in the coolness, then got quickly into bed.

A door opened somewhere and he could hear footsteps: leather shoes and heavy feet. Ford waited. What could he do—throw his catheter bag at the guy? A circle of light preceded the footsteps and then a man came into the room carrying an oil lamp. Ford pretended to be asleep, watching through cracked eyes. The man came closer, peering at him, and then Ford sat up abruptly. "Rivera!"

General Juan Rivera took two quick steps backward, touching his hand to his heart. "You would scare the life out of me, you crazy person!" But then he was smiling, the sudden anger gone. "Marion, you bad man, you are awake!"

"Sure I'm awake. I don't have any clothes. Get me my clothes, Juan."

Rivera put the lamp on the table, stepped over the

broken pitcher, and took Ford by the shoulders. "You have been asleep for so long that I began to worry you would never awaken. It presented certain difficulties. How can one properly bury a man who is still breathing? How could I get the Dodgers of Los Angeles to take notice of the greatest pitcher in Central America?" The big man was shaking Ford gently, laughing.

"Where are we?"

"In a convent above thirty kilometers from Tambor."

"How long, Juan? How long have I been out?"

"Um, three days . . . no, this is the fourth. Your friend the great DiMaggio pulled you out of the water. You were unconscious and had a small cut on the head— such a small cut to knock out a man of your size! My men captured you and wanted to kill you. Who can blame them? A gringo that looks like you. But then one of them recognized you as the great Johnny Bench. I give them strict orders not to shoot players of quality." He shrugged his shoulders humorously. "You were lucky that it was my best team I sent on the assault. They are all students of the game and so remembered you."

"Your men? But you said you wouldn't help."

Rivera said softly, "Do I need a gringo to tell me how to run my army? I had been planning the attack on Zacul long before you came to my camp."

"You didn't tell me that."

"Should I share such a secret with a capitalist dog like yourself? I did not become a general by doing stupid things."

Ford sat back in the bed, touching his hand to his head. Rivera said, "You are still weak. You will need sleep. And food. I will bring you something, but I warn you that these nuns eat the food of birds."

"Where's Tomlinson? I need to talk to him. He had a young boy with him—"

"They have both returned to the United States. The doctor who tended you said the boy was sick and that he should go home. The boy wanted very badly to go home. So the great DiMaggio went with him, but he said he would return if you did not get better."

"Then I need to call him—"

"I will have my men get word to him when they go to town. There's no phone here. Now you need food and rest."

Ford sat up once more, remembering something. "Pilar was here, Juan. She talked to me. I'd like to see her. Can you tell her that I'm awake?"

Rivera had picked up the lamp, and now he looked uncomfortable. "That would be difficult to do."

"Why? Did she already leave?"

Rivera looked at the flame in the lamp, not at Ford. "In a way she has left. Pilar Balserio is dead."

Ford stayed in the convent another night and another day, and then the doctor came—a small, bald man with a mustache—and said he would have to rest for at least one more night before starting the long trip home. Ford protested; Rivera insisted, and without Rivera's help there would be no leaving. So he stayed. The nuns nursed him. They brought him books and food, and he was never so anxious to leave a place in his life. The one thing he did enjoy was the chanting. He would sneak out and watch the nuns through the portal; watch them march solemnly around the domed chamber with its tiny penance cells where the nuns, by choice, could go to suffer alone on the cold rock floors or by tying themselves with the penance ropes that hung suspended from the ceiling.

Sometimes Rivera came to talk. Yes, Zacul was dead. They had found his body floating. The men had crossed themselves when they pulled his body from the water, so terrible was the expression of horror on his white face. The sharks had not bitten him, though. Even so, the mountain people were already saying that the sharks had taken him; that one more evil man had died from the bite of El Dictamen. Rivera said he was certain that someday the story would be told as truth throughout the mountains of Masagua.

Zacul's men had bolted, Rivera said, though some had already returned to join the Masaguan People's Army. Zacul's officers had been taken prisoner, though four had been found dead of some strange illness— wagging his eyebrows at this, for Tomlinson had already told him about the poison. With his own army now stronger, with Zacul's guerrillas scattered leaderless around the country, and with the government forces in Masagua City already fighting among themselves, Rivera's destiny seemed clear.

But he would not answer Ford's questions about Pilar Balserio. Once he came close.

"She's not dead, Juan. That was no dream I had. She was here."

"Always it's the same thing with you. Eat your nasty soup."

"I heard her. She talked to me."

"With a woman of her spirit, all things are possible. But the Pilar you knew is dead. It was a ghost. A holy vision from the gods."

"It wasn't a ghost, damn it!"

"Don't use such language when you speak of Ixku!" Flaring at him, really angry.

"*Ixku?* Who in the hell—"

"Yes Ixku! Would I agree to forgo my rightful presidency for anyone less?"

And that was all he would say.

Ford left on a Saturday, one week after the battle at Zacul's camp. Rivera brought him his clothes and made a request; a favor, though he insisted that Ford would be repaid. Ford agreed and said payment was not necessary. Rivera said it had already been done and left. That seemed rather cryptic until Ford put on his pants. The emeralds he had picked up that night on the dock were still in his pockets. Seven of them.

Three of Rivera's men took him to Utatlan where there, amazingly, was the Land Cruiser—not even a gas cap missing. He flew LACSA out of San José on Sunday, had a long layover in Miami, then flew Air Florida to Fort Myers.

It was 11 P.M. when the cab dropped him at Dinkin's Bay Marina. The island air was moist, like a warm veil, and the moon was three days past full, tumid with light.

Ford could smell jasmine as he walked down the dock to his stilt house.

TWENTY-TWO

His sharks were gone. Ford could see that even before he got the door open to turn on the lights. The water within the shark pen was cobalt in the moonglow and still. Dead water and fishless.

He popped the lock and stepped into the stale air of a house that hadn't been inhabited for nearly two weeks. There were several handwritten notes on the table but no mail. MacKinley had been keeping his mail at the marina. Ford put his bag on the floor, hit the outside lights, then walked down the steps to the fish tank. The fish stirred in the glare of the overhead bulb; the eyes of the shrimp glowed.

Two of his squid were gone and one of them floated, partially decomposed, in the ripple of the water jets.

Not a happy homecoming.

Ford stood on the lower porch looking at the bay. At the marina, the lights of the boats shimmered on the water, but it was quiet; a quiet Sunday night. Tomlinson's mast light was on, but the windows of his sailboat were dark, and that meant he wasn't aboard. Far out on the point, Jessica McClure's porch light was on; she was also away.

Ford went to the shark pen and confirmed that the bull sharks were gone. There was a great dent in the fencing, as if someone had purposely trampled it. Why would someone do that? Disgusted, he went inside and took a quart of cold beer from the little refrigerator. It was the first beer he'd had in nine days, and he drank from the bottle as he read the messages on the table.

Two were from Tomlinson.

The first note said that he'd noticed the dead squid and had Ford ever tested for electrolysis? Maybe that was the problem. He'd taken the liberty of testing the water with a meter and got a small reading—he hoped Ford wouldn't mind. So maybe if he added some lead plates to the ground cable, it might help.

Ford almost smiled. Electrolysis, sure, that could be the problem. He'd never built an aquarium this close to a modern marina before, and with all that electricity going into the water his ground line would be drawing it right into the tank. Adding lead to the cable would stop the migration of ions.

The second note read:

Doc, in case you get back before I do, I'm taking Jake to Harvey Hollins's in West Virginia. He says he could fly alone, but I think I'd better stick with him. That bitch he has for a mother shouldn't have been the one to tell him about his father's death. If

I'd known what she was like, I'd have told him my-self. She blamed Jake for running off with his father and for his father killing himself, which I guess was her excuse for not wanting him anymore. I'm not going to let Jake fly up there alone, not after what he's been through.

There was a message from Jeth Nicholes, so ner-vously written and apologetic that the block letters al-most seemed to stutter. Some kids or someone had busted down the shark pen and maybe got into the house through the window, but they didn't seem to take any-thing or leave any mess, but Jeth would pay for it if something was missing, only he didn't know how much sharks cost, but that's how bad he felt about it.

There were a couple of other notes from MacKinley. One said he had an important package sent registered mail, but he'd have to sign for it at the post office. An-other said a man had called from D.C. and left an urgent message. It didn't say who, but Ford knew. The message was: "The antique salesman jumped bail. Whereabouts unknown." The package, like the phone message, could only be from Donald Piao Cheng. The *Kin Qux Cho* was at the post office waiting for him.

Ford got to his feet and walked through the roofed passageway and unlocked the door of his lab. It looked just the way he had left it, nice and neat, with micro-scopes under their covers and stainless-steel tables glis-tening. He went to the shelves of marine specimens and began to inspect the jars of small sharks and shark embryos. He took one of the jars from the shelf. The lid

didn't seem to be screwed as tightly as he normally left
lids, and there seemed to be more preservative in the jar
than there should have been—an odd combination considering evaporation.

Ford put the jar back on the shelf and dialed Major
Les Durell's home number. Durell's wife answered,
sounding sleepy. Ford identified himself and said it was
important. Durell came on a few moments later, sounding even sleepier, and said without preamble, "You don't
follow directions very well, do you, boy?"

Ford, taken aback, said he didn't know about any
directions.

"Like you didn't get my letter, huh? Like the mail between Fort Myers and Sanibel's that bad. You're not
very good at playing innocent."

"I've been out of the country for two weeks, Les. I
just got back. I haven't even seen my mail."

"Oh. No kidding? Jesus, what time is it?" He made a
grunting noise as if trying to clear his head, or maybe
pulling a chair out to sit. "Well, it was in the letter. It
was an official letter. I told you not to contact me again
unless it was through your attorney. I told you we'd be
seating a grand jury in a couple of weeks to look into
that matter we discussed, and that any further testimony
you wanted to deliver would have to be through the
grand jury system."

"About Rafe's murder, you mean?"

"No, Sealife Corporation. The governor's office
sealed their records on Wednesday. Really took the bastards by surprise and got everything. I mean everything. Some of the assistant D.A.s have been going

through the stuff and they already have enough to put half the city officials behind bars and keep the other half in tax court for the next ten years. That includes that scuzzball Mario DeArmand. That bastard's going to jail, even if the feds don't come up with gun-smuggling charges."

Ford said, "They will," trying not to sound as pleased as he felt. Then: "What about Rafe?"

"What about him? If it makes you feel any better, that newspaper jackal Melinski has raked up enough muck on Hollins's ex-wife to get her and Judge what's-his-name run out of the city—if there's any city left when the grand jury gets through. He got some interesting stuff on when Hollins worked for Sealife, too, back when they were just starting to develop Sandy Key. They had a hell of a mosquito problem and they hired Rafe to fly their spray chopper. They had him spraying some kind of poison—quig-something-tox, I forget the name."

"Queleatox?" Ford said.

"Yeah, that's it. How did you know?"

Ford was thinking that if they had been spraying queleatox in the area, maybe his squid weren't dying from electrolysis after all. In Africa, queleatox was used to exterminate weaver birds; massive fish kills always followed for a long, long time afterward. Ford said, "Just an unlucky guess."

"Anyway, this poison was death on mosquitoes, but it was death on birds and fish, everything else, too, plus it was cumulative. It never went away. According to Melinski, Rafe found out what he was spraying, raised a fuss, and got himself fired. So you can bet the city fathers were more than happy to get rid of him nice and quiet and fast enough so reporters wouldn't get the idea of poking around into his background."

"He was murdered, Les, and he's got a nice little boy who's going to grow up thinking his father committed suicide and left him in a place you can't even imagine."

"Now you're starting to sound like Melinski. I'll bet you anything his story's going to make it all sound like my fault. That vulture has had me working day and night, looking over my shoulder, second-guessing me. What gives him the right? The shithead. I don't mind when reporters act like they've been elected. It's when they start pretending they've been ordained that I really get pissed off." Durell paused, catching himself before he got madder. "Why did you call me?"

"My house was broken into. I wanted to tell you—"

"Doc, I don't know how you got the idea I'm your own private police force, but get it out of your head. Like my letter says, we shouldn't talk anymore."

"But I think the person who broke in was—"

"If it's an emergency, the number is nine one one. If it's not, look it up in the book." And hung up.

Ford considered calling Don Cheng in D.C., but when he glanced out the window he noticed that Jessica's porch light was no longer on.

He locked the lab.

He would call Cheng in the morning.

He almost took his staff but that would be noisy. So he walked his bike down the dock and pedaled out to Periwinkle, Sanibel's main street. He rode the bikepath east past the restaurants and small boutiques. Coconut Grove, Mc T's, and the rest, then took Dixie Beach Road north to the water's edge where the road became shell, following the cusp of the peninsula to the mouth of Dinkin's Bay.

Jessica's house sat in the shadows of casuarina trees, its tin roof white beneath the summer moon. There were lights downstairs and he could hear music playing, saxophone and piano—public radio doing jazz. Ford leaned his bike against a tree. There was only one car in the drive, Jessica's car, and he touched the hood as he passed. It was cool. She had either been out walking, which seemed unlikely, or someone had dropped her off and left, or . . . there was another possibility. Staying in the shadows, he walked around the house to the dock. Her boat was still tied, shifting uneasily in the tidal flow. There were empty water jugs on the deck and something brown rolled into a bundle like a sleeping bag. He reached out and touched the small outboard engine. It was still warm.

Ford walked up the sand pathway to the porch but then he hesitated just before rapping on the door.

What was that noise?

The windows were open, and, through the screens, he could hear the music and he could hear the creak of the ceiling fans, but there was something else, too: a familiar low moan and the slap of belly skin against thigh.

The noise sensitized the hair on his neck even before he realized what it was, and Ford found himself being drawn inexorably to the expanse of living-room window.

The television was on and the room was aglow with mer-
curial light—a music video station, so it wasn't public
radio after all. The television's glare threw long shadows
and, on the screen, two black musicians sweated over
their saxophones. Ford watched the musicians for a time
because he found it difficult to look at Jessica.

Jessica McClure was on the couch with her back to
Ford. She sat astride some man who lay with his feet
aimed at the window, a faceless creature who was all
legs and long arms. Her head was cast back, auburn hair
in a sheet over her buttocks, and she massaged her
own breasts while pivoting on the man; lifting, sliding,
then ingurgitating him with all the precision of a Ger-
man clock. Every time she lifted, Ford could see the
underside of her like an anatomy lesson.

He stood watching for a moment, detached, feeling
no emotion stronger than disappointment, then turned
and walked quietly back to the dock. He sat on the dock
listening to the smack-thump of mullet jumping, swatting at mosquitoes. There were several big whelk shells
in the sand, shells Jessica had collected and left to bleach
in the sun. Ford picked up one of the shells, shook the
sand out, and fitted his hand through the aperture, gripping the spire so that it was like a boxing glove. After
about fifteen minutes, he saw silhouettes against the
window, then heard the toilet flush. Ford leaned over
the boat and yanked on the rope, starting the engine.
Then he grabbed the whelk shell and knelt beside the
low hedge of mangroves by the dock.

He heard their voices above the music, a quizzical
garble, then the screen door slammed and the man came

running out. Ford waited until the man was about to leap onto the dock, then swung out of the bushes and hit him in the face with the whelk shell. He mistimed the punch and the shell glanced off the man's cheek, but he still went down as if he had been shot. Then Ford stepped over the man expecting to see Benjamin Rouchard, the New York art dealer who had jumped bail. Instead, he saw Rafe Hollins.

Ford stood numbly as if in a dream, unable to speak, unable to move; stood wondering if maybe he wasn't having a hallucination from the concussion. But it was Rafe, all right, lying there blinking up at him, wearing only a T-shirt and Jockey shorts, holding his cheek, which was bleeding. Hollins began to slide away from him, backward in the sand, then slowly got to his feet. He said, "Is that any way to greet an old friend, Doc?" Then: "How in the hell did you find me?"

Ford was breathing heavily, still staring. He dropped the whelk shell, grabbed Hollins's T-shirt in both fists, and ran him backward into the mangroves, holding him against the limbs and yelling: "You son of a bitch, your little boy was dying down there. They had him living like an animal! I almost got killed getting him out."

Hollins wrapped his hands around Ford's arms, not fighting him but shaking him, as if trying to shake information out. "You mean you have him? Jake's alive?"

"As if you care."

"Is he okay?"

"Yes!"

"You've got to tell me where he is! I've got to go see him."

Ford smacked Hollins's hands away. "Real convincing. But then you always were good at tricks." And he hit Hollins in the face again. Hollins fell back into the mangroves, tried to catch his balance, but the limbs sprung him out into the sand.

Another voice said, "Go ahead, Ford. Go ahead and beat him to death." Jessica was walking toward them, barefooted, a robe pulled tight around her neck, and speaking softly in a husky alto voice that sounded cold, cold. "Make everything nice and neat, just the way you like it. Your dead friend isn't dead, so go ahead and solve the problem—eliminate the data that doesn't fit. Kill him."

Ford pointed his finger at her. "Why don't you run along and take a shower? You look a little dirty tonight."

"There! Now you've put me in my place. You're doing marvelously, Ford. Actually showing some emotion." She stepped onto the boat and shut off the engine. In the sudden silence she said, "I knew you had a heart banging around someplace in that big chest of yours."

Hollins was sitting up groggily, snorting blood into the sand, trying to breathe. "Don't hit me again, Doc. I mean it. If you hit me again I'm gonna have to fight back."

Ford said, "Don't make promises you can't keep."

"I don't want to fight you, but lay off, damn it."

"Jake was down there sleeping in his own crap. He's got open sores all over his legs. They had him chained to a wall. And your buddy Zacul came *this* close to getting his hands on him."

Hollins lowered his head, shaking it. "Ah, *Christ.*" A low agonized wail.

"Why don't you give him a chance, Ford? Or maybe it's more than just the boy. Maybe you did some window peeking and just didn't enjoy the show."

Ford snapped, "Why would an old pro like you care?" throwing the words at her—and was surprised to see her face register pain.

She turned her back to him. "Sometimes you're just so damn unfair."

Ford stared at the woman, then released a long breath. He said to her, "Go inside and get some ice. A washcloth, too. He's bleeding pretty bad," as he took Hollins's arm, helped him to his feet, and steered him toward the porch steps.

Hollins said, "I broke into your house."

"I know."

"I just wanted to tell you that right off the bat."

"Something honest for a change. There were grown men crying at your funeral, you asshole."

TWENTY-THREE

Hollins sat on the steps and the wood creaked beneath his weight. Jessica brought the washcloth out and he leaned his face against it, flinching at the cold. He said, "I needed money, Doc. I figured I needed ten or twelve grand to get Jake out, to make all the bribes and get the right papers—all that stuff. I couldn't ask you for that much, plus I thought I had a couple of other ways to get it. I'd been smuggling in Mayan artifacts and this art dealer, Ben Rouchard, was auctioning them off in New York—"

"I know all about that."

"You do?"

Ford looked at Jessica. "Yeah; almost all of it."

"Well . . ." Hollins was thinking, trying to put the rest of the story together. He said, "The other way I came up with getting quick cash was to offer the corporation that developed Sandy Key a deal. I used to work for those bastards, and I had some information that could

cost them a couple of million in fines if the Environ-
mental Regulation people found out."

"About them putting illegal insecticide in your helicopter."

"Jesus, you know about that, too?"

"I'm surprised they didn't kill you when you tried to
blackmail them. There's no statute of limitations on en-
vironmental offenses."

"That's the point. They tried. My old boss was a guy
named DeArmand, so I called him and offered him the
deal. I said if he brought me twenty grand in cash,
I'd sign a paper they could postdate saying that I understood that I'd been fired for spraying illegal chemicals
and accepted all responsibility, like the poison was my
idea. Like a confession. DeArmand's the sheriff there
now, and he threatened to have me put away for that kidnapping charge, the thing with Jake. I said fine, I'd go to
prison but he would, too, plus the corporation would go
bankrupt paying the DER fines. So DeArmand agreed
to meet me on the Tequesta Bank, just him alone with
the money.

"He was supposed to be there in the morning, the day
before you came. I watched him coming across the flats
in a small boat, kicking up mud the whole way because
he didn't know the cuts. But, when he lands, I see it isn't
DeArmand at all. It's this big guy about my size and I
know he's some professional DeArmand has brought in
to kill me. But I didn't give him a chance, Doc. We got
up there on the mound and I hit him with a club the first
chance I got. He went down and I couldn't believe it—
he was dead. That quick; just stopped breathing.

"I panicked. I was already wanted for kidnapping and now they'd get me for murder, too, and I'd never see Jake again. You know how upset I was when I talked to you on the phone that morning, but when that guy stopped breathing, I just went crazy. At first, I was going to run. Just get the hell out of there. But the idea of being wanted for murder was about the worst thing I'd ever felt, Doc. I'm not kidding. It made me want to run around in circles and bang into trees. Like some kind of animal being hunted. I wanted to vomit. So I got the idea of trying to make it look like an accident. I drug that guy's body all over the place, trying to make it look like he'd fallen or hit his head on a rock or something. But it just didn't work. Shit, there's no place to fall on that island and no rocks to hit—it's all shell.

"Then I got the idea of making it look like he'd killed himself. That seemed like the best idea. Even if I ended up in court, there were no witnesses and the jury would have to go by what the cops found. So I got a rope, and you know what I did with that. The dead guy looked like he'd come straight from the big city, so I tied bad knots like he'd probably tie and did a bunch of other stuff, trying to make it just right. But then it crossed my mind they'd do an autopsy and find out the guy had died from getting hit in the head and that just ruined everything. Right back to square one. I was about ready to cry by that time.

"So I left the guy hanging up there; took the boat and just went. God, I've never spent a night like that in my life. I holed up in a tidal creek under the mangroves, expecting police choppers to start buzzing me any minute. It was like I was crazy. I couldn't stop . . . stop crying. I spent all night in that boat, trying to figure out what to do, and it seemed like the best thing was to just hide the body and try to pretend like it never happened. By the time I got back to the island, though, the vultures had already been at this guy and his face was about gone. That's when it hit me. All my problems solved at once. They don't hunt a guy for kidnap and murder if he's already dead. The guy was about my size, had my hair, but wore clothes like I'd never wear. I swear to God, that was the worst part. Changing clothes with that corpse. It still gives me the shivers."

Ford said, "You told DeArmand if he'd push the body past the coroner, you'd give him a confession about the insecticide?"

"Right. That was the risk. Turned out, it wasn't much of a risk. I snuck over to the mainland that night and got DeArmand alone. He didn't give a damn about the guy I'd killed—he was just some Marielito from Miami, a professional killer. But the twenty grand would have come out of DeArmand's pocket. So that was the deal. I signed the paper and DeArmand would see to it this guy went to the grave as me, no questions asked. No money, but I got my freedom. And I'd planned on living with Jake in Costa Rica anyway."

Hollins cleared his throat uncomfortably and added, "I wanted to stay on the island and wait for you, Doc. I almost did. But I was still panicky and you always were kind of a stickler for the law. I figured I'd just head down to Masagua alone and try to get Jake out by myself, but when I got back to the island the emeralds were gone.

Shit, I had no money and no emeralds—nothing to trade. I woulda called you that night, but I knew the marina was closed. Then I figured the best thing to do was just sneak in and see you in person. But, by then, it was Tuesday night and you were already gone."

Ford said, "Zacul didn't want the emeralds. He wanted the book you stole."

Hollins sat up. "He wanted the *what*?"

Ford did not repeat himself; just stood looking at the man, watching it sink in.

Hollins said, "Christ, I gave that to Rouchard to auction off. I didn't think it was worth more than a couple hundred bucks. You're serious? And I thought it was the damn emeralds! That's why I broke into your house. They didn't mean money to me; they meant getting my little boy back. And I was beginning to think you were dead."

Ford looked at Jessica. She was leaning against the screen door, one hip thrown out, her copper hair hanging over the left side of her face. He said, "And you're the woman I could tell everything."

She made an open-handed gesture, as if pleading guilty. "Nice little trap, Ford. But don't you get a little nervous setting traps for people who love you? I mean, you're the one who gets hurt if the traps work."

Hollins reacted to that, glaring at Jessica. "Hey, wait a minute—you just told me you two were friends." He turned to Ford. "I swear to God, this girl didn't tell me that you and she were—"

"We're not." Ford was standing up, finding it hard to look at either one of them. "Rafe, you come over to my place in the morning, and we'll talk about your son."

"What?"

"You heard me."

"I can't just come out in broad daylight. I've been camping over on Chino Island so no one would see me. Jessica's been bringing me food and stuff until you got back. About her and me, I had no damn idea that you two were . . . and I hardly even knew her until about four days ago when Rouchard said—" He was stammering over a tough subject and making it tougher, so Jessica finished, "When Benny told him that any friend of his gets anything he wants from Jessica McClure. Right, Hollins?"

Rafe groaned. "Doc, I feel like a real shit about this. After all you've done for me."

Ford was already walking away. "Stop by in the morning, Rafe. You don't have to hide anymore. They couldn't prove you were murdered; they can't prove the Marielito was murdered. All the evidence is gone."

"But I'm supposed to be dead."

"You were out of the country with your son and returned to discover a terrible injustice had been done. You are shocked some stranger was mistaken for you."

"I left that stupid note—"

"I have the note, and I've already forgotten about it."

"And my wallet was on him."

"You mean the wallet was stolen? The Marielito died with a guilty conscience."

"But DeArmand knows—"

"DeArmand has his own problems to worry about. So does your ex-wife."

"They'll get me for kidnapping."

Ford stopped and turned toward him. "Right—and

gun running. You're going to have to face up to that anyway. Good fathers don't keep their kids hiding from the
law, Rafe. And you're going to be a good father. A very
damn good father. Or I'll unravel your story like a cheap
sweater and make sure you lose the boy."

Hollins's head was down and he said softly, "I guess
I have that coming. Maybe I do. But Doc—" He looked
at Ford, a steely look. "—don't ever threaten to take Jake
away from me again."

Ford said, "You keep your part of the bargain and I
won't."

Ford could hear Jessica's footsteps in the sand; could
feel her following him through the disc of porch light
to his bike. He turned and she came closer to him, still
holding the robe with one hand, but holding something
else in the other. She said, "You might as well take this
with you"—handing him a framed canvas—"since you
probably won't be coming by again." Not sounding cold
now, just weary.

Ford held the canvas out to the light and saw that she
had finished the painting: a man with glasses and a firm
expression wading the brass flats. It was Ford's face, but
she had idealized it; softened the rough features and
added virtues he had never seen in the mirror.

She said, "That's the way I see you." And they both
looked at the painting in a growing silence; then Jessica
said in a rush, "Doc, Rouchard has videos of me."

"Oh?"

"You don't want to hear it, do you?"

"I thought it might be something like that."

"I'm just trying to tell you why you saw what you saw—"

"You don't owe me an explanation."

"No, but you owe me the chance to offer, damn it." She was angry and close to tears, too. "That time in Greenwich Village, with the drugs and all. Well, it was a little bit worse than I told you. No, it was a lot worse. The drugs, mostly. Then I went to work for the marketing company in New York—"

"Seaboard Marketing. Unlimited."

She turned away from him, her hair swinging. "I don't even know why I bother. I should have known you'd already checked out every little detail. God, I feel like a fool."

Ford touched her shoulder and she pivoted slowly, not looking at him now. "You went to work for the company."

"Yes. I started to get my life straightened out a little. But I still had the drug problem. So Ben helped me out by supplying, but then he wanted me to help him, too. It didn't seem like I had much choice, that's how bad my problem was. So I began to do favors for him. Then he wanted me to do favors for his important clients when they came to the city. He didn't know it but he was giving me all the motivation I needed for getting off the drugs for good. By then he had the videos. I didn't even know he'd taken them."

"Nice guy, Ben."

"He's leaving the country Tuesday and I'll never have to do another thing for that man. He got busted last week and I'm helping him get out. I'll get the cassettes back in exchange."

"And Rafe is one of Ben's suppliers."

"I don't ask. He must have something on Ben, I don't know. I just do what they want, like taking medicine." She pressed her hands to his chest, not holding him away, but as if to make sure he stood and listened. "After Tuesday, it'll all be over, Doc. That whole damn segment of my life. Like it never happened. In a way, it didn't happen. Not to this me. The Jessica McClure you knew here in this house—that's who I am. It's who I would have been. Do you know how seriously the art critics would treat a coke whore? People don't just buy the painting. They buy the artist. I told you that once before."

Ford stood watching her, saying nothing as she let her hands slide to her sides.

She said, "Bad things happen to people, Ford. Bad random things that scar and humiliate. If you make one wrong choice, make one mistake, you can go from running your life to wanting to run from it. Like your friend Rafe Hollins. That painting you're holding was done by a person who never knew Ben Rouchard. It was done by a person who hadn't been scarred and was too strong to run. Take a close look at the face, Ford. It looks like you, but it's the way I should have been."

Ford said, "I like the woman I see in front of me just fine. I always have."

She slid her arm under his, wanting him to hug her. "I don't want to lose you, Ford, just because you stumbled onto a part of my life that is already over."

Ford almost said, "Jessica, you never had me." Instead, he kissed her on top of the head and rode away.

TWENTY-FOUR

On June 22, one day after the summer solstice, Ford was standing at the stove cooking when he heard a skiff outside, puttering toward his dock. He was expecting company and he stopped cutting onions long enough to glance out the window. It was Tomlinson—not the person he was expecting. He opened the little refrigerator and used his fingers to squeegee ice off two bottles of beer, then opened them both.

"Clare de Lune" was coming out of the Boise speakers, just getting to the nice harp part, the part where the music slowed and sparkled.

Tomlinson came up the steps, opened the door without knocking, and plopped down into a chair. He was carrying a newspaper. "Pilar Santana Fuentes Balserio isn't dead," he said.

Ford had gone back to the stove and, without looking up, he said, "There's a beer on the desk for you."

"She presided at the Ceremony of Seven Moons

yesterday. They invited the world press, like a coronation. They're calling it the bloodless revolution. Even the Miami *Herald* ran two . . . no, three pictures. I wonder why they didn't invite you—I mean, you sent Rivera the damn book back just like he asked."

Ford turned and said, "I've got a lady due to arrive in about fifteen minutes. I don't want to be rude, but she's not coming here to hear about current events. Then we're going up to Cabbage Key and dance. Rob Wells is having us to dinner."

"You're taking the news a little hard, aren't you?" Tomlinson was holding his bottle of beer, studying Ford's face.

"I'm cutting onions, you idiot."

"Oh yeah . . . It says here that Masaguans have accepted Pilar as the incarnation of Ixku, the Mayan goddess. Far out, huh? Ixku was the mother of Quetzalcoatl, the blond sun god. Pure spiritualism, man, I love it! 'She had disavowed her former life—'" Tomlinson was reading now. "'—and dedicated herself to promoting the political and social well-being of her people. An estimated two hundred thousand Maya made the pilgrimage to bow before the woman who led them in a ceremony that had not been performed since the arrival of the Spaniards in the sixteenth century.'" Tomlinson rattled the paper. "Goddamn, that woman's smart. In those Central American countries, they assassinate dictators like most people eat popcorn. But they won't lay a finger on a religious leader, no way. She'll govern that country until she dies at a ripe old age. She's a genius, I'm telling you."

Ford said, "You don't have to tell me."

Tomlinson was reading again. "'As a Mayan priestess, she must forsake all earthly pleasures and bonds. Even to speak her former name is considered heresy.' I guess that means she can't get married. Yeah, I'm sure that's what that means. See, Doc? It wasn't that she didn't want to see you again. That ought to cheer you up."

"Have I needed cheering up?"

"Naw, I guess not. You've been pretty cheery."

They'd both been pretty cheery. After selling off the emeralds, they each had enough money in the bank to do the work they wanted to do for a long, long time. So would Jake Hollins when he turned eighteen and the trust funds started paying off. And Rafe and Harvey Hollins would have enough money right along if all the stipulations of the trusts were honored.

"They got some quotes in here from Juan Rivera. He's going to be the high Ixku's prime minister. Some of them are pretty funny. You want me to read them?"

Tomlinson read the quotes aloud, and by the time he was done they were both laughing. Tomlinson said, "I'm telling you, the guy's going to be a great prime minister. That idea about getting a major league franchise in Masagua was the best. 'Provide us such a bond with capitalism and we will never turn away.' Pure poetry and, when you think of it, he's absolutely right."

Ford had already thought of it. It was his idea.

Tomlinson said, "You want to see the pictures they took of the ceremony? I'll leave the paper. Hey, I better get going if you have a lady coming over. Plus you combed your hair and, judging from that clean shirt, probably even took a shower." At the door he said again, "I think you ought to take a look at those pictures, Doc."

As Tomlinson's boat started, Ford picked up the paper. He looked at the photographs, then put the paper down. He found his glasses and considered the photographs once more, studying them carefully, moving very slowly, as a man in a dream might move. He took a long breath, then another. Then he carried the paper outside, where he stood, hands clenched white on the railing, and stared down into the pen where the two big bull sharks Jeth Nicholes had caught cruised like dark sentinels. Their dull goat's eyes seemed to stare back at him.

Someone was calling his name . . . a woman's voice.

He turned to see Dr. Sheri Braun-Richards grinning at him, looking fresh and professional in her summer dress and white jacket, just in from Iowa at his invitation, and saying "Hey, sailor, you got room for one very tired lady?"

"Huh?"

She came up the dock, gave him a big squeeze, then pulled the newspaper out of his hands playfully. "What's so important in here that you'd give your personal physical therapist such a dull greeting? Oh, I see now—some Latin beauty in a white robe. Nice picture; very nice." She folded the paper neatly and said, "But in case you didn't notice, that beautiful woman is holding a very fat, very healthy, little blond baby. She's obviously not available. But you know what?" She touched her fingertips to the slow, soft smile forming on Ford's face. "I am."